Praise for the **[Aubrey-Maturin Novels]** and Patrick O'Brian

"The best historical novels ever written."
—Richard Snow, *New York Times Book Review*

"I love these books.... [They offer] the same sense of lived experience as Hilary Mantel.... They will sweep you away and return you delighted, increased and stunned. If the phrase 'Napoleonic war fiction' fills you with anticipation, then you don't need me to convince you to read [Patrick] O'Brian. But for the rest of you.... [P]lease, just trust me."
—Nicola Griffith, NPR

"A few books work their way... onto [bestseller] lists by genuine, lasting excellence—witness *The Lord of the Rings*, or Patrick O'Brian's sea stories."
—Ursula K. Le Guin

"Like John le Carré, [O'Brian] has erased the boundary separating a debased genre from 'serious' fiction. O'Brian is a novelist, pure and simple, one of the best we have."
—Mark Horowitz, *Los Angeles Times Book Review*

"[Patrick O'Brian has] the power of bringing near to the reader... savagery and tenderness, beauty and mystery and boldness and dignity."
—Eudora Welty

"O'Brian's eloquent admirers include not merely distinguished critics and reviewers but... thousands upon thousands of fervent readers who thank the gods for him.... [H]is work accomplishes nobly the three grand purposes of art: to entertain, to edify, and to awe."
—Stephen Becker, *Paris Review*

"For escapist reading, I especially like the sea novels of Patrick O'Brian."
—Bill Bryson

"O'Brian's narrative . . . provides endlessly varying shocks and surprises—comic, grim, farcical and tragic. An essential of the truly gripping book for the narrative addict is the creation of a whole, solidly living world for the imagination to inhabit, and O'Brian does this with prodigal specificity and generosity."

—A. S. Byatt

"I prefer the Aubrey-Maturin series to all others. . . . Every book is packed to absolute straining with erudition, wit, history, and thunderous action."

—Joe Hill

"All of the Aubrey-Maturin series by Patrick O'Brian [is on my shelves]."

—Mindy Kaling, *New York Times*

"Although O'Brian is ingenious at devising new adventures, it is the richness of his characters which justifies his readers' continuing enthusiasm. . . . O'Brian acknowledges Jane Austen as one of his inspirations, and she need not be ashamed of the affiliation."

—*The New Yorker*

"I fell in love with [O'Brian's] writing straightaway, at first with *Master and Commander.* . . . Jack Aubrey and Stephen Maturin always remind me a bit of Mick and me."

—Keith Richards

"Aubrey and Maturin have been described as better than Holmes and Watson, the equal of Quixote and Panza. . . . All this is true. And the marvel is, it hardly says enough."

—John Balzar, *Los Angeles Times*

"The high seas are his home place—as they were for Melville and Conrad. And his time, the age and era of the great Nelson, is the altogether gracefully resurrected past. . . . But Patrick O'Brian is a novelist for here and now, someone who shares his splendid vision, his wonderful sense of character, with a growing number of lucky contemporary readers."

—George Garrett

"There are two types of people in the world: Patrick O'Brian fans, and people who haven't read him yet."

—Lucy Eyre, *Guardian*

The
Wine-Dark
Sea

THE WORKS OF PATRICK O'BRIAN

BIOGRAPHY

Picasso

Joseph Banks

AUBREY/MATURIN NOVELS IN ORDER OF PUBLICATION

The Truelove

The Wine-Dark Sea

The Commodore

The Yellow Admiral

The Hundred Days

Blue at the Mizzen

21: The Final Unfinished Voyage of Jack Aubrey

NOVELS

Testimonies

The Golden Ocean

The Unknown Shore

COLLECTIONS

The Rendezvous and Other Stories

The Uncertain Land and Other Poems

The sails of a square-rigged ship, hung out to dry in a calm.

1. Flying jib
2. Jib
3. Fore topmast staysail
4. Fore staysail
5. Foresail, or course
6. Fore topsail
7. Fore topgallant
8. Mainstaysail
9. Maintopmast staysail
10. Middle staysail
11. Main topgallant staysail
12. Mainsail, or course
13. Maintopsail
14. Main topgallant
15. Mizzen staysail
16. Mizzen topmast staysail
17. Mizzen topgallant staysail
18. Mizzen sail
19. Spanker
20. Mizzen topsail
21. Mizzen topgallant

PATRICK O'BRIAN

The Wine-Dark Sea

THE AUBREY/MATURIN SERIES

W. W. NORTON & COMPANY
Independent Publishers Since 1923

First published as a Norton paperback 1994, reissued 2022

For information about permission to reproduce selections from this book, write to
Permissions, W. W. Norton & Company, Inc., 500 Fifth Avenue, New York, NY 10110

For information about special discounts for bulk purchases, please contact
W. W. Norton Special Sales at specialsales@wwnorton.com or 800-233-4830

Manufacturing by Lakeside Book Company
Book design by Chris Welch
Production manager: Delaney Adams

Library of Congress Cataloging-in-Publication Data

Names: O'Brian, Patrick, 1914–2000, author.
Title: The wine-dark sea / Patrick O'Brian.
Description: New York, NY : W. W. Norton & Company, 2022. |
Series: The Aubrey/ Maturin Series
Identifiers: LCCN 2021049426 | ISBN 9781324021544 (pbk.)
Classification: LCC PR6029.B55 W5 2022 | DDC 823/.914—dc20
LC record available at https://lccn.loc.gov/2021049426

W. W. Norton & Company, Inc., 500 Fifth Avenue, New York, N.Y. 10110
www.wwnorton.com

W. W. Norton & Company Ltd., 15 Carlisle Street, London W1D 3BS

1 2 3 4 5 6 7 8 9 0

FOR RICHARD SIMON AND
VIVIEN GREEN

CHAPTER ONE

A purple ocean, vast under the sky and devoid of all visible life apart from two minute ships racing across its immensity. They were as close-hauled to the somewhat irregular north-east trades as ever they could be, with every sail they could safely carry and even more, their bowlines twanging taut: they had been running like this day after day, sometimes so far apart that each saw only the other's topsails above the horizon, sometimes within gunshot; and when this was the case they fired at one another with their chasers.

The foremost ship was the *Franklin*, an American privateer of twenty-two guns, nine-pounders, and her pursuer was the *Surprise*, a twenty-eight-gun frigate formerly belonging to the Royal Navy but now acting as a privateer too, manned by privateersmen and volunteers: she was nominally commanded by a half-pay officer named Thomas Pullings but in fact by her former captain, Jack Aubrey, a man much higher on the post-captain's list than would ordinarily have been found in so small and antiquated a ship – an anomalous craft entirely, for although she purported to be a privateer her official though unpublished status was that of His Majesty's Hired Vessel *Surprise*. She had set out on her voyage with the purpose of carrying her surgeon, Stephen Maturin, to South America, there to enter into contact with those leading inhabitants who wished to make Chile and Peru independent of Spain: for Maturin, as well as being a doctor of medicine, was an intelligence-agent exceptionally well qualified for this task, being a Catalan on his mother's side and bitterly opposed to Spanish – that is to say Castilian – oppression of his country.

He was indeed opposed to oppression in all its forms, and in his youth he had supported the United Irishmen (his father was a Catholic Irish officer in the Spanish service) in everything but the violence of 1798: but above all, far above all, he abhorred that of Buonaparte, and he was perfectly willing to offer his services to the British gov-

ernment to help put an end to it, to offer them *gratis pro Deo*, thus
doing away with any hint of the odious name of spy, a vile wretch
hired by the Ministry to inform upon his friends, a name associated
in his Irish childhood with that of Judas, Spy-Wednesday coming just
before the Passion.

His present undertaking, resumed after a long interruption caused
by the traitorous passing of information from London to Madrid, gave
him the greatest satisfaction, for its success would not only weaken
the two oppressors but it would also cause extreme anger and frus-
tration in a particular department of French intelligence that was trying to bring about the same result, though with the difference that
the independent South American governments should feel loving and
strategically valuable gratitude towards Paris rather than London.

He had had many causes for satisfaction since they left the Polynesian island of Moahu in pursuit of the *Franklin*. One was that the
American had chosen to rely on her remarkable powers of sailing very
close to the wind on a course that was leading them directly towards
his destination; another was that although her sailing-master, an old
Pacific hand from Nantucket, handled her with uncommon skill,
doing everything in his power to run clear or shake off his pursuer by
night, neither his guile nor his seamanship could outmatch Aubrey's.
If the *Franklin* slipped a raft over the side in the darkness, lighting
lanterns upon it, dowsing her own and changing course, she found
the *Surprise* in her wake when the day broke clear; for Jack Aubrey
had the same instinct, the same sense of timing and a far greater
experience of war.

Still another cause for satisfaction was that every successive
noonday observation showed them slanting rapidly down towards
the equator and some two hundred miles or more closer to Peru, a
country that Dr Maturin associated not only with potential independence but also with the coca plant, a shrub whose dried leaves he,
like the Peruvians, was accustomed to chew as a relief from mental
or spiritual distress and physical or intellectual weariness as well as a
source of benignity and general well-being. Rats, however, had eaten

his store of leaves somewhere south of Capricorn. Coca-leaves could not be replaced in New South Wales, where the *Surprise* had spent some dismal weeks, and he looked forward eagerly to a fresh supply: ever since he last heard from his wife – letters had caught up with the ship off Norfolk Island – he had felt a deep indwelling anxiety about her; and the coca-leaves might at least dispel the irrational part of it. They sharpened the mind wonderfully; and he welcomed the prospect of that familiar taste, the deadening of the inside of his mouth and pharynx, and the calming of his spirit in what he termed 'a virtuous ataraxy', a freedom that owed nothing to alcohol, that contemptible refuge, nor even to his old love opium, which might be objected to on physical and even perhaps on moral grounds.

This was scarcely a subject that so discreet, private and indeed secretive a person as Stephen Maturin was likely to discuss, and although it flashed into his mind as a piece of green seaweed rose momentarily on the bow-wave, all he said to his companion was 'It is a great satisfaction to see the ocean a colour so near to that of new wine – of certain kinds of new wine – as it comes gushing from the press.'

He and Nathaniel Martin, his assistant-surgeon, were standing in the frigate's beakhead, a roughly triangular place in front of and below the forecastle, the very foremost part of the ship where the bowsprit reached out, where the seamen's privy was to be found, and where the medicoes were least in the way, not only of the hands trimming the sails to capture the greatest possible thrust from the wind but, and above all, of the gunners serving the two bow-chasers on the forecastle, guns that pointed almost directly forward. The gun-crews in question were commanded by Captain Aubrey himself, who pointed and fired the windward chaser, a long brass nine-pounder called *Beelzebub*, and by Captain Pullings, who did the same for the leeward gun: they both had much the same style of firing, which was not surprising, since Captain Pullings had been one of Jack's midshipmen in his first command, a great while ago in the Mediterranean, and had learnt all his practical gunnery from him. They were now very carefully aiming their pieces at the *Franklin*'s topsail yards with the intent of cutting halliards, backstays and the whole nexus of cordage at the level of the mainyard and even with luck of wounding the mainyard itself: in any case of delaying her progress without damage to her hull. There was no point in battering the hull of a prize, and a prize the *Franklin* seemed fated to be in the long run – perhaps even today, since the *Surprise* was perceptibly gaining. The range was now a thousand yards or even a little less, and both Jack and Pullings waited for just before the height of the roll to send their shot racing over the broad stretch of water.

'The Captain does not like it, however,' observed Maturin, referring to the wine-dark sea. 'He says it is not natural. He admits the colour, which we have all seen in the Mediterranean on occasion; he admits the swell, which though unusually broad is not rare but the colour and the swell together . . .'

The crash and rumble of the Captain's gun, followed with scarcely a pause by Pullings's, cut him short: smoke and smouldering scraps of wad whistled about their heads, yet even before they swept away to leeward Stephen had his spy-glass to his eye. He could not catch the flight of the ball, but in three heart-beats he saw a hole appear low in the Frenchman's topsail, joining a score of others. To his astonishment he also saw a jet of water shoot from her lee scuppers, and above him he heard Tom Pullings's cry. 'They are starting their water, sir!'

'What does this signify?' asked Martin quietly. He had not applied to a very valuable source, Dr Maturin being strictly a land-animal, but in this case Stephen could truthfully reply 'that they were pumping their fresh water over the side to lighten the ship and make it go faster.' 'Perhaps,' he added, 'they may also throw their guns and boats overboard. I have seen it done.'

A savage cheer from all the Surprises in the fore part of the ship showed him that he was seeing it again; and having watched the first few splashes he passed Martin the glass.

The boats went overboard, and the guns: but not quite all the guns. As the *Franklin*'s speed increased, her two stern-chasers fired together, the white smoke streaming away across her wake.

'How disagreeable it is to be fired at,' said Martin, shrinking into as small a space as possible; and as he spoke one ball hit the best bower anchor close behind them with an enormous clang: the sharp fragments, together with the second ball, cut away almost all the foretopgallantmast's support. The mast and its attendant canvas fell quite slowly, spars breaking right and left, and the *Surprise*'s bow-chasers just had time to reply, both shots striking the *Franklin*'s stern. But before either Jack's or Pullings's crew could reload their guns they were enveloped in sailcloth, whilst at the same time all hands aft raised the cry *Man overboard* and the ship flew up into the wind, all her sails taken aback and clattering like a madhouse. The *Franklin* fired a single gun: an extraordinary cloud of smoke, and extraordinary report. But it was drowned by Captain Aubrey's roar of 'Clew up, clew up, there,' and emerging from the canvas 'Where away?'

'Larboard quarter, sir,' cried several hands. 'It's Mr Reade.'

'Carry on, Captain Pullings,' said Jack, whipping off his shirt and diving straight into the sea. He was a powerful swimmer, the only one in the ship, and from time to time he heaved himself high out of the water like a seal to make sure of his direction. Mr Reade, a midshipman of fourteen, had never been able to do much more than keep afloat, and since losing an arm in a recent battle he had not bathed at all. Fortunately the remaining arm was firmly hooked into the bars of a hen-coop that had been thrown to him from the quarterdeck, and though sodden and bruised he was perfectly in possession of his wits. 'Oh sir,' he cried from twenty yards, 'Oh sir, I am so sorry – oh how I hope we han't missed the chase.'

'Are you hurt?' asked Jack.

'Not at all, sir: but I am so sorry you should have . . .'

'Then clap on to my hair' – the Captain wore it long and clubbed, 'and so get set on my shoulders. D'ye hear me there?'

From time to time on the way back to the ship Reade apologized into Jack's ear, or hoped they had not lost the chase; but he was often choked with salt water, for Jack was now swimming against the wind and the set of the sea, and he plunged deep at every stroke.

Reade was less coldly received aboard than might have been expected: in the first place he was much esteemed by all hands, and in the second it was clear to any seaman that his being rescued had not in fact delayed the pursuit of the prize: whether Reade had gone overboard or not, the shattered crosstrees had to be replaced and new spars, sails and cordage had to be sent aloft before the frigate could resume her course. Those few hands who were not extremely busy with the tangle forward passed him the bight of a rope, hauled him aboard, asked him with real kindness how he did, and handed him over to Sarah and Emily Sweeting, two little black, black girls from a remote Melanesian island, belonging to Dr Maturin and attached to the sick-berth, to be led below and given dry clothes and a cup of tea. And as he went even Awkward Davies, who had been rescued twice and who often resented sharing the distinction, called out 'It was me as tossed you the hen-coop, sir. I heaved it overboard, ha, ha, ha!'

As for the Captain, he was already in conference with Mr Bulkeley the bosun, and the only congratulations he received were from Pullings, who said, 'Well, and so you've done it again, sir,' before going on to the foretopmost cheekblocks. Jack looked for no more, indeed not for as much: he had pulled so many people out of the water in the course of his time at sea that he thought little of it, while those who, like Bonden his coxswain, Killick his steward and several others, had served with him ever since his first command, had seen him do it so often that it seemed natural – some God-damned lubber fell in: the skipper fished him out – while the privateersmen and smugglers who made up most of the rest of the crew had acquired much of their shipmates' phlegm.

In any case they were all much too preoccupied with getting the barky into chasing trim again to indulge in abstract considerations; and to objective spectators like Maturin and his assistant it was a pleasure to see the intense, accurately-directed and almost silent energy with which they worked, a highly skilled crew of seamen who knew exactly what to do and who were doing it with whole-hearted zeal. The medicoes, having crawled from under the foretopmast staysail, had gone below to find Reade perfectly well, being fed with sick-berth biscuit by the little girls; and now they were watching the strenuous activity from the quarterdeck, where the ordinary life of the ship was going on in a sparse sort of way: West, the officer of the watch, was at his station, telescope under his arm; helmsmen and quartermaster by the wheel.

'Turn the glass and strike the bell,' cried the quartermaster in a loud official voice.

There was no one there of course to obey the order so he turned the glass himself and paced forward towards the belfry to strike the bell. But both gangways were obstructed with spars, cordage and a crowd of straining bodies, and he had to go down into the waist and pick his way among the carpenter and his crew as they worked sweating under the sun, now half-way to its height and terrible in the copper-coloured sky. They were shaping not only the new crosstrees but also the heel of the new topgallantmast, an intent body of men, working to very fine limits in a rolling ship, plying sharp-edged tools and impatient of the slightest interruption. But the quartermaster was a dogged soul; he had served with Nelson in the *Agamemnon* and the *Vanguard*; he was not going to be stopped by a parcel of carpenters; and presently four bells rang out their double chime. The quartermaster returned, followed by oaths and bringing with him the two helmsmen who were to take their trick at the wheel.

'Mr West,' said Stephen, 'do you suppose we shall eat our dinner today?'

Mr West's expression was difficult to read; the loss of his nose, frost-bitten south of the Horn, gave what had been a mild, good-humoured, rather stupid face an appearance of malignity; and this was strengthened by a number of sombre reflections, more recently acquired.

'Oh yes,' he said absently. 'Unless we are in close action we always shoot the sun and pipe to dinner at noon.'

'No, no. I mean our ceremony in the gunroom.'

'Oh, of course,' said West. 'What with Reade going overboard and the chase stopping us dead and tearing away like smoke and oakum just as we were overhauling her, it slipped my mind. Masthead, there,' he hailed. 'What do you see?"

'Precious little, sir,' the voice came floating down. 'It is cruel hazy – orange sorts of haze – in the south-east; but sometimes I catch what might be a twinkle of topgallants.'

West shook his head, but went on, 'No, no, Doctor; never you fret about our dinner. Cook and steward laid it on handsome, and though we may be a little late I am sure we shall eat it – there, do you see, the crosstrees go aloft. They will be swaying up the mast directly.'

'Will they indeed? Order out of chaos so soon?'

'Certainly they will. Never you fret about your dinner.'

'I will not,' said Stephen, who accepted what seamen told him about ships with the same simplicity as that with which they accepted what he told them about their bodies. 'Take this bolus,' he would say. 'It will rectify the humours amazingly,' and they, holding their noses (for he often used asafoetida) would force the rounded mass down, gasp, and feel better at once. With his mind at ease, therefore, Stephen said to Martin, 'Let us make our forenoon rounds,' and went below.

West, left to his solitude, returned to his own fretting – an inadequate word for his concern for the future and his anxiety about the present. Captain Aubrey had begun this much-interrupted voyage with his old shipmate. Tom Pullings acting as his first lieutenant and two broken officers, West and Davidge, as second and third. He did not know them as anything but competent seamen, but he was aware that the sentences of their courts-martial had been thought extremely harsh in the service – West was dismissed for duelling, Davidge for signing a dishonest purser's accounts without checking them – and that reinstatement was their chief aim in life. Up until recently they had been in a fair way to it; but when the *Surprise* was nearly a thousand miles out of Sydney Cove, sailing eastwards across the Pacific Ocean, it was found that a senior midshipman named Oakes had stowed a young gentlewoman away in the cable-tier; and this had led almost all the gunroom officers except Dr Maturin to behave extremely badly. Her instant marriage to Oakes had set her free in that she was no longer a transported convict liable to be taken up again, but it did not liberate her from the adulterous wishes, motions, and jealousies of her shipmates. West and Davidge were the worst and Captain Aubrey, coming late to an understanding of the position, had told them that if they did not put aside the barbarous open enmity that was spreading discord and inefficiency in the ship he would turn them ashore: farewell for ever to any hope of reinstatement.

Davidge had been killed in the recent action that made the Polynesian island of Moahu at least a nominal part of the British Empire and Oakes had gone off for Batavia with his Clarissa in a recaptured prize; but so far Captain Aubrey had said nothing. West did not know whether his zeal in the approaches to Moahu and in getting the carronades up through rough country and his modest part in the battle itself had earned him forgiveness or whether he should be dismissed when the ship reached Peru: an agonizing thought. What he did know, here and in the immediate present, was that a valuable prize, in which he would share even if he were later dismissed, had almost certainly escaped. They would never catch her before nightfall and in this hazy, moonless darkness, she could run a hundred miles, never to be seen again.

That was one torment to his spirit: another was that this morning Captain Aubrey had promoted Grainger, a forecastleman in the starboard watch, to fill the vacancy left by Davidge's death, just as he had raised a young fellow called Sam Norton to replace Oakes. West had to admit that Grainger was a capital seaman, a master-mariner who had sailed his own brig on the Guinea run until he was taken by two Salee rovers off Cape Spartel; but he did not like the man at all. He had already known what it was to be shut up in the gunroom with a

shipmate he detested, seeing him at every meal, hearing his voice; and
now it seemed that he should have to go through the odious experience again for at least the breadth of the Pacific. Yet more than that,
far more, he felt that the gunroom and the quarterdeck, the privileged
places in a man-of-war, were not only sacred in themselves but that
they conferred a kind of sanctity on their rightful inhabitants, a particular being and an identity. He felt this strongly, though he found the
notion difficult to express; and now that Davidge was dead there was
nobody with whom he could discuss it. Pullings was a small tenant-
farmer's son; Adams, though he acted as purser, was only the Captain's clerk; and Martin did not seem to think either family or caste
of much importance. Dr Maturin, who lived almost entirely with the
Captain, being his particular friend, was of illegitimate birth and
the subject could not be raised with him; while even if West had been
in high favour with his commander it would have been quite useless
to suggest that if it was necessary to promote foremast-jacks, as it was
in this case, then they might be made master's mates, herding with
the midshipmen, so that the gunroom should be preserved: useless,
because Jack Aubrey belonged to an older Navy in which a collier's
mate like James Cook could die a much-honoured post-captain, and a
foremast-hand like William Mitchell might begin his career by being
flogged round the fleet and end it as a vice-admiral, rather than to the
modern service, in which an officer had not only to pass for lieutenant
but also for gentleman if he were to advance.

Dr Maturin and his assistant had the usual seamen's diseases to
treat and a few wounds to dress, not from the recent battle, which
had been a mere point-blank butchery of an enemy caught in a narrow rocky defile, but from the wear and tear of dragging guns up and
down a jungly mountain-side. They also had one interesting case of a
sailor who, less sure-footed by land than by sea, had fallen on to the
pointed end of a cut bamboo, which let air into the cavity of his thorax, into his pleura, with the strangest effect on one lung. This they

discussed at length, in Latin, to the great satisfaction of the sick-berth, where heads turned gravely from one speaker to the other, nodding from time to time, while the patient himself looked modestly down and Padeen Colman, Dr Maturin's almost monoglot Irish servant and loblolly-boy, wore his Mass-going reverential face.

They never heard the orders that attended the swaying-up of the new topgallantmast, an anxious business at such a height and with such a swell; nor did they hear the cry of 'Launch ho!' as the bosun's mate at the topmast head banged the fid home through the heel of the topgallantmast, thus supporting it on the topmast trestle-tree. The complex business of securing the long unhandy pole escaped them too – an exceedingly complex business, for although before the swaying-up the shrouds had been placed over the head of the mast, followed by the backstays, the preventer-stays and the very stay itself, they all had to be made fast, bowsed upon and set up simultaneously with all possible dispatch so that they exerted an equally-balanced force fore and aft and on either side. The rigging of the topgallant yard with all its appurtenances also passed unnoticed; so did two typical naval illogicalities, for whereas by tradition and good sense only the lightest of the topmen laid out on the lofty yard to loose the sail, this time, once it was loosed, sheeted home and hoisted, the Captain, with his acknowledged sixteen stone, ran aloft with his glass to sweep what vague horizon could still be distinguished through the growing haze.

But the medical men and their patients did make out the cheer as the ship returned to her former course, and they did feel her heel as she gathered way, running with a far more lively motion, while all the mingled sounds of the wind in the rigging and the water streaming along her side took on the urgent note of a ship chasing once more.

Almost immediately after the *Surprise* had settled into her accustomed pace, shouldering the strange-coloured sea high and wide, the hands were piped to dinner, and in the usual Bedlam of cries and banging mess-kids that accompanied the ceremony, Stephen returned to the quarterdeck, where the Captain was standing at the windward rail, gazing steadily out to the eastward: he felt Stephen's presence and called him over. 'I have never seen anything like it,' he said, nodding at the sea and the sky.

'It is much thicker now than it was when I went below,' said Stephen. 'And now an umber light pervades the whole, like a Claude Lorraine run mad.'

'We had no noon observation, of course,' said Jack. 'There was no horizon and there was no sun to bring down to it either. But what really puzzles me is that every now and then, quite independent of the swell, the sea *twitches*: a quick pucker like a horse's skin when there are flies about. There. Did you see? A little quick triple wave on the rising swell.'

'I did, too. It is extremely curious,' said Stephen. 'Can you assign any cause?'

'No,' said Jack. 'I have never heard of such a thing.' He reflected for some minutes, and at each lift of the frigate's bows the spray came sweeping aft. 'But quite apart from all this,' he went on, 'I finished the draft of my official letter this morning, before we came within gun-shot, and I should be uncommonly obliged if you would look through it, strike out errors and anything low, and put in some stylish expressions, before Mr Adams makes his fair copies.'

'Sure I will put in what style there is at my command. But why do you say copies and why are you in haste? Whitehall is half the world away or even more for all love.'

'Because in these waters we may meet with a homeward-bound whaler any day.'

'Really? Really? Oh, indeed. Very well: I shall come as soon as our dinner is properly disposed of. And I shall write to Diana too.'

'Your dinner? Oh yes, of course: I do hope it goes well. You will be changing very soon, no doubt.' He had no doubt at all, because his steward Killick, who also looked after Dr Maturin on formal occasions, had made his appearance, standing at what he considered a respectful distance and fixing them with his shrewish, disapproving eye. He had been with them for many years, in all climates, and although he was neither very clever nor at all agreeable he had, by mere conviction of righteousness, acquired an ascendancy of which both were ashamed. Killick coughed. 'And if you should see Mr West,' added Jack, 'pray tell him I should like to see him for a couple of minutes. I do hope your dinner goes well,' he called after Stephen's back.

The dinner in question was intended to welcome Grainger, now Mr Grainger, to the gunroom; Stephen too hoped that it would go well, and although he ordinarily ate his meals with Jack Aubrey in the cabin he meant to take his place in the gunroom for this occasion: since in principle the surgeon was a gunroom officer his absence might be taken as a slight. Grainger, a reserved, withdrawn man, was much respected aboard, for although he had not belonged to the *Surprise* during her heroic days as a privateer, when she recaptured a Spaniard deep-laden with quicksilver, took an American commerce-raider and cut out the *Diane* from the harbour of St Martins, he was well known to at least half the crew. He had joined at the beginning of this voyage, very highly recommended by his fellow-townsmen of Shelmerston, a port that had provided the *Surprise* with scores of prime seamen, a curious little West Country place, much given to smuggling, privateering, and chapel-going. There were almost as many chapels as there were public houses, and Grainger was an elder of the congregation of Traskites, who met on Saturdays in a severe, sad-coloured building behind the rope-walk. Although the Traskites' views were controversial, he and the younger men who came aboard with him were perfectly at home in the *Surprise*, which was an ark of dissent, containing Brownists, Sethians, Arminians, Muggletonians and several others, generally united in a seamanlike tolerance when afloat and always in a determined hatred of tithes when ashore. Stephen was well acquainted with him as a shipmate and above all as a patient (two calentures, a broken clavicle) and he valued his many qualities; but he knew very well how such a man, dignified and assured in his own circle, could suffer when he was removed from it. Pullings would be kindness itself; so would Adams; but kindness alone was not necessarily enough with so vulnerable a man as Grainger. Martin would certainly mean well, but he had always been more sensitive to the feelings of birds than to those of men, and prosperity seemed to have made him rather selfish. Although he was sailing as Stephen's assistant he was in fact a clergyman and Jack had recently given him a couple of livings in his gift with the promise of a valuable third when it should fall in; Martin had all the particulars of these parishes and he discussed them over and over again, considering the possibility of different modes of gathering tithes or their equivalent and improvement of the glebes. But worse than the dullness of this conversation was a self-complacency that Stephen had never known in the penniless Martin of some years ago, who was incapable of being a bore. West he was not sure of. Here again there had been change: the moody, snappish, nail-biting West of their present longitude was quite unlike the cheerful young man who had so kindly and patiently rowed him about Botany Bay, looking for seaweed.

'Oh, Mr West,' he said, opening the gunroom door, 'before I forget it – the Captain would like to see you for a minute or two. I believe he is in the cabin.'

'Jesus,' cried West, looking shocked; then recollecting himself, 'Thank you, Doctor.' He ran into his cabin, put on his best coat, and hurried up the ladder.

'Come in,' called Jack.

'I understand you wish to see me, sir.'

'Oh yes, Mr West; but I shall not keep you a minute. Push those files aside and sit on the locker. I had meant to speak to you before, but I have been so taken up with paper-work that I have left it day after day: it is just to tell you that I was thoroughly satisfied with your conduct through our time at Moahu, particularly your exertion in getting the carronades up that infernal mountain: most officerlike. I have mentioned it in my official letter; and I believe that if only you had contrived to be wounded you might have been fairly confident of reinstatement. Perhaps you will do better next time.'

'Oh, I shall do my very best, sir,' cried West. 'Arms, legs, anything . . . and may I say how infinitely I am obliged to you for mentioning me, sir?'

'Mr Grainger, welcome to the gunroom,' said Tom Pullings, splendid in his uniform. 'Here is your place, next to Mr West. But first, messmates, let us drink to Mr Grainger's health.'

'Good health,' 'Hear him,' 'Huzzay,' and 'Welcome,' cried the other four, emptying their glasses.

'My dear love to you all, gentlemen,' said Grainger, sitting down in a good blue coat borrowed from his cousin the carpenter, looking pale under his tan, grim and dangerous.

But grimness could not withstand Pullings's and Stephen's goodwill, far less West's surprising flow of spirits: his happiness broke out in an extraordinary volubility – a thoroughly amiable volubility – and he rose high above his ordinary powers of anecdote and comic rhyme; and when he was not proposing riddles he laughed. There was no doubt that Grainger was pleased with his reception; he ate well, he smiled, he even laughed once or twice; but all the time Maturin saw his quick nervous eyes flitting from plate to plate, seeing just how the gunroom ate its dinner, managed its bread and drank its wine. Yet by pudding-time and toasts the anxiety was gone; Grainger joined in the song *Farewell and adieu to you fine Spanish ladies* and even proposed one of his own: *As I walked out one midsummer's morning, for to view the fields and the flowers so gay.*

'From what I could make out here on deck,' said Jack, when Stephen joined him for coffee, 'your dinner seemed quite a cheerful affair.'

'It went off as well as ever I had hoped,' said Stephen. 'Mr West was in a fine flow of spirits – jokes, riddles, conundrums, imitations of famous commanders, songs – I did not know he possessed such social gifts.'

'I am heartily glad of it,' said Jack. 'But Stephen, you look a little worn.'

'I am a little worn. All the more so for having first stepped on deck for a breath of air: the appearance of the ocean appalled me. I asked Bonden what he thought – was it often like this? He only shook his head and wished we might all be here come Sunday. Jack, what do you think? Have you considered it?'

'I considered it most of the time your Nebuchadnezzar's feast was going on, and I cannot remember ever having seen or read of anything like it; nor can I tell what it means. When you have glanced over my draft, perhaps we might go on deck again and see whether we can make it out.'

Jack always sat uneasy while his official letters were read: he always broke the current of the reader's thoughts by saying 'The piece about the carronade-slides ain't very elegantly put, I am afraid . . . this is just a draft, you understand, not polished at all . . . Anything that ain't grammar or that you don't quite like, pray dash it out . . . I never was much of a hand with a pen,' but after all these years Stephen took no more notice of it than the thin drifting Irish rain.

With Jack's voice in the background, the roll and pitch of the ship and the crash of the sea on her weather-bow never affecting his concentration he read a succinct narrative, cast in the wooden service style: the *Surprise*, proceeding eastwards in accordance with their Lordships' instructions, had been overtaken in latitude 28°31S, longitude 168°1'E by a cutter from Sydney with official information that the inhabitants of the island of Moahu were at war with one another and that the British seamen were being ill-used and their ships detained: Captain Aubrey was to deal with the situation, backing whichever side seemed more likely to acknowledge British sovereignty. He had therefore changed course for Moahu without loss of time, pausing only at Anamooka for water and provisions: here he found the whaler *Daisy*, recently from Moahu, whose master, Mr Wainwright, informed him that the war between the chief of the northern part of Moahu and the queen of the south was complicated by the presence of a number of French mercenaries on the chief's side and of a privateer under American colours, the *Franklin*, commanded by another Frenchman allied to the chief, a Monsieur Dutourd. Acting upon this information, Captain Aubrey therefore proceeded with the utmost dispatch to Pabay, the northern port of Moahu, in the hope of finding the *Franklin* at anchor. She was not there, so having released the detained British ship, the *Truelove*, together with her surviving crew, and having destroyed the French garrison with the loss of one officer killed and two seamen wounded, he hastened to the southern harbour, which was about to be attacked from the mountains by the northern chief and probably from the sea by the privateer. The *Surprise* arrived in time: her people had the happiness of defeating the northern land forces without loss before the arrival of the privateer, and Captain Aubrey received the assurance of the Queen's willingness to be a faithful ally to His Majesty. Here followed a more detailed account of the two actions and the letter returned to the appearance of the *Franklin* next morning – her inferior force – her flight – and Captain Aubrey's hope that in spite of her excellent sailing qualities she might soon be captured.

'It seems to me a perfectly straightforward seamanlike account,' said Stephen, closing the folder. 'Admirably calculated for Whitehall, apart from a few quibbles I have pencilled in the margin. And I see why West was so happy.'

'Yes: I thought it due to him; and perhaps I laid it on a little heavy, because I was so sorry about Davidge. Thank you, Stephen. Shall we go on deck?'

It was indeed a lurid and portentous sight, the sky quite hidden and the diffused glow, now more orange than umber, showed an irregularly turbulent sea flecked as far as the eye could see (which was not much above three miles) with broken water that should have been white and that in fact had taken on an unpleasant acid greenish tinge, most evident in the frigate's leeward bow-wave – an irregular bow-wave too, for now, although the swell was still very much present, rolling strongly from the north-east, the series of crests was interrupted by innumerable cross-seas.

They stood in silence; and all along the gangway and on the forecastle there were little groups of seamen, gazing in the same attentive way, with a few low murmured words.

'It is not unlike the typhoon that so nearly did for us when we were running for the Marquesas, south of the line,' observed Jack. 'But there are essential differences. The glass is perfectly steady, for one thing. Yet even so I believe I shall strike topgallantmasts.' Raising his voice he called for the bosun and gave the order; it was at once followed by the wailing of pipes and entirely superfluous cries of 'All hands to strike topgallantmasts. All hands. All hands, d'ye hear me there?'

Without a word of complaint or a wry look, for they were much of the Captain's mind, the patient Surprises laid aloft to undo all they had done with such pains in the forenoon watch. They cast off all that had to be cast off; they clapped on to the mast-rope and by main force raised the foretopgallant so that the fid could be drawn out again and the whole lowered down; and this they did to the others in succession, as well as running in the jib-boom, making all fast and double-griping the boats.

'A pretty halfwit I may look, if the poor souls have to sway them up again tomorrow,' said Jack in a low voice. 'But when I was very young I had such a lesson about not getting your upper masts down on deck in plenty of time – such a lesson! Now we are on deck I could tell you about it, pointing out the various ropes and spars.'

'That would give me the utmost pleasure,' said Stephen.

'It was when I was coming back from the Cape in the *Minerva*, a very wet ship, Captain Soules: once we were north of the line we had truly miserable weather, a whole series of gales from the westward. But the day after Christmas the wind grew quite moderate and we not only let a reef out of the maintopsail but also sent up the topgallant mast and yard: yet during the night it freshened once more and we close-reefed the topsails again, got the topgallant yard down on deck and shaped the mast.'

'Before this it was amorphous, I collect? Shapeless?'

'What a fellow you are, Stephen. Shaping a mast means getting it ready to be struck. But, however, while this was in train, with the people tailing on to the mast-rope, the one that raises it a little, do you see, so that it can have a clear run down, the ship took a most prodigious lee-lurch, flinging all hands, still fast to their rope, into the scuppers. And since they hung on like good 'uns this meant that they raised the heel of the mast right up above the crosstrees, so that although the fid was out it could not be lowered down. Do you follow me, Stephen, with my fid and heel and crosstrees?'

'Perfectly, my dear. A most uncomfortable position, sure.'

'So it was, upon my word. And before we could do anything about it the topmast-springstays parted, then the topmast stay itself; and the mast went, a few feet above the cap, and falling upon the lee topsail yardarm carried that away too. And all this mare's nest came down on the mainyard, parting the lee-lift – that is the lee-lift, you see? Then the weather quarter of the mainyard, hitting the top, shattered the weather side of the crosstrees; so that as far as the sails were concerned, the mainmast was useless. At that very moment the ship broached to, huge green seas coming aft. We survived; but ever since then I have been perhaps over-cautious. Though this afternoon I had meant to reduce sail in any event.'

'You do not fear losing the prize?'

'Certainly I fear losing the prize: I should never say anything so unlucky as *No, she is ours*. I may lose her, of course; but you saw her start her water over the side, did you not?'

'Sure I saw the water and the guns; and I saw how she drew away, free of all that weight. I spent a few moments liberating poor Mr Martin from behind the seat of ease where the wreckage had imprisoned him and he so squeamish about excrement, the creature, and when I looked up again she was much smaller, flying with a supernatural velocity.'

'Yes, she holds a good wind. But she cannot cross the Pacific with what very little water she may have left – they pumped desperate hard and I saw ton after ton shoot into the sea – so she must double back to Moahu. The Sandwich Islands are much too far. I think he will put before the wind at about ten o'clock, meaning to slip past us with all lights dowsed during the graveyard watch – no moon, you know – and be well to the west of us by dawn, while we are still crack-ing on like mad lunatics to the eastward. My plan is to lie to in a little while, keeping a very sharp look-out; and if I do not mistake she will be in sight, a little to the south, at break of day, with the wind on her quarter and all possible sail abroad. I should add,' he went on after a pause in which Stephen appeared to be considering, 'that taking into account her leeway, which I have been measuring ever since the chase began, I mean first to take the ship quite a long way south.'

'The very same thought was in my mind,' said Stephen, 'though I did not presume to utter it. But tell me, before you lie in, do you not think it might calm our spirits if we were to contemplate let us say Corelli rather than this apocalyptic sea? We have scarcely played a note since before Moahu. I never thought to dislike the setting sun, but this one adds an even more sinister tinge to everything in sight, unpleasant though it was before. Besides, those tawny clouds flying in every direction and these irregular waves, these boils of water fill me with melancholy thoughts.'

'I should like it of all things,' said Jack. 'I do not intend to beat to quarters this evening – the people have had quite enough for one day – so we can make an early start.'

A fairly early start: for the irregular waves that had disturbed Ste-phen Maturin's sense of order in nature now pitched him headlong down the companion-ladder, where Mr Grainger, standing at its foot, received him as phlegmatically as he would have received a half-sack of dried peas, set him on his feet and told him 'that he should always keep one hand for himself and the other for the ship.' But the Doc-tor had flown down sideways, an ineffectual snatch at the rail having turned him about his vertical axis, so that Grainger caught him with one iron hand on his spine and the other on his upper belly, winding him to such an extent that he could scarcely gasp out a word of thanks. Then, when he had at last recovered his breath and the power of speech, it was found that his chair had to be made fast to two ring-bolts to allow him to hold his 'cello with anything like ease or even safety.

He had a Geronimo Amati at home, just as Aubrey had a treasured Guarnieri, but they travelled with rough old things that could put up with extremes of temperature and humidity. The rough old things always started the evening horribly flat, but in time the players tuned them to their own satisfaction, and exchanging a nod they dashed away into a duet which they knew very well indeed, having played it together these ten years and more, but in which they always found something fresh, some half-forgotten turn of phrase or of particular felicity. They also added new pieces of their own, small improvisations or repetitions, each player in turn. They might have pleased Corelli's ghost, as showing what power his music still possessed for a later generation: they certainly did not please Preserved Killick, the Captain's steward. 'Yowl, yowl, yowl,' he said to his mate on hearing the familiar sounds. 'They are at it again. I have a mind to put ratsbane in their toasted cheese.'

'It cannot go on much longer,' said Grimble. 'The cross-sea is getting up something cruel.'

It was true. The ship was cutting such extraordinary capers that even Jack, a merman if ever there was one, had to sit down, wedging himself firmly on a broad locker; and at the setting of the watch, after their traditional toasted cheese had been eaten, he went on deck to take in the courses and lie to under a close-reefed main topsail. He had, at least by dead-reckoning, reached something like the point he had been steering for; the inevitable leeway should do the rest by dawn; and he hoped that now the ship's motion would be eased.

'Is it very disagreeable upstairs?' asked Stephen when he returned. 'I hear thunderous rain on the skylight.'

'It is not so much very disagreeable as very strange,' said Jack.

'As black as can be, of course – never the smell of a star – and wet; and there are strong cross-seas, apparently flowing in three directions at once, which is contrary to reason. Lightning above the cloud, too, showing deep red. Yet there is something else I can hardly put a name to.' He held the lamp close to the barometer, shook his head, and going back to his seat on the locker he said that the motion was certainly easier: perhaps they might go back to the andante?

'With all my heart,' said Stephen, 'if I might have a rope round my middle to hold me to the chair.'

'Of course you may,' said Jack. 'Killick! Killick, there. Lash the Doctor into his seat, and let us have another decanter of port.'

The andante wound its slow length along with a curious gasping unpredictable rhythm; and when they had brought it to its hesitant end, each looking at the other with reproach and disapproval at each false note, Jack said, 'Let us drink to Zephyrus, the son of Millpond.' He was in the act of pouring a glass when the ship pitched with such extraordinary violence – pitched as though she had fallen into a hole – that he very nearly fell, and the glass left the wine in the air, a coherent body for a single moment.

'This will never do,' he said: and then, 'What in Hell was that crash?' He stood listening for a moment, and then in reply to a knock on the door he called, 'Come in.'

'Mr West's duty, sir,' said Norton, the newly-appointed midshipman, dripping on the chequered deck-cloth, 'and there is firing on the larboard bow.'

'Thank you, Mr Norton,' said Jack. 'I shall come at once.' He quickly stowed his fiddle on the locker and ran on deck. While he was still on the ladder there was another heavy crash, then as he reached the quarterdeck and the pouring rain, several more far forward.

'There, sir,' said West, pointing to a jetting glow, blurred crimson through the milk-warm rain. 'It comes and goes. I believe we are under mortar-fire.'

'Beat to quarters,' called Jack, and the bosun's mate wound his call. 'Mr

West – Mr West, there. D'ye hear me?' He raised his voice immensely, calling for a lantern: it showed West flat on his face, pouring blood.

'Foretopsail,' cried Jack, putting the ship before the wind, and as she gathered way he told two of the afterguard to carry West below. 'Forestaysail and jib.'

The ship came to life, to battle-stations, with a speed and regularity that would have given him deep satisfaction if he had had a second to feel it.

Stephen was already in the sick-berth with a sleepy Martin and a half-dressed Padeen when West was brought down, followed by half a dozen foremast-hands, two of them walking cases. 'A severe depressed fracture on either side of the coronal suture,' said Stephen, having examined West under a powerful lantern, 'and of course this apparently meaningless laceration. Deep coma. Padeen, Davies, lift him as gently as ever you can to the mattress on the floor back there; lay him face down with a little small pad under his forehead the way he can breathe. Next.'

The next man, with a compound fracture of his left arm and a series of gashes down his side, required close, prolonged attention: sewing, snipping, binding-up. He was a man of exceptional fortitude even for a foremast-jack and between involuntary gasps he told them that he had been the larboard midship look-out when he saw this sudden spurt of red to windward and a glow under the cloud, and he was hailing the quarterdeck when he heard something like stones or even grape-shot hitting the topsail and then there was a great crash and he was down. He lay on the gangway staring through the scuppers with the rain soaking him through and through before he understood what had happened, and he saw that red spurt show twice: not like a gun, but more lasting and crimson: perhaps a battery, a ragged salvo. Then a cross-sea and a lee-lurch tossed him into the waist until old Plaice and Bonden fished him out.

The groaning from a man against the side grew almost to a scream. 'Oh, oh, oh. Forgive me, mates; I can't bear it. Oh, oh, oh, oh . . . '

'Mr Martin, pray see what you can do,' said Stephen. 'Sarah, my dear, give me the silk-thread needle.'

As she passed it Sarah said in his ear, 'Emily is frightened.'

Stephen nodded, holding the needle between his lips. He was not exactly frightened himself, but he did dread misplacing an instrument or probe. Even down here the ship was moving with a force he had never known: the lantern swung madly, with no sort of rhythm now; and he could scarcely keep his footing.

'This cannot go on,' he murmured. But it did go on; and as he and Martin worked far into the night that part of his mind which was not taken up with probing, sawing, splinting, sewing and bandaging heard and partly recorded what was going on around him – the talk between the hands treated or waiting for treatment, the news brought by fresh cases, the seamen's interpretation of the various sounds and cries on deck.

'There's the foretopmast gone.'

A long discussion of bomb-vessels and the huge mortars they carried: agreement: contradiction.

'Oh for my coca-leaves,' thought Stephen, who so very urgently needed a clear sharp mind untouched by sleep, and a steady hand.

The maintop was broken, injured or destroyed; but the half-heard voices said they should have had to get the topmast down on deck anyhow, with such a sea running and the poor barky almost arsy-versy every minute . . . poor sods on deck . . . it was worse than the tide-race off Sumburgh Head . . . 'This was the day Judas Iscariot was born,' said an Orkneyman.

'Mr Martin, the saw, if you please: hold back the flap and be ready with the tourniquet. Padeen, let him not move at all.' And bending over the patient, 'This will hurt for the moment, but it will not last. Hold steady.'

The amputation gave place to another example of these puzzling lacerated wounds; and Reade came below followed by Killick with a covered mug of coffee.

'Captain's compliments, sir,' said Reade, 'and he thinks the worst may be over: stars in the south-south-west and the swell not quite so pronounced.'

'Many thanks, Mr Reade,' said Stephen. 'And God bless you, Killick.' He swallowed half the mug, passing Martin the rest. 'Tell me, have we been severely pierced? I hear the pumps have been set a-going, and there is a power of water underfoot.'

'Oh no, sir. The masts and the maintop have suffered, but the water is only the ship working, hauling under the chains so her seams open a little. May I ask how Mr West comes along, and Wilcox and Veale, of my division?'

'Mr West is still unconscious. I believe I must open his skull tomorrow. We took Wilcox's fingers off just now: he never said a word and I think he will do well. Veale I have set back till dawn. An eye is a delicate matter and we must have daylight.'

'Well, sir, that will not be long now. Canopus is dipping, and it should be dawn quite soon.'

CHAPTER TWO

A reluctant dawn, a dim blood-red sun; and although the sea was diminishing fast it was still wilder than most sailors had ever seen, with bursting waves and a still-prodigious swell. A desolate ocean, grey now under a deathly white, rolling with enormous force, but still with no life upon it apart from these two ships, now dismasted and tossing like paper boats on a millstream. They were at some distance from one another, both apparently wrecks, floating but out of control: beyond them, to windward, a newly-arisen island of black rock and cinders. It no longer shot out fire, but every now and then, with an enormous shriek, a vast jet of steam leapt from the crater, mingled with ash and volcanic gases. When Jack first saw the island it was a hundred and eighty feet high, but the rollers had already swept away great quantities of the clinker and by the time the sun was clear of the murk not fifty feet remained.

The more northern of the ships, the *Surprise*, was in fact quite well in hand, lying to under a storm trysail on her only undamaged lower mast, while her people did all that very weary men could do – it had been all hands all night – to repair her damaged maintop and to cross at least the lower yard. They had the strongest motives for doing so, since their quarry, totally dismasted and wallowing gunwales under on the swell, lay directly under their lee; but there was no certainty that helpless though she seemed she might not send up some kind of a jury-rig and slip away into the thick weather with its promise of blinding squalls.

'Larbolines bowse,' cried Captain Aubrey, watching the spare topmast with anxious care. 'Bowse away. Belay!' And to his first lieutenant, 'Oh Tom, how I hope the Doctor comes on deck before the land vanishes.'

Tom Pullings shook his head. 'When last I saw him, perhaps an hour ago, he could hardly stand for sleep: blood up to the elbows and blood where he had wiped his eyes.'

'It would be the world's pity, was he to miss all this,' said Jack. He was no naturalist, but from first light he had been very deeply impressed not only by this mineral landscape but also by the universal death all round as far as eye could see. Countless fish of every kind, most wholly unknown to him, lay dead upon their sides; a sperm whale, not quite grey, floated among them; abyssal forms, huge squids, trailing half the length of the ship. And never a bird, never a single gull. A sulphurous whiff from the island half-choked him. 'He will never forgive me if I do not tell him,' he said. 'Do you suppose he has turned in?'

'Good morning, gentlemen,' said Stephen from the companion-ladder. 'What is this I hear about an island?' He was looking indescribably frowzy, unwashed, unshaved, no wig, old bloody shirt, bloody apron still round his waist; and it was clear that even he felt it improper to advance to the holy place itself.

'Let me steady you,' said Jack, stepping across the heaving deck. Stephen had dipped his hands but not his arms, and they looked like pale gloves against the red-brown. Jack seized one, hauled him up and led him to the rail. 'There is the island,' he said. 'But tell me, how is West? And are any of the others dangerously hurt?'

'West: there is no change, and I can do nothing until I have more light and a steadier basis. As for the others, there is always the possibility of sepsis and mortification, but with the blessing I think they will come through. So that is your island. And God help us, look at the sea! A rolling, heaving graveyard. Jesus, Mary and Joseph. Whales: seven, no eight, species of shark: scombridae: cephalopods . . . and all parboiled. This is exactly what Dr Falconer of the *Daisy* told us about — submarine eruption, immense turbulence, the appearance of an island of rock or cinders, a cone shooting out flames, mephitic vapours, volcanic bombs and scoriae — and I never grasped what was happening. Yet there I had the typical lacerated wounds, some-

times accompanied by scorching, and the evidence of heavy globu-
lar objects striking sails, deck, masts, and of course poor West. You
knew what was afoot, I am sure?'

'Not until we began knotting and splicing at first light,' said Jack,
'and when they brought me some of your bombs – there is one there
by the capstan must weigh fifty pound – and showed me the cinders
the rain had not washed away. Then I saw the whole thing plain. I
think I should have smoked it earlier if the island had blazed away
good and steady, like Stromboli; but it kept shooting out jets, quite
like a battery of mortars. But at least I was not so foolishly mistaken
about the *Franklin*. There she lies, right under our lee. You will have
to stand on the caronnade-slide to see her: take my glass.'

The *Franklin* was of infinitely less interest to Dr Maturin than
the encyclopaedia of marine life heaving on the swell below, but he
climbed up, gazed, and said, 'She is in the sad way altogether, with no
masts at all. How she rolls! Do you suppose we shall be able to catch
her? Our sails seem somewhat out of order.'

'Perhaps we shall,' said Jack. 'We should have steerage-way in about
five minutes. But there is no hurry. She has few hands on deck, and
those few cannot be called very brisk. I had much rather bear down
fully prepared, so that there can be no argument, no foolish waste of
life, let alone spars and cordage.'

Six bells, and Stephen said, 'I must go below.'

Jack gave him a hand as far as the ladder, and having urged him 'to
clap on for dear life' asked whether they should meet for breakfast,
adding that 'this unnatural hell-fire sea would go down as suddenly
as it had got up.'

'A late breakfast? I hope so indeed,' said Stephen, making his way
down by single steps and moving, as Jack noticed for the first time,
like an old man.

It was after this late breakfast that Stephen, somewhat restored and
by now reconciled to the fact that the dead marine animals were too

far altered by heat, battering and sometimes by great change of depth to be valued as specimens, sat under an awning watching the *Franklin* grow larger. For the rest, he and Martin contented themselves with counting at least the main genera and rehearsing all that Dr Falconer had said about submarine volcanic activity, so usual in these parts; they had little energy for more. The wind had dropped, and a squall having cleared the air of volcanic dust, the sun beat down on the heaving sea with more than ordinary strength: the *Surprise*, under forecourse and maintopsail, bore slowly down on the privateer, rarely exceeding three knots. Her guns were loaded and run out; her boarders had their weapons at hand; but their earlier apprehensions had died away entirely. The chase had suffered much more than they had; she was much less well equipped with stores and seamen; and she made no attempt to escape. It had to be admitted that with scarcely three foot of her main and mizzen masts showing above deck and the foremast gone at the partners her condition was almost desperate; but she could surely have done something with the wreckage over the side, still hanging by the shrouds and stays, something with the spars still to be seen in her waist, something with her undamaged bowsprit? The Surprises looked at her with a certain tolerant contempt. With the monstrous seas fast declining the galley fires had been lit quite early, and this being Thursday they had all eaten a pound of reasonably fresh pork, half a pint of dried peas, some of the remaining Moahu yams, and as a particular indulgence a large quantity of plum-duff; they had also drunk a quarter of a pint of Sydney rum, publicly diluted with three quarters of a pint of water and lemon-juice, and now with full bellies and benevolent minds they felt that the natural order of things was returning: the barky, though cruelly mauled, was in a fair way to being shipshape; and they were bearing down upon their prey.

Closer and closer, until the capricious breeze headed them and Jack steered south and west to run alongside the *Franklin* on the following tack. But as the *Surprise* was seen to change course a confused bawling arose from the *Franklin* and a kind of raft was launched over her side, paddled by a single man with a bloody bandage round his head. Jack let fly the sheets, checking the frigate's way, and the man, heaved closer by the swell, called, 'Pray can you give me some water for our wounded men? They are dying of thirst.'

'Do you surrender?'

The man half raised himself to reply – he was clearly no seaman – and cried, 'How can you speak so at such a time, sir? Shame on you.' His voice was harsh, high-pitched and furiously indignant. Jack's expression did not change, but after a pause in which the raft drifted nearer he hailed the bosun on the forecastle: 'Mr Bulkeley, there. Let the Doctor's skiff be lowered down with a couple of breakers in it.'

'If you have a surgeon aboard, it would be a Christian act in him to relieve their pain,' said the man on the raft, now closer still.

'By God . . . ' began Jack, and there were exclamations all along the gangway; but as Stephen and Martin had already gone below for their instruments Jack said no more than 'Bonden, Plaice, pull them over. And you had better pass that raft a line. Mr Reade, take possession.'

Ever since this chase began Stephen had been considering his best line of conduct in the event of its success. His would have been a delicate mission in any event, since it presupposed activities contrary to Spanish interests in South America at a time when Spain was at least nominally an ally of the United Kingdom; but now that the British government had been compelled to deny the existence of any such undertaking it was more delicate by far, and he was extremely unwilling to be recognized by Dutourd, whom he had met in Paris: not that Dutourd was a Buonapartist or in any way connected with French intelligence, but he had an immense acquaintance and he was incurably talkative – far too talkative for any intelligence-service to consider making use of him. Dutourd was the man on the raft, the owner of the *Franklin*, and the sequence of events that had brought about their curious proximity, separated by no more than twenty feet of towline, was this: Dutourd, a man of passionate enthusiasms, had like many others at the time fallen in love with the idea of a terrestrial Paradise to be founded in a perfect climate, where there should be perfect equality as well as justice, and plenty without excessive labour, trade or the use of money, a true democracy, a more cheerful Sparta; and unlike most others he was rich enough to carry his theories into something like practice, acquiring this American-built privateer, manning her with prospective settlers and a certain number of seamen, most of the people being French Canadians or men from Louisiana, and sailing her to Moahu, an island well south of Hawaii, where with the help of a northern chief and his own powers of persuasion, he hoped to found his colony. But the northern chief had misused some British ships and seaman, and the *Surprise*, sent to deal with the situation, destroyed him in a short horrible battle immediately before the *Franklin* sailed in from a cruise, a private ship of war wearing American colours. The chase had begun in what seemed another world; now it was ending. As the crowded boat rose and fell, traversing the last quarter of a mile, Stephen derived some comfort from the fact that during his earlier years in Paris he had used the second half of his name, Maturin y Domanova (Mathurin, spelt with an *h* but pronounced without it, having ludicrous associations with idiocy in the jargon of that time) and from the reflection that it was much easier to feign stupidity than wisdom – although it might be a mistake to know no French at all he did not have to speak it very well.

'Bring the raft against the chains,' called Reade.

'Against the chains it is, sir,' replied Bonden; and looking over his shoulder he pulled hard ahead, judging the swell just so. The raft lurched against the *Franklin*'s side, and she was so low in the water that it was no great step for Dutourd to go aboard directly. Two more heaves and Bonden hooked on. Dutourd helped Stephen over the shattered gunwale with one hand while with the other he swept off his hat, saying, 'I am deeply sensible of your goodness in coming, sir.' Stephen instantly saw that his anxiety had been quite needless: there was no hint of recognition in the earnest look that accompanied these words. Of course, a public man like Dutourd, perpetually addressing assemblies, meeting scores, even hundreds of people a day, would not remember a slight acquaintance of several years ago – three or four meetings in Madame Roland's salon before the war, at a time when his republican principles had already caused him to change his name from du Tourd to Dutourd, and then two or three dinners during the short-lived peace. Yet himself he would have known Dutourd, a curiously striking man, more full of life than most, giving the impression of being physically larger than he was in fact: an animated face, an easy rapid flow of speech. Upright: head held high. These thoughts presented themselves to his mind while at the same time he registered the desolation fore and aft, the tangle of sailcloth, cordage and shattered spars, the demoralization of the hands. Some few were still mechanically pumping but most were either drunk or reduced to a hopeless apathy.

Martin, Reade and Plaice boarded the *Franklin* on three successive swells, Bonden fending off; and in a high clear voice Reade, taking off his hat, said, 'Monsieur, je prends le commandement de ce vaisseau.'

'Bien, Monsieur,' said Dutourd.

Reade stepped to the stump of the mainmast: Plaice lashed a stray studding sail boom to it and amid the heavy indifference of the *Franklin*'s crew they hoisted British colours. There was a modest cheer from the *Surprise*. Dutourd said, 'Gentlemen, most of the wounded are in the cabin. May I lead the way?'

As they went down the ladder they heard Reade call to Bonden, who had an extremely powerful voice, telling him to hail the ship and ask for the bosun, his mate, Padeen and all the hands who could be spared: the prize was near foundering.

On the starboard side of the cabin a dozen men lay side by side and another was stretched out motionless on the stern-window locker; in this heat they were suffering terribly from thirst. But the ship had such a heel to larboard that on the other side there was a wretched tangle of living and dead washing about with every roll: screams, groaning, a shocking stench and cries for help, cries for rescue.

'Come, sir, take off your coat,' said Stephen. Dutourd obeyed and the three of them pulled and lifted with what care they could. The dead they dragged to the half-deck; the living they laid in something like an order of urgency. 'Can you command your men?' asked Stephen.

'Some few, I think,' said Dutourd. 'But most of them are drunk.'

'Then tell them to throw the dead overboard and to bring buckets and swabs to clean where the dead men lay.' He called to Bonden out of the shattered stern-window, 'Barret Bonden, now. Can you heave up the little keg till Mr Martin and I can catch a hold on it?'

'I'll try, sir,' said Bonden.

'We shall have to move this man,' said Stephen, nodding at the figure lying on the locker. 'In any case he is dead.'

'He was my sailing-master,' said Dutourd. 'Your last shot killed him, his mate and most of the crew. The other gun burst.'

Stephen nodded. He had seen a raking shot do terrible damage; and as for a bursting gun . . . 'Shall we ease him out of the window? I must look to these men at once.'

'Very well,' said Dutourd, and as the rigid corpse slid into the sea so Bonden called, 'On the rise, sir; clap on,' and the keg came aboard. Martin started the bung with a serving-mallet: he had only a filthy can to serve it out, but in this unnatural parching heat neither filth nor can was of the least account, only the infinitely precious water.

'Now, sir,' said Stephen to Dutourd, 'a pint is all, or you will bloat. Sit here and show me your head.' Beneath the handkerchief, dried blood and matted hair, there was a razor-like cut along the side of his scalp, certainly a piece of flying metal: Stephen clipped, sponged and sewed – no reaction as the needle went in – clapped a bandage over all and said, 'That should answer for the moment. Pray go on deck and set your men to pumping more briskly. They may have the other breaker.'

Stephen was thoroughly accustomed to the consequences of a battle at sea and Martin moderately so, but here the usual gunshot and splinter wounds and the frightful effects of a bursting gun were accompanied by the unfamiliar wounds caused by volcanic eruption, worse lacerations than they had seen in the *Surprise* and, since the *Franklin* had been closer to the vent, much more severe burning. They were both dog-tired, short of supplies, short of strength and of breath in the stifling heat of the cabin, and it was with relief that they saw Padeen arrive with lint, tow, bandages, splints, all that an intelligent man could think of, and heard Mr Bulkeley wind his call, ordering the Franklins to the pumps. They might not have understood the bosun's French, but there was no mistaking his rope's end, his pointing finger and his terrible voice. Jack had sent Awkward Davies over with Padeen, as well as the bosun and all the expert hands he could spare – Davies was biddable with Stephen – and with these two very powerful men to lift, hold and restrain, the medicoes dealt with their patients each in turn.

They were taking a leg off at the hip when Reade came below: averting his ashy face he said, 'Sir, I am to carry the *Franklin*'s master back to the ship with his papers. Have you any message?'

'None, thank you, Mr Reade. Padeen, clap on, now.'

'Before I go, sir, shall I get the bosun to unship the companion?'

Stephen did not hear him through the patient's long quavering scream, but a moment later the whole framework overhead was lifted off and the fetid room was filled with brilliant light and clean, almost cool sea-air.

From the first Jack Aubrey had disliked all that he had heard of Dutourd: Stephen described him as a good benevolent man who had been misled first by 'that mumping villain Rousseau' and later by his passionate belief in his own system, based it was true on a hatred of poverty, war and injustice, but also on the assumption that men were naturally and equally good, needing only a firm, friendly hand to set them on the right path, the path to the realization of their full potentialities. This of course entailed the abolition of the present order, which had so perverted them, and of the established churches. It was old, old stuff, familiar in all its variations, but Stephen had never heard it expressed with such freshness, fire and conviction. Neither fire nor conviction survived to reach Jack in Stephen's summary, however, but the doctrine that levelled Nelson with one of his own bargemen was clear enough, and he watched the approaching boat with a cold look in his eye.

The coldness grew to strong disapproval when Dutourd, coming aboard in the traditional manner with the side-men offering him hand-ropes, failed to salute the quarterdeck. He had also failed to put on a sword to make his formal surrender. Jack at once retired to his cabin, saying to Pullings, 'Tom, pray bring that man below, with his papers.'

He received Dutourd sitting, but he did not tell Killick to place a chair for the gentleman, while to Dutourd himself he said, 'I believe, sir, that you speak English fluently?'

'Moderately so, sir: and may I use what fluency I possess to thank you for your humanity to my people? Your surgeon and his assistant have exerted themselves nobly.'

'You are very good, sir,' said Jack with a civil inclination of his head; and after an enquiry about Dutourd's wound he said, 'I take it that you are not a seaman by profession? That you are not very well acquainted with the customs of the sea?'

'Scarcely at all, sir. I have managed a pleasure-boat, but for the open sea I have always engaged a sailing-master. I cannot describe myself as a seaman: I have spent very little time on the sea.'

'That alters the case somewhat,' thought Jack, and he said, 'Please to show me your papers.'

Dutourd's most recent sailing-master had been an exact and orderly person as well as a taut skipper and an excellent seaman, and Dutourd handed over a complete set wrapped in waxed sailcloth.

Jack looked through them with satisfaction; then frowned and looked through the parcels again. 'But where is your commission, or letter of marque?'

'I have no commission or letter of marque, sir,' replied Dutourd, shaking his head and smiling a little. 'I am only a private citizen, not a naval officer. My sole purpose was to found a colony for the benefit of mankind.'

'No commission, either American or French?'

'No, no. It never occurred to me to solicit one. Is it looked upon as a necessary formality?'

'Very much so.'

'I remember having received a letter from the Minister of Marine wishing me every happiness on my voyage: perhaps that would answer?'

'I am afraid not, sir. Your happiness has included the taking of several prizes, I collect?'

'Why, yes, sir. You will not think me impertinent if I observe that our countries, alas, are in a state of war.'

'So I understand. But wars are conducted according to certain forms. They are not wild riots in which anyone may join and seize whatever he can overpower; and I fear that if you can produce nothing better than the recollection of a letter wishing you every happiness you must be hanged as a pirate.'

'I am concerned to hear it. But as for prizes, as for the merely privateering aspects of the voyage, Mr Chauncy, my sailing-master, has a paper from his government. We sailed under American colours, you will recall. It is in a cover marked *Mr Chauncy's qualifications and references* in my writing-desk.'

'You did not bring it?'

'No, sir. The young gentleman with one arm told me there was not a moment to be lost, so I abandoned all my personal property.'

'I shall send for it. Pray describe the writing-desk.'

'An ordinary brass-bound walnut-tree writing-desk with my name on the plate; but there can be very little hope of finding it now.'

'Why do you say that?'

'My dear sir, I have seen sailors at work aboard a captured ship.'

Jack made no reply but glancing through the scuttle he saw that Bulkeley and his men had now raised a spar on the stump of her mizzenmast, and that with an improvised lugsail she was lying with her head to the sea, lying much easier. The *Surprise* would be alongside in a few minutes.

'Have you any officer surviving unhurt?' he asked.

'None, sir. They were both killed.'

'A servant?'

'Yes, sir. He hid below, with the ransomers.'

'Killick. Killick, there. Pass the word for Captain Pullings.'

'Aye aye, sir: Captain Pullings it is,' replied Killick, who could give a civil answer when guests or prisoners of rank were present: but instead of Pullings there appeared young Norton, who said, 'I beg pardon, sir, but Captain Pullings and Mr Grainger are at the mast-head, getting the top over. May I carry them a message?'

'Are they got so far so soon? Upon my word! Never worry them at such a delicate point, Mr Norton. Jump up on deck yourself, borrow a speaking-trumpet and hail the *Franklin*, telling Bonden and Plaice to have Mr Dutourd's servant, sea-chest and writing-desk ready to be brought across as soon as there is a moment to spare. But first take this gentleman into the gunroom and tell the steward to bring him whatever he calls for. I am going into the foretop.'

'Aye aye, sir. Mr Dutourd's servant, sea-chest and writing-desk as soon as there is a moment; and Mr Dutourd to the gunroom.'

Dutourd opened his mouth to speak, but it was too late. Jack, throwing off his coat, sped from the cabin, making the deck tremble as he went. Norton said, 'This way, sir, if you please,' and some minutes later the message reached Bonden's ear as he and his mates were hauling an uninjured topmast aboard by its shrouds. He in turn hailed the bosun: 'Mr Bulkeley, there. I must take Mr Dutourd's servant, chest and writing-desk across. May I have the skiff?'

'Yes, mate,' replied the bosun, his mouth filled with rope-yarns, 'unless you had sooner walk. And bring me back a pair of girt-lines and two long-tackle blocks. And the coil of one-and-a-half-inch manila abaft the fore-hatchway.'

Jack returned to the cabin with the liveliest satisfaction: in spite of
the absence of Mr Bulkeley and many very able seamen the *Surprise*
had made an extraordinary recovery. It was true that she had at least
half a dozen forecastlemen who, apart from the paper-work, could
have served with credit as bosun in a man-of-war, and it was true that
as Jack was wealthy she was uncommonly well supplied with stores;
yet even so the change from the chaos of first light to the present
approach to trim efficiency was very striking. At this rate the frigate, with four new pairs of preventer-stays set up in the morning,
would be able to carry on under topsails and courses tomorrow; for
the trades were already steadying over a more nearly normal sea.

'Pass the word for Mr Dutourd,' he called.

'Which his name is really Turd,' observed Killick to his mate
Grimshaw before making his way to the gunroom to wake the red-
eyed Frenchman.

'There you are, sir,' said Jack, as he was led into the cabin. 'Here
is your sea-chest, and here is what appears to be your writing-desk,'
pointing to a box whose brass plate, already automatically polished by
Killick, bore the name Jean du Tourd clear and plain.

'I am amazed,' cried Dutourd. 'I never thought to see them again.'

'I hope you will be able to find the cover you spoke of.'

'I am sure I shall: the desk is still locked,' said Dutourd, feeling for
his keys.

'I ask pardon, sir,' said Mr Adams, Jack's highly-valued clerk, 'but it
wants less than a minute to the hour.'

'Forgive me, Monsieur,' cried Jack, leaping from his seat. 'I shall be
back in a few moments. Pray search for your paper.'

He and Adams had been carrying out a chain of observations,
always made at stated intervals: wind direction and strength, estimated current, barometrical pressure, compass variations, humidity,
temperature of the air (both wet bulb and dry) and of the sea at given
depths together with the salinity at those depths, and the blueness of

the sky, a series that was to be carried round the world and communicated to Humboldt on the one hand and the Royal Society on the other. It would be a great pity to break its exact sequence at such a very interesting point.

A long pause; nautical cries; the click-click-click of capstan-pawls as a great spar rose up: and almost immediately after the cry of 'Belay!' Captain Aubrey returned.

'I have found the certificate,' said Dutourd, starting up from his half-doze and handing him a paper.

'I rejoice to hear it,' said Jack. He sat down at his desk; but having read the letter attentively he frowned and said, 'Yes, this is very well, and it allows Mr William B. Chauncy, who was I presume your sailing-master, to take, burn, sink or destroy ships or vessels belonging to His Britannic Majesty or sailing under British colours. But it makes no mention of Mr Dutourd. No mention at all.'

Dutourd said nothing. He was yellow-pale by now: he put his hand to his bandaged head, and Jack had the impression that he no longer cared whether he was to be hanged as a pirate or not, so long as he was allowed to lie down in peace for a while.

Jack considered for some moments and then said, 'Well, sir, I must say you are an anomalous kind of prisoner, rather like the creature that was neither flesh nor fowl nor good red herring but partook of each: the Sphinx. You are a sort of owner, a sort of commander, though absent from the muster-roll, and a sort of what I can only call a pirate. I am not at all sure what I ought to do with you. As you have no commission I cannot treat you as an officer: you cannot berth aft.' Another pause, during which Dutourd closed his eyes. 'But fortunately the *Surprise* is a roomy ship with a small company, and right forward on the lower deck we have made cabins for the gunner, the bosun and the carpenter. There are still two to spare and you shall have one of them. Since you have no surviving officers you will have to mess by yourself, but I dare say the gunroom will invite you quite often; and of course you may have the liberty of the quarterdeck.'

Dutourd made no acknowledgement of this offer. His head

drooped, and the next roll pitched him right out of his seat, head first. Jack picked him up, laid him on the cushioned stern lock and called for Killick.

'What are you a-thinking of, sir?' cried his steward. 'Don't you see he is bleeding like a pig from under his bandage?' Killick whipped into the quarter-gallery for a towel and thrust it under Dutourd's head. 'Now I must take all them covers off and soak them this directly minute in cold fresh water and there ain't no cold fresh water, which the scuttle-butt is empty till Chips comes back and shifts the hand-pump.'

'Never you mind the bloody covers,' said Jack, suddenly so angry with extreme weariness that it cowed even Killick. 'You and Grimshaw jump forward to the cabin next the bosun's: get a bed from Mr Adams, sling a hammock, and lay him in it. And have his sea-chest lighted along, d'ye hear me, there?'

Extreme weariness: it pervaded both ships, evening out the gloom of the defeated and the elation of the conquerors. Both sets of men would have resigned prize-money or freedom to be allowed to go below and take their ease. But it was not to be: the few able-bodied prisoners had to pump steadily to keep their ship clear, or haul on a rope at the word of command; and in both ships it was all hands on deck until enough canvas could be spread to allow them at least to lie to in something like safety if it came on to blow; for the glass was far from steady, and neither the midday nor the present evening sky was at all certain.

The only apparently idle hands in either ship were the medical men. They had returned to the frigate some time before; they had made the rounds of the sick-berth and its extensions and now they were waiting for a pause in the general activity, when someone would have time to pull Martin, who was to spend the night in the *Franklin*, across the lane of choppy water that separated the ships. Although both medicoes could row, after a fashion, neither could afford to have inept, clumsy fingers with so strong a likelihood of further surgery.

They were watching the extraction of the *Franklin*'s broken lower masts and their replacement by a jury-rig, and from time to time Stephen explained the various operations. 'There, do you see,' he said, 'those two very long legs joining at the top with a pair of stout pulleys at the juncture and their feet resting on planks either side of the deck, are the sheers I was speaking about. See, the men haul them upright by a rope, perhaps even a hawser, running through yet another pulley, or block as I should say, to the capstan; while at the same time any undue motion is restrained by the – Mr Reade, what is the name of those ropes fore and aft and sideways?'

'Guys, sir; and those at the bottom of the sheers are tail-tackles.'

'Thank you, my dear. Let me advise you not to run in that impetuous manner, however.'

'Oh sir, if I did not run in this impetuous manner . . .'

'Mr Reade, there. Have you gone to sleep again?' called Pullings, very hoarse, very savage.

'Now, as you see, Martin, the sheers are quite upright: they let down the lower pulley – the bosun attaches it to the broken mast by a certain knot – he bids them heave, or haul – he encourages them with cries – with blows. Those must be the idle prisoners. The stump rises – it is detached, cast off – they bring the new spar – I believe it is one of our spare topmasts – they make it fast – up it rises, up and up and up until it dangles over the very hole, the partners as the mariner calls it – and yet with the motion of the ship how it wanders! – Mr Bulkeley seizes it – he cries out – they lower away and the mast descends – it is firm, pinned no doubt and wedged. Someone – it is surely Barret Bonden – is hoisted to the trestle-trees to place the rigging over the upper end in due order.'

'If you please, sir,' said Emily, 'Padeen says may Willis have his slime-draught now?'

'He may have it at the third stroke of the bell,' said Stephen. She

ran off, her slim black form weaving unnoticed through gangs of seamen intent upon a great variety of tasks, too weary to be jocular, and
Stephen said, 'If one, then all; and we have mere chaos.'

He had often said this before, and Martin only nodded. They
watched in silence as the sheers moved forward to the stump of the
Franklin's mainmast, fitting to it a curious object made up of yet
another spare topmast and a hand-mast, the two coupled athwartships by two lower caps and a double upper cap above the refash-
ioned maintop.

Stephen did not attempt to explain the course of this particular
operation, which he had never seen before. Until now neither had
spoken of West's death apart from their brief exchange in the sick-
berth, but during a short pause in the hammering behind them and
the repeated shouts from the *Franklin* Stephen said, 'I am of opinion
that there was such damage to the brain that an even earlier, more
skilful intervention would have made no difference.'

'I am certain of it,' said Martin.

'I wish I were,' thought Stephen. 'Yet then again, what is gratifying
to self-love is not necessarily untrue.'

The arduous fitting of the double cap went on and on: they watched
in stupid, heavy-headed incomprehension.

'Such news, sir,' cried Reade, flitting by. 'The Captain is going to
send up a lateen on her mizzen. What a sight that will be! It will not
be long now.'

The sun was nearly touching the horizon, and both over the water
and in the *Surprise* the people could be seen coiling down and clearing away; the carpenters were collecting their tools; Stephen, sunk in
melancholy thought, recalled his motions with that singular clarity
which comes with certain degrees of tiredness and in some dreams.
He could feel the vibration of his trephine cutting through the injured
skull, an operation he had carried out many, many times without failure, the raising of the disk of bone, the flow of extravasated blood.

They were both far away in their reflections and Stephen had
almost forgotten that he was not alone when Martin, his eyes fixed on

the prize, said, 'You understand these things better than I do, for sure: pray which do you think the better purchase for a man in my position and with my responsibilities, the Navy Fives or South Sea stock?'

Stephen was called out only twice that night; and his third sleep was of the most delicious kind, changing, evolving, from something not unlike coma to a consciousness of total relaxation, of mental recovery and physical comfort; and so he lay, blinking in the early light and musing on a wide variety of pleasant things: Diana's kindness to him when he was ill in Sweden; goshawks he had known; a Boccherini 'cello sonata; whales. But a steady, familiar, discordant noise pierced through this amiable wandering: several times he dismissed his identification as absurd. He had known the Navy for many years; he was acquainted with its excesses; but this was too wild entirely. Yet at last the combination of sounds, grinding, scrubbing, bucket clashing, water streaming, swabs driving the tide into the scuppers, bare feet padding and hoarse whispers just over his head could no longer be denied: the larboard watch and the idlers were cleaning the deck, getting all the volcanic dust and cinders from under gratings, gun-carriages and such unlikely places as the binnacle drawers.

Yet as his conscious mind accepted this so yesterday came flooding back, and the extravagance of the sailors' activity disappeared. Mr West had died. He was to be buried at sea in the forenoon watch, and they were seeing to it that he should go over the side from a ship in tolerably good order. He was not an outstandingly popular officer; nor was he very clever, either, and sometimes he did tend to top it the knob, being more quarterdeck than tarpaulin; but he was not in the least ill-natured – never had a man brought up before the Captain as a defaulter – and there was no question at all of his courage. He had distinguished himself when the *Surprise* cut the *Diane* out at St Martin's, while in this last affair at Moahu he had done everything a good, active officer could do. But above all they were used to him: they had sailed with him for a great while now: they liked what they were used to; and they knew what was due to a shipmate.

If there had been any danger of Stephen's forgetting, then the appearance of the deck when he came up into the sparkling open air and the brilliant light after his long morning round would have brought it all to mind. Quite apart from the fact that the waist of the ship, the part between the quarterdeck and the forecastle, where ordinarily he saw a mass of spare masts, yards and spars in general covered with tarpaulins on the booms, the boats nestling among them, was now quite clear, the spars nearly all used and the boats either busy or towing astern, which gave her a singular clean-run austerity – quite apart from this there had been an extraordinary change from the apparent confusion and real filth of yesterday to a Sunday neatness, falls flemished, brass flaming in the sun, yards (such as there were) exactly squared by the lifts and braces. But there was an even greater change in the atmosphere, a formality and gravity shown at one end of the scale by Sarah and Emily, who had finished their duties in the sick-berth half an hour before and who were now standing on the forecastle in their best pinafores looking solemnly at the *Franklin*, and at the other by Jack Aubrey, who was returning from her in the splendour of a post-captain, accompanied by Martin and rowed with great exactness by his bargemen.

'There, sir,' said Reade at Stephen's side. 'That is what I meant by a splendid sight.'

Stephen followed his gaze beyond the Captain's boat to the *Franklin*. She had cast off her tow and she was sailing along abreast of the *Surprise*, making a creditable five knots under her courses, with the great triangular lateen drum-taut on her mizzen gleaming in the sun. 'Very fine, indeed,' he said.

'She reminds me of the old *Victory*,' observed Reade after a moment.

'Surely to God the *Victory* has not been sunk, or sold out of the service?' asked Stephen, quite startled. 'I knew she was old, but thought her immortal, the great ark of the world.'

'No, sir, no,' said Reade patiently. 'We saw her in the chops of the Channel, not two days out. What I mean is in ancient times, in the last age, before the war even, she used to have a mizzen like that. We have a picture of her at home: my father was her second lieutenant at Toulon, you know. But come, sir, you will have to shift your coat or go below. The Captain will be aboard any minute now.'

'Perhaps I should disappear,' said Stephen, passing a hand over his unshaven chin.

The *Surprise*, having checked her way, received her Captain with all the ceremony she could manage in her present state. The bosun's mates piped the side; Tom Pullings, acting as first lieutenant, Mr Grainger, the second, Mr Adams, the clerk and de facto purser, and both midshipmen, all in formal clothes, took off their hats; and the Captain touched his own to the quarterdeck. Then with a nod to Pullings he went below, where Killick, who had been watching his progress from the moment he left the *Franklin*, had a pot of coffee ready.

Attracted by the smell, Stephen walked in, holding a sharpened razor in his hand; but perceiving that Jack and Pullings meant to talk about matters to do with the ship he drank only two cups and withdrew to the fore-cabin in which he usually had his being. Jack called after him 'As soon as Martin has changed his clothes, he will be on deck, you know,' and at the same time Killick, whose never very amiable character had been soured still further by having to look after both Captain and Doctor for years and years, burst in at the forward door with Stephen's good coat over his arm. In a shrill, complaining voice he cried, 'What, ain't you even shaved yet? God love us, what a disgrace it will bring to the ship.'

'Now Tom,' said Jack Aubrey, 'I will tell you very briefly how things are in the *Franklin*. Grainger and Bulkeley and the others have done most uncommonly well and we can send up topmasts tomorrow. I have been considering the prize-crew, and although we cannot spare many, I think we shall manage. She has twenty-one hands left fit to serve, and together with what the Doctor can patch up and three of the English ransomers and a carpenter they took out of a Hull whaler to replace their own she should be adequately manned without weakening the *Surprise* too much. I mean they should be able to fight at least one side, not merely carry her into port. Most of the Franklins understood some English so I told them the usual things: those that saw fit to volunteer should berth with our own people on the lower deck, have full rations, grog and tobacco, and be paid off in South America according to their rating, while those that did not should be kept in the fore-hold on two-thirds rations, no grog and no tobacco and be carried back to England. One of the ransomers, a boy, spoke French as brisk as the Doctor, and what they did not understand from me they understood from him. I left them to think it over, and there is not much doubt about the result. When we have re-armed her with our carronades she will make an admirable consort. You shall have command of her, and I will promote Vidal here. We can certainly find you three men capable of standing a watch: Mr Smith, for one, and he will stiffen their gunnery. And even if we were not so well supplied, two of the ransomers were mates of their ship, the one a fur-trader on the Nootka run, the other a whaler. Have you any observations, Captain Pullings?'

'Well, sir,' said Pullings, returning his smile, but with a certain constraint, 'I take it very kindly that you should give me the command, of course. As for Vidal, he is a prime seaman, of course: there is no doubt of that. But he is the leader of the Knipperdollings, and the Knipperdollings and the Sethians have been at odds ever since the love-feast at the Methody chapel in Botany Bay. And as you know very well, sir, some of the most respected hands on board are Sethians or their close friends; and to have a Knipperdolling set over them . . . '

'Hell and death, Tom,' said Jack. 'You are quite right. It had slipped my mind.'

It should not have slipped his mind. For although Shelmerston was well known for bold enterprising expert seamen – Vidal himself had armed a ship and cruised upon the Barbary corsairs themselves with remarkable success – it was even better known for its bewildering variety of religious sects, some, like the Sethians, with origins hazy in the remote past, some, like the Knipperdollings, quite recent but a little apt to be quarrelsome by land if a point of doctrine were raised; and at the love-feast in Botany Bay a disagreement on the filioque clause had ended in many a black eye, many a bloody nose and broken head.

Jack repressed some reflections on seamen and theology, blue-light officers and tracts, and said, 'Very well. I shall rearrange the prize-crew. Peace at all costs. You shall have the Sethians and I shall bring back what Knipperdollings there may be in the *Franklin*. By the way, what is a Knipperdolling?'

Pullings looked perfectly blank, and slowly shook his head.

'Well, never mind. The Doctor will know, or even better Martin. I hear his voice on deck. They will start tolling the bell directly.'

CHAPTER THREE

They buried West in 12°35′N, 152°17′W; and some days later his clothes, according to the custom of the sea, were sold at the mainmast.

Henry Vidal, a master-mariner shipping as a forecastle-hand for this voyage, bought West's formal coat and breeches. He and his Knipperdolling friends removed all the lace and any ornament that could be taken for a mark of rank, and it was in these severe garments that he presented himself, on his promotion to acting second lieutenant, for his first dinner in the gunroom.

For this occasion too Stephen dined below; but the nature of the present feast was entirely different. For one thing the ship was still a great way from her settled routine; there was still a great deal to be done aboard the frigate and in the *Franklin*, and this could not be the leisurely ceremony with which Grainger had been welcomed. For another the atmosphere was much more like that of a civilian gathering, three of the eight people having nothing whatsoever to do with the Navy: at the foot of the table, on either side of Mr Adams, sat two ransomers, men taken from her prizes by the *Franklin* as security for the sum the ships had agreed to pay for their release; in Pullings's absence Grainger was at the head, with Stephen on his right and Vidal on his left, while in the middle of the table Martin sat opposite Dutourd, invited by Adams on a hint from the Captain.

It was therefore much less of an ordeal for Vidal: there was no intimidating gold lace; many of the people were as much strangers to the table as he was himself; and he was very well with his neighbours, Grainger, whom he had known from boyhood, and Dutourd, whom he found particularly sympathetic; while Dr Maturin, his shipmate in three commissions, was not a man to put a newcomer out of countenance.

Indeed, after their first kindly welcome of the new officer there was no need for taking any special care of him: Vidal joined in the fine steady flow of talk, and presently Stephen, abandoning his social duties, as he so often did, confined himself to his dinner, his wine and to contemplating his messmates.

The ransomers on either side of Adams, the one a supercargo and the other a merchant, both out of fur-traders, were still in the full joy of their liberation, and sometimes they laughed for no reason whatsoever, while a joke such as 'What answer was given to him, that dissuaded one from marrying a wife because she was now wiser? "I desire," said he, "my wife should have no more wit, than to be able to distinguish my bed from another man's," ' threw them into convulsions. It was noticeable that they were both on good terms with Dutourd; and this did not seem to Stephen to be merely the result of their being set free, but a settled state of affairs.

As for Dutourd himself, Stephen already knew him pretty well in his present condition, since Dutourd came every day to visit those Franklins who had been brought across to be cared for in the *Surprise*'s capacious sick-berth. Stephen necessarily spoke French to these patients, and with such frequent contact it would have been childish to conceal his fluency. Dutourd for his part took it for granted and made no comment, any more than Stephen took notice of Dutourd's English, remarkably exact and idiomatic, though occasionally marked by the nasal twang of the northern colonies, in which he had spent some early years.

He was sitting there in the middle of the table, upright, buoyant, wearing a light-blue coat and his own hair, cropped in the Brutus fashion, talking away right and left, suiting himself to his company and apparently enjoying his dinner: yet he had lost everything, and that everything was sailing along under the lee of the *Surprise*, commanded by those who had taken him prisoner. Insensibility? Stoicism? Magnanimity? Stephen could not tell: but it was certainly not mere levity, for what Stephen did know was that Dutourd was a highly intelligent man with an enquiring not to say an inquisitive mind. He was now engaged in extracting an account of English municipal government from Vidal, his right-hand neighbour and Stephen's vis-à-vis.

Vidal was a middle-aged seaman with much of the dignity that Stephen had often observed in those who were masters of their trade: yet apart from his earrings one would scarcely have taken him for a sailor. His face, though tanned mahogany, was more that of a good-natured reading man and it would have been no surprise to see him reach for a pair of spectacles. He had the habitual gravity expected of an elder, but his expression was far from humourless; there was nothing of the Holy Joe about him and he was perfectly at home in a ribald, profane ship's company and in a bloody, close-fought action. He laughed at his messmates' mediaeval jokes, at the young men's occasional horseplay, and at the facetiousness of his cousin the bosun; but no one, at any time, would have attempted to make game of him.

Stephen's mind wandered away on the subject of authority, its nature, origin, base or bases: authority whether innate or acquired, and if acquired then by what means? Authority as opposed to mere power, how exactly to be defined? Its etymology: its relation to *auctor*. From these thoughts he was aroused by an expectant silence opposite him, and looking up he saw Dutourd and Vidal looking at him across the table, their forks poised: reaching back in his mind he caught the echo of a question: 'What do you think of democracy?'

'The gentleman was asking what you thought of democracy, sir,' said Vidal, smiling.

'Alas I cannot tell you, sir,' said Stephen, returning the smile. 'For although it would not be proper to call this barque or vessel a King's ship except in the largest sense, we nevertheless adhere strictly to the naval tradition which forbids the discussion of religion, women, or politics in our mess. It has been objected that this rule makes for insipidity, which may be so; yet on the other hand it has its uses, since in this case for example it prevents any member from wounding any other gentleman present by saying that he did not think the policy that put Socrates to death and that left Athens prostrate was the highest expression of human wisdom, or by quoting Aristotle's definition of democracy as mob-rule, the depraved version of a commonwealth.'

'Can you suggest a better system?' asked Dutourd.

'Sir,' said Stephen, 'my words were those of some hypothetical person: where my own views are concerned, tradition seals my mouth. As I have told you, we do not discuss politics at this table.'

'Quite right too,' called out the merchant on Adams's left. 'If there is one thing I hate more than topics it is politics. Damn all talk of Whigs, Tories and Radicals, say I: and damn all topics too, like the state of the poor and slavery and reform. Let us talk about the enclosing of commons, annuities and South Sea stock, like this gentleman here, and how to make two groats where only one grew before, ha, ha!' He clapped Martin on the shoulder and repeated 'Two groats where only one grew before.'

'I am very sorry to have offended against your tradition, gentlemen,' said Dutourd, recollecting himself, 'but I am no seaman, and I have never before had the honour of sitting down in an English officers' mess.'

'A glass of wine with you, sir,' said Stephen, bowing to him across the table.

It had been foreseen that with so much work to do inboard and out the dinner would come to an early end; and once the cloth was drawn it moved on quickly to the loyal toast.

'You understand, sir,' said Grainger to Dutourd in terms that he had prepared beforehand, 'that those parties who have not the happiness of being his subjects are not required to drink the King.'

'You are very good, sir,' replied Dutourd, 'but I am perfectly willing to drink to the gentleman's good health: God bless him.'

Shortly after this the table emptied and Stephen and Martin took a turn on the quarterdeck until six bells, when they were invited to drink coffee with the Captain, who however hungry he might be was required by custom to dine later than anyone else. After the shadowy gunroom the full day was almost intolerably bright, a blue day with white clouds sailing on the warm breeze, a white ripple on the small cross-seas, no marked roll or pitch. They paced up and down with their eyes narrowed until they became used to the brilliance; and Martin said, 'An odd, somewhat disturbing thing happened to me this morning. I was coming back from the *Franklin* when Johnson pointed out a bird, a small pale bird that overtook us, circled the boat and flew on: certainly a petrel and probably Hahnemann's. Yet although I watched it with a certain pleasure I suddenly realized that I did not really care. I did not mind what it was called.'

'We have never yet seen Hahnemann's petrel.'

'No. That was what made it so disturbing. I must not compare great things with small, but one hears of men losing their faith: waking up one morning and finding that they do not believe in the Creed they must recite to the congregation in a few hours' time.'

'One does, too. And on a scale of infinitely less consequence but still distressing there was a cousin of mine in the County Down who found – one morning, just as you say – that he no longer loved the young woman to whom he had made an offer. She was the same young woman, with the same physical advantages and the same accomplishments; she had done nothing reprehensible; but he did not love her.'

'What did the poor man do?'

'He married her.'

'Was the marriage happy?'

'When you look about among your acquaintance do you find many happy marriages?'

Martin considered. 'No,' he said, 'I do not. My own is very happy, however; and with *that*,' nodding over the water at the prize, 'it is likely to be even happier. All the hands who have been on the Nootka run say she is extremely rich. And sometimes I wonder whether, with such a wife, a parish and the promise of preferment, I am justified in leading my present wandering life, delightful though it may be on such a day as this.'

Six bells, and they hurried down the companion-ladder. 'Come in, gentlemen, come in,' cried Jack. He was always a little over-cordial with Martin, whom he did not like very much and whom he did not invite as often as he felt he ought. Killick's arrival with the coffee and his mate's with little toasted slices of dried breadfruit masked the slight, the very slight, awkwardness and when they were all sitting comfortably, holding their little cups and gazing out of the sweep of windows that formed the aftermost wall of the great cabin, Jack asked, 'What news of your instrument, Mr Martin?'

The instrument in question was a viola, upon which, before it was broken, Martin played indifferently, having an uncertain ear and an imperfect sense of time. No one had expected to hear it again this voyage, or at least not until they touched at Callao; but the fortune of war had brought them a French repairer, a craftsman who had been sent to Louisiana for a variety of crimes, mostly crapulous, and who, escaping from bondage, had joined the *Franklin*.

'Gourin says that Mr Bentley has promised him a piece of lignum vitae as soon as he has a moment to spare: then it will be only half a day's work, and time for the glue to dry.'

'I am so glad,' said Jack. 'We must have some more music one of these days. There is another thing I wanted to ask, for you know a great deal about the various religious persuasions, as I recall?'

'I should, sir, because in the days when I was only an unbeneficed clergyman,' said Martin, with a bow towards his patron, 'I translated the whole of Muller's great book, wrote my version out again in a fair copy, saw it through the press and corrected two sets of proofs; every word I read five times, and some very curious sects did I come across. There were the Ascitants, for example, who used to dance round an inflated wine-skin.'

'The people I should like to know about are Knipperdollings.'

'Our Knipperdollings?'

'Oh, Knipperdollings in general: I do not mean anything personal.'

'Well, sir, historically they were the followers of Bernhard Knipperdolling, one of those Münster Anabaptists who went to such very ill-considered lengths, enforcing equality and the community of goods and then going on to polygamy – John of Leiden had four wives at a time, one of them being Knipperdolling's daughter – and I am afraid that even worse disorders followed. Yet I think they left little in the way of doctrinal posterity, unless they can be said to live on in the Socinians and Mennonites, which few would accept. Those who use the name at present are descendants of the Levellers. The Levellers, as you will recall, sir, were a party with strong republican views in the Civil War; they wished to level all differences of rank, reducing the nation to an equality; and some of them wanted land to be held in common – no private ownership of land. They were very troublesome in the army and the state; they earned a thoroughly bad name and eventually they were put down, leaving only a few scattered communities. I believe the Levellers as a body did not have a religious as opposed to a social or political unity, though I cannot think that any of them belonged to the Established Church; yet some of these remaining communities formed a sect with strange notions of the Trinity and a dislike of infant baptism; and to avoid the odium attached to the name of Levellers and indeed the persecution they called themselves Knipperdollings, thinking that more respectable or at least more obscure. I imagine they knew very little of the Knipperdollings' religious teaching but had retained a traditional knowledge of their notions of social justice, which made them think the name appropriate.'

'It is remarkable,' observed Stephen after a pause, 'that the *Surprise*, with her many sects, should be such a peaceful ship. To be sure, there was that slight want of harmony between the Sethians and the Knipperdollings at Botany Bay – and in passing I may once more point out, sir, that if this vessel supplied her people with round rather than square plates, these differences would be slighter still; for you are to consider that a square plate has four corners, each one of which makes it more than a mere contunding instrument.' He perceived from the civil inclinations of Captain Aubrey's head and the reserved expression on his face that the square plates issued to the *Surprise* when she

was captured from the French in 1796 would retain their lethal corners as long as he or any other right-minded sea-officer commanded
her: the Royal Navy's traditions were not to be changed for the sake
of a few broken heads. Stephen continued ' . . . but generally speaking
there is no discord at all; whereas very often the least difference of
opinion leads to downright hatred.'

'That may be because they tend to leave their particular obser-
vances on shore,' said Martin. 'The Thraskites are a Judaizing body
and they would recoil from a ham at Shelmerston, but here they
eat up their salt pork, aye, and fresh too when they can get it. And
then when we rig church on Sundays they and all the others sing the
Anglican psalms and hymns with great good-will.'

'For my own part,' said Captain Aubrey, 'I have no notion of dis-
liking a man for his beliefs, above all if he was born with them. I find
I can get along very well with Jews or even . . . ' The P of Papists was
already formed, and the word was obliged to come out as Pindoos.

Yet it had hardly fallen upon Stephen's ear before a shriek and
the crash of glass expelled embarrassment: young Arthur Wedell, a
ransomer of Reade's age, who lived and messed in the midshipmen's
berth, fell through the skylight into the cabin.

Reade had been deprived of youthful company for a great while,
and although he was often invited to the gunroom and the cabin
he missed it sorely: at first Norton, though a great big fellow for his
age, had been too bashful to be much of a companion in the berth,
but now that Arthur had been added to them his shyness wore away
entirely and the three made enough noise for thirty, laughing and
hooting far into the night, playing cricket on the 'tween-decks when
the hammocks were out of the way or football in the vacant larboard
berth when they were not; but this was the first time they had ever
hurled one of their number into the cabin.

'Mr Grainger,' said Jack, when it had been found that Wedell was
not materially injured and when the lieutenant had been summoned
from the head, 'Mr Wedell will jump up to the mizzen masthead
immediately, Mr Norton to the fore, and you will have Mr Reade

whipped up to the main. They will stay there until I call them down.
Pass the word for the carpenter; or for my joiner, if Mr Bentley is not
in the way.'

'I have rarely known such delightful weather in what we must, I suppose, call the torrid zone,' said Stephen, dining as usual in the cabin.
'Balmy zephyrs, a placid ocean, two certain Hahnemann's petrels,
and perhaps a third.'

'It would be all very capital for a picnic with ladies on a lake, particularly if they shared your passion for singular birds; but I tell you,
Stephen, that these balmy zephyrs of yours have not propelled the
ship seventy sea-miles between noon and noon these last four days.
It is true that we could get along a little faster ourselves, but clearly
we cannot leave the *Franklin* behind; and with her present rig she is
but a dull sailer.'

'I noticed that you have changed her elegant great triangular sail
behind.'

'Yes. Now that we are making progess with her lower masts we can
no longer afford that very long lateen yard: we need it for pole topgallants. Presently you will see that twin jury mainmast of hers replaced
by something less horrible made up from everything you can imagine
by Mr Bentley and that valuable carpenter we rescued: upper-tree,
side-trees, heel-pieces, side-fishes, cheeks, front-fish and cant-pieces,
all scarfed, coaked, bolted, hooped and woolded together; it will be
a wonderful sight when it is finished, as solid as the Ark of the Cov-
enant. Then with that in place, and the respectable fore and mizzen
we already possess, we can send up topmasts and the pole topgallants
I was telling you about. That will be best of what breeze there is. How
I long to see her royals! I have sworn not to touch my fiddle until they
are set.'

'You are in a great hurry to reach Peru, I find.'

'Of course I am. So would you be, could you see our bread-room,
our spirit-room, reckon up our water and count our pork and beef

casks, with all these new hands aboard. Above all our water. We had
no time to fill at Moahu, or the Franklin would have run clear. And
she having pumped all hers over the side, we are now in a sad way.
There is only one thing for it: no fresh water will be allowed for washing clothes or anything else: only a small ration for drinking – no
scuttle-butts standing about – and a minimum for the steep-tubs to
get what salt off the pork and beef that towing them in a net over the
side won't do.'

'But since we can go so much faster, could you not give the *Franklin* a modicum, sail briskly on and let her follow? After all, Tom found
his way here: he could surely find it back.'

'What a fellow you are, Stephen. My whole plan is to arm her with
our carronades and cruise in company, snapping up what China
ships, whalers and fur-traders may appear, then to send *Surprise* in
to Callao with I hope a captured ship or two so that they can be disposed of there and you can go ashore. Tom will be in command –
they are used to him in Callao because of the prizes he took on the
way out – and the barky will go on topping it the privateer. And while
you are looking after your affairs and Tom is victualling, watering
and getting in stores, I shall cruise alone offshore, sending in captures
from time to time or at all events a boat. But without we spread more
canvas we shall never get there before we die of thirst and starvation:
that is why I am so eager to see the *Franklin* fully masted and looking like a Christian ship at last, instead of a God-damned curiosity.'

'So am I, upon my word,' said Stephen, thinking of his coca-leaves.
'I can hardly wait.'

'Possess yourself in patience for a day or two, and you will see her
set her royals. Then that evening we shall have a concert – we may
even sing!'

At the time Stephen wondered that Jack should speak so thought-
lessly, tempting a Fate that he almost always placated with a *perhaps*
or *if we are lucky* or *tide and weather permitting*; and Stephen being

by now a thorough-going seaman at least as far as weak superstition was concerned he was more grieved than surprised when a top-maul fell upon Mr Bentley's foot early the next morning. The wound was not dangerous but it confined the carpenter to his cot for a while and in the mean time his crew, most unhappily, fell out with the carpenter from the *Franklin*. The privateer had taken him from a Hull whaler and he spoke a Yorkshire dialect almost entirely incomprehensible to the West-Country hands from Shelmerston, who looked upon him with dislike and suspicion as little better than a foreigner, a French dog or a Turk.

Work therefore went forward slowly, and not only work on the mast but the innumerable tasks that waited on its erection; and with an equal or even greater deliberation the two ships moved over the quiet sea through this perfect picnic weather. In spite of his eagerness to be in South America it pleased Stephen, who spread himself naked in the sun and even swam with Jack in the mornings: it pleased most of the people, who could devote themselves to a detailed reckoning of the *Franklin*'s worth and the value of the goods she had taken out of her various prizes and dividing the total according to each man's share; and it would have pleased the midshipmen if the Captain had not come down on them like a thousand of bricks. Football was abolished, cricket prohibited, and they were kept strictly to their duty, taking altitudes right and left, showing up their day's working (which rarely amounted to fifty miles of course made good) and writing their journals neat and fair. No blots were allowed, and a mistaken logarithm meant no supper: they walked about barefoot or in list slippers, rarely speaking above a whisper.

During this time Stephen often went forward to Mr Bentley's cabin to dress and poultice his poor foot, and on these occasions he sometimes heard Dutourd, whose quarters were close at hand, talking to his neighbour the bosun or to the visiting Grainger or Vidal: quite frequently to more, most of them forecastlemen during their watch below. Stephen did not listen particularly but he did notice that when Dutourd was speaking to one or two his voice was that of ordinary human conversation – rather better in fact, since he was unusually good company – but that when several were present he tended to address them in a booming tone and to go on and on. They did not seem to dislike it, though there was little new to be said about equality, the brotherhood of man, the innate goodness and wisdom of human nature unoppressed; but then, he reflected, Dutourd's hearers, Knipperdollings for the most part, were accustomed to much longer discourses at home.

Mr Bentley's innate wisdom told him that if he remained in the Doctor's list much longer the newcomer would get the credit for the *Franklin's* mainmast, now nearing completion in spite of doggedness on the part of the carpenter's crew, and this, though he was a good and benevolent man, he could not bear. In spite of the pain he crossed to the prize the morning the last of the *Franklin's* casualties were buried. The privateer's company had not been together long enough to form a united crew and the dead went over the side with little ceremony and less mourning, though in the general indifference Dutourd did say a few words, received with approving nods by his former shipmates before they went back to work: they had all volunteered to serve as temporary Surprises, mainly, it was thought, for the sake of the tobacco.

Mr Bentley was only just in time. The Captain had already gone aboard the *Franklin*, meaning to take advantage of the calm sea to carry out the delicate manoeuvre of getting the new mast in by the old, the composite old; for by now neither ship could provide adequate sheers. With propitious weather, an eager and highly competent skipper and an eager and highly competent first lieutenant, both of them capable of hard-horse driving, there was certainly not going to be any leisure for mocking at a Yorkshire word: there was not indeed going to be loss of a single minute, and the carpenter heaved himself up the side, limping to his place by the new mainmast's heel.

Nearly all the *Surprise's* hands were aboard the prize, prepared to haul, heave, or gather up the wreckage in the by no means improbable event of accident, and it was Stephen who rowed Bentley across in his little skiff: a frightening experience. Having delivered the carpenter, he brought Martin back. The medical men had no place on the crowded, busy, anxious deck: ropes ran in every direction, and wherever they stood they were liable to be in the way: in any case since those Franklins who had been left in the ship were now either healed or buried, Martin's duty there was at an end.

The frigate's cook, a fine great black man with one leg, and a bearded Thraskite helped them up the side, Martin carrying his mended viola; and leaving the boat to more skilful hands the medicoes leaned on the rail for a while, watching the operations over the water.

'I wish I could explain what they are about,' said Stephen, 'but this is so much more complex than the business with the sheers that with your own limited command of the seamen's language you might not be able to follow me. Indeed, I might even lead you into error.'

'How quiet it is,' said Martin. Uncommonly quiet: a gentle heave and set, the yards and rigging answering each with a murmur; but no break and run of water, no singing of the breeze, and scarcely a word from the few hands aboard, grouped on the forecastle and gazing steadily at the *Franklin*.

'So quiet,' said Stephen some minutes later, 'that I believe I shall take advantage of it to write in peace for a while. There will soon be a stamping as of wild beasts and cries of belay, avast, and masthead, there.'

'My dearest soul,' he wrote, continuing an unfinished sheet, 'I have just ferried Nathaniel Martin back, and I am afraid he regrets his return. He was happier messing along with Tom Pullings in the prize, and on the few occasions when he had come back to help me or to attend a particular dinner I have noticed that he has seemed more ill at ease in the gunroom than he was before. We now have added to our company one of the ransomer mates, recently discharged from the sick-berth, and the loud-voiced confident mirth of the supercargo, the merchant and this mate oppresses him; nor can it be said that the conversation of our two acting-lieutenants is enlivening: both are eminently respectable men, but neither has enough experience of this kind of mess to keep the ransomers in order, so that in Tom's absence the place is more like the ordinary of an inferior Portsmouth tavern than the gunroom of a man-of-war. The officers quite often invite Dutourd, and he does impose a certain respect; but unhappily he is a great talker and in spite of some tolerably emphatic checks he will drift towards philosophic considerations bordering upon politics and religion, the politics being of the Utopian pantisocratic kind and the religion a sort of misty Deism, both of which distress Martin. The poor fellow regrets Dutourd's absence and dreads his presence. I hope that our meals (and it is wonderful how long one spends at table, cooped up with the other members of the mess: it seems longer when some members belch, fart and scratch themselves) will become more tolerable when Tom returns, for I imagine the prize will be sold on the coast, and when Jack regularly dines with us.

'Yet even in that case I do not think Martin's is likely to be an enviable lot. In this ship there was always a prejudice against him as a cleric, an unlucky man to have aboard; and now that it is known he is a parson in fact, the rector of two of Jack's livings, the prejudice has grown. Then again, as a man of some learning, acquainted with Hebrew, Greek and Latin, he is awkward company for our sectaries: in the event of a theological disagreement, a differing interpretation of the original, they carry no guns at all. And of course by definition he is opposed to Dissent and favourable to episcopacy and tithes; as well as to infant baptism, abhorrent to many of our shipmates. At the same time, being a quiet, introspective man, he completely lacks the ebullient bonhomie that comes so naturally to Dutourd. It is acknowledged aboard that he is a good man, kind as a surgeon's mate, and in former commissions as a letter- or petition-writer (now there is little occasion for either and our few illiterates usually go to Mr Adams). But he is not cordially liked. He has been poor, miserably and visibly poor; now he is by lower-deck standards rich; and some suspect him of being over-elevated. But more than this it is known – in a ship everything is known after the first few thousand miles – that the Captain is not very fond of him; and at sea a captain's opinion is as important to his crew as that of an absolute monarch to his court. It is not that Jack has ever treated him with the least disrespect, but Martin's presence is a constraint upon him; they have little to say to one another; and in short Martin has not accomplished the feat of making a friend of his friend's closest associate. The attempt is rarely successful, I believe, and perhaps Martin never even ventured upon it. However that may be, they are not friends, and this means that he is looked upon by the people with less consideration than I think he deserves. It surprises me: I must say that I thought they would have used him better. Perhaps, as far as many of the ship's present crew are concerned, it is to some degree a question of these wretched tithes, which so many of them resent: and he is now one of those who receive or who will receive the hated impost.

'In any event, I am afraid he is losing his taste for life. His plea-sure in birds and marine creatures has deserted him; and an educated man who takes no delight in natural philosophy has no place in a ship, unless he is a sailor.

'Yet I remember him in earlier commissions, in much the same circumstances, rejoicing in the distant whale, the stink-pot petrel, his face aglow and his one eye sparkling with satisfaction. He was quite penniless then, apart from his miserable pay; and at those times when cause and effect seem childishly evident I am inclined to blame his prosperity. He now possesses, but has never enjoyed, two livings and what might be called a fair provision in prize-money: from a worldly point of view he is a much more considerable man than he ever has been before; although this makes no difference to his importance aboard it will do so by land, and I think it likely that he exaggerates the happiness which ease and consequence may bring – that he pines for the shore – and its compensation for the disappointments he has suffered at sea. I have disappointed him, I am afraid, and . . . ' Stephen held his pen in the air, reflecting upon Clarissa Oakes, a young woman to whom he was much attached, a convict transported for murder, who, escaping, had sailed in the frigate from Sydney Cove to Moahu. He reflected upon her, smiling, and then upon Martin's ambiguous relations with her, which might also have had a deep influence on the people's attitude. If a parson sinned (and Stephen was by no means convinced of it), his sin was multiplied by every sermon he preached. ' . . . so have other people, including no doubt himself. Yet like so many poor men he almost certainly mistakes the effect of wealth upon happiness in anything but the first fine flush of possession: he speaks of money very much more often than he did, more often than is quite agreeable; and the other day, referring to his marriage, which is as nearly ideal as can be, he was so thoughtless as to say that it would be even happier with his share of our current prize.' Stephen paused again, and in the silence of the ship he heard Martin playing his viola in his cabin opening off the gunroom: an ascending scale, true enough, then coming down, slower, more hesitant and ending in a prolonged, slightly false, B flat, infinitely sad.

'I do not have to tell you, my dear,' he went on, 'that although I speak in this high ascetic way about money, I do not, never have, despise a competence: it is the relation of *superfluity* to happiness that is my text, and I am holier than thou only after two hundred pounds a year.'

The viola had stopped, and Stephen, locking away his paper, walked into the great cabin, stretched out on the cushioned stern-window locker, gazed for a while at the reflected sunlight dancing overhead, and went to sleep.

He was woken, as long use had told him he would be woken, by a trampling as of wild beasts as the *Surprise*'s boats were hoisted in: hoarse cries – *Oh you impotent booby* – the shrilling of the bosun's call – the clash of tackles run up chock-a-block – *Handsomely, handsomely now, our William* (Grainger to an impetuous young nephew) – but then instead of the usual cries of avast and belay an unexpected unanimous good-natured cheer, accompanied by laughter. 'What can this signify?' he asked himself, and while he was searching for a plausible sea-going answer he became aware of a presence in the cabin, a suppressed giggle. It was Emily and Sarah, standing neatly side by side in white pinafores. 'We have been standing here a great while, sir,' said Sarah, 'whilst you was a-contemplating. The Captain says, should you like to see a marble?'

'Wonder,' said Emily.

'Marble,' said Sarah, adding, 'You impotent booby' in a whisper.

'There you are, Doctor,' cried the Captain as Stephen came on deck, still looking rather stupid. 'Have you been asleep?'

'Not at all,' said Stephen. 'I very rarely sleep.'

'Well, if you had been asleep, here is a sight that would wake you even if you were a Letter to the Ephesians. Look over the leeward quarter. The *leeward* quarter.'

'Jesus, Mary and Joseph,' cried Stephen, recognizing the *Franklin* at last. 'What a transformation! She has three tall Christian masts and a vast great number of sails – what splendour in the sun! Sails of every kind, I make no doubt, including topgallant-royals.'

'Exactly so, ha, ha, ha! I never thought it could have been done in the time. She spread them not five minutes ago, and already she has gained on us a cable's length. A neat little craft, upon my word. We shall have to set our own. Mr. Grainger' – in a louder voice – 'I believe we must show her our royals.'

The *Surprise*'s royals, which were set flying, had already been bent to their yards, with the halliards hitched to the slings and the starboard arm stopped to them, the hands fidgeting to be at it; but no man laid a finger on a rope until Mr Grainger called, 'Now then, our George, haul away,' and the long slim yards fairly shot up through the rigging, up and up, threading lengthways through a cat's-cradle of cordage, up to the masthead, where the light and nimble Abraham Dorkin cut the small stuff stopping the yard to the halliards, swung it on to the horizontal plane of the topgallant yard, fixed it there with a becket, lashed the clews of the sails, its lower corners, to the topgallant yardarm, cast off the beckets, and cried, 'Way-oh!'

His cry almost exactly coincided with others from the fore and mizzen mastheads, and the royals flashed out at the same moment, filling at once to the gentle breeze. The Surprises cheered; from over the water the weary Franklins did the same; and Jack turned a beaming face to Stephen, his eyes more startlingly blue than ever. 'Ain't that capital?' he cried. 'Now we can have our concert at last.'

'Very capital indeed, upon my soul,' said Stephen, wondering why they were all so delighted. Certainly the ships, particularly the *Franklin*, were more beautiful by far with their towering clouds of ordered whiteness reducing their hulls to low slim elegant forms: and as he watched the sun lit the *Franklin* with more than common force, causing all the staysails to make strong exactly-curved shadows on the square courses, topsails and topgallants behind them. Very fine indeed, and perhaps there was a just-perceptible increase in their gentle pace, a very slightly greater lean from the breeze.

'Mr Reade,' called Jack, 'pray heave the log.'

'Aye aye, sir: heave the log it is,' replied Reade, all duty and submission still. The usual ceremony followed: the log-ship splashed over the leeward quarter, went astern at a walking pace until it was free of what mild eddies the *Surprise* might make, watched with the closest attention by all hands. The moment the bunting that marked the end of the stray-line went over the rail Reade cried 'Turn,' and Norton turned the twenty-eight-second sand-glass, holding it close to his eye. As the last grain fell he bawled 'Stop' and Reade nipped the line a little after the second knot had passed. The quartermaster holding the log reel gave the line a tweak, dislodging a pin so that the log-ship floated sideways, and wound it in. Reade measured the distance between his nip and the second knot with a knowing eye: 'Two knots and a trifle better than one fathom, sir, if you please,' he reported, bareheaded, to the Captain.

'Thank you, Mr Reade,' said Jack, and to Stephen, 'There, Doctor: ain't you amazed? Two knots and a little more than a fathom!'

'Profoundly amazed; yet I seem to remember having gone even faster.'

'Why God love you, of course you have,' cried Jack. 'It is not the absolute speed that I am talking about but the relative speed, the speed in this miserable zephyr of yours. Good Lord, if we can both make better than two knots in an air that would scarcely bend a candle-flame, there is precious little can escape us, without it has wings or carries seventy-four guns.'

'Hear him, hear him,' said somebody in the waist of the ship, and both helmsmen and quartermaster chuckled.

'To be sure, there is always the joy of the chase,' said Stephen with what enthusiasm he could command; and after a pause in which he felt he had been disappointing he said, 'For our concert, now, have you anything particular in mind?'

'Oh, old favourites, for sure,' said Jack. 'I remember your telling me long ago, when we were beating out of Port Mahon in the *Sophie*, that in Spain they had a saying "Let no new thing arise." I thought at the time it might do very well for the Navy; and I am not so sure there is not something to be said for it in music.'

It was a very old favourite they began with that evening, Benda's violin and 'cello duet in C minor, and they played it unusually well. There is a great deal to be said for a steady deck under a 'cello: a great deal to be said for a cheerful heart behind a fiddle: and they would have brought it to an unusually handsome close if Killick had not blundered in, tripping over a little stool, unseen because of his tray, and saving their supper only by a miracle of juggling.

At one time this supper had consisted of toasted cheese held in a remarkably elegant piece of Irish silver, a covered outer dish that held six within it, the whole kept warm over a spirit-stove: the dish was still present, gleaming with a noble brilliance, but it held only a pap made of pounded biscuit, a little goat's milk, and even less of rock-hard cheese-rind rasped over the top and browned with a loggerhead, so that some faint odour of cheddar could still just be made out.

Jack Aubrey weighed sixteen or seventeen stone, Stephen barely nine, and to avoid the tedium of self-sacrifice, protests against the sacrifice, and privy maundering afterwards it had long been agreed that they should share accordingly: finishing his fourth dish, therefore, Jack also finished his explanation of the remarkable sailing qualities of both the *Franklin* and the *Surprise*: ' . . . so as I say, although at present we have the current setting against us, I believe I can promise we shall make as much of what breeze there is as any two ships afloat: from the look of the sky and the glass I should not be astonished if we achieved five knots tomorrow. And then, you know, as we slant down towards the equator, there is the counter-current in our favour.'

'So much the better,' said Stephen. 'Now what do you say to our Boccherini in D major? The minuet has been running in my head these last two or three days; but we have still to work out the adagio.'

'I should like it of all things,' said Jack. 'Killick. Killick, there. Clear the decks and bring another decanter of port.'

'Which it is getting wery low, sir,' said Killick. 'At this rate we shall have to rouse up your feast-day eighty-nine, or be satisfied with grog.'

'Rouse it up, Killick: let us live whilst we are alive.' When Killick was gone, looking pinched and disapproving, Jack went on. 'That reminds me of Clarissa Oakes. She said something of the same kind in Latin, you told me, and translated it for her husband. Lord, Stephen, that was a fine young woman. How shamefully I lusted after her: but it would not do, of course, not in my own ship. And I believe poor Martin was much smitten. Sheep's eyes were not in it. However, I do so hope she will be happy with Oakes. He was not perhaps quite up to her mark, but he was a tolerable seaman.'

'Little do I know of port wine,' said Stephen. 'Was eighty-nine an uncommon year?'

'Pretty good,' said Jack, 'but I love it because of its associations. I never drink it without thinking of the Spanish Disturbance.'

'My dear, you have the advantage of me.'

'Really? Well, I am amazingly glad to know something you do not. It had to do with Nootka Sound, the place where the fur-traders go. Captain Cook, that great man, discovered it during his last voy-

age, when he was running up the north-west coast of America; and
our people had been trading there and to the northwards for years
and years when all at once the Spaniards said it was a continuation
of California and therefore Spanish. They sent up a twenty-six-gun
frigate from Mexico and seized the English ships and the settlement.
It made a great noise when the news reached home, above all as we
had not long since been beaten in America; people were furiously
angry – my cousin Edward stood up in Parliament beside himself
with rage and said England was going to the dogs and the House
cheered him – and when the Spaniards would not listen to reason
the Ministry began hurrying ships out of ordinary, manning them
with a hot press, and laying down new ones. Lord, we were so happy,
we sailors turned ashore after the American disaster! One day I was
only a wretched master's mate with no half pay, glum, blue, hipped,
sitting on the beach and adding salt tears to the bitter flood, and the
next I was Lieutenant Aubrey, fifth of the *Queen*, covered with glory
and gold lace, or at least as much as I could get on credit. It was a
wonderful stroke of luck for me; and for the country too.'

'Who could deny it?'

'I mean it was wonderfully well timed, since it meant we had a
well-manned, well-equipped Navy to cope with the French when
they declared war on us a little later. Bless the Spanish Disturbance.'

'By all means. But, Jack, I could have sworn your commission was
dated 1792. Sophie showed it to me with such pride. Yet our wine
is 1789.'

'Of course it is. That was when the Disturbance started – the very
beginning, when those wicked dogs seized our ships. The talking
and the re-armament went on until ninety-two, when the Spaniards
pulled in their horns as they did over the Falklands some time before.
But it all began in eighty-nine. A precious date for me: a wonderful
year and I had great hopes of it as soon as the news came home.' He
paused for a while, sipping his port and smiling at his recollections;
then he said, 'Tell me, Stephen, what were you doing in eighty-nine?'

'Oh,' said Stephen vaguely, 'I was studying medicine.' With this he set down his glass and walked into the quarter-gallery. He had been studying medicine, it was true, walking the wards of the Hôtel-Dieu, but he had also spent a great deal of the time running about the streets of Paris in the headiest state of happy excitement that could be imagined, or rather exaltation, in the dawn of the Revolution, when every disinterested, generous idea of freedom seemed on the point of realization, the dawn of an infinitely finer age.

When he came back he found Jack arranging the score of their next duet on their music stands. Like many other heavy men Jack could be as sensitive as a cat on occasion: he knew that he had touched on some painful area – that in any case Stephen hated questions – and he was particularly attentive in laying out the sheets, pouring Stephen another glass of wine, and, when they began, in so playing that his violin helped the 'cello, yielding to it in those minute ways perceptible to those who are deep in their music if to few others.

They played on, and only once did Jack raise his head from the score: the ship was leaning half a strake, and beneath their strings the sound of the rigging could just be heard. At the end of the allegro he said, turning the page with his bow, 'She is making four knots.'

'I believe we may attack the adagio directly,' said Stephen. 'The wind is in our poop, and we have never played better.'

They swept into the next movement, the 'cello booming nobly, and carried straight on without a pause, separating, joining, answering one another, with never a hesitation nor a false note until the full satisfaction of the end.

'Well done, well done,' said Dutourd: he and Martin were standing in the warm darkness abaft the lit companion, alone on the quarterdeck apart from Grainger and the men at the wheel. 'I had no idea they could play so well – no contention, no striving for pre-eminence – pray which is the 'cello?'

'Dr Maturin.'

'And Captain Aubrey the violin, of course: admirable tone, admirable bowing.'

Martin did not care for Dutourd in the gunroom: he thought that the Frenchman talked far too much, that he tended to harangue the company, and that his ideas though no doubt well-intended were pernicious. But en tête-à-tête Dutourd was an agreeable companion and Martin quite often took a turn on deck with him. 'You play yourself, sir, I collect?' he said.

'Yes. I may be said to play. I am not of the Captain's standard, but with some practice I believe I could play second fiddle to him without too much discredit.'

'Have you a violin with you?'

'Yes, yes. It is in my sea-chest. The man who repaired your viola renewed the pegs just before we set off from Molokai. Do you often play in the cabin?'

'I have done so, though I am an indifferent performer. I have taken part in quartets.'

'Quartets! What joy! That is living in the very heart of music.'

The next morning Jack Aubrey came up from a conference, a pursers' conference with Mr Adams: Jack, like Cook and many a far-ranging captain before him, was nominally his own purser, just as Adams was nominally the captain's clerk; but by dividing the work between them they accomplished both it and their own specific duties quite well, particularly as the anomalous status of the *Surprise* meant that her accounts would never have to pass the slow, circumspect eyes of the Victualling Office, for whom all persons in charge of His Majesty's stores were guilty of embezzlement until with countersigned dockets of every conceivable nature they could prove their innocence. At this conference they had weighed a number of sacks of dried peas, and Jack, taking advantage of the steelyard hanging from a convenient beam, had also weighed himself: to his shame he found that he had put on half a stone, and he meant to walk it off as soon as possible. He wished to hear no more flings about obesity, no more facetious remarks about letting out his waistcoats, no grave professional warnings about the price big heavy men of a sanguine temperament had so often to pay for taking too little exercise, too much food and too much drink: apoplexy, softening of the brain, impotence.

Fore and aft, fore and aft, pacing the windward side of the quarterdeck, his own private realm, a narrow unencumbered path on which he had travelled hundreds, even thousands of miles since he first commanded the *Surprise*; an utterly familiar terrain on which his mind could let itself run free. The breeze was too far before the beam for the ships, steering south-east, to set studdingsails, but they were wearing everything they possessed, including that uncommon object a middle staysail, and they were making four knots. They were an elegant sight indeed, from any distance; but from close to, a seaman's eye could still see many signs of the battering they had been

through: some knots had yet to be replaced by splices or new cordage; the fine finish of the decks had not yet been restored – in some
places what ordinarily resembled a ball-room floor still looked more
like a bloody shambles; and clouds of hot volcanic ash and scoriae had
played Old Harry with the paintwork and the blacking of the yards,
to say nothing of the tar. An immense amount of small, unspectac-
ular, highly-skilled work was going on from one end of the ship to
the other, and Captain Aubrey's walk was accompanied by the steady
thump of caulker's mallets.

It was early in the day, and although the weather was as fair as
could be wished, apart from the lack of wind, the quarterdeck had
nobody upon it who was not called there by duty: Vidal and Reade,
officer and midshipman of the watch; the men at the helm; the carpenter and two of his crew at the taffrail, putting the frigate's modest
decorative carving, her gingerbread-work, to rights. The usual daily
procession of Jemmy Ducks, Sarah and Emily, carrying hen-coops
and leading the goat Amalthea, had come and gone; and as usual
Jack, reflecting upon the rapid growth of the little girls, thought of his
own daughters, their present height, weight and happiness, their possible but unlikely progress in deportment, French and the pianoforte
under Miss O'Mara. But neither Stephen nor Martin had appeared,
nor any of the ransomers. A mile and a half of steady pacing followed
these reflections about home, and then two distinct thoughts arose:
'I must ask Wilkins whether he will act as third lieutenant until we
reach Callao: they say he was a master's mate in *Agamemnon*.' This
second thought ran on into a consideration of those young men who,
having passed the Navy's examination for a lieutenant, remained
senior midshipmen or master's mates because they did not also 'pass
for a gentleman,' a mute, unwritten, unacknowledged examination
whose result was announced only by the absence of a commission
– a practice that was becoming more and more frequent. He considered the advantages often put forward – a more homogeneous mess,
less friction, the hands' greater respect for gentlemen than for their
own kind – and the disadvantages – the exclusion of such men as

Cook, the unstated qualifications and the varying standards of those who did the choosing, the impossibility of appeal. He was still considering when, on reaching the rail and turning, he noticed that the young man in question, one of the ransomer mates, was now present, together with some others of those who were allowed to walk the quarterdeck.

Four turns later he heard Reade's shrill cry of 'Oh no, sir, no. You cannot talk to the Captain,' and he saw Dutourd headed off, admonished, led firmly back to the group to leeward.

'But what did I do?' he cried, addressing Stephen, who had just come up the companion-ladder. 'I only wished to congratulate him on his playing.'

'My dear sir, you must not address the Captain,' said Stephen.

'You cannot possibly go over to the windward side, without you are invited,' said Wilkins.

'Even I may not speak to him, except on duty,' said Reade.

'Well,' said Dutourd, recovering from his surprise and concealing a certain vexation moderately well, 'you are a markedly formal, hierarchical society, I see. But I hope, sir' – to Maturin – 'that I may without sin tell you how very much I enjoyed your music? I thought the Boccherini adagio masterly, masterly . . .'

They walked off, still speaking of the Boccherini, with real knowledge and appreciation on Dutourd's part. Stephen, who in any case was not of an expansive nature, tended to avoid the Frenchman on general principles; but now he would voluntarily have remained in his company had not six bells struck. The sixth was followed by pandemonium fore and aft as the launch, towing astern, was hauled alongside to receive Mr Reade, her crew, barrels of water for the parched *Franklin*, and two carronades. The precious water, mercifully, could be pumped from the hold into barrels in the boat, but in the nature of things carronades could not: they were lowered down from the reinforced main yardarm, lowered with an infinity of precautions as though each were made of spun glass rather than of metal, and they were received with even more. They were ugly, squat little objects

yet they had their advantages, being only a third the weight of the
Surprise's regular twelve-pounder cannon but firing a ball twice as
heavy; furthermore they could be fought by a much smaller crew –
two zealous hands at a pinch, as opposed to the seven or eight gathered round a long twelve. On the other hand they could not fire their
heavy ball very far nor very accurately, so Jack, who loved the fine-
work of gunnery, disabling an opponent from a distance before bearing down and boarding him, carried them chiefly as ballast, bringing
them up only when he contemplated a cutting-out expedition, dashing into a harbour and blazing away at nearby batteries and the like
while the boats set about their prey. Or on an occasion such as this,
when the disarmed *Franklin* could be equipped with a two-hundred-
and-forty-pound broadside.

'If this weather continues,' said Jack ' – and the glass is perfectly
steady – the *Franklin* should soon be a very useful consort: and we
are, after all, getting somewhat nearer the path of merchantmen, to
say nothing of roving whalers.'

'I wish it may go on,' said Stephen. 'The temperature in Paradise
must have been very like this.'

It did go on, day after golden day: and during the afternoons Martin and Dutourd could often be heard playing, sometimes evidently
practising, since they would take a passage over and over again.

Yet in spite of his music, and in spite of the fact that he played better with the Frenchman far forward than he did in the cabin, Martin was not happy. Stephen was rarely in the gunroom – apart from
anything else Dutourd, a frequent guest, was an inquisitive man, apt
to ask questions, by no means always discreet; and evading enquiries
was often potentially worse than answering them – and apart from
the general taking of air on the quarterdeck Stephen and his assistant
met for the most part either in the sick-berth or in Stephen's cabin,
where their registers were kept. Both were much concerned with the
effects of their treatment: they had kept accurate records over a long
period, and at present it was the study and comparison of these case-
histories that made up the great part of their professional duty.

At one of these meetings Stephen said, 'Once again we have not exceeded five knots at any time in the day, in spite of all this whistling and scratching of backstays. And it makes a great while since fresh water has been allowed for washing anything but the invalids' clothes, in spite of our prayers for rain. Yet providing we do not die of thirst, I comfort myself with the thought that even this languid pace brings us nearly a hundred miles closer to my coca-leaves – a hundred miles closer to wallowing in some clear tepid stream, washing the ingrained salt from my person and chewing coca-leaves as I do so, joy.'

Martin tapped a sheaf of papers together and after a moment he said, 'I have no notion of these palliatives, which so soon become habitual. Look what happened to poor Padeen, and the way we are obliged to keep the laudanum under lock and key. Look at the spirit-room in this ship, the only holy of holies, necessarily guarded day and night. In one of my parishes there are no less than seven ale-houses and some of them sell uncustomed spirits. I hope to put all or at least some of them down. Dram-drinking is the curse of the nation. Sometimes I turn a sermon in my mind, urging my hearers to bear their trials, to rely on their own fortitude, on fortitude from within, rather than their muddy ale, tobacco, or dram-drinking.'

'If a man has put his hand into boiling water, is he not to pull it out?'

'Certainly he is to pull it out – a momentary action. What I deprecate is the persistent indulgence.'

Stephen looked at Martin curiously. This was the first time his assistant had spoken to him in a disobliging if not downright uncivil manner and some brisk repartees came into his mind. He said nothing, however, but sat wondering what frustrations, jealousies, discontents had been at work on Nathaniel Martin to produce this change not only of tone but even of voice itself and conceivably of identity: the words and the manner of uttering them were completely out of character.

When the silence had lasted some heavy moments Martin said, 'I hope you do not think there is anything personal about my remarks. It was only that your mention of coca-leaves set my mind running in another direction . . . '

The shattering din of the *Franklin* as she fired first her starboard and then her larboard broadside and as her captain desired his men to 'look alive, look alive and bear a hand,' interrupted him. There were only these two, to test the slides and tackle, but they were rippling broadsides and they lasted long enough to drown Martin's last words and the first of those spoken by the newly-arrived Norton, although he roared them: he was therefore obliged to repeat, still as though he were hailing the masthead, 'Captain's compliments to Mr Martin and would be glad of his company at dinner tomorrow.'

'My duty and best compliments to the Captain, and shall be happy to wait on him,' said Martin.

'And *Franklin* has hailed to say that Captain Pullings has put his jaw out again,' – this to Dr Maturin.

'I shall be over in a moment,' said Stephen. 'Pray, Mr Norton, get them to lower down my little skiff. Padeen,' he called in Irish to his huge loblolly-boy, 'leap into the little boat, will you now, and row me over.'

'Shall I bring bandages and perhaps the Batavia salve?' asked Martin.

'Never in life. Do not stir: I have known this wound since it was made.'

That was many years since, in the Ionian Sea, when a Turk gave Pullings a terrible slash on the side of his face with a scimitar, so damaging his cheekbone and the articulation of the joint that it often slipped, particularly when Captain Pullings was calling out with more than usual force. Stephen had put it more or less right at the time, and now he did so again; but it was a delicate little operation, and one that required a hand with a knowledge of the wound.

This was the first time Stephen had been aboard the *Franklin* for any length of time since the earlier critical days, when his horizon was almost entirely bounded by the walls of his operating and dressing stations – blood and bones, splints, lint, tow and bandages, saws, retractors, artery-hooks – and he had had little time to see her as a ship, to see her from within. Nor of course had Tom Pullings been able to show the Doctor his new command, already very near to his heart. 'I am so glad you was not obliged to come across before we had our whole armament aboard,' he said. 'Now you will see how trim and neat they sit in their ports, and how well they can traverse, particularly those amidships; and I will show you our new cross-catharpins, rigged this very afternoon. They bring in the foremast and aftermast shrouds, as I dare say you noticed when Padeen was pulling you over. And there are a vast number of other things that will astonish you.'

A vast number indeed: a vaster number of objects than Dr Maturin had supposed to exist in any ship afloat. Long, long ago, at the beginning of Stephen's naval career, Pullings, then a long, thin midshipman, had shown him over His Majesty's ship *Sophie*, a brig, Jack Aubrey's first, dwarfish command: he had done so kindly, conscientiously, but as a subordinate displaying her main features to a landsman. Now it was a captain showing his new ship to a man with many years of sea-experience, and Stephen was spared nothing at all: a fancy-line rigged on new principles, these cross-catharpins of course, drawings of an improved dumb-chalder to be shipped when she docked at Callao. Yet although his guide was now burlier by far, and almost unrecognizable from his frightful wound, there was the same ingenuous open friendliness, an unchanged pleasure in life, in sea-going life, and Stephen followed him about, admiring, and exclaiming, 'Dear me, how very fine' until the sun set, and the twilight, sweeping over the sky with tropical rapidity, soon left even Pullings without anything to point at.

'Thank you for showing me your ship,' said Stephen, going over the side. 'For her size, she is the beauty of the world.'

'Not at all,' said Tom, simpering. 'But I am afraid I was too long-winded.'

'Never in life, my dear. God bless now. Padeen, shove away. Give off.'

'Good night, sir,' said the seven Sethians, their smiles gleaming in the massive beards, as they thrust the skiff clear with a boom.

'Good night, Doctor,' called Pullings. 'I forgot the plan of the new fairleads, but I promise to show it you tomorrow: the Captain has invited me to dinner.'

'I am glad of that,' thought Stephen, waving his hat. 'It will make the party less awkward.'

He did not see Martin again that evening, but he thought of him from time to time; and when he had turned in, when he was lying in his cot, very gently rocking on the quiet sea, he reflected not so much upon the outburst of that afternoon as upon the notion of changing identity. He had known it often enough. A delightful child, even a delightful early adolescent, interested in everything, alive, affectionate, would turn into a thick, heavy, stupid brute and never recover: ageing men would become wholly self-centred, indifferent to those who had been their friends, avaricious. Yet apart from the very strong, very ugly passions arising from inheritance or political disagreement he had not known it in men neither young nor old. He swung, and thought, his mind wandering free, sometimes to the allied but quite distinct subject of inconstancy in love; and presently he found that this too was to be a sleepless night.

The moon was high when he came on deck, and there was a heavy dew. 'Why, then,' he asked, feeling the rail wet under his hand, 'with so heavy a dew is the moon not veiled? Nor yet the stars?'

'Have you come on deck, sir?' asked Vidal, who had the middle watch.

'I have, too,' said Maturin, 'and should be obliged if you would tell me about the dew. One says it falls: but does it fall in fact? And if it fall, where does it fall from? And why in falling does it not obscure the moon?'

'Little do I know of the dew, sir,' said Vidal. 'All I can say is that it loves a clear night and air as near still as can be: and every sailor knows it tightens all cordage right wicked, so you must slacken all over if you do not want your masts wrung. It is a very heavy dew tonight, to be sure,' he went on, having reflected, 'and we have clapped garlands on the masts to collect it as it trickles down: if you listen you can hear it running into the butts. It don't amount to much, and it don't taste very good, the masts having been paid with slush; but I have known many a voyage when it was uncommon welcome. And in any case it is fresh, and will wash a shirt clear of salt; or even better' – lowering his voice – 'a pair of drawers. The salt is devilish severe on the parts. Which reminds me, sir: I must beg some more of your ointment.'

'By all means. Look in at the sick-berth when I make my morning rounds, and Padeen will whip you up a gallipot directly.'

Silence: a vast moonlit space, but no horizon. Stephen gazed up at the dew-soaked sails, dark in the moon-shadow, the topgallants and topsails rounding just enough to send the ship whispering along, the courses hanging slack.

'As for the dew,' said Vidal after a while, 'you might ask Mr Dutourd. There's a learned gentleman for you! Not in physic, of course, but more in the philosophical and moral line: though as I understand it he has many friends in Paris who make experiments with the electric fluid, gas-balloons, the weight of air – that kind of thing – and perhaps dew might have come into it. But what a pleasure it is to hear him talk about moral politics! The rights of man, brotherhood, you know, and equality! He has edified us many an hour with his observations, you might almost say his oratory, on the just republic. And the colony he planned – no privileges, no oppression; no money, no greed; everything held in common, like in a mess with good shipmates – no statutes, no lawyers – the voice of the people the only law, the only court of justice – everybody to worship the Supreme Being just as he sees fit – no interference, no compulsion, complete freedom.'

'It sounds like the earthly Paradise.'

'That is what many of our people say. And some declare they would not have been so eager to stop Mr Dutourd if they had known what he was about – might even have joined him.'

'Do they not reflect that he was preying on our whalers and merchantmen, and helping Kalahua in his war with Puolani?'

'Oh, as for the privateering side, that was entirely his Yankee sailing-
master, and they would certainly never have joined in that – not against
their own countrymen, though natural enough, in war-time, on the
part of a foreigner. No: it was the colony that pleased them so, with its
peace and equality and a decent life without working yourself to the
bone and an old age that don't bear thinking on.'

'Peace and equality, with all my heart,' said Stephen.

'But you shake your head, sir, and I dare say you are thinking
about that war. It was sadly misrepresented, but Mr Dutourd has
made everything quite clear. The sides had been spoiling for a fight
time out of mind, and once Kalahua had hired those riff-raff Frenchmen from the Sandwich Islands with muskets there was no holding
him. They had nothing to do with Mr Dutourd's settlers. No. What
Mr D meant to do was to sail in with a show of force and set himself
between them, then establish his own colony and win both sides over
by example and persuasion. And as for persuasion . . . ! If you had
heard him you would have been convinced directly: he has a wonderful gift, you might say an unction, even in a foreign language. Our
people think the world of him.'

'He certainly speaks English remarkably well.'

'And not only that, sir. He is remarkably good to what were his
own men. You know how he sat up with them night after night in
the sick-berth until they were either cured or put over the side. And
although the master of the *Franklin* and his mates were right hard-
horse drivers, the men who are with us now say Mr D was always
stepping in to protect them – would not have them flogged.'

At this point, just before eight bells, a sleepy, yawning Grainger
came on deck to relieve his shipmate; and the starboard watch, most
of whom had been sleeping in the waist, began to stir: the ship came
to a muted sort of life. 'Three knots, sir, if you please,' reported young
Wedell, now an acting midshipman. And in the usual piping, calling,
hurrying sounds of the change – all fairly discreet at four o'clock in

the morning – Stephen slipped away to his cabin. There was something curiously pleasing about the Knipperdollings' credulity, he
reflected as he lay there with his hands behind his head: an amiable
simplicity: and he was still smiling when he went to sleep.

To sleep, but not for long. Presently the idlers were called, and they
joined the watch in the daily ritual of cleaning the decks, pumping
floods of sea-water over them, sanding, holystoning and swabbing
them, flogging them dry by the rising of the sun. There were hard-
ened sailors who could sleep through all this – Jack Aubrey was one,
and he could be heard snoring yet – but Stephen was not. On this
occasion it did not make him unhappy or fretful, however, and he lay
there placidly thinking of a number of pleasant things. Clarissa came
into his mind: she too had something of that simplicity, in spite of a
life as hard as could well be imagined.

'Are you awake?' asked Jack Aubrey in a hoarse whisper through a
crack in the door.

'I am not,' said Stephen. 'Nor do I choose to swim; but I will take
coffee with you when you return to the ship. The animal,' he added to
himself. 'I never heard him get up.' It was true. Jack weighed far too
much, but he was still remarkably light on his feet.

With this fine brisk start to the day Dr Maturin was early for his
morning rounds, a rare thing in one with so vague a notion of time.

These rounds amounted to little from the strictly surgical point of
view, but Stephen still had some obstinate gleets and poxes. In long,
fairly quiet passages these and scurvy were the medical man's daily
fare; but whereas Stephen could oblige the seamen to avoid scurvy by
drinking lemon-juice in their grog, no power on earth could prevent
them from hurrying to bawdy-houses as soon as they were ashore.
These cases he treated with calomel and guaiacum, and it was usual
for the draughts to be prepared by Martin: Stephen was not satisfied
with the progress of two of his patients and he had resolved upon
dosing them in the far more radical Viennese manner when he saw

a beetle on the deck just this side of the half-open door, clear in the light of the dispensary lantern, a yellow beetle. A longicorn of course, but what longicorn? An active longicorn, in any event. He dropped on to his hands and knees and crept silently towards it: with the beetle in his handkerchief, he looked up. His advance had brought the door directly in front of him, with the whole dispensary lit, clear, and as it were in another world: there was Martin, gravely mixing the last of his row of draughts, and as Stephen watched he raised the glass and drank it off.

Stephen rose to his feet and coughed. Martin turned sharply. 'Good morning, sir,' he said, whipping the glass under his apron. The greeting was civil, but mechanically so, with no spontaneous smile. He had obviously not forgotten yesterday's unpleasantness and he appeared both to resent his exclusion from the passage to the *Franklin* and to expect resentment on Stephen's part for his offensive remarks. Stephen was in fact of a saturnine temperament, as Martin knew: he could even have been called revengeful, and he found it difficult to forgive a slight. But there was more than this; it was as though Martin had just escaped being detected in an act he was very willing to conceal, and there was some remaining tinge of defiant hostility about his attitude.

Padeen came in, and having called on God to bless the gentlemen he announced, with some difficulty, that the sick-berth was ready for their honours. The medical men went from cot to cot, Stephen asking each man how he did, taking his pulse and examining his peccant parts: he discussed each case briefly with his assistant, in Latin, and Martin wrote down his observations in a book: as the book closed so Padeen gave each seaman his draught and pills.

When it was over they returned to the dispensary and while Padeen was washing the glasses Stephen said, 'I am not satisfied with Grant or MacDuff and intend to put them on the Viennese treatment next week.'

'My authorities speak of it, but I do not recall that they name its principle.'

'It is the murias hydrargi corrosivus.'

'The phial next to the myrrh? I have never known it used.'

'Just so. I reserve it for the most obdurate cases: there are grave disadvantages . . . Now, Padeen, what is amiss?'

Padeen's stammer, always bad, grew worse with emotion, but in time it appeared that there had been ten glasses in the cupboard an hour ago, not even an hour ago, and they shining: now there were only nine. He held up his spread hands with one finger folded down and repeated 'Nine.'

'I am so sorry, sir,' said Martin. 'I broke one when I was mixing the draughts, and I forgot to tell Padeen.'

Both Jack Aubrey and Stephen Maturin were much attached to their wives, and both wrote to them at quite frequent intervals; but whereas Jack's letters owed their whole existence to the hope that they would reach home by some means or another – merchantman, man-of-war or packet – or failing that that they would travel there in his own sea-chest and be read aloud to Sophie with explanations of just how the wind lay or the current set, Stephen's were not always intended to be sent at all. Sometimes he wrote them in order to be in some kind of contact with Diana, however remote and one-sided; sometimes to clarify things in his own mind; sometimes for the relief (and pleasure) of saying things that he could say to no one else, and these of course had but an ephemeral life.

'My dearest soul,' he wrote, 'when the last element of a problem, code or puzzle falls into place the solution is sometimes so obvious that one claps one's hand to one's forehead crying, "Fool, not to have seen that before." For some considerable time now, as you would know very well if we had some power of instant communication, I have been concerned about the change in my relations with Nathaniel Martin, by the change in him, and by his unhappiness. Many and sound reasons did I adduce when last I wrote, naming an undue concern with money and a conviction that its possession should in common jus-

tice win him more consideration and happiness than he possesses, as
well as many other causes such as jealousy, the boredom of unconge-
nial companions from whom there is no escape, a longing for home,
wife, relations, consequence, peace and quiet, and a fundamental
unsuitability for naval life, prolonged naval life. But I did not mention
the efficient cause because I did not perceive it until today, though
it should have been evident enough from his intense application to
Astruc, Booerhaave, Lind, Hunter and what few other authorities
on the venereal distemper we possess (we lack both Locker and van
Swieten), and even more from his curiously persistent eager detailed
enquiries about the possibility of infection from using the same seat
of ease, drinking from the same cup, kissing, toying and the like.
Whether he has the disease I cannot tell for sure without a proper
examination, though I doubt he has it physically: metaphysically however he is in a very bad way. Whether he lay with her or not in fact
he certainly wished to do so and he is clerk enough to know that the
wish is the sin; and being also persuaded that he is diseased he looks
upon himself with horror, unclean without and within. Unhappily he
has taken yesterday's disagreement more seriously than I did – our
relations are a cool civility at the best – and in these circumstances
he will not consult me. Nor obviously can I obtrude my services. Self-
hatred usually seems more likely to generate hatred of others (or at
least surliness and a sense of grievance) than mansuetude. Poor fellow, he is invited to dine in the cabin this afternoon, and to bring his
viola. I dread some kind of éclat: he is in a very nervous state.'

There was a confident knock on the door and Mr Reade walked
smiling in, quite sure of his welcome. From time to time what was left
of his arm needed dressing, and this was one of the appointed days:
Stephen had forgotten it; Padeen had not, and the bandage stood
on the aftermost locker. While it was putting on, fold after exactly-
spaced fold, Reade said, 'Oh sir, I had a wonderful thought in the
graveyard watch. Please would you do me a great kindness?'

'I might,' said Stephen.

'I was thinking about going to Somerset House to pass for lieutenant when we get home.'

'But you are not nearly old enough, my dear.'

'No, sir: but you can always add a year or two: the examining captains only put "appears to be nineteen years of age," you know. Besides, I shall be nineteen in time, of course, particularly if we go on at this pace; and I have my proper certificates of sea-time served. No. The thing that worried me was that since I am now only a tripod rather than a quadrupod, they might be doubtful about passing me. So I have to have everything on my side. These calm days I have been copying out my journals fair – you have to show them up, you know – and in the night it suddenly occurred to me that it would be a brilliant stroke and amaze the captains, was I to add some seamanlike details in French.'

'Sure it could not fail to do so.'

'So I thought if I took Colin, one of the Franklins in my division, a decent fellow and prime seaman though he has scarcely a word of English, on to the forecastle in the first dog, shall we say, sir, and pointed to everything belonging to the foremast and he told me the French and you told me how to write it down, that would be very capital. It would knock the captains flat – such zeal! But I am afraid I am asking for too much of your time, sir.'

'Not at all. Hold this end of the bandage, will you, now? There: belay and heave off handsomely.'

'Thank you very much indeed, sir. I am infinitely obliged. Until the first dog, then?'

'Never you think so, Mr Reade, sir,' said Killick, coming in with Stephen's new-brushed good blue coat and white kersey-mere breeches over his arm. 'Not the first dog, no, nor yet the last. Which the Doctor is going to dine with the Captain, and they won't be done in the melodious line before the setting of the watch. Now, sir, if you please,' – to Stephen – 'let me have that wicked old shirt and put this one on, straight from the smoothing-iron. There is not a moment to be lost.'

In fact the dinner went off remarkably well. Martin might not carry
Jack Aubrey in his heart, but he respected him as a naval commander
and as a patron: it would be ungenerous to say that his respect was
increased by the prospect of another benefice to come, but at some
level the fact may well have had its influence. At all events, in spite
of looking drawn and unwell he played his part as a cheerful, appre-
ciative guest quite well, except that he drank almost no wine; and
he told two anecdotes of his own initiative: one of a trout that he
tickled as a boy under the fall of a weir, and one of an aunt who had
a cat, a valuable cat that lived with her in a house near the Pool of
London – the animal vanished – enquiries in every direction – tears
that lasted a year, indeed until the day the cat walked in, leapt on to
its accustomed chair by the fire and began to wash. Curiosity had led
it aboard a ship bound for Surinam, a ship from the Pool that had
just returned.

After dinner it was proposed that they should play, and since one
of the chief purposes of the feast was to give Tom Pullings pleasure
they played tunes he knew very well. Songs, as often as not, and
dances, some delightful melodies with variations on them; and from
time to time Jack and Pullings sang.

'Your viola has profited immensely from its repair,' said Jack when
they were standing up for leave-taking. 'It has a charming tone.'

'Thank you, sir,' said Martin. 'Mr Dutourd has improved my fin-
gering, tuning and bowing – he knows a great deal about music – he
loves to play.'

'Ah, indeed?' said Jack. 'Now, Tom, do not forget your horizon-
glass, I beg.'

In his role of virtually omnipotent captain Jack could be deaf to a
hint, particularly if it reached him indirectly: Stephen was less well
placed, and two days later when Dutourd, having wished him a good

morning and having spoken of the pleasure it had given him to linger on the quarterdeck all the time they played, went on to say, with
an ease that surprised Maturin until he recalled that wealthy men
were used to having their wishes regarded, 'It would perhaps be too
presumptuous in me to entreat you to let Captain Aubrey know that
it would give me even greater pleasure to be admitted to one of your
sessions: I am no virtuoso, but I have held my own in quite distinguished company; and if I were allowed to play second fiddle we
might embark upon quartets, which have always seemed to me the
quintessence of music.'

'I will mention it if you wish,' said Stephen, 'but I should observe
that in general the Captain looks upon these as little private affairs,
quite unbuttoned and informal.'

'Then perhaps I must be content to listen from afar,' said Dutourd,
taking no apparent offence. 'Yet it would be benevolent in you to
speak of it, if a suitable occasion should offer.' He broke off to ask what
was going on aboard the *Franklin*. Stephen told him that they were
rigging out the foretopgallant studdingsail booms. 'Les bouts-dehors
des bonnettes du petit perroquet,' he added, seeing Dutourd's look of
blank ignorance, an ignorance equal to his own until yesterday, when
he had helped Reade to write the terms in his journal. From this they
moved on to a consideration of sails in general; and after a while,
when Stephen was already impatient to be gone, Dutourd, looking
him full in the face, said, 'It is surely very remarkable that you should
know the French for studdingsail booms as well as for so many animals and birds. But it is true that you have a remarkable command of
our language.' A meditative pause. 'And now that I have the honour
of being better acquainted with you it seems to me that we may have
met before. Do not you know Georges Cuvier?'

'I have been introduced to Monsieur Cuvier.'

'Yes. And were you not at Madame Roland's soirées from time to
time?'

'You are probably thinking of my cousin Domanova. We are often
confused.'

'Perhaps so. But tell me, sir, how do you come to have a cousin called Domanova?'

Stephen looked at him with astonishment, and Dutourd, visibly drawing himself in, said, 'Forgive me, sir: I am impertinent.'

'Not at all, sir,' replied Stephen, walking off. His inward voice ran on, 'Is it possible that the animal has recognized me – that he has some notion however vague of what we are about – and that this is in some degree a threat?' Dutourd's was not an easy face to read. Superficially it had the open simplicity of an enthusiast, together with the politeness of his class and nation; these did not of course exclude everyday cunning and duplicity, but there was also something else, a slight insistence in his look, a certain self-confidence, that might mean far deeper implications. 'Shall I never learn to keep my mouth shut?' he muttered, opening the sick-berth door, and aloud, 'God and Mary and Patrick be with you,' in answer to Padeen's greeting. 'Mr Martin, a good morning to you.'

'How these halcyon days go on and on, the one following the other with only a perfect night between,' he said, walking into the cabin. 'We might almost be on dry land. But tell me, Jack, will it never rain at all – hush. I interrupt your calculations, I find.'

'What is twelve sixes?' asked Jack.

'Ninety-two,' said Stephen. 'My shirt is like a cilice with the salt. I should wear it dirty and reasonably soft, but that Killick takes it away – he finds it out with a devilish ingenuity and flings it into the sea-water tub and I am convinced that he adds more salt from the brine-tubs.'

'What is a cilice?'

'It is a penitential garment made of the harshest cloth known to man and worn next the skin by saints, hermits, and the more anxious sinners.'

Jack returned to his figures and Stephen to his disagreeable reflections. 'What goeth before destruction?' he asked. 'Pride goeth before destruction, that is what. I was so proud of knowing those spars in English, let alone in French, that I could not contain, but must be blabbing like a fool. Hair-shirt, indeed: the Dear knows I deserve one.'

In time Jack put down his pen and said, 'As for rain, there is no hope of it, according to the glass. But I have been casting the prize accounts, as far as I can without figures for the *Franklin*'s specie: a roundish figure, which is some sort of consolation.'

'Very good. To predatory creatures like myself there is something wonderfully fetching about a prize. The very word evokes a smile of concupiscent greed. Speaking of the *Franklin* reminds me that Dutourd wishes you to know that he would be glad of an invitation to play music with us.'

'So I gather from Martin,' said Jack, 'and I thought it a most uncommon stroke of effrontery. A fellow with wild, bloody, regicide revolutionary ideas, like Tom Paine and Charles Fox and all those wicked fellows at Brooks's and that adulterous cove – I forget his name, but you know who I mean – '

'I do not believe I am acquainted with any adulterers, Jack.'

'Well, never mind. A fellow who roams about the sea attacking our merchantmen with no commission or letter of marque from anyone, next door to a pirate if not actually bound for Execution Dock – be damned if I should invite him if he were a second Tartini, which he ain't – and in any case I disliked him from the start – disliked everything I heard of him. Enthusiasm, democracy, universal benevolence – a pretty state of affairs.'

'He has qualities.'

'Oh yes. He is not shy; and he stood up very well for his own people.'

'Some of ours think highly of him and his ideas.'

'I know they do: we have some hands from Shelmerston, decent men and prime seamen, who are little better than democrats – republicans, if you follow me – and would easily be led astray by a clever political cove with a fine flow of words: but the man-of-war's

men, particularly the old Surprises, do not like him. They call him
Monsieur Turd, and they will not be won round by smirking and leer-
ing and the brotherhood of man: they dislike his notions as much as
I do.'

'They are tolerably chimerical, admittedly, and it is surprising that
a man of his age and his parts should still entertain them. In 1789 I
too had great hopes of my fellows, but now I believe the only point on
which Dutourd and I are in agreement is slavery.'

'Well, as for slavery . . . it is true that I should not like to be one
myself, yet Nelson was in favour of it and he said that the country's
shipping would be ruined if the trade were put down. Perhaps it comes
more natural if you are black . . . but come, I remember how you tore
that unfortunate scrub Bosville to pieces years ago in Barbados for
saying that the slaves liked it – that it was in their masters' interest to
treat them kindly – that doing away with slavery would be shutting
the gates of mercy on the negroes. Hey, hey! The strongest language
I have ever heard you use. I wonder he did not ask for satisfaction.'

'I think I feel more strongly about slavery than anything else, even
that vile Buonaparte who is in any case one aspect of it . . . Bosville . . .
the sanctimonious hypocrite . . . the silly blackguard with his "gates of
mercy," his soul to the Devil – a mercy that includes chains and whips
and branding with a hot iron. Satisfaction. I should have given it him
with the utmost good-will: two ounces of lead or a span of sharp steel;
though common ratsbane would have been more appropriate.'

'Why, Stephen, you are in quite a passion.'

'So I am. It is a retrospective passion, sure, but I feel it still. Thinking of that ill-looking flabby ornamented conceited self-complacent
ignorant shallow mean-spirited cowardly young shite with absolute
power over fifteen hundred blacks makes me fairly tremble even
now – it moves me to grossness. I should have kicked him if ladies
had not been present.'

'Come in,' called Jack.

'Mr Grainger's duty, sir,' said Norton, 'and the wind is hauling aft.
May he set the weather studdingsails?'

'Certainly, Mr Norton, as soon as they will stand. I shall come on deck the moment I have finished these accounts. If the French gentleman is at hand, pray tell him I should like to see him in ten minutes. Compliments, of course.'

'Aye aye, sir. Studdingsails as soon as they will stand. Captain's compliments to Monsieur Turd . . . '

'Dutourd, Mr Norton.'

'Beg pardon, sir. To Monsieur Dutourd and wishes to see him in ten minutes.'

On receiving this message Dutourd thanked the midshipman, looked at Martin with a smile, and began walking up and down from the taffrail to the leeward bow-chaser and back again, looking at his watch at each turn.

'Come in,' cried Jack Aubrey yet again. 'Come in, Monsieur – Mr Dutourd, and sit down. I am casting my prize-money accounts and should be obliged for a statement of the amount of specie, bills of exchange and the like carried in the *Franklin*: I must also know, of course, where it is kept.'

Dutourd's expression changed to an extraordinary degree, not merely from confident pleasurable anticipation to its opposite but from lively intelligence to a pale stupidity.

Jack went on, 'The money taken from your prizes will be returned to its former owners – I already have sworn statements from the ransomers – and the *Franklin*'s remaining treasure will be shared out among her captors, according to the laws of the sea. Your private purse, like your private property, will be left to you; but its amount is to be written down.' Dutourd's wits had returned to him by now. Jack Aubrey's massive confidence told him that any sort of protest would be worse than useless: indeed, this treatment compared most favourably with the *Franklin*'s, whose prisoners were stripped bare; but the long pause between capture and destitution, so very unlike the instant looting he had seen before, had bred illogical hopes. He managed a look of unconcern, however, and said, 'Vae victis' and produced two keys from an inner pocket. 'I hope you may not find that my former shipmates have been there before you,' he added. 'There were some grasping fellows among them.'

There were some grasping fellows aboard the *Surprise* too, if men who dearly loved to get their hands upon immediate ringing gold and silver rather than amiable but mute, remote, almost theoretical pieces of paper, are to be called grasping. There had been the sound of chuckling throughout the ship ever since Oracle Killick let it be known 'that the skipper had got round to it at last,' and a boat carrying Mr Reade, Mr Adams and Mr Dutourd's servant had pulled across to the *Franklin*, returning with a heavy chest that came aboard not indeed to cheers, for that would not have been manners, but with great cheerfulness, good-will, and anxious care while it hung in the void, and witticisms as it swung inboard, to be lowered as handsomely as a thousand of eggs.

Even until the next day, however, Stephen Maturin remained unaware of all this, for not only had he dined by himself in the cabin, Jack Aubrey being aboard the *Franklin*, but his mind was almost entirely taken up with cephalopods; and as far as he took notice of the gaiety at all (by no means uncommon in the *Surprise*, that happy ship) he attributed it to the freshening of the breeze, which was now sending the two ships along at close on five knots with promise of better to come. He had had to make his morning rounds alone, Martin having remained in bed with what he described as a sick headache; Jack's breakfast and Stephen's had for once failed to coincide, and they had exchanged no more than a wave from the sea to the deck before Stephen sat down to his collection. Some of the cephalopods were dried, some were in spirits, one was fresh: having ranged the preserved specimens in due order and checked the labels and above all the spirit level (a necessary precaution at sea, where he had known jars drained dry, even those containing asps and scorpions) he turned to the most interesting and most recent creature, a decapod that had fixed the terrible hooks and suckers of its long arms into the net of salt beef towing over the side to get rid of at least some of the salt before the pieces went into the steep-tub – had fixed them with such obstinate strength that it had been drawn aboard.

With Sarah and Emily standing in opposite corners of the cabin and holding the squid's arms just so, Stephen snipped, drew, and described, dissecting out various processes for preservation: there was alas no possibility of keeping the entire animal even if he had possessed a jar large enough, since it was Mr Vidal's property, he having detached it from the beef at the cost of some cruel wounds (a spiteful decapod) and having promised it to the gunroom cook for today's feast, this Friday being the day when, on the other side of the world, Shelmerston, forgetting all differences of creed, lit bonfires and danced round them singing a chant whose meaning was now lost but which as late as Leland's time was clearly in honour of the goddess Frig; and even today the words retained such power that as Stephen well knew no Shelmerstonian born and bred would willingly omit them.

The little girls were usually as good and silent as could be on these occasions, but now the coming of the feast and the arrival of the prize-money overcame Sarah's discretion and she said, 'Jemmy Ducks says Monsieur Turd's nose is sadly out of joint. He kicked Jean Potin's arse. Jean Potin is his servant.'

'Hush, my dear,' said Stephen. 'I am counting the suckers. And you are not to say Monsieur Turd: nor arse.'

Emily prized Stephen's attention and approval more than her immortal soul: though an affectionate child, she would betray her best friend to obtain it and now she called out from her corner, 'She is always saying Monsieur Turd. Mr Grainger checked her for saying it only yesterday: he declared it was wicked to speak so of such a benevolent gentleman.'

'Heave that tentacle taut,' said Stephen. 'Never mind your pinafores.' He knew the squid's destination and he was working fast,

with great concentration. Yet well before the description was complete there was a gunroom cook's mate begging his pardon, but so
horny an old bugger, if his honour would excuse the word, needed
a good hour in the pot: his honour sighed, quickly removed one last
ganglion and sat back. 'Thank you, my dears,' he said to the little girls.
'Give Nicholson a hand with the longer arms. And Sarah, before you
go, pass me the frigate-bird, will you, now?'

He was pretty well acquainted with frigate-birds, as any man who
had sailed so far in tropical waters must be, and he had skinned quite
a number, distinguishing three or perhaps four closely-allied species and making careful descriptions of their plumage; but he had
never thoroughly dissected one. This he now settled himself to do,
meaning first to examine the flight muscles, for in their lofty soaring the frigate-birds were perhaps even more remarkable than the
albatrosses: and he had scarcely laid bare the breast before he had a
premonition that he might be on the verge of the finest anatomical
study of his career.

The bird, naturally enough, possessed a wishbone: yet from the
very first it had seemed extraordinarily, unnaturally, firm under his
touch. As his scalpel worked delicately down towards the keel of the
breastbone, a spatula easing the muscles aside, he was perfectly deaf
to the ring of coins and the powerful voices on the other side of the
bulkhead – Captain Aubrey, the two oldest forecastle-hands (rather
hard of hearing), and Mr Adams telling over the treasure of the *Franklin*, converting it into Spanish dollars and reckoning the shares – and
to those on the quarterdeck: an extraordinary number of hands had
found tasks that kept them within earshot of the open companion,
and they kept up a murmured commentary upon the amounts, pro-
venence and rates of exchange of the coins handled below, showing
a wonderful grasp of the European and American system, switching
from Dutch rixdollars to Hanover ducats with as much ease as from
Barcelona pistoles to Portuguese joes, Venice sequins or Jamaica
guineas. The murmur, the remarkably strong murmur, ceased when
hands were piped to dinner, but the telling in the great cabin con-

tinued, while Stephen, without a thought for anything else, steadily exposed the upper thorax of the frigate-bird.

He had not quite bared all the essentials by the time Killick and Padeen came in fairly skipping with impatience to say that the gun-room was assembling – the feast was almost under way. He submitted to their attentions and hurried below properly dressed, fairly clean, with his wig straight on his head and a look of shining delight still on his face.

'Why, gentlemen,' he cried on entering the gunroom, 'I am afraid I was almost late.'

'It is no matter,' said Grainger. 'We had another whet and feel the better for it. But now I will ask Mr Martin to say grace, and we will set to.'

Martin had been moved to make room for two more Shelmerstonians from the prize and now he was on Stephen's right. He was looking ill and thin and when they sat down Stephen said to him in a low voice, 'I trust I see you tolerably well?'

'Perfectly so, I thank you,' said Martin without a smile. 'It was only a passing malaise.'

'I am glad to hear it; but you must certainly stay on deck this evening,' said Stephen; and after a pause, 'I have just made a discovery that I think will please you. In the frigate-bird the symphysis of the furcula coalesces with the carina and the upper end of each ramus with the caracoid, while in its turn each caracoid coalesces with the proximal end of the scapula!' His look of modest triumph faded as he saw that Martin's anatomy did not appear to reach so far, or at least not to grasp at the consequences, and he went on, 'The result, of course, is that the whole assembly is entirely rigid, apart from the slight flection of the rami. I believe this to be unique among existing birds, and closely related to the creature's flight.'

'It is of some interest, if your example was not a sport,' said Martin, 'and perhaps it justifies taking the bird's life away. But how often have we seen hecatombs that yield nothing of significance – hundreds and hundreds of stomachs opened, all with much the same result. Even

Mr White of Selborne shot very great numbers. Sometimes I feel that
the dissection may take place merely to warrant the killing.'

Stephen had often known patients eager to be disagreeable: a common morbid irritability, especially in putrid fevers. But it was almost
invariably kept for their friends and relations, rarely extending to their
medical men. On the other hand, although Martin was undoubtedly
sick, Stephen was not in fact his physician; nor was it likely that Martin would consult him. He made no reply, turning to Mr Grainger
with praise of the squid soup; but he was wounded, deeply disappointed, far from pleased.

Opposite him sat Dutourd, apparently in much the same unenviable
state of mind. Both men however kept up a creditable appearance of
urbanity for some time: they even exchanged remarks about the squid,
though it was clear to most of the table that not only was Dutourd's
nose out of joint but that he held the Doctor in some degree responsible. For Grainger, Vidal and the rest, privateers or man-of-war's men,
taking or being taken was as much part of sea-going life as fair weather
or foul and they accepted these things as they came; but they knew
that this was the first time Dutourd had been stripped – relatively
stripped – and they treated him with a particular deferential gentleness, rather as though he were recently bereaved. This had the effect
of making him more loquacious than usual: towards pudding-time his
voice rose from the tone of conversation to something nearer that of
public address and Stephen realized with dismay that they were to hear
a discourse on Rousseau and the proper education of children.

The plum-duff vanished, the cloth was drawn, the decanters
moved steadily round, Dutourd boomed on. Stephen had stopped listening several glasses back: his mind turned sometimes with glowing
joy to his discovery, more often with intense irritation at Martin's
obvious desire to wound. It was true that Martin was much more an
observer of birds – an accurate, highly experienced observer – than a
systematic ornithologist, basing his taxonomy upon anatomical principles, yet even so . . .

Dr Maturin had curiously pale eyes, which he often covered with blue spectacles. He was not wearing them at present, and this pallor was much accentuated by the mahogany tan of his face on the one hand and on the other by the cold displeasure with which he reflected upon his assistant, now sitting by him in dogged silence.

He was gazing straight before him in one of these reveries when Dutourd, pouring himself yet another glass of port, caught his eye and taking the glare as a personal reflection he said, 'But I am afraid, Doctor, that you do not share our opinion of Jean-Jacques?'

'Rousseau?' said Stephen, returning to the immediate present and composing his features to a more sociable amenity or at last adopting a less grim and even sinister expression. 'Rousseau? faith, little do I know of him, apart from the Devin du Village, which I enjoyed; but his theories have been floating about me for ever, and once an admirer made me swear to read the Confessions. I did so: an oath is sacred. But all the time I was reminded of a cousin, a priest, who told me that the most tedious, squalid and disheartening part of his duty was listening to penitents who having made the act of contrition recounted imaginary, fictitious sins, unclean phantasms. And the most painful was the giving of an absolution that might be blasphemous.'

'You surely did not doubt Rousseau's truthfulness?'

'Out of common charity I was obliged to do so.'

'I do not understand you, sir.'

'You will recall that in this book he speaks of four or five children his mistress bore him, children that were at once dismissed to the foundling hospital. Now this does not agree very well with his praise of the domestic affections, still less with his theories of education in Emile. So unless I was to think of him as a hypocrite where bringing up the young was concerned, I was compelled to regard him as a begetter of false babies.' The ransomer merchants at the end of the table, earthy creatures who unlike their serious hosts had been growing more and more restless, burst into a great horse-laugh at the words *false babies*, and clawing one another on the back they called out, 'Hear him. Very good. Hear him.'

'Those children can perfectly well be explained to a candid mind,' cried Dutourd over the hubbub, 'but where there is a fixed prejudice, an evident hatred of progress and enlightenment, a love of privilege and outworn custom, a denial of the essential goodness of man, a settled malevolence, I have nothing to say.'

Stephen bowed, and turning to the troubled acting first lieutenant he said, 'Mr Grainger, sir, you will forgive me if I leave you at this point. Yet before I go, before I *sling my hook*, allow me to propose a toast to Shelmerston. Bumpers, gentlemen, if you please; and no heel-taps. Here's to Shelmerston, and may we soon sail in over her bar with never a scrape.'

'Shelmerston, Shelmerston, Shelmerston for ever,' they cried as he walked off, returning to the great cabin and feeling the ship's much stronger pitch and roll as he went. He found Jack well into his dinner and sat down beside him. 'Will I confess a grave sin?' he asked.

'Do, by all means,' said Jack, looking at him kindly. 'But if you managed to commit a grave sin between the gunroom and here you have a wonderful capacity for evil.'

Stephen took a piece of biscuit, tapping it mechanically, brushed away the weevil-frass, and said, 'I was in a wicked vile temper, so I was too, and I flew out at Dutourd and Rousseau.'

'He was in an ugly frame of mind as well, very willing to have a fight. He could only just be civil when I made him give up the *Franklin*'s money; yet God knows it was natural enough.'

'So you took his money away? I did not know.'

'Not *his* money – we left him his purse – his *ship's* money: booty from her prizes, cash carried for stores and supplies. It is always done, you know, Stephen. You must have seen it scores of times. The chest came aboard in the forenoon watch.'

'Oh certainly, certainly. Only I was not on deck at the time, and I do not believe anybody mentioned the fact. Yet I did observe a general gaiety; and Sarah stated that Dutourd's nose was out of joint.'

'Indeed he took it very ill. He had a great deal of money aboard. But what could he expect? We are not a philanthropic institution. Adams and I and two of the hands were telling it all the morning: there were some very curious pieces, particularly among the gold. I kept this little heap to show you.'

'Little do I know of money,' said Stephen, 'but these are surely bezants; and is not this very like an archaic gold mohur? Pierced and worn as a charm, no doubt.'

'I am sure of it,' said Jack. 'And what do you make of this broad piece? It is rubbed almost smooth, but if you hold it sideways to the light you can make out a ship with a forward-raking mast, very heavy shrouds, and an absurd high-perched poop or after-castle.'

In time Jack finished his dinner, and when they were drinking their coffee Stephen said, 'I made a remarkable discovery this morning. I believe it will make a great stir in the Royal Society when I read my paper; and Cuvier will be *amazed*.' He described the extraordinarily unyielding nature of the frigate-bird's bosom, contrasting it with that of other fowl, no more rigid than an indifferent wicker basket, and spoke of its probable connection with the creature's soaring flight. As it was usual with them when they spoke of the lie of the land, naval manoeuvres or the like he traced lines on the table with wine, and Jack, following with keen attention, said, 'I take your point, and I believe you are right. For this, do you see' – drawing a ship seen from above – 'is the mainyard when we are close-hauled on the starboard tack. It is braced up sharp with the larboard brace – here is the larboard brace – the sheet hauled aft, the weather leeches hauled forward with bowlines twanging taut, and the tack hauled aboard, brought down to the chess-trees and well bowsed upon. When all this is done in a seamanlike manner there is precious little give – flat as a board – and a stiff, well-trimmed ship fairly flies along. Surely there is a parallel here?'

'Certainly. If you will come next door I will show you the bones in question and their coalescence, and you will judge the degree of rigidity yourself, comparing it with that of your sheets and chess-trees. I was called away before the dissecting was quite complete – before everything was as white and distinct as a specimen or example mounted for an anatomy lesson – but *you* will never dislike a little blood and slime.'

Stephen was not a heavy, impercipient man in most respects, yet he had known Jack Aubrey all these years without discovering that he disliked even a very little blood and slime extremely: that is to say, cold blood and slime. In battle he was accustomed to wading ankle-deep in both without the least repulsion, laying about him in a very dreadful manner. But he could scarcely be brought to wring a chicken's neck, still less watch a surgical operation.

'You will take the exposed furcula between your finger and thumb,' Stephen went on, 'and all proportions guarded you will gauge its immobility.'

Jack gave a thin smile: seven excuses came to his mind. But he was much attached to his friend; and the excuses were improbable at the best. He walked slowly forward into what had once been his dining-cabin and was now, to judge from the reek, a charnel-house.

He did indeed take the exposed furcula as he was desired to do, and he listened to Stephen's explanations with his head gravely inclined: he looked not unlike a very large dog that was conscientiously carrying out an unpleasant duty: but how happy he was when the duty was done, when the explanations came to an end, and when he could walk out into the fresh air with a clear conscience!

'Everything is laid along, sir,' said Vidal, meeting him at the head of the companion-ladder. 'The chest is up, the Frenchmen ordered below, and Mr Adams is by the capstan with the muster-book.'

'Very good, Mr Vidal,' said Jack, breathing deep. He glanced at the sky, he glanced aft, where the *Franklin* lay on the frigate's quarter a cable's length away, throwing a fine bow-wave. 'Let us take in royals and topgallant studdingsails.'

Vidal had hardly relayed the order before the topmen were racing aloft: the royals and topgallant studdingsails vanished, the ship's way sensibly decreased, and Jack said, 'All hands aft, if you please.'

'Mr Bulkeley, pipe all hands aft,' said Vidal to the bosun, who replied, 'All hands aft it is, sir,' and instantly wound his call – sharp blasts followed by a long quavering shriek.

This was the first official information to reach the foremast-hands, but if anyone aboard was so simple as to expect them to be surprised at the news he was wholly mistaken: they had all contrived to be clean, shaved, sober and properly dressed; they all had their hats; and now they all swarmed aft along the larboard gangway, overflowing on to the quarterdeck in the usual shapeless heap. There they stood grinning and sometimes nudging one another, and Jack called out, 'Now, shipmates, we are going to proceed to a provisional sharing-out. But this is all to be by silver, Spanish dollars or pieces of eight, shillings and bits, or by gold that everybody knows: guineas, louis d'or, ducats, joes and the like. The old-fashioned, outlandish pieces will be sold by weight and shared accordingly. Mr Wedell, hands out of beckets.' The unhappy boy blushed crimson, whipped his hands from his pockets and crept behind the taller Norton with what countenance he could summon. 'Paper notes and bills, and of course hull, fittings, goods and head-money, come in the final reckoning.'

'If spared,' murmured Mr Vidal.

'Just so,' said Jack. 'If spared. Mr Adams, carry on.'

'Ezekiel Ayrton,' cried Mr Adams, his finger on the open muster-book, and Ayrton, foretopman, starboard watch, came aft, happy though somewhat conscious of being alone and in the public gaze. He walked across the quarterdeck, taking off his hat as he came, but instead of passing straight on beyond the Captain to the windward gangway and so forward as he would have done at an ordinary muster, he advanced to the capstan. There, upon the capstan-head, Adams paid down two guineas, one louis d'or, two ducats (one Venetian, the other Dutch) and enough pieces of eight and Jamaica bits to bring the sum to twenty-seven pounds six shillings and fourpence. Ayrton swept them into his hat with a chuckle, moved on two paces and touched his forehead to the Captain. 'Give you joy of them, Ayrton,' said Jack, smiling at him. So it went throughout the alphabet, with more laughter and outbursts of wit than would have been countenanced in a more regular man-of-war, until a minute after John Yardley, yeoman of the sheets, had joined his jocose, wealthy companions on the forecastle, when all merriment was cut to instant silence by the hail from the masthead: 'On deck there: object fine on the starboard bow. Which I believe it is a barrel.'

T he barrel, the first inanimate object they had seen outside their own wooden world for what already seemed an age, was watched intently by all hands as it bobbed closer; and when at last it came aboard, seized with some difficulty by Bonden and Yardley, tossing on the choppy sea in the Doctor's skiff, most of the *Surprise*'s former whalers came as far aft alongside the gangway as was decent, for the cask was seen to be bound with withies, not with iron hoops, not man-of-war fashion nor even that of a China-going ship.

'Mr Vidal,' said Jack, 'you have been in the South Sea fishery: what do you make of it?'

'Why, sir,' said Vidal, 'I should say it is a Yankee barrel; but I sailed out of London River, and never was in those ports. Simon and Trotter would know more.'

'Pass the word for Simon and Trotter,' said Jack, and they instantly stepped on to the quarterdeck.

'Martha's Vineyard,' said Trotter, turning the barrel in his hands.

'Nantucket,' said Simon. 'I was married there, once.'

'Then how come it has Isaac Taylor's mark?' asked Trotter.

'Well, any road,' said Simon, looking fixedly at Jack, 'this here is a Yankee barrel, sir, what they call a Bedford hog in New England; and it has not been in the water a couple of days. There is no sea-clummer on it. And the dowels is sound. They would never have heaved it over the side without they had a full hold. A full hold and homeward-bound.'

All within earshot nudged one another, grinning: their prize-money clanked in their loaded hats; they were delighted at the idea of even more.

Jack considered the sky, the set of the sea, the breeze and the current. The whole ship's company, eminently professional, did the same. The only exception was Dr Maturin, who considered a thin line of

birds, high and remote: when he had fixed them in his pocket-glass
(no simple feat with the increasing swell) he put them down as southern cousins to the kittiwake: they were gliding steadily east-south-
east. For a moment he thought of offering Martin the little telescope;
but he decided against it. For their part Martin and Dutourd were
contemplating the seamen, their profoundly serious, concentrated
weighing of the sea, the weather, the possibilities of a capture, and
Stephen heard Martin say, 'Homo hominis lupus.'

Jack called the *Franklin* up by signal and when she was within half
a cable's length he stepped right aft and called out, 'Tom, we have
picked up a barrel, seemingly fresh, perhaps from a Yankee whaler.
Bear away to leeward and let us sweep on our former course.'

Not a great deal was left of the tropical day, but until the very
dipping of the sun every masthead was manned and relieved each
bell; and some lingered on throughout the brief twilight. Even the
most sanguine had known that the chance of finding a ship in this
immensity of ocean with no more than a barrel and the known habits
of South Sea whalers for guidance was very remote, although hope
was sustained by the presence of sea-birds (rather uncommon in
these blue waters) travelling in the same direction. The chief basis of
this hope was a fervent desire that it should be fulfilled, and it sank
steadily with the coming of the night, sweeping up deep purple from
the east, already flecked with stars. Now, in the last dog-watch, as the
last men came slowly down, dispirited, it revived, rising high above
its former merely speculative pitch, for the *Franklin*, far over to leeward, sent up a blue flare, followed shortly after by a night-signal, a
hoist of lanterns.

Reade was signal-midshipman, and with his telescope poised on
Wedell's shoulder he read off the hoist to his Captain in a firm, official
voice. 'Telegraphic, sir: alphabetic. K. R. E. N. G. Kreng, sir: I hope I
have got it right,' he added in a more human tone.

'Kreng, ha, ha ha!' cried a dozen voices on the gangway; and the
helmsman, in a low, kindly murmur said to Reade, 'That's what we

call a corpus, sir: a carcass with his head emptied of spermaceti and the blubber all stripped off.'

Jack took the *Franklin*'s bearing, said, 'Mr Reade, acknowledge and make the signal *Course SSE by E: close-reefed topsails.*'

This same course took the *Surprise* past the dead whale soon after the moon had risen: white birds whirled and flashed through the beams of the stern-lantern. They could scarcely be identified – some pied petrels and possibly a few of the small albatrosses, apart from gulls – but on the other hand the huge carcass, rolling in the phosphorescent sea, was perfectly clear. 'I reckon he would have been an old eighty-barrel bull,' observed Grainger, standing at the rail by Stephen's side. 'They are not as troublesome as the young ones, not being so nimble, but they sound mighty deep – I have known one take out the line of four boats an-end, eight hundred fathom, can you imagine it? – and when they come up they are apt to turn awkward and snap your boat in two. But may I say, Doctor,' he added in a hesitant murmur, 'I saw your mate catting over the side – to windward, poor soul – and then he went below, looking right sickly. Could he have eaten something, do you suppose?'

'Perhaps he may. Though possibly it is the lively motion of the ship, with these short sudden seas and all this spray.'

'To be sure, the breeze is dead against the current now: and the stream has grown stronger with the main not so very far away.'

However, Martin seemed reasonably well for their morning rounds, though the sea was livelier still, and the ship pitched with more than ordinary force as they sailed large under mere topsails and they close-reefed, sweeping as wide an expanse of the somewhat hazy sea as ever they could, perpetually looking for their quarry or to their consort for a signal. Theoretically each could see at least fifteen miles in all directions; and even with the necessity for keeping within clear signalling distance they covered a vast area, but the veering wind brought low scud and it was not until early in the forenoon watch, with the misty sun two spans above the horizon, that the exultant hail 'Sail ho!' came down from the masthead, echoing below, even into the sick-berth itself.

'We've found them!' cried Martin with a triumph that contrasted strangely with his now habitually anxious, withdrawn, cheerless expression.

'Go along, my dears,' said Stephen to the little girls, whose duties were already over, and with the sketch of a bob they flitted away into the dark orlop, scattering rats and cockroaches as they ran, invisible but for their white pinafores. Stephen finished rubbing blue ointment into Douglas Murd, washed his hands, tossed Martin the towel, called to Padeen, 'Let the glasses dry of themselves,' and ran on deck, joining almost all the ship's company who were not aloft.

'Ho, Doctor,' called Jack from the starboard rail, 'here's an elegant spectacle.' He nodded forward over the short tossing angry sea, and as he nodded a sperm whale rose not ten yards out, blew a fine spout, breathed audibly and dived, a great smooth roll. The spout swept aft along the deck and beyond it Stephen saw the whaler clear, directly to windward: beyond her, two boats close together, and farther still, a mile and more to the east, three more. 'They were so busy with their fish they did not see us till a moment ago. The boats in the north-north-east have not seen us yet. But look at the men on board the ship – parcel of old women.' He passed the telescope and at once that remote deck sprang close, sharp and distinct, visibly dirty and disordered even from here. Not many people still aboard, but those few running about with great activity and little apparent purpose, while a person in the crow's nest waved his arms with uncommon vehemence, pointing to the south.

'Mr Grainger,' called Jack, 'pray explain the situation to the Doctor.' He took back his telescope, slung it, and ran up to the masthead like a boy.

'Why, sir,' said Grainger in his comfortable West Country voice, 'those far-off boats away to the eastward are fast to a gurt old bull, running like a coach and six on a turnpike. George, tell our William to bring my other spy-glass, and bear a hand, bear a hand. Now, do you see,' he went on, when it came, 'there is the headsman standing in the bows with his lance, to kill the whale when he rises. It was the boat-steerer sent the harpoon home, of course; and now he is in the stern again.'

'A very broad-shouldered man.'

'They generally are. The other boats are standing by, right close, ready to pass their lines in case he sounds again and deeper still. Now if you look back to the ship, sir, you will see they have had a fine morning: two whales killed and fast to a third. They are empty-ing the first one's head alongside now, or were until they saw us and started their capering; and an awkward time they were having of it, with the short seas breaking over all. And the two boats close to are towing in the second fish. Those fast to the gurt old bull ain't seen us yet, watching so eager; but I dare say the ship will give them a gun presently.'

Stephen gazed and gazed. The little figures hurrying and jerking about in the distant whaler, though clear, were perfectly mute, inau-dible, which added a ludicrous side to their distress: some, including a man who was presumably the master, since he beat and cuffed the others, were struggling round the great try-pots set up amidships to melt the blubber – struggling to get a gun clear of all the trying-out gear, the casks and the general whaler-like disorder.

'The man in the crow's nest seems very earnest in urging them to go away to the right. He leaps up and down.'

'Why, yes, sir. The *Franklin* lies there in the west. Ain't you noticed?'

'To tell you the truth, I had not. But why should he want them to go to her?'

'Because she is wearing American colours, in course, whereas we wear the ensign. That is the Captain's guile, do you see? In any case they certainly know her, she having been a-privateering in these waters since March; and the look-out wants them to make sail for her while there is yet time: they do not know she is took. As the breeze lays now we should need two long boards or tacks if you follow me to come up with her, and by then she could just squeeze under the *Franklin*'s lee.'

'Little good would it do them.'

'None at all, Doctor. But they don't know it. Nor they don't know what metal we carry.'

'Would it not mean abandoning their friends over there in the east?'

'Oh yes. And it would mean abandoning three good fish, enough to break a whaler's heart. I doubt they do it: they are more likely to wait for the *Franklin* to come up, and then brazen it out the two of them, either hoping we will sheer off, or putting before the wind and running for it, the one supporting the other. But her master might possibly think it worth while to save a full hold; and then you know, sir' said Grainger in a low confidential tone, 'a whaler's crew ships by the lay – no wages but a share in the profits – so the fewer come home the more the survivors gain. Oh, by God, they are doing it!' he cried. 'They are leaving their friends behind.' Indeed, the hands had dropped the gun for the yards and braces; and the nearer boats, having cast off their whale, were racing for the side, tearing through the broken sea. The sails dropped, the yards rose up, the ship's head turned, and as the men from the two boats scrambled aboard she gathered way. She had a fine topgallant breeze on her quarter and she moved at a surprising pace.

Her people packed on sail faster than would have been believed possible for so few hands, and their calculations were right: the whaler, wearing American colours on every mast, reached the *Franklin* well before the *Surprise*, which had paused to take the eastern boats in tow.

When the whaler was within pistol-shot the *Franklin* hauled down her Stars and Stripes, hoisted the ensign and sent a twenty-four-pound ball skipping across the whaler's forefoot. She let fly her sheets and Tom Pullings hailed her in a voice of brass: 'Strike your colours and come under my lee.'

She was still lying there when the *Surprise* came up with the eastern boats strung out behind her; Jack rounded to and ranged up on the whaler's starboard side.

'I have left her for you, sir,' called Pullings across the prize's deck.

'Quite right, Tom,' replied Jack, and wiping the spray from his face – for even here, in the lee of two ships, the waves were chopping high – he gave the order 'Blue cutter away. Mr Grainger, go across, if you please: take possession and send the master back with his papers. The whaler, ahoy!'

'Sir?'

'Start a couple of casks fore and aft, d'ye hear me, there?'

'Aye aye, sir,' said the master, a sparse, hard-featured man, now awkwardly willing to please; and a moment later whale-oil poured from the scuppers, spreading with extreme rapidity. The sea did not cease heaving, but the spray no longer flew – there was no white water, no breaking between the ships nor away to leeward.

'Should you like to go, Doctor?' asked Jack, turning kindly. 'I believe you have always wanted to look into a whaler.' Stephen bowed, and quickly tied a length of bandage over his hat and wig, tying it under his chin. Jack directed his voice towards the half-swamped whale-boats astern: 'You fellows had better go aboard, before you are drowned.'

It took some little time to get the Doctor safely down into the blue cutter; it took longer to get him up the oily side of the whaler, where the master stretched down an officious hand and Bonden thrust him from below. But he was scarcely on the filthy deck before the whale-boat crews came swarming aboard with their gear, the headsmen carrying their lances, the boat-steerers their shining harpoons. They boarded mostly on the quarter, coming up nimbly as cats, and raced forward with a confused bellow. The master backed to the mainmast.

'You left us to starve on the ocean, you rat,' roared the first headsman.

'You made all sail and cracked on – cracked on,' roared the second, shaking his lance, barely articulate.

'Judas,' said the third.

'Now Zeek,' cried the master, 'you put down that lance. I should have picked you up . . .'

The broad-shouldered harpooner, the man who had been fast to the big bull whale, was last up the side; he heaved his way through the shouting, tight-packed throng; he said nothing but he flung his iron straight through the master's breast, deep into the wood.

Returning to the *Surprise* covered with blood – a useless investigation, heart split, spinal cord severed – Stephen was met with the news that Martin had been taken ill. He dabbled his hands in a bucket of sea-water and hurried below. In spite of the activity on deck the gunroom was an example of the inevitably promiscuous nature of life at sea, with two anxious-looking officers sitting at the table with biscuit and mugs of soup in front of them, the cook standing at the door with the bill of fare in his hand and the grizzle-bearded lady of the gunroom at his side, all of them listening with concern to Martin's groans and stifled exclamations in the quarter-gallery, or rather the nasty little enclosure just aft by the bread-bins that served the gunroom for a quarter-gallery or house of ease, the deck being too low for anything more luxurious than a bucket.

Eventually he came out, fumbling at his clothes, looking inhuman; he staggered to his cabin and fell on to his cot, breathing quick and shallow. Stephen followed him. He sat on a stool and said in a low voice, close to Martin's head, 'Dear colleague, I am afraid you are far from well. May I not do something – mix a gentle palliative, a soothing draught?'

'No. No, I thank you,' said Martin. 'It is a passing . . . indisposition. All I need is rest . . . and quiet.' He turned away. It was clear to Stephen that at this stage there was nothing more he could usefully say. And when Martin's breathing grew easier he left him.

The rest of the ship was full of life, with prisoners coming aboard with their chests and a prize-crew going across to take over; and as usual the whaler's hands were being checked against her muster-book by Mr Adams, the Captain's clerk, in the great cabin. Jack and Tom Pullings were there, watching the men, listening to their answers, and making up their minds how they should be divided. They were heavy, sad, disappointed men at present, with the whole of their three-years cruise taken from them in a moment; but their spirits would revive, and many an enterprising band of prisoners had risen upon their captors and seized the ship. Moreover sailors from the northern colonies could prove as troublesome and pugnacious as Irishmen.

It appeared, however, that no more than a score of them belonged to the original crew from Nantucket, Martha's Vineyard and New Bedford. In three years many had died by violence, disease or drowning, whilst two or three had run, and their places had been filled with South Sea islanders and what could be picked up in the odd Pacific port: Portuguese, Mexican, half-castes, a wandering Chinese. A fairly simple division, though the *Surprise* was already somewhat short of hands.

The last, a thick-set youngish man who had lingered behind, came to a halt before the table and called out, 'Edward Shelton, sir, headsman, starboard watch: born in Wapping,' in a strong, undoubted Wapping voice.

'Then what are you doing in an enemy ship?' asked Adams.

'Which I went a-whaling during the peace and joined this here ship long before the American war was declared,' said Shelton, his words carrying perfect conviction. 'May I speak a word to the Captain?'

Adams looked at Jack, who said, 'What have you to say, Shelton?' in a tone that though mild enough promised nothing.

'You don't know me, sir,' said Shelton, putting a doubled forefin-

ger to his forehead in the naval way, 'but I seen you often enough in
Port Mahon, when you had the *Sophie*: I seen you come in with the
Cacafuego at your tail, sir. And many a time when you came aboard
Euryalus, Captain Dundas, Captain *Heneage* Dundas, in Pompey: I
was one of the side-men.'

'Well, Shelton,' said Jack, after a question or two for conscience'
sake, 'If you choose to return to your natural service, to enter volun-
teerly, you shall have the bounty and I will find you a suitable rating.'

'Thank you kindly, your honour,' said Shelton. 'But what I mean
is, we cleared from Callao on the seventh, and while we were getting
our stores aboard – tar, cordage, sailcloth and stockfish – there was
a merchantman belonging to Liverpool, homeward-bound from the
northwards, in dock, tightening up for her run round the Horn. We
cleared on the seventh which it was a Tuesday, homeward-bound too
though not really full: not a right good voyage, not heart's content as
you might say, but middling. And off the Chinchas at break of day,
there was a four-masted ship directly to windward. Man-of-war fashion. The master said, "I know her, mates: she's friend. A Frenchman
out of Bordeaux, a privateer," and he lay to. There was nothing else
he could do, dead to leeward of a ship of thirty-two guns with yards
like Kingdom Come and the black flag flying at her masthead. But as
we lay there he walked fore and aft, gnawing his fingers and saying,
"Jeeze, I hope he remembers me. God Almighty, I hope he remembers
me. Chuck" – that was his mate and aunt's own child – "Likely he'll
remember us, don't you reckon?"

'Well, he did remember us. He hauled down his black flag and
we lay alongside one another, matey-matey. He asked after the Liverpool ship and we told him she would be out of dock in under a
month. So he said he would stretch away to the westward for a while
on the chance of an English whaler or a China ship and then lie off
the Chinchas again: and he told us the sea thirty leagues to the west-
north-west was full of whales, thick with whales. We sailed together,
separating gradually, and the day after we had sunk his topgallants
there we were in the middle of them, spouting all round the compass.'

'Tell me about her guns.'

'Thirty-two nine-pounders, sir, or maybe twelves; in any case all brass. Besides her chasers. I never seen a privateer so set out. But I did not like to go aboard or look too curious, let alone ask no questions, not with that crowd of villains.'

'Was their black flag in earnest?'

'Oh yes, sir; deadly earnest. They were as thorough-paced a no-quarter-given-or-asked as ever I see – trample the Crucifix any day of the week. But you and your consort could deal with her. I dare say *Surprise* could do so on her own, though it might be nip and tuck; and she would buy it very dear, they having to sink or be sunk. Which I mean if they are killed they are deaders, and if they are taken they are hanged. It is half a dozen of the one and . . .' His voice died away; he hung his head, a certain coldness having told him that he had been talking too much.

'As taut as it is long,' said Jack, not unkindly. 'Well, Shelton, is Mr Adams to write you down as pressed or volunteer?'

'Oh volunteer, sir, if you please,' cried Shelton.

'Make it so, Mr Adams, and rate him able for the moment: starboard watch,' said Jack. He wrote on a piece of paper. 'Shelton, give this to the officer of the watch. Well, Tom,' he went on after the man had gone, 'what do you think?'

'I believe him, sir, every word,' said Pullings. 'I am not to put my opinion before yours; but I believe him.'

'So did I,' said Jack, and the old experienced Adams nodded his head. Jack rang the bell. 'Pass the word for Mr Vidal.' And a few moments later, 'Mr Vidal, when we have seen the whaler's mate and her charts, and when we have shifted as much water out of her as can be done in thirty minutes, you will take command and steer for Callao under moderate sail. We are running down no great way in the hope of a Frenchman, and it is likely we shall overtake you. If we do not, wait there. Mr Adams will give you the necessary papers and the name of our agent: he looked after the frigate's prizes on the way out. You may take the whaler's mate, bosun and cook – no arms, of course, either on themselves or in their chests – and several of our people.'

'Very good, sir,' said Vidal, unmoved.

'As for getting the water across, you have half an hour: there is not a minute to lose; and since the sea is a little choppy, spend the oil and spare not. A couple of casks are neither here nor there.'

'Aye, aye, sir: spend and spare not it is.'

'Jack!' cried Stephen, coming in to their strangely late and even twilit dinner, 'did you know that those active mariners have brought a large number of hogsheads aboard, and they filled with fresh water?'

'Have they, indeed?' asked Jack. 'You amaze me.'

'They have, too. May I have some to sponge my patients and have their clothes washed at last?'

'Well, I suppose you may have a little for sponging them – a very small bowl would be enough, I am sure – but as for washing clothes – washing *clothes*, good Lord! That would be a most shocking expenditure, you know. Salt does herrings no harm, nor lobsters; and my shirt has not been washed in fresh water since Heaven knows how long. It is like coarse emery-paper. No. Let us wait for the rain: have you looked at the glass?'

'I have not.'

'It began dropping in the first dog. It has already reached twenty-nine inches and it is still falling: look at the meniscus. And the wind is hauling aft. If the rain don't come down in great black squalls tonight or tomorrow, you shall have one of these hogsheads – well, half a hogshead – for your clothes.'

After a short, dissatisfied silence Dr Maturin said, 'It will be no news to you, sure, that the whaler has slipped away, going, they tell me, to Callao, if ever they can find the place God be with them.'

'I had noticed it,' said Jack through his sea-pie.

'But you may not know that two of her men forgot their pills entirely or that in his legitimate agitation Padeen gave Smyth a liniment, not telling him it was to be rubbed in rather than drunk. However, nobody, *nobody* has told me why we are rushing in this impetuous manner through the turgid sea, with sailors whose names I do not even know, rushing almost directly away, to judge by the sun, away from the Peru I had so longed to see and which you had led me confidently to expect before Bridie's birthday.'

'I never said which birthday, this or the next.'

'I wonder you can speak with such levity about my daughter. I have always treated yours with proper respect.'

'You called them a pair of turnip-headed swabs once, when they were still in long clothes.'

'For shame, Jack: a hissing shame upon you. Those were your very own words when you showed them to me at Ashgrove before our voyage to the Mauritius. Your soul to the Devil.'

'Well, perhaps they were. Yes: you are quite right – I remember now – you warned me not to toss them into the air, as being bad for the intellects. I beg pardon. But tell me, brother, has nobody told you what is afoot?'

'They have not.'

'Where have you been?'

'I have been in my cabin downstairs, contemplating on mercury.'

'A delightful occupation. But he is not to be seen now, you know: he is too near the sun. And to tell you the truth he is neither much of a spectacle nor a great help in navigation, though charming from the purely astronomical point of view.'

'I meant the metallic element. In its pure state quicksilver is perfectly neutral; you may swallow half a pint without harm. But in its various combinations it is sometimes benign – where would you portly men be without the blue pill? – and sometimes, when exhibited by inexpert hands, its compounds are mortal in doses so small they can hardly be conceived.'

'So you know nothing of what is going forward?'

'Brother, how tedious you can be, on occasion. I did hear some cries of "Jolly rogers – jolly rogers – we shall roger them." But in parenthesis, Jack, tell me about this word *roger*. I have often heard it aboard, but can make out no clear nautical signification.'

'Oh, it is no sea-term. They use it ashore much more than we do – a low cant expression meaning to swive or couple with.'

Stephen considered for a moment and then said, 'So roger joins bugger and that even coarser word; and they are all used in defiance and contempt, as though to an enemy; which seems to show a curious light on the lover's subjacent emotions. Conquest, rape, subjugation: have women a private language of the same nature, I wonder?'

Jack said, 'In some parts of the West Country rams are called Roger, as cats are called Puss; and of course that is their duty; though which came first, the deed or the doer, the goose or the egg, I am not learned enough to tell.'

'Would it not be the owl, at all?'

'Never in life, my poor Stephen. Who ever heard of a golden owl? But let me tell you why we are cracking on like this in what promises to be a very dirty night. There was an Englishman called Shelton in the whaler's crew, a foremast-jack in *Euryalus* when Heneage Dundas had her: he told us of a French four-master, fitted out man-of-war fashion, *Alastor* by name, that attacks anything she can overpower, whatever its nation; a genuine pirate, wearing the black flag, the Jolly Roger, which means *strike and like to or we shall kill every man and boy aboard. We ask no quarter: we give no quarter.* We have checked Shelton's account; we have looked at the whaler's chart, pricked all the way from their leaving Callao to yesterday at sunset; and we know just about where the *Alastor* must be. She means to sail back to the coast and wait off the Chinchas for a Liverpool ship now docking at Callao for the homeward run. Listen!'

The companion overhead lit with three flashes of extreme brilliance; thunder cracked and bellowed at masthead height; and then came the all-pervading sound of enormous rain, not exactly a roar, but of such a volume that Jack had to lean over the table and raise his powerful voice to tell Stephen that 'now he could sponge his patients, aye, and wash them and their clothes too – there would be enough for the whole ship's company – the first ten minutes would carry off all the filth and then they would whip off the tarpaulins and fill the boats and scuttle-butts.'

The rain had no great effect on the swell, rolling strong from the north-west, but it flattened the surface almost as effectually as oil, doing away with countless superficial noises, so that the great voice of the rain came right down into the sick-berth itself, and Stephen, on his evening rounds, had to repeat his exclamation, 'I am astonished to see you here, Mr Martin: you are not fit to be up, and must go back to bed directly.' Of course he was not fit to be up. His eyes were deep-sunk in his now boney head, his lips were barely visible; and although he said, 'It was only a passing indisposition as I told you; and now it is over,' he had to grip the medicine-chest to keep upright. 'Nonsense,' said Stephen. 'You must go back to bed directly. That is an order, my dear sir. Padeen, help Mr Martin to his cabin, will you, now?'

When Stephen's work was done he walked up the ladder and into the gunroom: his was not exactly a seaman's step – there was something too tentative and crablike for that – but no landsman would have accomplished it, paying so little attention to the motion in that pitching ship as she raced with a full-topsail gale three points on her quarter, her stern rising up and up on the following swell; nor would a landsman have stood there, barely conscious of the heave, as he considered his messmates' dwelling-place.

It was a long dim corridor-like room, some eighteen feet wide and twenty-eight in length, with an almost equally long table running down the middle and the officers' cabin doors opening on to the narrow space on either side – opening outwards, since if they opened the other way they must necessarily crush the man within. There was no one in the gunroom at present apart from a seaman who was polishing the table and the foot of the mizzenmast, which rose nobly through it half-way along, though Wilkins, whose watch had just been relieved, could be heard snoring in the aftermost larboard dog-hole; yet at four bells the table would be lined with men eager for their supper. Dutourd was likely to be invited, and he was certain to talk: the ransomers were nearly always noisy: it was no place for a sick man. He walked into Martin's cabin and sat down by his cot. Since Martin had retired by order their relations were now changed to those between physician and patient, the physician's authority being enormously enhanced by the Articles of War. In any case a certain frontier had been crossed and at present Stephen felt no more hesitation about dealing with this case than he would have done if Martin had all at once run mad, so that he had to be confined.

Martin's breathing was now easy, and he appeared to be in a very deep, almost comatose sleep; but his pulse made Stephen most uneasy. Presently, shaking his head, he left the cabin: at the foot of the ladder he saw young Wedell coming down, soaked to the skin. 'Pray, Mr Wedell,' he said, 'is the Captain on deck?'

'Yes, sir. He is on the forecastle, looking out ahead.' Stephen grasped the hand-rail, but Wedell cried, 'May I take him a message, sir? I am wet as a whale already.'

'That would be very kind. Pray tell him, with my compliments, that Mr Martin is far from well; that I should like to move him to the larboard midshipmen's berth; and that I should be obliged for two strong sensible hands.'

The hands in question, Bonden and a powerful forecastleman who might have been his elder brother, took a quick, seamanlike glance at the situation and with no more than a 'By the head, mate. Handsomely, now,' they unshipped Martin's cot, carrying him forward in it at a soft barefoot trot to the empty larboard berth, where Padeen had cleared the deck and hung a lantern. They were of opinion that 'the Doctor's mate was as drunk as Davy's sow,' and indeed the inert relaxation, the now-stertorous breathing, gave that impression.

It was not the case, however. Nathaniel Martin had lain down in his clothes and now as Stephen and Padeen undressed him, as limp as a man deeply stunned, they saw the recent and exacerbated sores over much of his body.

'Would this be the leprosy, your honour?' asked Padeen, his low, hesitant speech made slower, more hesitant by the shock.

'It would not,' said Stephen. 'It is the cruel salt on a very sensitive skin, and an ill habit of constitution. Go and fetch fresh water – it will be to be had by now – warm if ever the galley is lit, two sponges, two towels, and clean sheets from the chest by my bed. Ask Killick for those that were last washed in fresh.'

'Salt and worse on a sensitive mind; an unhappy mind,' he added to himself. Leprosy he had seen often enough; eczemas of course and prickly heat carried to the extreme, but never anything quite like this. There were many things about Martin's state that he could not make out; and although analogies kept flitting through his mind like clues to the solution of a puzzle, none would settle or cling to its fellows.

Padeen returned and they washed Martin with warm fresh water all over twice, then laid on sweet oil wherever it would do good, wrapping him at last naked in a clean sheet: no nightshirt was called for in this steady warmth. From time to time he groaned or uttered a disconnected word; twice he opened his eyes, raised his head and stared about, uncomprehending; once he took a little water with inspissated lemon-juice in it; but generally speaking he was wholly inert, and the habitual look of anxiety had left his face.

When he sent Padeen to bed Stephen sat on. In sponging Martin he had looked very attentively for signs of the veneral disorder that he had at one time suspected: there were none. As a naval surgeon he had a great experience of the matter, and there were no signs at all. He knew, as any medical man must know, that mind could do astonishing things to body – false pregnancies, for example, with evident, tangible lactation and all the other marks of gravidity – but the lesions now before him were of another kind, and more virulent. Martin might believe himself poxed, and the belief might induce skin troubles, some forms of paralysis, constipation or uncontrolled flux, and in a man like Martin all the consequences of extreme anxiety, guilt and self-loathing; but not these particular miseries: he had seen something of the same nature in a patient whose wife was steadily poisoning him. More from intuition than any clear reasoning he expected a crisis of distress either about three in the morning, during what the Navy emphatically called the graveyard watch, when so many people die, or else at dawn.

He sat on: and although the ship was full of sound – the hissing rush of water along her side, the combined voices of all her rigging under a press of sail, the churn of the pumps, for with such a wind and such a sea she was hauling under the chains and making a fair amount of water, and from time to time the drumming of yet another squall – he was by now so accustomed to it that through the general roar he caught the strokes of the frigate's bell marking the watches through, and they often coincided with the minute silvery chime of the watch in his pocket.

He was accustomed to the room, too. At one time the frigate, as a regular man-of-war, had carried several midshipmen, master's mates and others and she needed two berths for them; now, in her present ambiguous position of His Majesty's hired vessel *Surprise*, engaged in an unavowable intelligence mission but going through the motions of being a privateer, by way of cover, she carried only three, and a single berth, that on the starboard side, was enough. Earlier in the voyage from Sydney Cove, when the stowaway Clarissa was discovered and instantly married to the young gentleman who had concealed her, the couple had had this larboard berth to themselves, and he had often sat with her when the weather was foul and the deck impossible; though their frequent consultations had always taken place in his cabin, where the light was better.

Dr Maturin, as the frigate's surgeon, belonged officially to the gun-room mess: in fact he nearly always lived in the great cabin with his particular friend Jack Aubrey, sleeping in one of the smaller cabins immediately forward of it, but he remained a member of the mess; and he was the only member of whom poor long-horned Oakes was not jealous. Yet he was the only member who was deeply attached to Clarissa as a person rather than as a means to an end, and the only one who could have taken her affection away from Oakes, if it was affection that the young man valued. To be sure, Stephen was perfectly conscious of her desirability; he was an ordinary sensual man in that respect and although in his long period of opium-eating his ardour had so declined that continence was no virtue, it had since revived with more than common force; yet in his view amorous conversation was significant only if the desire and the liking were shared, and early in their acquaintance it had become clear to him that physical love-making was meaningless to Clarissa, an act of not the slightest consequence. She took not the least pleasure in it and although out of good nature or a wish to be liked she might gratify a 'lover' it might be said that she was chastely unchaste. At that time no moral question was involved. The experience of her childhood – loneliness in a remote country house, early abuse, and a profound ignorance of the ordinary world – accounted for her attitude of mind: there was no bodily imperfection. None of this was written on her forehead, however, nor was she apt to confide in anyone but her physician, and she was packed off with her husband in a prize bound for Batavia amid general disapprobation. They were to go home in an Indiaman, and there, perhaps, Mrs Oakes would stay with Diana while her husband returned to the sea: he was passionately eager to succeed in the Navy.

Stephen thought about her most affectionately: it was her courage that he most admired – she had had a very hard life in London and an appalling one in the convict settlement of New South Wales, but she had borne up admirably, retaining her own particular integrity: no self-pity, no complaint. And although he was aware that this courage might be accompanied by a certain ferocity (she had been transported for blowing a man's head off) he did not find it affected his esteem.

As for her person, he liked that too: little evident immediate prettiness, but a slim, agreeable figure and a very fine carriage. She was not as beautiful as Diana with her black hair and blue eyes, but they both had the same straight back, the same thoroughbred grace of movement and the same small head held high; though in Clarissa's case it was fair. Something of the same kind of courage, too: he hoped they would be friends. It was true that Diana's house contained Brigit, the daughter whom Stephen had not yet seen, and upon the whole Clarissa disliked children; yet Clarissa was a well-bred woman, affectionate in her own way, and unless the baby or rather little girl by now were quite exceptionally disagreeable, which he could not believe, she would probably make an exception.

Bells, bells, bells, and long wandering thoughts between them: Martin quiescent.

Eight bells, and the starbowlines, after a trying watch with frequent trimming of sail, taking reefs in and shaking them out, with much toil and anxiety over the rain-water, separating the foul from the clean, and with very frequent soakings, hurried below through the downpour to drip more or less dry in their hammocks.

Jack remained on deck. The wind had slackened a little and it was now coming in over the frigate's quarter; the sea was less lumpy: if this continued, and it was likely to do so, he could soon set topgallants. But neither the set of the sea nor the wind was his first concern at present. During the night they had lost the *Franklin*, and unless they could find her again their sweep would be nothing like so efficient; besides, with even the remote prospect of an action his aim was always to bring a wholly decisive force into play. He was scarcely what would be called a timid man, but he far preferred a bloodless battle; often and often he had risked his people and his ship, yet never when there was a real possibility of having such a weight of metal within range that no enemy in his right mind would resist – colours struck, no blood shed, no harm done, valuable powder returned to the magazine, and honour saved all round. He was, after all, a professional man of war, not a hero. This fellow, however, was said to be a pirate. Shelton had seen the black flag. And if he was a pirate there was likely to be resistance or flight. Yet might it not have been that the Jolly Roger was hoisted for a cod, or as a way of disarming his legitimate privateer's prey by terror? Jack had known it done. True piracy was almost unheard of in these waters, whatever might be the case elsewhere; though some privateers, far and far from land, might some-times overstep the mark. And surely no downright pirate would have let a well-charged whaler go? The *Surprise* cared for neither flight nor fight: but still he did not want her scratched, nor any of her precious sailcloth and cordage hurt, and few sights would be more welcome than the *Franklin*.

Her top-lantern had vanished during the first three squalls of the night, reappearing in her due station on the starboard beam as each cleared, as much as it did clear in this thick weather. Yet after the long-lasting fourth it was no longer to be seen. At that time the wind was right aft, and this was the one point of sailing in which the *Franklin*, a remarkably well-built little craft, could draw away from the *Surprise*: Tom Pullings, the soul of rectitude, would never mean to do so, but with such a following sea the log-line was a most fallible guide and Jack therefore gazed steadily through the murk forward, over the starboard bow.

Even the murk was lessening, too: and although the southeast was impenetrably black with the last squall racing from them there were distinct rifts in the cloud astern, with stars showing clear. He had a momentary glimpse of Rigel Kent just above the crossjack yard; and with Rigel Kent at that height dawn was no great way off.

He also caught sight of Killick by the binnacle, holding an unnec-essary napkin. 'Mr Wilkins,' he said to the officer of the watch, 'I am going below. I am to be called if there is any change in the wind, or if any sail is sighted.'

He ran down the companion-ladder and into the welcome scent of coffee, the pot sitting there in gimbals, under a lantern. He gathered his hair – like most of the ship's company he wore it long, but whereas the seamen's pigtails hung straight down behind, Jack's was clubbed, doubled back and held with a bow: yet all but the few close-cropped men had undone their plaits to let their salt-laden hair profit from the downpour; and very disagreeable they looked, upon the whole, with long dank strands plastered about their upper persons, bare in this warm rain – he gathered his hair, wrung it out, tied it loosely

with a handkerchief, drank three cups of coffee with intense appreciation, ate an ancient biscuit, and called for towels. Putting them
under his wet head he stretched out on the stern locker, asked for
news of the doctor, heard Killick's 'Quiet as the grave, sir,' nodded,
and went straight to sleep in spite of the strong coffee and the even
stronger thunder of the wave-crests torn off by the wind and striking
the deadlights that protected the flight of stern-windows six inches
from his left ear.

'Sir, sir,' called a voice in his right ear, a tremulous voice, the tall,
shy, burly Norton sent to wake his commander.

'What is it, Mr Norton?'

'Mr Wilkins thinks he may hear gunfire, sir.'

'Thank you. Tell him I shall be on deck directly.'

Jack leapt up. He was draining the cold coffee-pot when Norton
put his head back through the door and said, 'Which he sent his compliments and duty, too, sir.'

By the time the *Surprise* had pitched once, with a slight corkscrew
roll, Jack was at the head of the ladder in the dim half-light. 'Good
morning, Mr Wilkins,' he said. 'Where away?'

'On the starboard bow, sir. It might be thunder, but I thought . . .'

It might well have been thunder, from the lightning-shot blackness
over there. 'Masthead. Oh masthead. What do you see?'

'Nothing, sir,' called the look-out. 'Black as Hell down there.'

Away to the larboard the sun had risen twenty minutes ago. The
scud overhead was grey, and through gaps in it lighter clouds and even
whitish sky could be seen. Ahead and on the starboard bow all was
black indeed: astern, quite far astern, all was blacker still. The wind
had hauled forward half a point, blowing with almost the same force;
the sea was more regular by far – heavy still, but no cross-current.

All those on deck were motionless: some with swabs poised, some
with buckets and holystones, unconscious of their immediate surroundings, every man's face turned earnestly, with the utmost concentration, to the blue-black east-south-east.

A criss-cross of lightning down over there: then a low rumble, accompanied by a sharp crack or two. Every man looked at his mate, as Wilkins looked at his Captain. 'Perhaps,' said Jack. 'The arms chests into the half-deck, at all events.'

Minutes, indecisive minutes passed: the cleaning of the deck resumed: a work of superogation, if ever there was one. Wilkins sent two more hands to the wheel, for the squall astern was coming up fast in their wake. 'This may well be the last,' said Jack, seeing a patch of blue right overhead. He walked aft, leant over the heaving taffrail and watched the squall approach, as dark as well could be and lit from within by innumerable flashes, like all those that had passed over them that night. The blue was utterly banished, the day darkened. 'Come up the sheets,' he called.

For the last quarter of a mile the squall was a distinct entity, sombre purple, sky-tall, curving over at the top and with white water all along its foot, now covering half the horizon and sweeping along at an inconceivable speed for such a bulk.

Then it was upon them. Blinding rain, shattered water driving so thick among the great heavy drops that one could hardly breathe; and the ship, as though given some frightful spur, leapt forward in the dark confused turmoil of water.

While the forefront of the squall enveloped them and for quite long after its extreme violence had passed on ahead, time had little meaning; but as the enormous rain dwindled to little more than a shower and the wind returned to its strong steady southeast course, the men at the wheel eased their powerful grip, breathing freely and nodding to one another and the sodden quartermaster, the sheets were hauled aft, the ship, jetting rainwater from her scuppers, sailed on, accompanied for some time by low cloud that thinned and thinned and then quite suddenly revealed high blue sunlit sky: a few minutes later the sun himself heaved out of the lead-coloured bank to larboard. This had indeed been the last of the series: the *Surprise* sailed on after it, directly in its track as it raced to the south-east, covering a vast breadth of sea with its darkness.

On and on, and now with the sun they could clearly distinguish the squall's grim front from its grey, thinner tail, followed by a stretch of brilliant clarity: and at a given moment the foremast look-out's screaming hail 'Sail ho! Two sail of ships on the starboard bow. On deck, there, two sails of ships on the starboard bow' brought no news, for they were already hull-up as the darkness passed over and beyond them, suddenly present and clear to every man aboard.

Jack was on his way to the foretop before the repetition. He levelled his glass for the first details, though the first glance had shown the essence of the matter. The nearer ship was the four-masted *Alastor*, wearing the black flag; she was grappled tight to the *Franklin*; they were fighting hand to hand on deck and between decks and now of course there was no gunfire. Small arms, but no cannon.

'All hands, all hands,' he called. 'Topgallants.' He gauged their effect; certainly she could bear them and more. From the quarterdeck now he called for studdingsails alow and aloft, and then for royals.

'Heave the log, Mr Reade,' he said. He had brought the *Alastor* right ahead, broadside on, and in his glass he could see her trying to cast off, the *Franklin* resisting the attempt.

'Ten and one fathom, sir, if you please,' said Reade at his side.

Jack nodded. The grappled ships were some two miles off. If nothing carried away he should be alongside in ten minutes, for the *Surprise* would gather speed. Tom would hold on for ten minutes if he had to do it with his teeth.

'Mr Grainger,' he said, 'beat to quarters.'

It was the thunder of the drum, the piping and the cries down the hatchways, the deep growl and thump of guns being run out and the hurrying of feet that roused Martin. 'Is that you, Maturin?' he whispered, with a terrified sideways glance.

'It is,' said Stephen, taking his wrist. 'Good day to you, now.'

'Oh thank God, thank God, thank God,' said Martin, his voice broken with the horror of it. 'I thought I was dead and in Hell. This terrible room. Oh this terrible, terrible room.'

The pulse was now extremely agitated. The patient was growing more so. 'Maturin, my wits are astray – I am barely out of a night-long nightmare – forgive me my trespasses to you.'

'If you please, sir,' said Reade, coming in, 'the Captain enquires for Mr Martin and desires me to tell the Doctor that we are bearing down on a heavy pirate engaged with the *Franklin*: there will be some broken omelets presently.'

'Thank you, Mr Reade: Mr Martin is far from well.' And calling after him, 'I shall repair to my station very soon.'

'May I come?' cried Martin.

'You may not,' said Stephen. 'You can barely stand, my poor colleague, sick as you are.'

'Pray take me. I cannot bear to be left in this room: I hate and dread it. I could not bring myself to pass by its door, even. This is where I . . . this is where Mrs Oakes . . . the wages of sin is death . . . I am rotting here in this life, while in the next . . . Christe eleison.'

'Kyrie eleison,' said Stephen. 'But listen, Nathaniel, will you? You are not *rotting* as the seamen put it: not at all. These are salt-sores: they are no more, unless you have taken some improper physic. In this ship you could not have contracted any infection of that kind. There has been no source of infection, whether by kissing, toying, drinking in the same cup, or otherwise: none whatsoever. I state that as a physician.'

The wind had hauled a little farther forward, and with her astonishing spread of drum-tight canvas the *Surprise* was now running at such a pace that the following seas lapped idly alongside. From high aloft Jack made out the confused situation with fair certainty: the ships were still grappled fast: the Alastors had boarded the *Franklin*'s waist but Tom had run up stout close-quarters and some of his people were holding out behind them while others had invaded the *Alastor*'s forecastle and were fighting the Frenchmen there. Some of the Alastors were still trying to cast off, and still the Franklins prevented them – Jack could see the bearded Sethians in the furious struggle that flung three Frenchmen bodily off the lashed bowsprits. Another group of pirates were turning one of the *Franklin*'s forward carronades aft to blast a way through the close-quarters; but the mob of their own men and deadly musket-fire from their own forecastle hindered them, and the carronade ran wild on the rolling deck, out of control.

Jack called down: 'Chasers' crew away. Run them out.' He landed on the deck with a thump, ran through the eager, attentive, well-armed groups to the bows, where his own brass *Beelzebub* was reaching far out of the port. 'Foretopsail,' he said, and they heaved the gun round. He and Bonden pointed it with grunts and half-words, the whole crew working as one man. Glaring along the sights Jack pulled the laniard, arched for the gun's recoil beneath him and through the bellowing crash he roared, 'T'other.'

The smoke raced away before them, and barely was it clear before the other chaser fired. Both shots fulfilled their only function, piercing the foretopsail they were aimed at, dismaying the Alastors – few ships could fire so clean – and encouraging the Franklins, whose cheer could now be heard, though faint and thin.

But these two shots, reverberating through the ship's hollow belly, sent poor Martin's weakened mind clear off its precarious balance and into a delirium. His distress became very great, reaching the screaming pitch. Stephen quickly fastened him into his cot with two bandages and ran towards the sick-berth. He met Padeen on his way to tell him that quarters had been beaten. 'I know it,' he replied. 'Go straight along and sit with Mr Martin. I shall come back.'

He returned with the fittest of his patients, a recent hernia. 'See that all is well below, Padeen,' he said, and when Padeen had gone he measured out a powerful dose from his secret store of laudanum, the tincture of opium to which he and Padeen had once been so addicted. 'Now, John,' he said to the seaman, 'hold up his shoulders.' And in pause, 'Nathaniel, Nathaniel my dear, here is your draught. Down it in one swallow, I beg.'

The pause drew out. 'Lay him back, lay him back gently,' said Stephen. 'He will be quiet now, with the blessing. But you will sit with him, John, and soothe his mind if he wakes.'

'Shipmates,' cried Jack from the break of the quarterdeck, 'I am going to lay alongside the four-master as easy as can be. Some of our people are on her forecastle; some of theirs are trying to work aft in the *Franklin*. So as soon as we are fast, come along with me and we will clear the four-master's waist, then carry on to relieve Captain Pullings. But Mr Grainger's division will go straight along the *Alastor*'s gun-deck to stop them turning awkward with their cannon. None of you can go wrong if you knock an enemy on the head.'

The seamen – a savage-looking crew with their long hair still wild about them – the seamen cheered, a strangely happy sound as the frigate glided in towards those embattled ships: roaring shouts, the clash of bitter fighting clear and clearer over the narrowing sea.

He stepped to the wheel, his heavy sword dangling from his wrist by a strap and he took her shaving in, his heart beating high and his face gleaming, until her yards caught in the *Alastor*'s shrouds and the ships ground together.

'Follow me, follow me,' he cried, leaping across, and on either side of him there were Surprises, swarming over with cutlasses, pistols, boarding-axes. Bonden was at his right hand, Awkward Davies on his left, already foaming at the mouth. The Alastors came at them with furious spirit and in the very first clash, halfway across the deck, one shot Jack's hat from his head, the bullet scoring his skull, and another, lunging with a long pike, brought him down.

'The Captain's down,' shrieked Davies. He cut the pikeman's legs from under him and Bonden split his head. Davies went on hacking the body as the Franklins came howling down and took the Alastors in the flank.

There was an extremely dense and savage mêlée with barely room to strike – cruel blows for all that and pistols touching the enemy's face. The battle surged forward and back, more joined in, forward and back, turning, trampling on bodies dead and living, all sense of direction lost, a slaughter momentarily interrupted by the crash of the *Franklin*'s carronade, turned and fired at last, but misfired, misaimed so that it killed many of those it was meant to help. The remaining Alastors came flooding back into their own ship, instantly pursued by Pullings's men, who cut them down from behind while the Surprises shattered them from in front and either side, for they had all heard the cry 'The Captain's down – they've got the Captain' and the fighting reached an extraordinary degree of ferocity.

Presently it was no more than broken men, escaping below, screaming as they were hunted down and killed: and an awful silence fell, only the ships creaking together on the dying sea, and the flapping of empty sails.

A dozen black slaves were found shut in the Alastor's orlop, as well as a few wretched little rouged and scented boys; and they were put to throwing the dead over the side. Long before they reached his part of the deck Jack Aubrey heaved himself from beneath three bodies and one desperately wounded man. 'It was as bloody a little set-to as ever I have seen,' he said to Pullings, sitting by him on the coaming, trying to staunch the flow from his wound and dabbing at his bloody eye. 'How are you, Tom?' he asked again. 'And how is the ship?'

'It would be only with the greatest reluctance that I should consent to leave you,' said Stephen, sitting there in the *Franklin*'s cabin.

'It is most obliging of you to say so,' replied Jack with a hint of testiness, 'and I take it very kindly; but we have been through this many times and once again I am obliged to point out that you have no choice in the matter. You must go into Callao with the others as soon as everything is ready.'

'I do not like your eye, and I do not like your leg,' said Stephen. 'As for the scalp-wound, though spectacular it is of no great consequence. I dare say it will hurt for some weeks and your hair will go white for an inch or two on either side; but I do not think you need fear any complications.'

'It still makes me stupid and fretful at times,' said Jack, and then with the slightly false air of one who is deliberately changing the subject, 'Stephen, should Sam come aboard – of course it is very unlikely – why should he indeed, or even still be in Peru? But should he come aboard, pray give him my love, tell him that I hope to bring the *Franklin* in, and that we should be very happy if he would dine with us. And for the moment, I mean if he should come, which I doubt, please ask him what we can do with the blacks we took in *Alastor*. They are not seamen in any sense of the term and they are really no use to us at all. But they were slaves, and Peru is a slave country; so I do not like to put them ashore, where they may be seized and sold. I particularly dislike it since having been aboard an English ship they are now, as I understand it, free men. Quite how this squares with the slave-trade I cannot tell, but that is how I understand the law.'

'Sure, you are right: there was that case in Naples, where some slaves came aboard a man-of-war and wrapped themselves in the ensign. They were never given up. And in any case Government abolished the trade in the year seven. The law may be disobeyed; slavers may still sail. But they do so illegally, since Government certainly abolished the vile traffic.'

'Did they indeed? I was not aware. Where were we in the year seven?' He pondered for a while on the year seven, tracing back voyage after voyage, and then he said, 'By the by, I am sending in the Frenchmen who do not choose to carry on with us and who are not seamanlike enough for us to keep – I promised to pay them off in Callao, you remember – and now I come to think of it there is one in this ship' – they were sitting in the cabin of the *Franklin*, to which Jack had removed – 'who was an apothecary's assistant in New Orleans. He wished to stay, and he might be of some use to you, short-handed as you are. Martin found him quite helpful, I believe.'

'Then you must certainly keep him,' said Stephen.

'No,' said Jack in a determined voice. 'Killick has looked after me, under your orders, ever since before the peace. This man's name is Fabien. I shall send him over.' Stephen knew that argument would be useless; he said nothing, and Jack went on, 'I shall be sending a whole parcel of them over, those who wish to go.'

'You would never be sending Dutourd, at all?' cried Stephen.

'I had thought of doing so, yes,' said Jack. 'He sent me a polite little note, asking leave to make his adieux, thanking us for our kindness and undertaking not to serve again.'

'From my point of view it might be impolitic,' said Stephen.

Jack looked at him, saw that the matter had to do with intelligence and nodded. 'Are there any others you would object to?' he asked. 'Adams will show you a list.'

'Never a one, my dear,' said Stephen, and he looked at the opening door.

'If you please, sir,' said Reade, 'Captain Pullings sends his compliments, and all is laid along.'

'The Doctor will be with you directly,' said Captain Aubrey.

'In five minutes,' said Dr Maturin. He lifted the bandage over Jack's eye: he looked at the pike-wound. 'You must swear by Sophie's head to suffer Killick to dress both these places with their respective lotions and pommades before breakfast, before dinner, and before retiring: I have given him precise instructions. Swear.'

'I swear,' said Jack, holding up his right hand. 'He will grow absolutely insupportable, as usual. And Stephen, pray give Martin my most particular compliments. It was noble of him to try to come on deck to bury our people: I have never seen a man look so like death: gaunt, grey, sunken. He could barely stand.'

'It was not only weakness: he has lost his sense of balance entirely. I do not think he will regain it. He must leave the sea.'

'So you told me. Leave the sea . . . poor fellow, poor fellow. But I quite understand; and he must certainly go home. Now, brother, your boat has been hooked on this age. You will be much better by yourself for a while. I am afraid I have been like a bear in a whore's bed these last few days.'

'Not at all, not at all: quite the reverse.'

'As for Dutourd, Adams will reply to his note saying it is regretted his request cannot be complied with and he is required to remain aboard the *Franklin*. Compliments, of course, and a civil word about accommodation. And Stephen, one last word. Have you any notion of how long your business will keep you on shore? Forgive me if I am indiscreet.'

'If it is not over in a month it will not be over at all,' said Stephen. 'But I will leave word in the ship. God bless, now.'

The ships were not to part until the sun was low, in the first place because Captain Aubrey had to speak at some length to the other commanders and redistribute the crews and in the second because he wished to deceive a remote sail on the western horizon, a potential quarry. He intended this distant ship to suppose that an unhurried convoy slowly heading east by south, often peaceably gossiping alongside, would carry straight on to Callao, and he did not intend to make the signal to part company until the stranger's topgallants were out of sight even from the main jack-crosstrees.

Long before this time however Dr Maturin had to attend to his
duties as the frigate's surgeon. Having regained the *Surprise* he stood
for a while at the taffrail, looking aft along the line of ships: the *Alas-*
tor, thinly manned but unharmed in masts and rigging and now
almost clean; the whaler, in much the same case; and the *Franklin*,
her wounded bowsprit now repaired with spars from the four-master:
a fine array of yards and canvas, and the kind of tail that had so often
followed the *Surprise*, that predatory ship, into various ports.

'I beg pardon, sir,' said Sarah, just behind him, 'but Padeen says
will you be long at all?'

After a moment she tugged his coat and speaking rather louder
said, 'I beg pardon, sir; Padeen wonders will you ever be a great while
surely not for the love of God.'

'I am with you, child,' said Stephen, gathering his wits. 'I thought
I heard a sea-lion bark.' He plunged down to the sick-berth, tolerably fetid still in spite of double windsails, although it was not so
crowded as it had been in the first few days after the battle, when
he could hardly step between his patients, and they laid here and
there about the orlop. Padeen, his loblolly-boy, was as kind and
gentle a creature as ever came from Munster, and long use had not
blunted his humanity; he was weeping now over a wretched man
from the *Alastor* who having fallen out of his cot was lying there on
his shattered arm, wedged under a helpless neighbour and resisting all attempts at help by clinging with maniac force to a ring-bolt.
He was indeed out of his mind, not only because of the terrifying
end of the battle and the horrible future, but also because his fever
had now almost drowned what little reason he had left. However,
what Padeen's kindness and great though cautious strength and the
little girls' expostulation could not do, Dr Maturin's cool authority
accomplished, and with the wretched man restored to his bed, fastened to it, his hopeless wound re-dressed, Stephen began his long
and weary round. There had been few survivors from the *Alastor*
and of those few three had already died of their injuries; most of the

rest swore they were prisoners, and certainly they had taken no part in the fight, having crammed themselves unarmed into the manger or the forepeak.

All the others were his shipmates, men he had known and liked for many voyages, sometimes for as long as he had been in the Navy. Bonden's great cutlass-slash, which had called for such anxious sewing, was doing well, but there were cases where he saw the probable necessity for resection – foresaw it and its dangers with a grief increased by the seamen's total, unfounded confidence in his powers, and by their gratitude for his treatment.

A wearing round, and it should have been followed by his visits forward, to the little berths where the warrant-officers slept: Mr Smith, the gunner, was not aboard the *Franklin* and Stephen had put Mr Grainger into his place, as more suitable for a wounded man than his official cabin aft. He was on his way there, accompanied by Sarah carrying basin, lint, bandages, when as they passed through the chequered shafts of daylight coming down from the deck they heard the call, 'Signal for parting company, sir,' and Pullings's reply, 'Acknowledge and salute.'

'Oh sir,' cried Sarah, 'may we run up and look?'

'Very well,' said Stephen, 'But put down your basin and the lint, and walk soberly.'

The ships separated with the smooth inevitability of a sea-parting, slow at first, still within calling-distance, and then, if one's attention were distracted for a few moments by a bird, a floating patch of seaweed, the gap had grown to a mile and one's friends' faces were no longer to be made out, for with the warm steady southerly breeze ships sailing in opposite directions drew apart at fifteen or sixteen knots, even with no topgallants abroad.

The *Franklin*, Captain Aubrey, headed west to cruise upon the enemy until he should hear that the *Surprise* had been docked and was now fit for a passage of the Horn, that the prizes had been disposed of, and above all that Stephen, having accomplished what he had set out to do, was ready to go home. The *Franklin* would, he hoped with reasonable confidence, send in prizes from time to time; but in any event he had a fine half-decked schooner-rigged launch belonging to the *Alastor* that could be dispatched from well out in the offing to fetch stores and news from Callao.

The *Surprise*, Captain Pullings, on the other hand, stood a little south of east for Peru, whose prodigious mountains were already said to be visible from the masthead and whose strange cold north-flowing current was undoubtedly present; and in duty bound her two prizes sailed after her, each at two cable's lengths.

The sun set, with the *Franklin* clear on the horizon, and it left a golden sky of such beauty that Stephen felt a constriction in his throat. Sarah too was moved but she said nothing until they were below again, when she observed, 'I shall say seven Hail Marys every day until we see them again.'

The bosun was their first patient. He had gone aboard the *Alastor* roaring drunk, and there pursuing a pair of enemies into the maintop he had fallen, landing in the waist of the ship on to a variety of weapons. He was a mass of cuts and abrasions: yet it was a great wrench where his leg had caught in the catharpins that kept him from his duty. He was drunk again now, and he endeavoured to disguise his state by saying as little as possible, and that very carefully, and by directing his breath down towards the deck. They dressed his many places, Sarah with something less than her habitual tenderness – she hated drunkenness and her disapproval filled the little cabin, making the bosun simper in a nervous, placating manner – and when he was bound up they parted, Sarah to go back to the sick-berth and Stephen to call on Mr Grainger, who had been brought down by a musket-shot: the ball had followed one of those strange indirect courses so unlike the path of a rifle-bullet and after a prolonged search Stephen had found it lodged, visibly pulsating, just in contact with the subclavian artery. The wound was healing prettily, and Stephen congratulated Grainger on having flesh as clean and sweet as a child's; yet although the patient smiled and made a handsome acknowledgement of the Doctor's care it was plain that he had something on his mind.

'Vidal came over from the *Franklin* to see me a little while ago,' he said, 'and he was in a great taking about Mr Dutourd. He had heard that Mr D's request to be sent in to Callao with the other Frenchmen had been refused. As you know, Vidal and his friends think the world of Mr Dutourd; they admire his sentiments on freedom and equality and no tithes – no interference with worship. Freedom! See how he spoke up for those poor unfortunate blacks out of the *Alastor*, offering to pay the Jamaica price out of his own pocket for their liberty, pay it down on the capstan-head for the general prize-fund.'

'Did he, indeed?'

'Yes, sir, he did. So Vidal and his relations – most of the Knipperdollings are cousins in some degree or another – are most uneasy at the thought of his being taken back to England and perhaps taken up before the Admiralty Court on a point of law and ending up at Execution Dock, hanged for a pirate, just because he did not have a piece of paper. Mr Dutourd a pirate? It makes no sense, Doctor. Those wicked men in the *Alastor* were pirates, not Mr Dutourd. They were the sort of people you see hanging in chains at Tilbury Point, a horrid warning to them as sails by; not Mr Dutourd, who is a learned man, and who loves his fellow-beings.'

Grainger's drift was clear enough, and he could not be allowed to reach a direct request. Stephen had the medical man's recourse: during a pause for emphasis he desired Grainger to hold his breath, took his pulse, and having counted it, watch in hand, he said, 'Do you know we parted company an hour ago? I must go and tell Mr Martin: with this breeze I understand we should be in quite soon, and I should like to set him on dry land as early as possible.'

'Parted company so soon?' cried Grainger. 'I never knew; nor did Vidal when he spoke to me this morning.' Then recovering himself, 'Mr Martin, of course. Pray give the poor gentleman my kind good-

day. We were right moved to hear he had tried to creep on deck to
bury our shipmates.'

'Nathaniel Martin,' said Stephen, 'I am sorry to have left you so long
untended.'

'Not at all, not at all,' cried Martin. 'That good Padeen has been by,
Emily brought me a cup of tea, and I have slept much of the time: I am
indeed very much better.'

'So I see,' said Stephen, bringing his lantern down to look into Martin's face. He then turned back the sheet. 'The disorders of the skin,'
he observed, gently feeling the ugliest lesion, 'are perhaps the most
puzzling in all medicine. Here is a sensible diminution within hours.'

'I slept as I have not slept for – for Heaven knows how long, my
body lying peacefully at last: no incessant irritation, no pain from the
slightest pressure, no perpetual turning in vain for ease.'

'There is nothing to be done without sleep,' said Stephen, and he
continued with his examination. 'Yet,' said he, replacing the sheet, 'I
shall be glad to set you on shore. Your skin may well be on the mend,
but I am not at all satisfied with your heart or your lungs or your
elimination; and from what you tell me the vertigo is as bad as ever,
even worse. Firm land under foot may do wonders; and a vegetable
diet. The same is to be said for several of our patients.'

'We have so often known it to be the case,' said Martin. 'In parenthesis, may I tell you a strange thing? Some hours ago, as I was coming out of a blessed doze, I thought I heard a sea-lion bark, and my
heart lifted with happiness, as it did when I was a boy, or even in New
South Wales. How close are we to the shore?'

'I cannot tell, but they said before we parted company – for the
Captain is standing to the westward: he leaves you his particular
compliments – that the Cordillera was distinctly to be seen from the
masthead; and there may well be some rocky islands close at hand
where sea-lions live. For my own part I have seen a file of pelicans,
and they are not birds to go far from land.'

'Very true. But pray tell me about the present state of the sick-berth. I am afraid you have been cruelly overworked.'

They talked for a while about the recent incised, lacerated, punctured and gunshot wounds, the fractures simple, compound or comminuted that had come below, and Stephen's success or failure in dealing with them, speaking in an objective, professional manner. In a less detached tone Martin asked after the Captain. 'It is the eye that troubles me,' said Stephen. 'The pike-thrust is healing by first intention; the head-wound, though its stunning effect is still evident to a slight degree, is of no consequence; nor is the loss of blood. But the eye received the wad of the pistol-bullet that tore his scalp, a thick, gritty, partially disintegrated wad. I extracted many fragments and I believe there was no grave scoring of the cornea nor of course any penetration. But there is great and persistent hyperaemia and lachrymation . . . ' He was about to say that 'such a patient was not to be relied upon – would double doses – would swallow them together with any quack panacea – would listen to the first cow-leech he might encounter,' but he restrained himself and their conversation returned to the sick-berth as Martin had left it, to their old patients.

'And how are Grant and MacDuff?' asked Martin.

'Those who had the Vienna treatment? Grant died just before the action, and clearly I did not have time to open him: but I strongly suspect the corrosive sublimate. MacDuff is well enough for light duties, though his constitution is much shattered; I doubt his full recovery.'

After a pause, and in an altered voice, Martin said, 'I must tell you that I too took the Vienna treatment.'

'In what dose?'

'I could find nothing in our authorities, so I based myself on the amount we used for our calomel draughts.'

Stephen said nothing. The bolder Austrian physicians might administer a quarter of a grain of the sublimate: the usual dose of calomel was four.

'Perhaps I was rash,' said Martin. 'But I was desperate; and the calomel and guaiacum seemed to do no good.'

'They could not cure a disease you did not have,' said Stephen. 'But in any event I shall be glad to have you in hospital, where you can with something like decency and comfort be purged and purged again. We must do everything possible to rid your system of this noxious substance.'

'I was desperate,' said Martin, his mind fixed on that dreadful past. 'I was unclean, unclean: rotting alive, as the seamen say. A shameful death. And I think my mind was disturbed. Until you absolutely asserted that these were salt-sores I was wholly convinced that they were of sinful origin: you will admit they were very like. They were very like, were they not?'

'When they had been exacerbated by an immoderate use of mercury, perhaps they were; though I doubt an impartial observer would have been deceived.'

'The wicked fleeth where no man pursueth,' said Martin. 'Dear Marturin, I have been a very wicked fellow. In intention I have been a very wicked fellow.'

'You must spend the night in drinking fresh rain-water,' said Stephen. 'Every time you wake, you must swallow down a glass at least, to get rid of all you can. Padeen will bring you a rack of necessary-bottles and I trust I shall see them filled by morning: but I cannot wait to get you ashore and to start more radical measures; for indeed, colleague, there is not a moment to lose.'

There was not a moment to be lost, and happily the harbour formalities in Callao bay did not take long, the *Surprise* and her valuable train being so welcome to the agent, who had dealt with her prizes on the outward voyage, and to his brother, the captain of the port: as soon as they were over Stephen went ashore pulled by Jemmy Ducks in his little skiff. Well over on the left hand they passed a remarkable amount of shipping for so small a town: vessels from Chile, Mexico and farther north, and at least two China ships. 'Right on our beam, beyond the yellow schooner, in the dockyard itself, that must be the barque from Liverpool,' said Jemmy. 'They are busy in her tops.'

It was high tide on the dusty strand, and as Stephen walked up it towards an archway in the wall a gritty cloud swept across from the earthquake-shattered ruins of Old Callao. When it had cleared he saw a group of ill-looking men of all colours from black to dirty yellow standing under the shelter. 'Gentlemen,' he said in Spanish, 'pray do me the kindness of pointing out the hospital.'

'Your worship will find it next to the Dominican church,' said a brown man.

'Sir, sir, it is just before Joselito's warehouse,' cried a black.

'Come with me,' said a third. He led Stephen through the tunnel into an immense unpaved square with dust whirling in eddies about it. 'There is the Governor's house,' he said, pointing back to the seaward end of the square. 'It is shut. On the right hand,' he went on, holding out his left, 'your worship has the Viceroy's palace: it too is closed.'

They turned. In the middle of the square three black and white vulturine scavengers with a wingspan of about six feet were disputing the dried remains of a cat. 'What do you call those?' asked Stephen.

'Those?' replied his guide, looking at them with narrowed eyes. 'Those are what we call *birds*, your worship. And there, before Joselito's warehouse, is the hospital itself.'

Stephen looked at it with some concern, a low building with very small barred windows, the flat mud roof barely a hand's reach from the filthy ground. Prudent, no doubt in a country so subject to earthquakes, but as a hospital it left to be desired.

'The hospital, with a hundred people at the least, lying on beds raised a good span from the ground. And there I see a vile heretic coming out of it, with his countryman.'

'Which? The little small fat yellow-haired gentleman, who staggers so?'

'No, no, no. He is an old and mellow Christian – your honour too is an old and mellow Christian, no doubt?'

'None older; few more mellow.'

'A Christian though English. He is the great lawyer come to lecture the university of Lima on the British constitution. His name is Raleigh, don Curtius Raleigh: you have heard of him. He is drunk. I must run and fetch his coach.'

'He has fallen.'

'Clearly. It is the tall black-haired villain who is picking him up, the surgeon of the Liverpool ship, that is the heretic. I must run.'

'Do not let me detain you, sir. Pray accept this trifle.'

'God will repay your worship. Farewell, sir. May no new thing arise.'

'May no new thing arise,' replied Stephen. With his pocket spyglass he watched the birds for a while, their name hovering on the edge of his mind. Presently, as don Curtius's coach rolled into the square, silent on the dust, they flew off, one carrying the desiccated cat, and the other snatching at it. They flew inland, towards Lima, a splendid-looking white-towered city five or six miles away with an infinitely more splendid series of mountains behind it, rising higher and higher in the distance, their snow at last blending with the white sky and the clouds.

The carriage rolled away, drawn by six mules, don Curtius singing Greensleeves.

Stephen approached the remaining Englishman, took off his hat, and said, 'Francis Geary, a very good day to you, sir.'

'Stephen Maturin! I thought for a moment it looked like you, but my spectacles are covered with dust.' He took them off and peered myopically at his friend. 'What happiness to see you! What joy to find a Christian in this barbarous land!'

'You are just come out of the hospital, I find.'

'Yes, indeed. One of my people – I am surgeon of the *Three Graces* – has what looks to me very like the marthambles, and I wished to isolate him, under proper care, until it declares itself, rather than infect the whole ship. It is as deadly as measles or the smallpox to islanders, and we have many of them aboard. But no. They would not hear of it. So I went to see Mr Raleigh, who had travelled out with us, and who is a Roman, in case he could persuade them – he lectures on law at the university: an influential man. But no, no and no. They gave him a bottle or two of excellent wine, as I dare say you noticed, but they would not yield. On the way from Lima he told me that he did not expect to succeed, their memory of the buccaneers, the sacking of churches and so on being so very vivid; and he was right, I suppose. At all events they do not choose to have anything to do with me or my patient.'

'Then I am afraid my case is hopeless, for my patient is not only a Protestant but a clergyman too. Come and drink a cup of coffee with me.'

'I should be very happy. But your case would have been hopeless had he been the Pope. The place is so low and airless and fetid, the numbers so great and indiscriminately heaped upon one another, that they would never have left your parson there.'

Geary and Maturin had studied medicine together: they had shared a skeleton and several unclaimed victims of the Liffey or the Seine. Now, as they sat in the shade, drinking coffee, they spoke with the uninhibited directness of medical men. 'My patient,' said Stephen, 'is also my assistant. He was as devoted to natural philosophy as you, particularly to birds, and although he had followed no regular course, attended no lectures, walked no wards, he became a useful surgeon's mate by constant attendance in the sick-berth and frequent dissection; and since he was a well-read, cultivated man, he was also an agreeable companion. Unhappily, he recently came to suspect that he had contracted a venereal disease, and when during an exceptionally long period without fresh water to wash our clothes he developed salt-sores, he thought his suspicions were confirmed: it is true that his mind was very much perturbed at the time for reasons that it would be tedious to relate and almost impossible to convey – the distress of jealousy, imagined ill-usage and homesickness entered into it – and that his lesions were far more important than any I have seen at any time. Yet even so, how a man of his experience could persuade himself that they were syphilitic I cannot tell; but persuaded he was, and he dosed himself privately with calomel and guaiacum. Naturally enough these had no effect; so he took to the corrosive sublimate.'

'Corrosive sublimate?' cried Geary.

'Yes, sir,' said Stephen, 'and in such amounts that I hesitate to name them. He brought himself very low indeed before he told me: our relations were by then far from cordial, though there remained a deep latent affection. Fresh water, the proper lotions and a conviction that he was not diseased have improved the state of his skin remarkably, but the effects of this intolerable deal of sublimate remains. Young gentlewoman,' he called towards the dim recesses of the wine-shop, 'be so good as to prepare me a ball of coca-leaves.'

'With lime, sir?'

'By all means; and a trifle of llipta too, if you have it.'

'What are the symptoms at this point?' asked Geary.

'Strongly marked vertigo, perhaps aggravated by the loss of an eye some years ago; difficulty in following the sequence of letters; some degree of mental confusion and distress; great physical weakness of course; a most irregular pulse; chaotic defecation. Thank you, my dear' – this to the girl with the coca-leaves.

They carried on with Martin's present state, and when Stephen had said all that occurred to him without reference to his notes Geary asked, 'Is there on the one hand a difficulty in telling right from left, and on the other a certain loss of hair?'

'There is,' said Stephen: he stopped chewing and looked attentively at his friend.

'I have known two similar cases, and in Vienna itself I heard of several more.'

'Did you hear of cures, at all?'

'Certainly. Both my men walked away from the hospital unaided, one quite well, the other with only a slight impediment: though in his case there had been a baldness of the entire person and loss of nails, which Birnbaum cites as the criterion; but the treatment was long and delicate. What do you intend to do with your patient?'

'I am at a loss. My ship is about to be docked, and he cannot remain aboard. I had hoped to find him a room in the hospital until I could arrange for his passage home in a merchantman: we may cruise for a great while, and in any case a privateer is no place for an invalid. Perhaps Lima . . . ' Stephen fell silent.

'When you speak of a passage,' said Geary, 'I presume the gentleman is not the usual indigent surgeon's mate?'

'Never in life. He is an Anglican clergyman with two livings; and he has done well in prize-money. If you were to look into the bay you would see two captured ships, a clearly-determined share of which belongs to him.'

'I say this only because our captain, a paragon of nautical virtue and of many others, is answerable to his owners, insatiable men who know nothing of charity or good-will. Yet since there is no question of either, why does not your patient sail in the *Three Graces*? We have two empty state-rooms amidships; and she is a remarkably steady ship.'

'This is very precipitate, Francis Geary,' said Stephen.

'So it is,' replied Geary, 'but the voyage itself will be tranquil and deliberate: Captain Hill very rarely spreads royals; we are to touch at Iquique and Valparaiso and perhaps at another port in Chile – so many pauses for refreshment on shore – and we are to prepare ourselves at the entrance to the Magellan Straits at the very best time of the year for the eastward passage. Captain Hill does not choose to risk his owners' spars off the Horn: furthermore, he is an acknowledged expert on the intricate navigation of the channel – has threaded it again and again. It would be infinitely more suitable for a man in a delicate state of health. Will you not come with me and look at the ship?'

'If you please, sir,' said Jemmy Ducks, 'the tide is on the turn: which we ought to shove off directly.'

'Jemmy Ducks,' said Stephen, 'when you have drank a moderate dram, you shove off by yourself. I am going to walk to the dockyard to see the Liverpool ship.'

'My dear love to you, sir,' said Jemmy Ducks, lowering a quarter of a pint of Peruvian brandy without a wink, 'and my duty to the gentleman.'

As they walked back from the tall headland from which they had waved to the *Three Graces* for a great while as she sailed away into the south-west, Stephen, Padeen and the little girls were low in their spirits, mute. It was not that the tropical day was oppressive, for an agreeable breeze blew in from the sea, but the dry hard pale-yellow ground under foot had nothing whatsoever growing on it, no life of any kind, and the arid sterility had a saddening effect on minds already disappointed. The distance to their lofty cliff had been greater than they thought, their pace slower; the Liverpool ship was already clear of the coast by the time they got there, and even with Stephen's spy-glass they could not be sure they had seen Martin, though he had gone aboard with no more than a hand to help him over the gangway and had promised to sit there by the taffrail.

In silence they walked, therefore, with the ocean on their left and the Andes on their right, both admittedly majestic, indeed sublime, but perhaps beyond all human measure, at least to those who were sad, hungry and intolerably dry; and it was not until their stark plateau fell abruptly away, showing the green valley of the Rimac far below, with Lima apparently quite close at hand, sharply defined by its walls, and in the other direction Callao, the busy port, the dockyard and the exactly squared town, that they came to sudden cheerful life, calling out to one another 'There is Lima, there is Callao, there is the ship, poor thing' – for to their astonishment she was already in the yard, stripped to the gant-line and partially heaved down – 'And there,' cried Sarah, pointing to the shipping along the mole, 'there is the *Franklin*'s handmaiden.'

'You mean tender,' said Emily.

'Jemmy Ducks says handmaiden,' replied Sarah.

'Sir, sir,' cried Emily, 'she means the *Alastor*'s big schooner-rigged launch, lying there next to the Mexico ship.'

'With the barky all sideways, will there ever be tea?' asked Padeen, with quite extraordinary fluency for him.

'There will certainly be tea,' said Stephen, and he stepped forward briskly to the path winding down the slope.

He was mistaken, however. The *Surprise* was in far too much of a hullaballoo for any form of quiet enjoyment. The word that she might be heaved down without waiting for her turn had reached Tom Pullings only after Stephen set out, and he and the carpenter and the only valid bosun's mate were already as busy as bees among the port's stores of copper, cordage, ship's timber and paint, with Jack's words 'Spend and spare not' in their ears when the launch appeared, sent in to carry out a large number of men for the short-handed *Franklin*.

'We had foreseen it, in course,' said Pullings, receiving Stephen on the sloping deck. 'The Captain would not have had enough people to send a prize in, else. But it came at an awkward moment, before we could arrange for a gang of dockyard mateys. As soon as I heard we could dock well before our time, I hauled alongside the *Alastor* and shifted all your things and the sick-berth into her: and then when we were in dock and barely half stripped, the launch brought her orders and everything had to be changed. She also brought a hand by the name of Fabien, who belonged to the *Franklin* and who helped Mr Martin when he was aboard; the Captain had meant to send him across before we parted company, but he forgot. Oh, Doctor,' he cried, striking his forehead, 'here am I, forgetting likewise – when we were all ahoo a clergyman came aboard, the same that we saw on the way out; the gentleman very like the Captain, only rather darker. He had heard the Captain was wounded – was much concerned – enquired for you – said he would come again at noon tomorrow – begged for paper and ink and left you this note.'

'Thank you, Tom,' said Stephen. 'I shall read it aboard the *Alastor*. May I beg for a boat? And perhaps the man the Captain sent might come with us.'

In the *Alastor*'s great cabin, now thoroughly clean at last and smelling only of sea-water, tar and fresh paint – there had been a truly shocking carnage – Stephen sat drawing in sips of scalding tea, a drink he ordinarily despised, though not as much as he despised Grimshaw's coffee, but one that he found comforting after the high Peruvian desert; and as he did so he re-read the note.

> My dear Sir,
>
> When I came back from a retreat with Benedictines of Huangay last night I heard that the *Surprise* had put into Callao once more, and I had great hopes of news of you and of Captain Aubrey. But on sending to your agent in the morning it appeared that although he had indeed been aboard her he was now in the captured American privateer *Franklin*: at the same time to my consternation I learnt that he had been wounded in taking the infamous *Alastor*. I hurried down to the port at once where Captain Pullings reassured me to some degree and told me of your very welcome presence.
>
> I propose therefore to do myself the honour of waiting on you at noon tomorrow, to assure you that I remain, dear Sir,
>
> your most humble, obliged, and obedient servant,
>
> Sam Panda

Neither Jack nor Sam acknowledged the relationship in so many words but it was clearly understood by both, as it was by all those members of the crew who had first seen the younger man come aboard the *Surprise* in the West Indies: it was indeed obvious to anyone who saw them together, for Sam, borne by a Bantu girl after Jack had left the Cape station, was an ebony-black version of his father:

THE WINE-DARK SEA 149

somewhat larger, if anything. Yet there were differences. Jack Aubrey neither looked nor sounded sharply intelligent unless he were handling a ship, fighting a battle, or speaking of navigation: in fact he also possessed uncommon mathematical powers and had read papers on nutation to the Royal Society; but this did not appear in his ordinary conversation. Sam, on the other hand, had been brought up by singularly learned Irish missionaries; his command of languages, ancient and modern, did the Fathers infinite credit; and he had read voraciously. Stephen, a Catholic himself with a certain amount of influence in Rome, had procured him the dispensation necessary for a bastard to be ordained priest, and now Sam was doing remarkably well in the Church: it was said that he might soon become a prelate, not only because at present there were no black monsignori – some yellowish or quite dark brown, to be sure, but none of such a wholehearted gleaming black as Sam – but also because of his patristic learning and his exceptional and evident abilities.

'I look forward to seeing him,' said Stephen; and after a pause in which he drank yet another cup of tea, 'I believe I shall walk along the road to Lima and meet him half way. Who knows but what I may see a condor?' He hailed William Grimshaw, Killick's mate, who had been detached to look after him, in spite of the fact that Tom Pullings had a perfectly good steward of his own. 'William Grimshaw,' he said, 'pray desire the Franklin the Captain sent to step below.' And when the Franklin appeared, a tall, thin, nervous young man with receding hair, he went on, 'Fabien, sit down on that locker. I understand you were an apothecary's assistant in New Orleans – but first tell me which language you speak more readily.'

'They are much the same, sir,' said Fabien. 'I was apprenticed to a horse-leech in Charleston when I was a boy.'

'Very well. Now I understand you helped Mr Martin when he was aboard your ship.'

'Yes, sir. Since the surgeon and his mate were both killed I was all he could find.'

'But I am sure you were very useful to him, with your experience as

an apothecary: indeed I seem to remember his mentioning you with
commendation, before he grew so ill.'

'It did not amount to much, sir: most of my time in the shop I spent
skinning or stuffing birds, or drawing them, or colouring plates. Yet I
did learn to make up the usual prescriptions – blue and black draught
– and I did help Monsieur Duvallier in his practice – just the simple things.'

'In New Orleans, is it customary for apothecaries to stuff birds?'

'No, sir. Some like to have rattlers in the window or a baby in spirits, but we were the only one with birds. Monsieur Duvallier had a
school-friend who engraved them and he wanted to compete with
him, so when he found me drawing a turkey-buzzard and then setting it up, he offered me a place.'

'The horse-leech's calling did not please you?'

'Well, sir, he had a daughter.'

'Ah.' Stephen made himself a ball of leaves and said, 'No doubt you
were well acquainted with the birds of your country?'

'I read what I could find to read – Bartram, Pennant and Barton –
but it did not amount to much; yet still and all,' – smiling – 'I reckon I
had an egg and some feathers of every bird that nested within twenty
miles of New Orleans or Charleston; and drawings of them.'

'That must have interested Mr Martin.'

Fabien's smile left him. 'They did at first, sir,' he said, 'but then he
seemed not to care. The drawings were not very good, I guess. Monsieur Audubon took little notice of them – said they were not lively
enough – and Monsieur Cuvier never answered when my master sent
two or three he had touched up.'

'I should like to see some when we are at leisure; but at present I
still have a few patients in the sick-berth. My engagements may take
me away from the ship, and until I have made proper arrangements
for them on shore I should like to leave a man aboard to whom I can
send instructions. There are no longer any urgent cases: it is a matter
of changing dressings and administering physic at stated intervals. I
have an excellent loblolly-boy, but although he understands English

quite well he speaks little, and all the less in that he has a severe stammer; and he can neither read nor write. On the other hand he has a great gift for nursing, and he is much loved by the people. I should add that he is enormously strong, and although mansuetude, although gentleness is written on his face, he is capable of terrible rage if he is provoked. To offend him, and thus to offend his friends, in a ship like this would be mortal folly. Come with me till I show you our sick-berth. There are only three amputations left, and they are in a very fair way, they will need dressing for a week or two more, and some physic and lotions written on a sheet with their times. You will meet Padeen there, and I am sure you will conciliate his good-will.'

'I certainly shall, sir. Anything for a quiet life is my motto.'

'And yet you were in a privateer.'

'Yes, sir. I was running away from a young woman: the same as when I left the Charleston horse-leech.'

The road to Lima ran between great irrigated mud-walled fields of sugar-cane, cotton, alfalfa, Indian corn, and past carob-groves, with here and there bananas, oranges and lemons in all their variety; and where the sides of the valley rose, some distant vines. At times it followed the deep-cut bank of the Rimac, now a fine great roaring torrent from the snows that could be seen a great way off, and here were palms, strangely interspersed with fine great willows of a kind Stephen had not seen before. Few birds, apart from an elegant tern that patrolled the quieter side-pools of the river, and few flowers: this was the dry season of the year, and except where the innumerable irrigation-channels flowed nothing but a grey wiry grass was to be seen.

There was a good deal of traffic: casks and bales travelling up from the port or down to it in ox- or mule-drawn wagons that brought the Spain of his youth vividly to mind – the same high-crested yokes, the same crimson, brass-studded harness, the same ponderous creaking wheels. Some few horsemen, some people sitting on asses, more going

by foot: short, strong Indians with grave or expressionless copper
faces, sometimes bowed under enormous burdens; some rare Spaniards; many black Africans; and every possible combination of the
three, together with additions from visiting ships. All these people
called out a greeting as they passed, or told him that 'it was dry, dry,
intolerably dry'; all except the Indians, who went by mute, unsmiling.

It was Stephen's custom, particularly when he was walking in a flat
country, to turn his face to the zenith every furlong or so, in order not
to miss birds soaring above the ordinary range of vision. When he had
been walking for an hour he did this again after a longer pause than
usual and to his infinite delight he saw no less than twelve condors
wheeling and wheeling high in the pale sky between him and Lima.
He walked a few paces more, sat on a mile-stone and fixed them with
his pocket-glass. No possibility of error: enormous birds: not perhaps
as wide as the wandering albatross but more massive by far – a different kind of flight, a different use of the air entirely. Perfect flight,
perfect curves: never a movement of those great wings. Round and
round, rising and falling, rising and rising still until at the top of their
spiral they glided away in a long straight line towards the north-east.

He walked on with a smile of pure happiness on his face; and presently, just after he had passed a posada where carts and wagons stood
under the shade of carob-trees while their drivers drank and rested,
he felt his smile return of its own accord: there on the road ahead
was a tall black horse carrying a taller, blacker rider at a fine easy
trot towards Callao. At the same moment the trot changed to a brisk
canter, and a yard from Stephen Sam leapt from the saddle, his own
smile still broader.

They embraced and walked slowly along, each asking the other
how he did, the horse gazing into their faces with some curiosity.

'But tell me, sir, how is the Captain?'

'His main being is well, thanks be to God –'

'Thanks be to God.'

' – but he had the wad of a pistol in his eye. The bullet itself
rebounded from his skull – a certain concussion – a certain passing

forgetfulness – no more. But the wad set up an inflammation that had not yet quite yielded to treatment by the time I left him – by the time he *ordered* me to leave him. And he had a pike-thrust in the upper part of his thigh that is probably healed by now, though I wish I could be assured of it . . . But before I forget, he sends his love, says he hopes to bring the *Franklin*, his present ship, into Callao quite soon, and trusts that you will dine with him.'

'Oh how I hope we shall see him well,' cried Sam. And after a moment, 'But my dear sir, will you not mount? I will hold the stirrup for you; he is a quiet, gentle horse with an easy walk on him.'

'I will not,' said Stephen, 'though he is the dear kind creature, I am sure,' – stroking the horse's nose. 'Listen: there is a little small she-been two minutes back along the road. If you are not desperate for time, let you put him up in the shelter there and return to Callao with me. There is nothing to touch walking for conversation. Reflect upon it, my dear: me perched up on this high horse, and he is seventeen hands if he is an inch, calling down to you, and yourself looking up all the while like Toby listening to the Archangel Raphael – edifying, sure, but it would never do.'

Sam left not only his horse but his black clerical hat, disagreeably hot through the beaver with the sun reaching its height, and they walked along with an agreeable ease. 'There is another thing that the Captain wished to speak to you about,' said Stephen. 'Among other prizes we took a pirate, the *Alastor*: she is in the port at this moment. Most of her crew were killed in the desperate fighting – it was in this battle that the Captain was hurt – and Captain Pullings has delivered up those who were not to the authorities here; but she also had a few seamen prisoners whom we have set free to go ashore or stay, as they please, and a dozen African slaves, the property, if I may use the word, of the pirates; they were shut up below and they took no part in the fighting. There is no question of their being sold to increase our people's prize-money, since the most influential men in our crew, deeply religious men, are abolitionists, and they carry the others with them.'

'Bless them.'

'Bless them indeed. But the Captain does not like to turn the black men ashore; he fears they may be taken up and reduced to servitude again: and although he does not feel so strongly about slaves as I do – it is one of the few points on which we differ – he is of opinion that having sailed for even so short a time under the British flag they ipso facto became free, and that it would be an injustice to deprive them of their liberty. He would value your advice.'

'I honour him for his care of them. Properly vouched for, they may certainly live here in freedom. Have they a trade, at all?'

'They were being carried from one French sugar-plantation to another when their vessel was taken: as far as I can make out – their French amounts to a few words, no more – that is all the work they understand.'

'We can find them places here easily enough,' said Sam, waving towards a sea of green cane. 'But it is hard work and ill-paid. Would the Captain not consider keeping them aboard?'

'He would not. We have only able seamen or highly-skilled tradesmen – the sailmakers, coopers, armourers – and landsmen could never be countenanced in such a vessel as ours. Yet surely even a low wage with freedom is better than no wage and lifelong slavery?'

'Anything at all is better than slavery,' cried Sam with a surprising degree of passion in so large and calm a man. 'Anything at all – wandering diseased and three parts starved in the mountains, roasted, frozen, naked, hunted by dogs, like the wretched Maroons I sought out in Jamaica.'

'You too feel very strongly about slavery?'

'Oh indeed and indeed I do. The West Indies were bad enough, but Brazil was worse by far. As you know, I worked for what seemed an eternity among the black slaves there.'

'I remember it well. That was one of the many reasons that I looked forward so to seeing you again in Peru.' He looked attentively at Sam; but Sam's mind was still in Brazil and in his deep voice, deeper than Jack's, he went on, 'There may be a tolerable domestic slavery – who has not seen something like it in slave-countries? – but the temptation is always there, the possibility of excess, the latent tyranny, the latent servility; and who is fit to be continually exposed to temptation? On the other hand it seems to me that there is no possibility whatsoever of a tolerable industrial slavery. It rots both sides wholly away. The Portuguese are a kindly, amiable nation, but in their plantations and mines . . . '

After a while, the road flowing past them and the river on the right-hand side, Sam checked abruptly and in a hesitant, faltering tone he said, 'Dear Doctor, sir, pray forgive me. Here am I prating away for ever and in a loud voice to you, a man that might be my father. Sure you know all this better than I do, and have reflected on it since before ever I was born: shame on my head.'

'Not at all, not at all, Sam. I have not a tenth part of your experience. But I know enough to be sure that slavery is totally evil. The early generous revolution in the France of my youth abolished it: Buonaparte brought it back; and he is an evil man – his system is an evil system. Tell me, does the Archbishop feel as you do?'

'His Grace is a very ancient gentleman. But the Vicar-General, Father O'Higgins, does.'

'Many of my friends in Ireland and England are abolitionists,' observed Stephen, deciding to go no farther at this point. 'I believe I can make out the *Alastor* among the shipping to the left of the Dominican church. She is painted black, and she has four masts. That is where we live while the *Surprise* is being repaired: her knees cause some anxiety, I understand. I look forward to presenting my little girls to you, Sarah and Emily, who are good – well, fairly good – Catholics, though they have barely seen the inside of a church, to showing you the Captain's unhappy, bewildered, half-liberated black men, and to asking your help in housing my patients if the prize is sold from under them before they are quite well. And Sam,' he went on as they entered Callao, 'at some later time when you are free I should very much like to talk to you about the state of public opinion here in Peru: not only about abolition, but about many other things, such as freedom of commerce, representation, independence, and the like.'

The little girls, stiff with pride and amazement, and fairly soused with holy water, were handed into the carriage after pontifical High Mass in Lima cathedral. They smoothed their white dresses, their broad blue Marial sashes and sat quite straight, looking as happy as was consistent with a high degree of pious awe: they had just heard the tremendous voice of an organ for the first time; they had just been blessed by an archbishop in his mitre.

The crowded steps and pavement thinned; the viceroy's splendid coach rolled away, escorted by guards in blue and scarlet, to his palace fifty yards away; the great square became clearly visible.

'There in the middle is the splendid fountain of the world,' said Sam.

'Yes, Father,' they replied.

'Do you see the water spouting from the top?' asked Stephen.

'Yes, sir,' they answered, and they ventured no more until they came to Sam's quarters in an arcaded court behind the university, not unlike a quadrangle in one of the smaller Oxford colleges. 'Yes, Father: yes, sir,' was their total response to the news that the fountain was forty foot high, not counting the figure of Fame on the top; that it was surrounded by four and twenty pieces of artillery and sixteen iron chains of unusual weight; that the Casa de la Inquisición had scarcely a rival but the one in Madrid; that two of the streets through which they passed had been entirely paved with silver ingots to welcome an earlier viceroy; and that because of the frequent earthquakes the upper and sometimes the lower floors of the house were built of wooden frames filled with stout reeds, plastered over and painted stone or brick colour, with appropriate lines to help the illusion – that the great thing to do, in the event of an earthquake, was to open the door: otherwise it might jam and you would be buried under the ruins.

They grew a little less shy, a little more human, when they were led indoors and fed. Sam's servant Hipolito pleased them by wearing a sash broader than their own but clerical violet; they were delighted to see that the door was indeed kept open by a wedge, and even more so by the discovery of a ludicrous resemblance between Hipolito and Killick – the same look of pinched, shrewish discontent, diffused indignation; the same put-upon air; and the same restless desire to have everything proceed according to his own idea of order – but with this essential difference, that whereas Killick relied on the Captain's cook for all but coffee and the simplest breakfast dishes, Hipolito could provide a capital dinner with no more help than a boy to carry plates. This meal, however, being very early and the guests very young, was as plain as well could be: gazpacho, a dish of fresh anchovies, a paella: with them a little flowery wine from Pisco. Then came fruit, including the Peruvian version of the custard-apple, the chirimoya at its best, of which the little girls ate so greedily that they were obliged to be restrained – so greedily that they could manage few of the little almond cakes that would have ended their feast if they had been allowed to remain. But happily Hipolito had been born old, and neither Sam nor Stephen had any notion of entertaining the young apart from putting volumes of Eusebius on their chairs so that they might dominate their food. Their wine-glasses had been regularly filled; they had as regularly emptied them; and when towards the end of the meal the boy, standing in the doorway, saw fit to make antic gestures behind his master's back they were unable to restrain themselves. Stifled laughter swelled to uncontrollable giggles – neither could look at the other, still less at the boy in the doorway; and both were rather relieved than otherwise when they were turned out into the quadrangle and told 'to run about and play very quietly, until Jemmy Ducks comes to fetch you in the gig.'

'I am so sorry, Father,' said Stephen. 'They have never behaved like this before: I should have whipped them had it not been Sunday.'

'Not at all, not at all, God love you, sir. It would be the world's pity if they were kept to a Carmelite silence – sure a healthy child must laugh from time to time; it would be a dismal existence otherwise.

Indeed they were very good, sitting up straight with their napkins held just so.' He passed almond cakes, poured coffee, and went on, 'As for public opinion here in Peru, I should say that there is reasonably strong feeling for independence, particularly as the present Viceroy has made some very unpopular decisions in favour of those born in Spain as opposed to those born here. In some cases it is combined with a desire to see the end of slavery, but I do not think this is so much so as it is in Chile. After all, there are perhaps ten times as many slaves here, and many of the plantations depend entirely on their labour: yet there are many highly-respected, influential men who hate it. I have two friends, two colleagues, who know very much more about the matter than I do: the one is Father O'Higgins, the Vicar-General and my immediate superior – he is very, very kind to me – and the other is Father Iñigo Gomez, who lectures on Indian languages in the university. He is descended from one of the great Inca families on his mother's side – you know, I am sure, that there are still many of them, even after the last desperate rising. That is to say, those who were opposed to the rebellious Inca Tupac Amaru; and they still have many followers. Clearly, he understands that side better than any Castillian. Should you like to meet them? They are both abolitionists, but they would do their best to speak without prejudice, I have no doubt at all.'

The chiming watch in Stephen's fob, so often his conscience before, now warned him once again. He started up and in a low hurried voice he said, 'Listen, Sam, I do not wish to abuse your friends' confidence, far less your own. You must know that I am not only bitterly opposed to slavery but also to the dependence of one country upon another – you may smile, Sam, brought up as you were by Irish missionaries, God be with them – yet I mean the dependence of any country at all upon another; therefore I may be suspected of political, even subversive motives by those in authority. Do not run yourself or your friends into danger; for where those who are called intelligence-agents or their allies are concerned the Inquisition is mildness itself in comparison with those who maintain the established order.' He saw the half-suppressed, not wholly unexpected smile on Sam's face, heard him say, 'Doctor dear, you are beyond measure more candid than the Frenchmen here, the serpents,' and went on, 'But tell me now, Sam, where is the calle de los Mercadores? If it takes ten minutes I shall be twenty minutes late.'

'If I let you out by the stable door it will be the third on your right hand: and I will give the little girls over to the sailor when he comes with the gig.'

In spite of his name Pascual de Gayongos was a Catalan, and when by a series of arbitrary questions and answers Stephen had established his identity it was in Catalan that he said, 'I had expected you long, long before this.'

'I regret it extremely,' said Stephen. 'I was caught up in a particularly interesting conversation. But, my dear sir, does not a *long, long time* almost border on the excessive for twenty minutes?'

'I was not speaking of twenty minutes, no, nor of twenty weeks. These funds have been in my hands for an even greater time.'

'Certainly. Some information about our undertaking had been betrayed to Spain' – Gayongos nodded – 'and it was thought expedient that I should change to another ship, rejoining the *Surprise* at a stated rendezvous. An intelligent plan, and one that would have caused no great delay; but it did not foresee that this second vessel should be wrecked in a remote part of the East Indies, nor that the inevitable pauses in Java and New South Wales should eat up days, weeks, months that will never return.'

'And in that period,' said Gayongos in a discontented voice, 'the situation here has changed radically: Chile is now a very much more suitable plan for the enterprise, the whole series of undertakings.'

Stephen looked at him attentively. Gayongos was a big heavy man, well on in middle age; he gave the impression of general greyness and he was over-weight: at this point his fat trembled with passion, fairly well concealed. His commercial dealing had already made him rich: he had nothing to gain and his motives seemed wholly pure, if indeed hatred could be called pure: hatred of the Spaniards for their treatment of Catalonia; hatred of the Revolutionary and Buonapartist French for ravaging the country.

'Is Government aware of this?' asked Stephen.

'I have made representations through the usual channels, and I have been told to mind my own business: the Foreign Office knows best.'

'I have known the same treatment.' Stephen reflected and went on, 'But at this point I am necessarily bound by my instructions: any alteration must take six months to reach me and those six months, added to the present delay, will see the decay of the whole structure built up here and in Spain. I shall have to do the best I can: yet at the same time I shall endeavour to avoid committing what we have at our disposal until we see some·strong probability of success.'

After a silence Gayongos made a gesture of resignation and said, 'If the Foreign Office were a firm of marine insurers they would be bankrupt within a year. But it must be as you wish, and I shall arrange the agreed meetings, or at least those that are still of any consequence, as soon as possible.'

'Before we speak of them, be so good as to tell me, very briefly, how the situation has changed.'

'In the first place General Mendoza is dead. His horse threw him and he was picked up dead. He was one of the most popular men in the army, particularly among the Creoles, and he might well have carried half the officers with him. In the second the Archbishop is now – I hardly like to use the word senile about so good a man and so outspoken an abolitionist: but we are deprived of the full force of his support. In the third place Juan Muñoz has returned to Spain, and he has been replaced as far as governmental enquiries, secret service and unavowable activities are concerned by Garcia de Castro, too timid to be equally corrupt and in any event wholly unreliable: clever perhaps but oh so weak – terrified of the new Viceroy, terrified of losing his place. He is not a man to have anything to do with, near or far.'

'The absence of Muñoz disturbs me,' said Stephen. 'If Castro has access to his papers, my position is very nearly untenable.'

'I do not think you should feel anxious,' said Gayongos. 'We did handsomely by Muñoz; and quite apart from the presents he was wholly on our side. I do not pretend that handsome presents, or places in my concerns for his nephew and natural sons, did not have their effect on him, but he was not a weak unprincipled man like this Castro, and he was capable of taking decisive action in support of his friends. The reports about our possible intervention here – never taken very seriously in Madrid, by the way – passed through his hands in the first place and he virtually smothered them: it was easy enough, since the then Viceroy was about to leave, very ill, sick of the country and everything to do with it. And when the *Surprise* appeared – I mean when she came in first without you – he went privately down to Callao, ascertained that she was what she purports to be, a privateer, and had her officially inspected and passed the next day. Before he left Peru he destroyed a great many files. If any of the more bulky routine commonplace innocuous registers were kept you would appear only under your name of Domanova: but I very much doubt it. And I do not believe the privateer's captain was ever named at all.'

'That is comforting, to be sure,' said Stephen, cocking his ear to the window. All over Lima church and chapel bells began ringing the Angelus with no more than a few seconds between them, a remarkable medley of tones: both men crossed themselves and remained silent for a while. Looking up again Stephen said, 'Except in certain forms the Church is not a well-organized body – scarcely an organized body at all – yet sometimes flashes of sharp, co-ordinated intelligence pierce through and they are the more formidable for being unexpected. There is perhaps a certain analogy here with the Spanish government.'

Gayongos digested this, and then said, 'Let us turn to the administration. The new Viceroy is not intelligent, but he wished to distinguish himself by being active and zealous: he is wholly committed to the King – quite unapproachable by any means – and so are the people he brought with him, his immediate staff. But fortunately most of the secretariat remains unaltered, and I have some reports that will interest you. As for the chief office-holders, there is little change, except at the head of Indian affairs, which is now occupied by a highly-respected man, a friend of Humboldt's and like him an abolitionist; while in the department dealing with trade and customs the deputy-controller has taken over from his chief, but he continues the same kindness towards me, and sometimes with my wide connections I am able to let him know of a profitable venture, as I did for his predecessor.'

In a kind of parenthesis they talked about trade for a while: it was a subject upon which Gayongos, with his correspondents and business associates up and down the Pacific coast and beyond the isthmus, even as far as the United States, was unusually well qualified to speak. He had many activities but the chief was the insurance of ships and their cargoes, sometimes joining in a scheme he thought unusually sound; and to make a success of these an accurate knowledge of conditions, public feeling and official intention in the various provinces was of the first importance. 'As I am sure you know,' he observed, 'the governors of all the considerable cities, garrisons and districts send confidential reports to the Viceroy. It was Muñoz who first suggested that we should use them, when I began to let him have a share in some of my undertakings; and now of the seven copies made one comes to me as a matter of course: they are particularly interesting at this juncture, since they have an appendix on the political opinion and loyalty of many officers, ecclesiastics and servants of the crown.' He looked at Stephen to see the effect of his words, and with some satisfaction he went on, 'This brings us naturally to the army. But before we speak of the soldiers, may I ask whether you know there is a French mission here?'

'I do,' said Stephen, smiling. 'It would be strange if there were not. But I know only of its existence. Pray tell me what the mission consists of, and how they are coming along.'

'There are five of them, all said to be Swiss, Catholic Swiss. The leader and his brother, the two Brissacs, are mathematicians, measuring the force of gravity and the height of various mountains; the other two are said to be naturalists. The fifth, who speaks very good Spanish, seems merely to arrange their expeditions. They brought a letter of introduction from Humboldt, or what purported to be a letter of introduction from Humboldt, and they were well received at the university. They are evidently men of considerable learning.'

'What progress have they made?'

'Not very much. The elder Brissac, Charles, is a man of real ability and he has entered into serious conversation with some who are in favour of the new order. But the present French position on slavery cannot please the sort of people he usually sees, who are abolitionists, and he has nothing like enough money to tempt those who are both open to temptation and worth tempting. On the other hand, in spite of everything, *everything*, there is still a glamour attaching to France, and combined with the name of Napoleon and the idea of independence it moves some young men to a giddy enthusiasm; and the two naturalists, who appear to have served in the Italian campaign, have a number of followers. Castro may be one of them. He often invites the younger, Latrobe, and he arranged for their journey to the place where Humboldt stayed near Quito, so far up in the Andes that you can touch the moon from the ground floor.'

'That would have been Antisana for sure; and if I do not mistake the house is at more than thirteen thousand feet. If these French agents were not truly devoted naturalists, it must have been the weary, weary climb for them. But Lord, what an opportunity! I long to see the high Andes – to tread the virgin snow, and view the condor on her nest, the puma in his lair. I do not mention the higher saxifrages.'

'I went to Quito once,' said Gayongos, 'which is only nine thousand odd: up and up, always up and up, your lungs bursting, the muscles of your shins on fire; for you often have to lead your mule. Never, never again. I had rather be taken by the Inquisition. And there – how curious – there, hesitating to cross the street – ' They were sitting in a protruding louvered balcony from which they could see without being seen – 'there, the gentleman in black, is a familiar of the Inquisition. Yes. Yes. So he is. That reminds me: Castro is a Marrano – his great-grandmother was a Toledo Jewess – and perhaps that is what makes him so anxious to be cherished by the Viceroy while at the same time he longs to insure himself on the other side.'

'A difficult position,' observed Stephen. 'A Marrano cannot afford to make enemies: one alleged dislike of pork – one seven-branched candlestick found in his house – no matter who put it there – and the familiars come for him. He is accused of Hebrew practices, and you know the rest. Castro had much better keep quiet.'

'Castro is not capable of keeping quiet,' said Gayongos, and from that they went on to discuss the soldiers: it appeared from Gayongos's informed comments and from his appendices that there was a considerable amount of idealism and of support for independence, particularly among the captains and lieutenants; the senior officers were for the most part chiefly concerned with power and personal advantage; and they tended to hate one another. 'There are already bitter quarrels about how various commands and ministries are to be shared out,' said Gayongos. But he also vouched for three relatively disinterested generals and stated that if they were properly approached they might move in concert and precipitate the revolution: this would be all the more feasible if they were supplied with donatives to win the support of five or six regiments in key positions. 'This we can afford to do,' said Gayongos, 'whereas the French can not. Yet these are difficult, imperious men, and the presentation of the scheme is of the very first importance; and in any case it is you who have to decide on their value and on the present situation. General Hurtado is by far the most influential, and he is in Lima at present: should you like to go shooting with him early on Friday morning?'

'Very much. It would I think be indiscreet to ask to borrow your confidential reports.'

'They are indeed very bulky; and although I could explain their presence, no one else outside the palace could do so. May I look through them for some particular point?'

'I should be interested in any recent mention of Father O'Higgins the Vicar-General, of Father Gomez and of Father Panda.'

'Now that the Archbishop is failing, the Vicar-General is the most important man in the diocese. He is an abolitionist and he would be entirely on our side but for the fact that he deplores violence and that the English are for the most part heretics. Father Panda, a tall African, is his confidential assistant; he does not seem to mind violence nearly so much. Although he is so young they say he is very well seen in Rome, and is likely to be a prelate soon: the Vicar-General thinks the world of him. He too is an abolitionist of course. Of Father Gomez I only know that he is descended from Pachacutic Inca, that he is much reverenced by the Indians, and that he is very learned, which is not my line at all.'

'I believe I shall meet them privately quite soon.'

'Very good,' said Gayongos. 'And for these gentlemen?' He held up his list of agreed meetings.

'General Hurtado on Friday morning by all means; but it might be wiser to give the Vicar-General priority over the others – to see them having learnt his views.'

'Very much wiser.'

There seemed little more to be said at this first interview, apart from settling the place and time of Friday's expedition; but after a moment Gayongos said, 'This may be an absurd suggestion – it is most unlikely that you should have the time – but you said you longed to see the high Andes: Antisana, Cotopaxi, Chimborazo and the like. Now I shall presently have messengers going to Panama and Chagres by way of Quito. I should in any case have offered their services for any letters you might wish to have sent from the Atlantic side of the isthmus; but it occurs to me that some of these interviews may take a long while to arrange, a long while for emissaries to come and go – Potosí, Cuzco, for example – and that possibly you might find time to travel with them as far as Quito, reliable men who know the road and who could show you prodigious prospects of snow, rock and ice, volcanoes, bears, guanacoes, vicuñas, eagles . . . '

'You tempt me strangely: I wish it could be so. I dearly love a mountain,' said Stephen. 'But I could not square it with my conscience. No. I am afraid it will have to wait until our design is carried out. But I shall certainly burden your people with my letters, if I may: many, many thanks to you, my dear sir.'

For days the wind had kept in the east, and by now there was a considerable sea running across the northward current, causing the *Franklin* to roll and pitch rather more than was comfortable, rather more than was usual for mustering the ship's company by divisions; but this was Sunday, the first Sunday that Jack had felt reasonably sure that his wounded leg would bear the exercise, and he decided to carry on. At breakfast the word had been passed 'clean to muster' and now the bosun was bawling down the hatchways, 'D'ye hear, there, fore and aft? Clear for muster at five bells. Duck frocks and white trousers,' while his only remaining mate roared, 'D'ye hear, there? Clean shirts and shave for muster at five bells.' Many of the seamen were of course old Surprises: for them all this was part of immemorial custom, as much part of natural life as dried peas on Wednesday, Thursday and Friday, and they had already washed their best shirts in readiness while on Saturday evening or early on Sunday they had combed out their pigtails and replaited them, each man for his tie-mate, before or after cornering the ship's barber for their shave. Now, apart from fitting the poor bewildered blacks into their purser's slops, brushing and tidying them as well as they could and comforting them by calling out, 'It's all right, mate: never fret,' and patting them on the back or shoulders, they were quite ready.

So was their Captain. He was about to pull on his ceremonial breeches when, through the open door, Killick cried, 'No you don't. Oh no you don't, sir. Not until I have looked at those there wounds and that there eye. It was the Doctor's orders, sir, which you cannot deny it. And orders is orders.'

He had an overwhelming moral advantage, and Jack sat down, showing his thigh, a damned great slit that had been very painful at first but that had healed to a fair extent, just as his scalp had done, though walking was still awkward. Unwillingly Killick admitted that they needed no more than the ointment; but when he unrolled the bandage covering the Captain's eye he cried, 'Now we shall have to have the drops as well as the salve – a horrid sight: like a poached egg, only bloody – and I tell you what, sir, I shall put a little Gregory into the drops.'

'How do you mean, *Gregory*?'

'Why, everybody knows Gregory's Patent Liquid, sir: it rectifies the humours. And don't these humours want rectifying? Oh no, not at all. I never seen anything so ugly. God love us!'

'Did the Doctor mention Gregory's Patent Liquid?'

'Which I put some on Barret Bonden's wound, a horrible great gash: like a butcher's shop. And look at it now. As clean as a whistle. Come on, sir. Never mind the smart; it is all for your own good.'

'A very little, then,' said Jack, who had in fact known of Gregory's Liquid together with Harris's Guaranteed Unguent, Carey's Warranted Arrowroot, brimstone and treacle on Friday and other staples of domestic medicine, all as much a part of daily life on land as hardtack and mustering by division on Sunday at sea.

With his hat very carefully arranged over his new bandage – for in spite of his innumerable faults Killick did not lack a kind of sparse tenderness – Jack made his way up the companion-ladder at half a glass before five bells in the forenoon watch, hauling himself up step by step. It was an exceptionally beautiful day, brilliant, cloudless, with the immense sky a deeper, more uniform blue than usual and the sea, where it was not chopped white, an even deeper shade, the true imperial blue. The wind was still due east, singing quite loud in the rigging; but although the *Franklin* could have spread topgallantsails she was in fact lying to, bowing the uneven seas with her maintopsail aback and a balancing mizzen. Under her lee lay her most recent prize, a fur-trader down from the north, a fat, comfortable vessel, but naturally so unweatherly and now so foul-bottomed as well that she was utterly incapable of working to windward at all, and Captain Aubrey was waiting for the return of the south-east or south-south-east trade to see her in. She carried no extraordinary cargo – she had meant to fill up her hold with seals' skin down at Más Afuera – but those Surprises, and there were several of them, who had been on the Nootka run and who had conversed with their prisoners, knew that in sea-otter skins and beaver alone the able seaman's share of the prize would be in the nature of ninety-three pieces of eight; and it was a cheerful ship that her Captain was now about to inspect.

The starboard watch had already brought up their clothes bags, arranging them in a low pyramid on the booms, and the larbowlines were laying theirs in a neat square far aft on the quarterdeck when Jack appeared. As he had done a thousand times on such occasions he cast an eye at the sea, the sky, and the ship's trim: literally *an* eye, for even if the other had not been hidden by a bandage it could not bear this brilliant light, whilst in the dimness of his sleeping-cabin its sight was troubled, uncertain. He also absorbed the mood of the ship's company, and in spite of the severe indwelling pain and anxiety some of their cheerfulness came into his mood.

Five bells, and he nodded to Vidal, the acting first lieutenant, who cried, 'Beat to divisions.' So many people were away in various ships that the order did not run down the usual series of repetitions but came into instant effect with the thunder of the roaring drum. The recently-promoted stopgap officers, most of them Shelmerstonian master-mariners in their own right, reported that their divisions were 'present, properly dressed and clean'.

Vidal crossed the deck, took off his hat, and said, 'All the officers have reported, sir.'

'We will go round the ship, then, if you please,' replied Jack.

And round they went in the traditional manner, except that Bonden, as Captain's coxswain, accompanied them in case of a false step on the blind side: for though Bonden's ribs and breastbone had been exposed to public view in the taking of the *Alastor*, his wound had healed fast and his friends had taken seamanlike steps to ensure that it should not open again: first a girth of linen rubbed with hog's lard, then two of number eight sailcloth, then the same of number four, and over all a span-broad white-marline plait ending in stout knittels that could be and were hauled taut with a heaver, so taut that he could breathe only with his belly.

The afterguard and waisters under Slade formed the first division, and here were most of the Alastor's black slaves, naturally enough, since they were the merest landsmen, useful only for holystoning the deck in smooth weather, swabbing and sweeping it, or hauling on a rope under strict supervision: abruptly Jack found that he did not know their names – could not tell one from another – and was unable to exchange the usual word. They were beautifully clean, shining clean, and perfectly dressed in their new duck frocks and trousers, and they had been taught to stand up and pull off their hats, but they looked nervous, far from happy: their eyes rolled with apprehension. The next group had two more as well as some remaining Franklins, and although Jack knew the white men tolerably well he was surprised to see them in this division. But the people under his command had necessarily been given such different duties and moved to and fro between such different ships that even a captain who had not been knocked on the head and obliged to keep his cabin for some time might have been confused. It was better when he came to the gunners and the forecastlemen, the oldest hands aboard, ludicrously under Reade, whose voice had not yet finished breaking; but Jack was still worried when he went below with his escort to inspect the galley, the berth-deck and all the rest. He had always felt that it was an officer's absolute duty to know all his men, their watch, rating, abilities, and of course their name and division: he, Vidal and Bonden at length returned to the daylight, filed past the remaining seamen prisoners and so to the leeward side of the quarterdeck where the captured officers stood. 'It is a pleasure to see you walking about and looking so well, sir,' said one of them.

'You are very good, sir,' replied Jack. Then, conscious of an absence, he ran his eye sharply over the little band and cried, 'Where is Mr Dutourd? Bonden, jump down to his cabin and rouse him out. Find his servant.'

There was no Dutourd: nor could his servant be found though the ship; the prize and the schooner-rigged launch towing astern were searched through and through with all the skill of those accustomed to hiding goods from customs officers and men from impressments. His sea-chest, with the plate reading Jean du Tourd, was in his cabin, and all his clothes; his writing-desk, open and disordered, with some papers presumably taken from it; but his purse, which Jack had restored, was not to be seen.

The testimonies were extraordinarily varied: they agreed only in that Dutourd had not dined in the gunroom for quite a while and that he had seemed to be offended – was thought to be messing by himself. But how long that time was no one could tell for certain. Even Killick, the most inquisitive man aboard, had no sure, clearly-dated knowledge, and to Jack's astonishment he was not even aware that Dutourd had been refused leave to go to Callao in the *Surprise* with his former shipmates – did not even know that he had asked for permission. No one could swear to having seen him on the quarterdeck after the *Franklin* had parted company: none could swear to the contrary: most had the impression that he was keeping his cabin, studying or sick.

There were several possibilities, and Jack turned them over in his mind as he sat, alone at last, in the *Franklin*'s stern-window: Dutourd might have brought his belongings over from the *Surprise* to the *Franklin*, returning on some pretext and there concealing himself. He might have walked into the *Alastor* when she was alongside, transferring stores: the same applied to the whaler. And there was the launch, sent in to bring hands from Callao.

It was the outcome that really mattered, however: in his reserved way Stephen had said that sending Dutourd in to Callao 'might be impolitic'; and there was no doubt that Dutourd was in Callao at this moment.

'Pass the word for Mr Vidal,' he called, and when Vidal came, 'Sit down, Mr Vidal. Who took the launch into Callao?'

'I did, sir,' said Vidal, changing colour.

'How did she handle?'

'Sir?'

'How did she handle? Is she a weatherly boat? Does she hold a good wind?'

'Yes, sir. She points up very close indeed: makes almost no leeway, close-hauled, a jewel of a . . . ' His voice died away.

'Very well. Pray have her victualled and stored, with masts stepped, before the first dog.'

' . . . craft,' said Vidal, finishing his words.

'Do not let them forget fishing-tackle and a casting net: it may need two or three days to beat in if this wind don't change. I shall take Bonden, Killick, Plaice, William Johnson: and your Ben.' The last he named after an infinitesimal pause, for while they were speaking he had come to an intimate conviction that Dutourd had gone ashore in the schooner and that taking Ben would if nothing else prevent any foolish action on Vidal's part: it might have been wiser to take Vidal himself, but with so many of the most responsible and experienced men away or wounded Vidal was by far the best to leave in charge: he might have chapelish, democratic, even republican views, but he had been the master of a ship larger than the *Franklin*, he was a prime seaman, thoroughly respected, and he had a large following. 'You will take command while I am away,' he said after a silence. 'If the wind keeps in the east, as I believe it will, you will not be able to carry the prize a single mile nearer Callao, though you beat up day and night. Should it change you may come in, and if you cannot fetch Callao we will rendezvous off the Chinchas. But I shall give you your orders in writing, together with a list of meeting-places from the Lobos Rock far to the southward.'

Indeed, to make any real progress in a breeze as strong and steady as this a vessel had to be rigged fore and aft, and nothing could have been more wholly fore and aft than the *Alastor*'s elegant mahogany launch with her remarkably flat-cut sails: in spite of his deep uneasiness Jack took a pleasure in getting all that he could from her, bringing her up to the very edge of shivering, falling off just that much and sending her fast through the coming sea. The launch was as responsive as a well-mannered, spirited horse; it was beamy and stiff enough for this kind of weather; and well before nightfall they had sunk the *Franklin*'s topsails in the west.

When Jack Aubrey was strongly moved he seemed to grow taller and broader-shouldered, while without the slightest affectation or morosity his ordinarily good-humoured expression became remote. Killick was not easily put down: ordinary fits of anger over dropped bottles, inept orders from Whitehall or the flag left him totally unmoved, so did reproach and even abuse, but this rare, particular gravity intimidated him and when he dressed leg, eye and scalp that evening he did so with no more words than were necessary, and those uttered meekly.

The decked part of the launch was divided fore and aft into two long cuddies, each with headroom enough to sit up; it was here that Jack stretched out on a mattress over the grating a little after the setting of the watch. Although the forward part of the cuddy was filled with canvas and cordage there was plenty of room for him and according to his life-long habit he fell asleep within minutes, in spite of pain and anxiety. His neighbours in the larboard cuddy, Johnson and young Ben Vidal, did much the same. Johnson, a black man from the Seven Dials, began telling Ben about his triumph over the whoreson pinchfart master-at-arms in *Bellerophon* when first he went to sea, but his voice dwindled when he found he had no hearer.

It had been laid down that they should be at watch-and-watch, and a few minutes before midnight Jack woke straight out of what had seemed a deep and dreamless sleep. Yet some parts of his mind must have been active, since he knew perfectly well that the launch had gone about four times and that the wind had diminished to a moderate breeze. He made his way out of the cuddy into the light of the moon, a true clock if one knew her age and her exact place among the stars for the beginning of each watch. Suddenly, as he stood there swaying to the quieter sea and wishing he could stretch over the lee rail and dash water into his face, it occurred to him that his eye scarcely hurt at all: there was still a certain irritation, but the deep pain was not there. 'By God,' he said, 'perhaps I shall be able to swim again in a week or two.'

'You are a good relief, sir,' said Bonden, yielding the tiller; and he gave an exact account of the courses steered – two reaches as near south-east by east as possible and two north-east by east – and their speed, rising to ten knots one fathom now that the head-seas had grown less lumpish. Behind them there was the muffled sound of the changing watch, the very small watch; and Jack said, 'Well, turn in, Bonden, and get what sleep you can.'

He settled into the helmsman's place with the living tiller under his hand and forearm, and while his companions pumped and baled the launch dry – a good deal of water had come aboard earlier, but now there was no more than the odd waft of spray – his mind moved back to its essential preoccupations. His moral conviction that Vidal had been party to Dutourd's escape was irrational in that it was based on no more than an instinctive distrust of Vidal's first reply; but now that he reflected, gathering all he had ever heard of Dutourd's views and those of the Knipperdollings, all that he knew about enthusiasm and the lengths to which it might lead the enthusiast, it appeared to him that here reason and instinct coincided, as they sometimes did when he fought a battle over again in recollection or at least those phases such as boarding and the hand-to-hand encounter in which there was really no time for deliberation, no time at all. And his reflecting mind approved of his having Ben here in the launch: it might do great good; it would do no harm at all.

Yet how Dutourd had managed to get away was scarcely worth pondering about for any length of time: all that signified was that he *had* got away and that Stephen had said he should be kept aboard. 'From my point of view it might be impolitic' for him to be set ashore in Peru.

Stephen's point of view had of course to do with intelligence, as Jack knew very well: during an earlier voyage he had seen him drop a box which, bursting, revealed a sum so vast that it could only have been intended for the subversion of a government; and he strongly suspected him of having dished two English traitors, Ledward and Wray, attached to a French mission to the Sultan of Prabang.

In a parenthesis he heard Stephen's voice: 'Tell me, Jack, my dear, is *dish* a nautical term?'

'We often use it in the Navy,' Jack replied. 'It means to ruin or frustrate or even destroy. Sometimes we say *scupper*; and there are coarser words, but I shall not embarrass you by repeating them.'

On the windward bow Canopus was just clearing the horizon. 'Stand by to go about,' he called, and his companions ran to their stations. He eased off half a point, cried, 'Helm's a-lee,' and ducking under the boom he brought the launch round in a true smooth curve, filling with barely a check on the starboard tack.

The moon was lowering now, and dimmed by a high veil she gave so little light that he scarcely saw Johnson come aft. 'Shall I spell you now, sir?' he asked, and his teeth showed in the darkness.

'Why, no thank you, Johnson,' said Jack. 'I shall sit here for a while.'

The launch sailed on and on, almost steering herself as the breeze grew lighter: and as the seas declined – no breaking crests at all – so the water became alive with phosphorescence, a pale fire streaming away and away in her wake but also gleaming in vast amorphous bodies at depths of perhaps ten or even twenty fathoms, and at various levels the movement of fishes could be seen, interweaving lanes or sudden flashes.

Jack returned to his reflections: Stephen's point of view had of course to do with intelligence. This had almost certainly been the case for many, many years, and on occasion Jack had been officially required to seek his advice on political matters. But he had no notion of Stephen's present task: he did not wish to know, either, ignorance being the surest guarantee of discretion. Nor could he imagine how such a man as Dutourd could be any hindrance to whatever task it was. Surely no government, however besotted, could ever think of using such a prating, silly fellow as an intelligence-agent or any sort of envoy.

He turned the matter over this way and that. It was an exercise as useful as trying to solve an equation with innumerable terms of which only two could be read. To windward there was a vast expiring sigh as a sperm whale surfaced, black in a corruscation of green light, an enormous solitary bull. His spout drifted across the launch itself, and he could be heard drawing in the air, breathing for quite some time; then easily, smoothly, he shouldered over and dived, showing his flukes in a final blaze.

Jack continued with his pointless exercise, with one pause when Johnson spelled him, until the end of the watch, ending with no more valuable observation than that with which he had begun: if Dutourd was in any way a threat to Stephen on shore it was his clear self-evident duty to get the man aboard again if it could be done, and if it could not, then at least to take Stephen off.

From the end of the watch at four he slept until six, blessing himself for this eye, but uneasy about the failing breeze, still right in their teeth, but barely carrying the launch close-hauled at more than five knots, and they measured by a hopeful mind.

It did not surprise him to wake to a calm, but for a moment he was surprised by the strong smell of frying fish: there was still an hour to go before breakfast.

'Good morning, sir,' said Killick, creeping in with his dressings. 'Flat calm and an oily swell.' But this he said without his usual satisfaction in bringing unwelcome news, and he went on, 'Which Joe Plaice asks pardon, but could not help having a cast; and breakfast will be ready in ten minutes. It would be a shame to let it grow cold.'

'Then bring me the hot water, and as soon as I am shaved I shall come on deck. You can do my eye afterwards: it is much better.'

'I knew as how Gregory would do it,' cried Killick, a look of triumphant happiness on his face. 'I shall double the dose. I knew I was right. It rectifies the humours, you understand.'

Joe Plaice, a steady forecastle-hand, was good at all the countless skills required of an able seaman, but he was an absolute artist in the use of a casting-net: poised on the bowsprit, with his left hand on the stay, he swung the net with his right, throwing it with an exactly-calculated twist that spread its weighted edge so that the whole fell flat as a disk on the surface just over one of the countless bands of anchovies that surrounded the launch for miles in every direction. The little fishes stared in amazement or even tried to leap upwards. The weights quickly carried the edge of the net down and inwards; a string drew them together; and the imprisoned fish were drawn aboard. Half the first cast had been eaten by the helmsman, who was always fed first; the second half and two more were eaten fresh and fresh by all hands, sitting on the deck round a large pan, itself poised over charcoal on a raised iron plate.

'By God, this is good,' said Jack, sweeping up the juice with his biscuit. 'There is nothing better than your really fresh anchovy.' 'It must die in the pan,' observed Plaice. 'It is deadly poison else.' There was a general murmur of assent. 'Very true,' said Jack. 'But I tell you what, shipmates,' he went on, nodding towards the east-south-east, 'you had better blow your kites out, you had better eat all you can, because God knows when you will have another hot meal. Or a cold one, for that matter. Ben, do you know what a wind-gall is?'

The very young man blushed, choked on his fish, and in a strained voice, looking nervously at his companions, said, 'Well, sir, I seen the ordinary kind.'

'Look out to leeward, a little afore the beam, and you will see one a long way out of the ordinary.'

'It was not there when we set to breakfast,' said Joe Plaice.

'And to leeward too, oh dear, oh dear,' said Johnson. 'God bless us.'

'Amen,' said the others.

Far over, in the ill-defined region between sea and sky, there was an iridiscent patch, roughly oval, of the size that an outstretched hand might cover; and its colours, sometimes faint, sometimes surprisingly vivid, shifted right through the spectrum.

'A wind-gall to windward means rain, as you know very well,' said Jack. 'But a wind-gall to leeward means very dirty weather indeed. So Joe, you had better make another cast: let us eat while we can.'

The other sea-creatures were of the same opinion. The launch was now in the middle of the northward-flowing Peruvian current and for some reason the animalculae that lived there had begun one of those immense increases in population that can colour the whole sea red or make it as turbid as pea-soup. The anchovies, blind with greed, devoured huge quantities; medium-sized fishes and squids ate the anchovies with reckless abandon, scarcely aware that they themselves were being preyed upon by fishes much larger than themselves, the bonitoes and their kind, by sea-lions, by great flights of pelicans, boobies, cormorants, gulls and a singularly beautiful tern, while agile penguins raced along just beneath the surface.

The launch's crew spent most of the forenoon making all fast, sending up preventer-stays and shrouds and preparing what number one canvas they possessed. A little before dinner-time, when a tall white rock, a sea-lions' island much haunted by birds, the sea-mark for Callao Head, showed plain on the starboard bow, nicking the horizon ten miles away, with the remote almost cloud-like snow-topped Andes far beyond, the wind began blowing out of a clear high pale-blue sky. It could be seen coming, a dun-coloured haze from the east, right off shore; it did not come with any sudden violence, but it increased steadily to a shrieking blast that flattened the sea, bringing with it great quantities of very fine sand and dust that gritted between their teeth and blurred their sight.

In the interval between the first pleasant hum in the rigging that woke the launch to life and the scream that overcame everything but a shout they came abreast of the tall white rock, Jack at the tiller, all hands leaning far out to windward to balance the boat and the launch tearing through the water at a pace somewhere between nightmare and ecstasy. As they passed under the lee of the island they heard the sea-lions barking and young Ben laughed aloud. 'You would laugh the other side of your face, young fellow, if you could feel how this God-damned tiller works with the strain,' said Jack to himself, and he noticed that Plaice was looking very grave indeed. Joe Plaice, he reflected, must be close on sixty: much battered in the wars.

And now at last the wind was working up an ugly sea: the waves had no great fetch and they were short and steep, growing rapidly steeper, with their crests streaming off before them. As soon as the boat was past the rock it was clear that she could not go on under this press of sail. The seamen looked aft: Jack nodded. No word passed but all moving together they carried out the perilous manoeuvre of wearing, carrying the launch back into the lee, there close-reefing the main and foresail, sending up a storm forestaysail and creeping out to sea again.

For the rest of daylight – and brilliant daylight it was, with never a cloud to be seen – this answered well enough and they supped by watches on biscuit and oatmeal beaten up with sugar and water: grog, of course, served out by Captain Aubrey. There was even enough of a pause for Killick to dress Jack's eye and to tell him he would certainly lose it if he did not put back to the barky, where it could be kept dry.

'Nonsense,' said Jack. 'It is much better. I can see perfectly well: it is only the bright light I cannot stand.'

'Then at least let me cut a patch out of the flap of your hat, sir, so you can wear the two together, like Lord Nelson, tied over your head with a scarf, if it blows.'

It blew. The patch was barely on before the making of it would have been impossible: the voice of the wind in the rigging rose half an octave in half an hour and the boat was flung about with shocking violence. Most of that night they were obliged to lie to under a storm trysail and a scrap of the jib – a night of brilliant moon, beaming over a sea white from horizon to horizon.

Tomorrow it must blow out, they said; but it did not. The days followed one another and the nights, everything on the point of carrying away, a perpetual series of crises; sometimes they advanced until they were in sight of the island guarding Callao and the cliffs: sometimes they were beaten back; and presently, though this was approaching the austral midsummer, the wind, blowing off the high Cordillera, grew perishing cold to those who were always dripping wet. Wet, and now hungry. The unhappy Ben contrived not only to scrape his shins to the bone but also to lose their precious keg of oatmeal overboard; and on Thursday their rations were cut by half.

When Jack announced this in a shout as they huddled together in the starboard cuddy he added the ritual

> 'Two upon four of us
> Thank God there are no more of us,'

and he was pleased to see an answering smile upon those worn, cruelly tired faces.

But there was no smile on Sunday, when at dawn they heard the sea-lions quite close at hand and realized that they had been driven back for the seventh time by a wind that was stronger still and even growing, a wind that must have blown the *Franklin* and her prize far, far into the western ocean.

CHAPTER EIGHT

L ong practice and a certain natural ability enabled Stephen
Maturin to compose a semi-official report of some length in his
head and to encode a condensed version from memory, leaving no
potentially dangerous papers after the message itself had gone. This
required an exceptional power of recollection, but he *had* an exceptional power of recollection and it had been trained from boyhood in
rote-learning: he could repeat the entirety of the Aeneid, and he had
the private code by heart – the code, that is to say, in which he and
Sir Joseph Blaine, the head of naval intelligence, wrote to one another.

'God between us and evil, my dear Joseph,' he began, 'but I believe
I can report an uncommonly promising beginning, an uncommonly
promising situation, with things moving at an extraordinary, dream-
like speed. To begin with I was introduced to General Hurtado, a
former Knight of Malta, who, though a soldier, is very much in favour
of independence, partly because Charles IV was rude to his father
but even more because both the present Viceroy and his predecessor seemed to him trifling ill-bred upstarts; this is not an unusual
pattern in Spain and here the animosity is very much increased by
the fact that in a letter the present Viceroy omitted the Excelenzia to
which Hurtado is by courtesy entitled; yet what is more unexpected
by far is that he is strongly opposed to slavery and that although he
holds a command from which most officers have hitherto retired
with enough wealth to ballast the ship that took them back to Spain,
he is quite poor. As for his hatred of slavery, he shares it with several
of my friends who were also Knights of Malta and I believe it comes
from his time in the galleys of the Order: and as for the king's rude-
ness, it consisted of addressing the general's father as 'my relative'
rather than 'my cousin,' which was due to his rank, an offence never
to be forgotten, since Hurtado is immeasurably proud.

'It was indeed the Knights of Malta who brought us cordially well acquainted, for although I had an excellent introduction from a political point of view, it was our many common friends in the Order that gave our meeting quite a different aspect – our common friends and our common attachment to the Sierra Leone scheme for settling liberated slaves, to which we are both subscribers.

'The first occasion was a ride in the barren wastes that lie beyond the reach of irrigation all round Lima. These expeditions are called hunting, and on feast-days the more athletic citizens urge their horses about the stony deserts in search of a more or less fabulous creature said to resemble a hare and blaze away at the very few things that move, usually a dingy, inedible passerine which I take to be a dwarvish subspecies of Sturnus horridus. I collected three beetles for you, of which all I can say is that they belong to the pentamera and that I am astonished that even such meagre, attenuated creatures could scrape a living from the desolation we travelled over. The General was more fortunate. He brought down a singularly beautiful tern, the Sterna ynca of Suarez: I can only suppose that it was taking a direct path from a curve in the river to some better fishing-ground along the coast; but the event was so rare, so nearly unknown, that it gave the General the utmost satisfaction – he declared there could be no finer omen for our future conversations.

'A good omen is always welcome: yet if it were not presumptuous I should feel inclined to say that there is comparatively little doubt about the outcome of these conversations, three of the high ecclesiastics and four governors being already wholly committed to us, together with those for whom they speak; while the officers in command of the regiments that must be moved are tolerably venal men, and we have ample funds at hand. Yet at the same time certain forms must still be observed: there must be persuasion, a gentle violence, before they can decently fall.

'We are to have a preliminary meeting without these gentlemen on Wednesday to arrange the details of payment and to decide whether Castro should be invited to the main conference on Friday. He is being very discreetly sounded at this moment, in the palace itself: the empty palace, for the Viceroy is hurrying to quell a disturbance in far northern Peru. He left with his military household and some other troops soon after I had met the last of our friends here who were still in Lima and he is already ten days' journey along the road.

'I could not have come at a more fortunate moment, when the Viceroy had alienated so many of the Creoles and so much of the army; when the desire for independence had risen to such a height; when he was about to remove himself and his surest friends from the capital; and when the ground had been to a certain extent prepared. It would perhaps have been wiser to start with Chile, where Bernardo O'Higgins (close kin to our Vicar-General) has so considerable a following; but given the present aspect of affairs, to say nothing of my direct, explicit instructions, I believe we may do very well here. It is true that time is all-important, with that smooth co-ordination of troop-movements, declarations, and the summoning of a Peruvian council that will present the Viceroy with a fait accompli on his return, a very well established fait accompli, with all these movements carried out and an overwhelming force in the citadel; yet most fortunately General Hurtado has an unusual sense of the passing hour, and he is a most capable chief of staff, the most capable in the Spanish service.

'How I wish I could give you the results of the full conference or even of the preliminary meeting, but I am to ride into the mountains directly, and the messengers who carry this to the Atlantic coast will be gone before I can be back. May I beg you to send the enclosed half-sheet down to Hampshire?'

'My dear,' he wrote on the half-sheet in question, 'this is the merest hasty scribble to bring you both my fondest love from our most recent port of call, and to tell you that all is well with us, except for poor Martin, who has been obliged to be sent home for his health. With the blessing, this note will reach you some three months before he arrives: please tell his wife that I am confident she will see him quite restored.

'This is a pleasant climate, for gentle sea-breezes temper the heat; but they assure me it never rains at all, not at all, ever; and although there are damp fogs throughout the winter they are not enough to relieve the almost total sterility of the desert, stony or sandy, that lies along the coast, the virtual absence of life, animal or vegetable. Yet I have already achieved one of my greatest ambitions: I have seen the condor. And you will be pleased to learn that I have already collected seven distinct species of mouse (five inhabit the fringe of the desert, one its very heart, and the seventh was making a nest in my papers), while the rivers, of course, which are fed from the high far-off snows and which therefore flow their strongest in the summer, provide their valleys and their irrigated fields with a valuable flora and fauna. But it is the high mountain that I long to see, with its plants and creatures unlike any others in the world; at this moment I am booted and spurred for a journey to the moderate heights. My mule stands in a courtyard close at hand, and across his saddle-bow he bears a poncho, an oblong piece of cloth with a hole in the middle, through which I shall put my head when I reach five or six thousand feet.

'Now God bless you, my dearest love; and pray kiss Brigit for me.'

He sat back, reflecting with the utmost tenderness upon his wife Diana, that fierce, spirited young woman, and upon their daughter, whom he had not seen but whom he pictured as a very small child in a pinafore, walking by now, perhaps already conversable. Once again his watch broke in upon his wandering thoughts: a watch that would have been a more valuable guide if he had wound it the night before. He folded his papers, carried them into Gayongos's private room, and rehearsed his direction once more. 'You cannot miss it,' said Gayongos, 'but I wish you may get there before nightfall. You are starting more than three hours late.' Stephen bent his head; he could not but

admit it. 'And there is a cruel wind blowing right in your face,' added
Gayongos. He led Stephen through a daedal of passages and stables
to a courtyard where the mule was standing, a tall, intelligent animal
that recognized their destination after their first two or three turns
through Lima streets, making his way through the gate beyond the
Misericordia convent without guidance and striking into the road
that ran a little north of east towards the mountains along the left
of the river, a fine turbulent great stream, growing day by day as the
season advanced.

The road was not much frequented at present, though on Friday
and Saturday it would be full of people going up to the shrine of Our
Lady of Huenca; and it grew less beyond the limits of irrigated land.
The mule was an ambler with a long easy motion and Stephen sat
quite relaxed upon his back: the river-banks had a reasonable population of birds, while the occasional reptile crossed the road and
large flying beetles were common as long as the carob-groves lasted.
Part of Stephen's mind recorded them, but the strong east wind and
the dust made it hard to see with any sharp definition and in any
case the rest of his being was so taken up with the possibility, indeed
the strong probability, of a brilliant success for his mission within
the next eight days or even less that he never stopped or reached for
his pocket-glass. The whole scheme had matured so quickly, because
of his excellent relations with Hurtado and O'Higgins and above all
because of the Viceroy's departure, that his spirits, usually so well
under control, were now in something of a fluster. This was a condition he had seen often enough in his colleagues, but finding it in himself put him somewhat out of countenance.

Once more he went over the various moves, the replacing of stated
regiments by others, the convocation of wholly committed support-
ers, the summoning of a council, the issue of a proclamation, the
rapid dispatch of guns to command three essential bridges: as he
named them in order they seemed simple enough, and his heart beat
so that he could hear it. Yet he had some acquaintance with the military mind, the Spanish military mind, and with that of the Spanish

conspirator; and before now he had seen a series of actions that were simple in themselves, but that had of necessity to be carried out in sequence, fall into hopeless chaos for want of a sense of time, for want of common efficiency, or because of hidden jealousies.

He wished he had not used such confident, presumptuous words in writing to Blaine. From very early times men had believed that it was unwise, even impious, to tempt fate: the ancient generations were not to be despised. The confident system of his youth – universal reform, universal changes, universal happiness and freedom – had ended in something very like universal tyranny and oppression. The ancient generations were not to be despised; and the seamen's firm belief that Friday was unlucky was perhaps less foolish than the *philosophe*'s conviction that all the days of the week could be rendered happy by the application of an enlightened system of laws. He wished the main conference had not been set for Friday.

Blushing at his momentary weakness, he turned his mind to Hurtado. The General might have some small absurdities such as a delight in being fine (he wore the stars of his three orders at all times) and setting an inordinate value on pedigree: he took more pleasure in recounting the stages of his descent, through his maternal grandmother, from Wilfred the Shaggy than in speaking of the four brilliant victories he had won as commander or the other battles in which he had served with such distinction. On all other subjects however he was not only a rational being but one with an unusually acute and ready mind: an active man, a born organizer, and an uncommonly effective ally in such a concern. His abilities, his known honesty, his high reputation in the army, and his influence throughout Peru made him the most valuable friend that ever Stephen could have found.

The white mile-stones filed by, and many crosses commemorating death by earthquake, murder, accident. For some little while the mule had not been pacing uphill with the same steady determination. He had been gazing from side to side; and now, giving Stephen a significant look, he turned off the road into the last carob-trees. By this point the road had wound some way from the Rimac, which could be heard roaring in the gorge below, but a small tributary stream ran through among the trees and in this Stephen and the mule drank heartily.

'You are a good honest creature, sure, and you bear an excellent character,' said Stephen, 'so I shall take off your saddle, confident you will not play the fool.'

The mule flung himself to the ground and rolled, waving his legs; and while Stephen sat under the lee of a carob's wall (each tree was surrounded by what looked like a well-head) grazed on what meagre herbage the grove could provide. Stephen ate bread and good Peruvian cheese with Peruvian wine; and in doing so he thought of the little girls, their apology the next day (Sarah: 'Sir, we are come to ask pardon for our wicked drunken folly.' Emily: 'For our wanton drunken folly.') and their words to Mr Wilkins, their voices piping alternately, clearly audible from below when Stephen had been chivvied right forward by Pullings and Mr Adams, who were bargaining with some merchants who wished to buy the *Alastor*: 'Yes, sir, and after Mass' – 'There was an organ: do you know what an organ is, sir?' – 'We went aboard a grand carriage drawn by mules with *purple* harness together with the Doctor and Father Panda.' 'There was a square with a lady on a column in the middle' – 'The column was forty foot high' – 'And the lady was made of bronze' – 'She had a trumpet and water came out of it' – 'And it came out of eight lions' heads too' – 'Out of twelve lions' heads, booby' – 'It was surrounded by six huge enormous iron chains' – 'And four and twenty twelve-pounders' – 'The merchants paved two of the streets with silver ingots once' – 'They weighed ten pounds apiece' – 'About a foot long, four inches broad, and two or three inches deep.'

He had nearly finished his meal when he felt the mule's breath on the back of his neck: then the long, smooth, large-eyed face came down and delicately took the last piece of bread from his knee, a crust. 'You are a sort of tame mule, I find,' he said. And indeed the creature's gentleness, the kind way in which he stood to be saddled and his fine willing stride gave Stephen a higher opinion of his owner, the Vicar-

General, an austere man in his ordinary dealings. The mule's name was Joselito.

Stephen mounted: out of the grove there was more wind now, more wind by far, right in their faces, and the road climbed, winding and for ever rising with tall, very tall, many branched columnal cactuses on either hand and little else apart from smaller cactuses with even crueller thorns. This was the first time in Stephen's life that he had ever ridden in a strange country paying so little attention to his surroundings; and although on occasion he had had a hand, even a directing hand, in matters of great importance, this was the first time that so much depended on his success, and the first time that the crisis, the decision, was drawing so near with such speed. He did not even notice two barefoot friars though the mule had been pointing his ears in their direction for a quarter of a mile until he was almost upon them and they standing on an outward corner, their beards streaming in the wind, looking back to the sound of hoofs. He pulled off his hat, called out a greeting and pushed on, hearing their 'Go with God' as he turned in yet another traverse, the road now high up on the steep side of the valley, with the stream a great way below.

He met a few small scattered groups, Indians coming down from the high pasture; and presently the road climbed to a saddle where the wind, a cold wind now, took them with great force. Before crossing it he steered Joselito into a less exposed hollow, where travellers before him had lighted fires, burning whatever little scrub they could find. Here, at what he judged to be some five thousand feet, he gave the mule his other loaf – no great sacrifice, since anxiety of a vague, diffused nature had eaten his own appetite – and put on the poncho, a simple garment with no sleeves, easier to manage than a cloak. The sky was still a fine light blue above them, unclouded here by dust; before him, when he turned, stretched the foothills and the plain, somewhat veiled, with the Rimac running through it to the immense Pacific, the coastline as clear as a map, and the island of San Lorenzo, beyond Callao, rising sharply from it, with the sun directly beyond,

two hours from the somewhat blurred horizon. No ships in the offing that he could see, but below him on the road, no great way off,
there was a party of horsemen, quite a large party, bound no doubt
for the monastery of San Pedro or that of San Pablo, both of them in
the mountains far ahead and both of them frequented for retreats,
particularly by soldiers.

The poncho was a comfort; so was the way the road went down
after they had crossed the saddle to a new valley with higher, farther
mountains rising beyond, range after range. But this did not last long.
Soon it began to rise once more and they climbed steadily mile after
mile, sometimes so steeply that Stephen dismounted and walked
beside the mule; and steadily the landscape grew more mineral.

'I wish I had paid more attention to geology,' said Stephen, for on
his right hand on the far side of the gorge the bare mountainside
showed a great band of red, brilliant in the declining sun against the
grey rock below and the black above. 'Would that be porphyry, at all?'

On and on: up and always up. The air was thinner by now, and
Joselito was breathing deep. Before they crossed the head of this valley they passed a man in a cloak whose horse had apparently both
lost a shoe and picked up a stone: there was no telling, since he led
his animal limping off the road and stood behind it, well out of hail.
Of infinitely greater consequence was the prospect of yet another
blessed downward stretch on the far side of the pass; yet here Stephen, if not the mule, was disappointed, for this before them was not
the last valley but only the prelude to an even higher range; and still
the road climbed.

A new and immediate anxiety added itself to the rest in Stephen's
head and bosom, that of being benighted: already the sun was low
behind them; there was twilight down there in the lower part of their
present valley; and the western sky was assuming a violet tinge.

Another half hour, a hard half hour, with Joselito grunting as he
strode on, and there before them was a new ridge and the parting of
the ways. The road split into two thinner paths, that on the right leading to the Benedictine house of San Pedro, the other to the Domin-

icans of San Pablo. Shading his eyes against the powerful wind, Stephen could see them both quite clearly, a hand's breadth above the rising shadow of the night.

Without the least hesitation Joselito took the right-hand path, and Stephen was glad of it. He respected the Dominicans' austere way of life, but he knew just how far Spanish piety could go and he had no wish to share their severity tonight. 'It would not have seemed so far, if I had not been so long at sea,' he said aloud. 'But as it is, I am destroyed entirely. What a delight to think of a good supper, a glass of wine and a warm bed.' The mule caught his cheerfulness if not his literal meaning and pressed on with renewed energy.

It was still only twilight, but darkening fast, when they came to the convent. Outside the grey wall, before the gate, a tall solitary figure was pacing to and fro, and the mule ran the last hundred yards or so, uttering a feeble hoarse noise – he could utter no more – and nuzzled the Vicar-General's shoulder. Father O'Higgins's particularly Irish clerical face, humourless and stern, changed to a look of simple pleasure, much of which remained when he turned to Stephen, now dismounted, and asked him whether he had had a pleasant ride, whether it had not seemed too long, with this untimely wind?

'Not at all, Father,' said Stephen. 'If I had not been so fresh from the sea, with my legs unused to the unyielding ground, it would not have seemed a great way at all, far from it indeed, particularly with so grand and high-stepping a mule as Joselito, God bless him.'

'God bless him,' said Father O'Higgins, patting the mule's withers.

'Yet the wind makes me anxious for those at sea: we can take shelter, where they can not.'

'Very true, very true,' said the priest, and the wind howled over the convent wall. 'Poor souls: God be with them.'

'Amen,' said Stephen, and they walked in.

Compline, at San Pedro's, was traditionally very long, and the choir-monks were still singing the Nunc dimittis when Stephen was woken and led through passages behind the chapel. The pure, impersonal, clear plainchant, rising and falling, moved his sleepy mind: the strong cold east wind outside the postern cleared it entirely.

The path led him and the others, a line of lanterns, over a ridge behind the monastery and down into the high but comparatively fertile plateau beyond – excellent grazing, he had been told – and so towards a large summering-house, a borda or shieling, ordinarily used by those who looked after the flocks. From the low voices before and behind him Stephen gathered that some men must have come in not only after his arrival but after he had gone to bed. Presently he saw a similar line of lanterns coming down from San Pablo, and the two little groups joined in the barn-like shieling, friends recognizing one another with low discreet greetings and feeling their way towards the benches – few lights and those high up.

First there was a long prayer, chanted, to Stephen's surprise, by the ancient prior of the Matucana Capuchins: he had not known that the movement had so wide a base as to reconcile Franciscan and Dominican.

The proceedings themselves did not interest him very much: there was clearly much to be said for admitting Castro; but equally clearly there was much to be said against it. Stephen did not possess enough knowledge either of Castro or of those who were speaking for or against his admission to form an opinion of much value: in any case he did not think it mattered a great deal one way or another. The support or opposition of so ambiguous a character was neither here nor there, now that great armed forces were about to be moved.

He listened to the general line however, sometimes dozing although the backless bench was a cruel seat for his weary frame, until with relief he heard Hurtado's strong soldierly voice: 'No, no, gentlemen, it will not do. There is no trusting a man who watches the cat so long and closely to see which way it will jump. If we succeed he will join us. If we do not he will denounce us. Remember José Rivera.'

'That seems to have settled the question,' reflected Stephen. 'What joy.' And soon after one line set out for San Pedro, another for San

Pablo, lit by a lop-sided moon, which was just as well, the wind being now so strong that lanterns could not be relied on.

Dear bed again, a remote sense of prime being sung; then an Indian lay-brother with a basin of quite warm water; early Mass: and breakfast in the small refectory. His neighbours were the Vicar-General, who greeted him kindly but who was taciturn at most times and even more so in the morning, and Father Gomez, who was not taciturn at all, though from his impassive, markedly Indian face – a brown Roman emperor – he might well have been. He drank a large quantity of maté from a gourd, observing, 'I know, my dear sir, that it is a waste of time trying to wean you from your coffee; but allow me to pass you these dried apricots from Chile. These dried Chilean apricots.' And after another gourd he said, 'I remember too that you spoke of your wish to see the high mountain, and some of the great Inca buildings. This, of course, is not the high mountain; yet it does approach some quite lofty ground – not the puna, you understand, but quite lofty – and my nephew will be here this morning to look at one of our llama stations. If only the weather were not so disagreeable he could show you something of the country. I spoke of you when last we met, and he begged me to present him. "Ah," cried he, clasping his hands, "someone at last who can tell me of the birds of the southern ocean!" '

'I should be charmed to tell him what little I know,' said Stephen. 'And surely the weather is not so very severe?'

'Eduardo would not think so,' replied Father Gomez. 'But then he is a great hunter. And he creeps up mountains through ice and snow: he is made of brass. He had climbed Pinchincha, Chimborazo, Cotopaxi itself.'

Stephen had rarely taken to a new acquaintance as he took to Eduardo. To be sure, he had always liked the friendly, straightforward, wholly unaffected young on those few occasions he had met them, but here these rare and amiable qualities were combined with a deep interest in living things, birds, animals, reptiles, even plants, and a surprising knowledge of those of his own immense and immensely varied country. Not that Eduardo was so very young, either – such a mass of experience could not be accumulated in a few years – but he had retained the directness, modesty and simplicity that so often disappear as time goes on. Furthermore he spoke a perfectly fluent but agreeably accented Spanish filled with pleasant archaisms, which reminded Stephen of the English in the former northern colonies; though Eduardo's language lacked the somewhat metallic overtones of Boston.

They sat in the cloister with their backs to the east wall, and when Stephen had told him all he knew about albatrosses, which was not inconsiderable, he having sat with them for hours at their nesting places on Desolation Island, sometimes lifting them off to look closely at their eggs – all he knew, particularly about their flight, Eduardo spoke with great eagerness of the guacharo, a very singular bird he had discovered in a vast cavern near Cajamarca in the Andes, a vast cavern indeed, but scarcely large enough for the prodigious number of guacharos that tried to get in, so that some were left outside. It was one of these that Eduardo came upon, fast asleep at noon in the darkest place it could find, the hollow underside of a fallen tree, a bird about the size of a crow, something like a nightjar, something like an owl, brown and grey, flecked with white and black, large winged, fast flying. A strictly nocturnal bird, yet feeding solely on oily nuts, seeds and fruit.

'You astonish me,' cried Stephen.

'I too was dumbfounded,' replied Eduardo. 'Yet such is the case. In the season of the year the people of the village climb up to the cave, take all the young they can reach – mere balls of fat – and melt them down for oil, a pure transparent oil which they use for lamps or for cooking. They showed me the cauldron, they showed me the brimming oil-jars, astonished at my ignorance. I went far into the cave, wearing a broad hat against their droppings, and while they screeched and clattered over my head – it was like being in the midst of a huge swarm of bees, gigantic bees, and a din so that one could hardly think – I saw a small forest of wretched light-starved dwarvish trees, sprung from seeds they had voided.'

'Pray tell me of their eggs,' said Stephen, for whom this was a cardinal taxonomic point.

'They are white and unshining, like an owl's, and they have no sharp end. But they are laid in a well-shaped rounded nest made of . . . what is it?' he asked a hovering lay-brother.

'There is a gentleman who would like to see the Doctor,' said the lay-brother, handing a card. It bore an agreed name and Stephen excused himself.

'He is cooling his horse outside the gatehouse,' said the lay-brother.

There were two or three other people doing the same after their ride up the last steep hill and Stephen had to look quite hard before he made out Gayongos in military uniform, cavalry moustache and a great slouch hat, which surprised him, disguise being almost unknown at this level of intelligence; but he had to admit that although unprofessional it was effective. Gayongos had a powerful, well-lathered stone-horse in his hand: the animal had clearly come up the road at a great pace.

'A man called Dutourd has reached Lima from Callao,' he said in a low tone as they walked the horse up and down. 'He is running about saying that he was ill-treated as a prisoner in the *Surprise*: ill-treated and robbed, that Captain Aubrey is not what he seems, that the *Surprise* is not a privateer but a King's ship, and that you are probably a British agent. He has found out some of the French mission and he harangued them in a loud voice in Julibrissin's crowded coffee-house until they became uneasy and walked off. Then he told another tale about an ideal projected republic. He makes a great deal of noise. His Spanish is incorrect but ready enough. He says he is an American, and he had a privateer sailing under American colours.'

'How did he get away, I wonder?' asked Stephen inwardly: the probable answer came at once. 'It is vexing,' he said to Gayongos. 'And at an earlier time it might have been most inconvenient, even disastrous; but now it is of no great consequence. The French will never

take him seriously – will never compromise themselves with such
a talkative enthusiast: with such a fool. He is incapable of keeping
quiet. Nor will anyone else. In any case, I believe things have moved
too far to be affected by his vapours. Consider: any complaint, any
representations that he may make would have to be dealt with by the
civil authorities. In a matter of twenty-four hours or so a military
government will have taken power and until independence is pro-
claimed the civil authorities will not exist.'

'Yes,' said Gayongos. 'That was my view: but I thought you ought to
be told. How did the meeting go?'

'It was decided not to admit Castro.'

Gayongos nodded, but his face was somewhat doubtful as he
remounted. 'What shall I do with Dutourd?' he asked 'Shall I have
him suppressed? He makes *such* a noise.'

'No. Denounce him to the Inquisition,' said Stephen, smiling. 'He
is a most infernal heretic.'

Gayongos however was not much given to merriment and there
was no answering smile on his face as he set off in a shower of small
stones and a cloud of dust for San Pablo, to give his journey another
face. The dust drifted westward, perceptibly slower than it would
have done a few hours earlier.

'Their nest is made of mud,' said Eduardo; and while Stephen was
digesting this he prepared a ball of coca-leaves, passed his soft leather
bag, and observed, 'The wind is dropping somewhat.'

'So it is indeed,' said Stephen, glancing at a group of people, who
had just come into the cloister: early pilgrims were beginning to
arrive in both monasteries. 'I hope you will not find your journey to
the llama-farm too arduous.'

'Oh, not at all: though I thank you for your kindness. I am accustomed to the mountain, even to the puna, the very high mountain;
though I confess that such a blow, at this time of the year and on this
side of the Cordillera, is almost unheard of. How I wish it would drop
a little more – and from the sky I believe it may – so that you might
be induced to come at least as far as Hualpo, our main llama station.'

'Fortified by coca-leaves, I should have no hesitation in setting out within the next quarter of an hour,' said Stephen. 'Once their virtuous principle is infused into my whole being, I shall bare my bosom to the blast with perfect equanimity. It will not be long; already I feel that agreeable insensibility invading my pharynx. But first pray tell me about the llama. I am pitifully ignorant of the whole tribe – have never seen a living specimen and only very few indifferent bones.'

'Well, sir, there are only two wild kinds, the vicuña, a little orange creature with a long silky fleece that lives high up, close to the snow, though sometimes we see a few above Hualpo, and the guanaco. We see some of them too – where would the puma be, were it not for the guanaco? – but they are more usual in Chile and right down to Patagonia. They are more easily tamed than the vicuña, and they are the ancestors of the llama and the alpaca, the llamas being bred for riding and carrying burdens, and the alpaca, smaller animals that we keep higher up, just for wool. Both give quite good meat, of course, though some say not nearly as good as mutton. In my opinion, mutton . . .' He coughed, blew his nose, and rolled another ball of coca-leaves; but to a reasonably attentive, sympathetic listener it was clear that the Inca – for Eduardo was of the pure blood – regarded sheep as an unwelcome Spanish introduction.

This became more apparent later in the day, when they rode eastward across the plateau, and rounding a knoll studded with the tallest many-branched cactuses Stephen had yet seen, came upon a flock gathered in a sheltered hollow, grazing close together, all facing one way. For the last few miles Eduardo had been talking away with the greatest animation, telling Stephen of a white-muzzled bear he had once met in a coca-grove and pointing out a variety of small birds (this country, though bare, was very far from being the desert of the coastal plain), but his cheerful face changed on seeing the flock running away, all in the same direction. 'Sheep. Well may they be called sheep,' he said indignantly, and putting his fingers to his mouth he uttered a piercing whistle which set them running faster still. This brought the Indian shepherds out from behind the rocks and while one, with the dogs, brought the sheep to order, the others raced towards the horses, calling out in submissive tones. But Eduardo rode on, and it was some minutes before he recovered his gaiety, describing the lake of Chinchaycocha, no great way farther to the east, but something of a climb, being at thirteen thousand feet: it was surrounded by reed-beds and it had a wonderful population of water-fowl. 'But unhappily,' he said, 'I know their names only in Quichua, the language of my people: I have found no learned descriptions, with Latin names, genus and species. For example there is a splendid goose we call huachua which has dark green wings, merging to violet . . . '

The plateau broke away in broad sloping terraces to a stream far below, and here the country was richer by far, with stretches of a crop called quinua, a species of chaenopodium, and fields of barley with dry-stone walls – stone in great plenty, lying in shattered heaps – and on the edge of one field a stray sheep. 'Sheep again,' said Eduardo with disapproval. Down the stream, far on the right hand, there was an Indian village, but he turned to the left, telling Stephen a little anx-iously that although the lofty slope on the other side looked high it was not really very steep or far, that the llama-farm was only just over the top – really a little low for llamas – and this path would get them there much quicker.

So it did, but only, as far as Stephen was concerned, at the cost of much gasping and great concentration as he led his horse up the cruel shaley track, keeping up with Eduardo's elastic step as well as he could but necessarily losing his explanation of several small birds and plants and a lizard. Beetles crossed the path unexamined, uncol-lected. As they climbed they were under the lee of the eastern wall: they could hear the wind high overhead but they felt no more than the occasional eddy; and in the still thin clear air the sun beat down. Whenever Eduardo found that he had drawn more than a few yards ahead he paused to cough or blow his nose; and this was the first time Stephen had ever known consideration for his age cause a young man to check his pace. He took another ball of coca-leaves, bent his head and watched his feet. Although his words to Gayongos had been perfectly sound, the wretched Dutourd would thrust his way up into some level of Stephen's mind just below full consciousness, an unreasonable haunting anxiety. Physical exertions helped; the coca-leaves had their usual charming effect; but it was not until a great gust struck him that he realized they were at the top and that the anxiety gave way to a lively interest in the present.

'Here we are,' cried Eduardo. And there they were indeed: massy stone buildings on yet another high plateau, corrals, distant herds, an Indian girl mounted on a llama who threw herself off and came running to kiss Eduardo's knee.

Stephen was led to a respectable barn, seated on a faggot covered with a herb related to lady's bedstraw, and handed a gourd of maté with a silver tube. The Indians were perfectly civil and obliging, but they had no smile for him: this had been the case with all the few Indians he had met: a gloomy nation by all appearances, unsocial, quite withdrawn. It was therefore with some amazement that he observed their delight in Eduardo's presence, their cheerfulness, and even, in spite of their profound respect, their laughter, which he had never heard before. Eduardo spoke to them only in Quichua, which came trippingly off his tongue: he had apologized to Stephen beforehand, saying that most of them did not know Spanish and that some of those who did preferred to conceal their knowledge.

Now, however, turning to Stephen he said in that language, 'Sir, allow me to show you a guanaco in the field outside. He is the wild ancestor of the llama, as you will recall, but this one was caught young, and now he is quite tame.'

'A fine animal,' said Stephen, looking at the slim elegant fawn-coloured white-bellied creature, which held its long neck high and returned his gaze quite fearlessly. 'About twelve hands, I believe.'

'Twelve hands exactly, sir. And here, coming up the path, is our best llama: his name in Quichua means spotless snow.'

'An even finer animal,' said Stephen, turning to watch the llama walk delicately up the path with an Indian boy, balancing its head delicately from side to side. He had barely fixed his attention upon the llama, estimating its height and weight, before the guanaco, gathering itself, bounded forward with both front knees bent and struck him a little below the shoulder-blades, sending him flat on his face.

In the general outcry while Stephen was picked up and dusted and the guanaco led away by the ears, the llama stood unmoved, looking scornful.

'Mother of God,' cried Eduardo, 'I am so sorry, so ashamed.'

'It is nothing, nothing at all,' said Stephen. 'A childish tumble on the grass, no more. Let us ask the llama how he does.'

The llama stood his ground as they approached, eyeing Stephen with much the same look as the guanaco, and when he was well within range, spat in his face. The aim was perfect, the saliva extraordinarily copious.

Outcry and hullabaloo again, but only Eduardo seemed really deeply moved and as Stephen was being washed and wiped he saw two Indian children in the far background fairly twisting themselves double with delight.

'What can I say?' asked Eduardo. 'I am desolated, desolated. It is true they sometimes do that to people who vex them, and sometimes to white men who do not. I should have thought of it . . . but after we had been talking for a while I forgot your colour.'

'May I beg for some maté?' asked Stephen. 'That most refreshing drink.'

'Instantly, instantly,' cried Eduardo, and coming back with the gourd he said, 'Just beyond that small sharp peak is where we keep the alpacas. From there one can sometimes see a band of vicuñas, and quite often too the small fluttering rock-creeper we call a pito; it is no great way, and I had hoped to carry you up there, but now I am afraid it is too late. And perhaps you have had enough of llamas and their kind.'

'Not at all, not at all,' cried Stephen. 'But it is true that I must not be late at the convent.'

Going down, Eduardo grew sadder as they lost height: his spirits declined with the slope of the path, and as they rested among the shattered boulders of another gigantic rock-fall, the result of the most recent earthquake and barely lichened yet, Stephen, to divert his mind, said, 'I was pleased to see your people so happy and gay. I had formed a false notion from my trifling experience in and about Lima, supposing them to be almost morose.'

'A people that has had its ancient laws and customs taken from it, whose language and history count for nothing, and whose temples have been sacked and thrown down is apt to be morose,' replied Eduardo: then, recollecting himself, 'I do not say that this is the state of affairs in Peru; and it would be the grossest heresy to deny the benefits of the true religion: I say only that this is what some of the more obstinate Indians, who may secretly practise the old sacrifices, believe; and – pray do not move,' he said in a low urgent voice, nodding towards the far side of the valley, there where the terraces and fields ran down to the stream. Against the mountain a band of condors were circling, rising, but to no great height; and as Stephen watched, three of them perched on convenient rocks.

'If you train your little spy-glass on the edge of the barley, half-way down,' said Eduardo in little more than a whisper, 'you will see the stray sheep, ha, ha.' Stephen rested the glass in a crack between two rocks, brought the edge of the field into focus, travelled down to a patch of white: but there was a tawny puma covering most of it, slowly eating mutton.

'They often do that,' murmured Eduardo. 'The condors come quite soon after he has killed his prey – they seem to watch him as he travels – and wait until he is gorged. Then he creeps off into shelter and they come down; but he cannot bear seeing them at it – he rushes out – they rise – he eats a little more – retires – and they return. There. He is going off already.'

'Our vultures are more circumspect,' said Stephen. 'They will wait for hours, whereas these are in directly. Lord, how they eat! I should not have missed this for the world. Thank you, my dear Eduardo, for showing me the puma, that noble beast.'

Riding back they discussed the whole event in minute detail – the exact angle and splay of the condors' primaries as they settled on a crag, the movement of their tails, the dissatisfied look on the puma's face when it came back for the third time to nothing but a heap of the larger bones. Having talked themselves hoarse, almost shouting over the declining but still powerful wind, they reached the monastery in reasonable time. Here they supped with a numerous company in the main refectory and Stephen retired to his cell as soon as grace was said.

He had not eaten much, he had drunk less, and now (another usual consequence of ingesting coca) he lay unsleeping, but not unhappy with it, his mind running over the day just past, regretting the untimely though surely unimportant Dutourd but taking much pleasure in the rest. At the same time he followed the chanting of the monks. This particular Benedictine house was unusually rigorous, separating mattins from lauds, singing the first at midnight, a very long service indeed with the full nocturn, lessons and Te Deum, and the second so that its middle psalm coincided with the rising of the sun.

He was in a half sleep, thinking of Condorcet, a very, very much larger man than Dutourd but equally foolish in his regard for that silly villain Rousseau, when his ear caught a footstep in the passage and he was wide awake when Sam came in, holding a shaded candle.

He was about to make some remark in Jack Aubrey's style, such as, 'Have you come up to the monastery, Sam?' when Sam's gravity quenched his smile. 'Forgive me for waking you, sir, but Father O'Higgins begs he might have a word.'

'Certainly he may,' said Stephen. 'Pray pass me my breeches in the corner there. As you see I lie in my shirt.'

'Doctor,' said the Vicar-General, rising and placing a chair, 'you know there is a clandestine French mission to the independentists here?' Stephen bowed. 'They have recently been joined or rather sought out by a noisy talkative enthusiast who has already thrown much discredit on them – I believe they will slip out of the country – and who has almost directly asserted that you are a British agent. It is true that the Holy Office has taken him up for some shocking blasphemies in the style of Condorcet uttered in public, but Castro has already seized upon the event to ingratiate himself with the Viceroy. "Heretical foreign gold" he cries: he has had one small mob bawling outside the British consulate and another has broken the windows of the house where the Frenchmen were staying. Until the Viceroy comes back he can do no more, and General Hurtado will probably knock him on the head tomorrow – I mean reduce him to silence. But the General is not to be found in Lima, nor is he at his brother's: he is much given to gallantry. We shall not see him until the conference at noon, and although I think it is weakness on my part I feel somewhat uneasy. A man of Castro's stamp is incapable of doing much good but he may do a great deal of harm, and I think we were unwise in rejecting him. I tell you these things, because if you share my weakness you may wish to take your measures, in the event of our being right.'

Stephen made suitable acknowledgements and observed, 'As far as regretting the rejection of an unreliable man is concerned, I think you may be mistaken. He could never have been trusted, and he would have come into the possession of a great many names.'

He returned to his cell carrying pens, ink and a quire of paper; and as he went he reflected on the unsoundness of his words. The rest of the night he spent writing. At sun-rise, still not at all sleepy, he folded his papers, put them into his bosom, and walked into the chapel to hear the Benedictus.

In the later part of the morning large numbers of people began to arrive at the two monasteries, many of them pilgrims coming early for the exposition, some of them members of the league, among whom there was a general tendency to silence and anxious looks. Messengers had been posted on the road to intercept General Hurtado with a letter telling him of Castro's activities so that he should be prepared to reassure the meeting and to take instant decisive measures.

He did not come. In his place there appeared Gayongos, old, grey, his face destroyed: he told Stephen, the Vicar-General, Father Gomez and Sam that Hurtado, extremely moved, had declared that with these cries of foreign gold abroad, repeated on every hand, and in this atmosphere of corruption he could not, as a man of honour, consider any further action at this moment.

They wasted no time in expostulation. Stephen asked whether Castro could possibly seize the ship. 'Certainly not,' said Father O'Higgins. 'Not until the Viceroy returns, and even then it is extremely improbable. But he may well risk a provisional arrest of your person on some pretext or other. You must go to Chile. I have prepared a letter to my kinsman Bernardino for you. He will take you to Valparaiso, where you can go on board your ship.'

'Eduardo will show you the way,' said Father Gomez. 'You will be in no danger with him,' he added with a curious smile.

Turning to Gayongos Stephen asked whether any of the actual treasure had been transferred. 'No,' said Gayongos. 'Apart from a few thousands, nothing but drafts on the provisional government. The gold was to have been distributed tomorrow afternoon.'

'Then pray retain it in a readily movable form until you receive word,' said Stephen, and to Sam, 'Father Panda, here is the merest note for Captain Aubrey: he will be in quite soon I am sure and you will explain things far better than I could do.'

They all shook hands, and in the doorway Gayongos said, 'I feel so much for your disappointment. Pray accept this parting gift.' Silent tears, utterly astonishing on that grey, dewlapped face, ran down as he handed Stephen an envelope.

CHAPTER NINE

E arly on Wednesday the east wind, which had been dying all night, at last expired in a peaceful calm: no more whirling dust, no more banging shutters, falling tiles; a blessed quietness. By the time the sun had risen ten degrees or so the sea-breeze began to waft in and by mid-morning it was blowing a moderate gale from the south-west: the *Surprise* could have carried full topsails, but Tom Pullings, less given to cracking on than his Captain, would have had a reef in them.

It blew steadily all that day and the next and on Friday Tom pulled over to San Lorenzo once more, walked across the island and so up to a point below the beacon, from which he commanded an immense stretch of ocean bounded by a hard, unusually distinct horizon.

He swept this clear line with his glass, and there indeed, due west, was what he had been looking for yesterday afternoon and evening, slowly drinking cold tea as he did so – a remote fleck of white in the sun between sea and sky. He climbed up to the beacon itself, sitting where a rock-fall gave him a firm rest for the telescope and focussed with the utmost care. At this height she was already topsails up, with another ship behind her; and well before likelihood became certainty his heart was eased, filled with happiness. She was surely the *Franklin*, and she was bringing in a prize.

Presently, when the sun was hot on the back of his head, she was hull-up, and he was wholly satisfied, head and heart. He had commanded her, and now he could not be mistaken. He might go back to the *Surprise* with an easy mind and sit in peace, admiring her new rigging, all fresh-rove and set up, all blacked where blacking was called for; yards likewise. And he could tell Father Panda.

For days now Tom had been growing more and more worried, with the Doctor away and the Reverend coming every night for news of the Captain, clearly anxious, clearly aware that something ugly was up,

bringing the sick back, advising him to close with the men bargaining for the prizes, to get the barky out of the yard, watered, victualled
and ready to weigh, all shore-leave stopped. And certainly there was
something very odd about the town, with people running about and
behaving strange. Some who had always been civil and more than
civil had grown rather shy. The master of the rope-walk for example:
all smiles and a glass of vino on Sunday, reserved, if not downright
chuff, on Monday. The ship-chandlers and the dockyard people had
become very eager for their money. On the other hand three considerable merchants had come to see him after dark (most visiting
took place by night at present) and had asked him to carry treasure
down to Valparaiso. Mr Adams, who spoke Spanish almost as well
as the Doctor and who managed all business affairs, said that when
the Viceroy came back there would be a fine old rumpus, all Hell to
pay, with people copping it right and left. Quite why he could not tell,
there being so many different rumours; but it seemed that the soldiers had been misbehaving, and perhaps some civilians too.

He reached his boat – the Doctor's skiff, newly painted green –
shoved off and made his way through some small-craft setting lobster-
pots. He had noticed a good many a mile or so offshore, fishing in
their primitive way. Slab-sided objects, and some of them mere dug-
out canoes. There was not a seaman among them, and at no time
did he pay any attention to their more or less facetious cries of 'Spik
English, yis, yis,' 'Marrano,' 'Herético pálido.'

One particularly obstinate bugger, a good way off, in a disgraceful
battered old thing almost the size of a man-of-war's longboat but only
pulling three lackadaisical oars, kept barking like a comic sea-lion,
on and on, anything for a laugh. Pullings frowned and rowed a little
faster, his head turned from the distant boat, a craft of no known
form, with bits and pieces dangling over the gunwale. He was after
all a commander, R.N., by courtesy called Captain; and he was not to
be barked at by a parcel of seals.

As his pace increased so the sea-lions began to bawl out all together
– a pitiful exhibition and much too hoarse to be amusing – but as the

THE WINE-DARK SEA   205

sudden clamour died away a single disgusted voice, not very loud, came clear across the quiet water: 'Oh the fucking sod.'

That was no native cry, no heathen mockery: that was a naval expression, familiar to him from childhood, and uttered in a naval voice. He turned, and with a mixture of horror and delight he saw the massive form of his Captain heaving up for a final hail, clinging to the stump of a mast; and he recognized the shattered hull of the *Alastor*'s launch.

Having whipped the skiff round and come alongside he wasted no time in asking what had happened or telling them they looked terrible, but gave them his bottle of cold tea – they were almost speechless from thirst, lips black, faces inhuman – passed a line and began towing the launch towards the shore.

He rowed with prodigious force, rising on the stretcher and pulling so that the sculls creaked and bent under his hands. He had never seen the Captain look more destroyed, not even after the *Alastor* action: the bloody bandage over his eye had something to do with it, but quite apart from that his bearded face was thin and drawn, barely recognizable, and he moved with difficulty, like an old man, heaving slowly on his oar. From the skiff Pullings looked straight into the launch: the Captain, Darky Johnson and Bonden were doing what they could, labouring with uneven sweeps, roughly shaped from broken spars; Killick was bailing; Joe Plaice and young Ben were stretched out, motionless. The two boats scarcely seemed to move; there were nearly three miles to go, and at this rate they would not be able to go half-way before the ebb set in, carrying them far out to sea.

Yet the *Surprise*, lying there in the road, had three midshipmen aboard, and what they lacked in intelligence they made up for in physical activity. Reade, having but one arm, could no longer go skylarking, hurling himself about the upper rigging regardless of gravity, but his messmates Norton and Wedell would hoist him by an easy purchase to astonishing heights, and from these, having still one powerful hand and legs that could twist round any rope, he would plunge with infinite satisfaction. He was at the masthead, negligently

holding the starboard main topgallant shrouds with the intention of
sliding straight down the whole length of the topgallant backstay, well
over a hundred feet, when his eye, wandering towards San Lorenzo,
caught the odd spectacle of a very small boat trying to tow a much
larger one. Even at this distance the very small boat looked surprisingly like the Doctor's pea-green skiff. Leaning down he called, 'Norton.' 'Ho,' replied his friend. 'Be a decent cove for once and send me
up my glass.'

Norton, an invariably decent cove, did more than that: he swarmed
aloft like an able-bodied baboon, begged Reade to shift over and
make room on his tiny foothold, unslung the telescope and handed
it over, all this with no more gasping than if he had walked up one
pair of stairs. Reade using a telescope from the masthead was a sight
to turn a landsman pale: he had to pull the tubes right out, twist his
one arm through the shrouds, set the small end to his eye and bring
all into focus by a steady pressure. Norton was used to it however
and he only said, 'Let's have a go, mate, when you've done: don't be all
bloody night.'

Reade's reply was a hail as loud as his breaking voice could make
it. 'On deck, there. On deck. Mr Grainger, sir. Right on the beam.
Captain Pullings is trying to tow the *Alastor*'s launch. Launch all
mangled: something cruel. They are bailing: in a bad way. Captain is
pulling, and I can make out Bonden, but . . . '

The rest was drowned in the vehement cry of all hands and the
launching of boats regardless of new paint not yet dry.

The *Alastor*'s launch and the skiff came alongside under the larboard chains, Bonden mechanically hooked on; and as hands ran
down with the man-ropes Pullings came scrambling aft to help his
Captain go aboard. 'Where is the Doctor?' asked Jack, looking up at
the rail.

'He's ashore, sir, and has been these five or six days: he sent to say
he was a-naturalizing in the mountains.'

'Very good,' said Jack, strangely disappointed, aware of an emptiness. He managed to get up the side with a shove, but only just. Even in his present state he loved his ship and he was heartily glad to be alive and aboard her again, but he could not cope with the quarterdeck's awed congratulations nor with the open amazement of all hands before the mast. He went as steadily as he could down the companion-ladder and to his cabin, and when he had drunk four pints of water – more, he thought vaguely, would amount to that excess so fatal to cows, horses and sheep – he looked at Plaice and Ben in their hammocks, washed the filth from his person, threw off his clothes, ate six eggs with soft-tack, followed by a whole water-melon, and stretched out on his cot, his eyes closing as his head went down.

A little after sunset he climbed up from a bottomless sleep, in a ship as silent as the grave, the light fading fast. He gathered himself into the present, collecting the immediate past, thanked God for his delivery, and then said, 'But what's amiss? Am I really here and alive?' He moved, feeling himself: the weakness was authentic, so was his gummed-up, itching eye and his unshaven face. So was his consuming thirst. 'Ahoy, there,' he called, but without much conviction.

'Sir?' cried Grimble, Killick's mate.

'Light along a jug of water, just tinged with wine.' And when he had drained it he asked, gasping, 'Why is the ship so quiet? No bells. Is anyone dead?'

'No, sir. But Captain Pullings said any sod as woke you should have a hundred lashes.'

Jack nodded and said, 'Let me have some warm water, and pass the word for Padeen and the Doctor's young man.'

They came, but a grim, bent Killick came hobbling in with them and for a moment Jack thought he would have to top it the Tartar, which he could hardly bear: he had under-estimated their kindness, however, for without any wrangling they divided the task. Padeen, the acknowledged surgical dresser, very gently removed the soaking bandage; Fabien replaced the exhausted salves with others from the medicine-chest; Killick applied them, stating that as far as he could see in this light the eye had not suffered but that he would give a considered judgment come the morning; and Padeen dressed the place again. 'Will I shave you at all, sir dear?' he asked. 'Sure you would lay . . . lay . . .'

'More easy,' said Killick.

Shaved and looking almost like a man that might live, Jack received Pullings at the setting of the watch. 'How do you feel, sir?' asked Tom in a hushed voice.

'Pretty well, I thank you,' said Jack. 'But tell me, have you had any word of Dutourd?'

'Dutourd? No, sir,' said Tom, amazed.

'He has contrived to run, stowing away either in the launch or possibly the *Alastor* herself. The Doctor told me to keep him aboard, and we must get him back.'

'How shall we set about it, sir?' asked Pullings.

'That indeed is a question. Perhaps the Doctor will come back tonight. Perhaps I shall be cleverer in the morning. But meanwhile, how does the barky come to look so trim and spry? How does she come to be out of the yard so soon?'

'Why, sir,' said Pullings, laughing. 'We were all very much at sea, our notions all ahoo. When the shipwrights had her clear, all we found was a stretch of copper clean gone, not much bigger than that table – a whale, no doubt. But the worm had been at it quite amazingly. It still kept the water out, more or less, but all the members around it worked something horrid in anything of a sea. They cut the whole piece back to sound wood, replaced it as pretty as ever Pompey could have done, and clapped on new copper twice as thick as ours. There were those few knees that we knew about and some we did not; but the wrights were honest fellows – they made little of it – and now we are as stiff as ever you could wish.'

'Just where . . .' began Jack, but on deck the cry 'The boat ahoy. What boat is that?' interrupted him.

'I dare say that will be Father Panda,' said Pullings. 'He usually comes about this time, asking for news of you.'

'Does he, Tom?' cried Jack, flushing. 'Let him be brought below at once. And Tom, keep the after part of the quarterdeck clear, will you?'

'Of course, sir,' said Pullings: and inclined his head to catch the deep, resonant answer to the frigate's hail; he said, 'That's him, all right. Perhaps he may be able to tell us how to get hold of Dutourd.' During the inexpert thumping and rattling of the boat along the side and the cries of 'Ship your oar, sir – clap on to the painter, Bill – here's t'other man-rope, Father: hold tight' he said, 'Oh sir, I forgot to tell you *Franklin* is in the offing with what looks like a prize. I will go and bring the Reverend below.'

Sam was even taller and more massive than when he and his father had last met. Jack rose with a double effort, put his hands on those broad shoulders, and said, 'Sam, how very glad I am to see you.'

Sam's great flashing smile lit up his face and he, clasping Jack, cried, 'Oh sir . . .' Then his expression changed to one of the utmost concern as he saw the bandage and he went on, 'But you are wounded – you are ill – let you sit down.' He guided Jack to his chair, lowered him gently into it, and sat under the hanging lamp gazing at him, drawn, lined and ravaged as he was, with such troubled affection that Jack said, 'Never take on so, dear Sam. My eye is all right, I believe – I can see pretty well. And for the rest, we had a rough time of it on a lee-shore in the *Alastor*'s launch during the easterly blow – she was stove, dismasted – lost our food and water – nothing to eat but a raw sea-lion. We had been forced back past the sea-lion island seven times and I said, "Shipmates, if we don't get round and run clear on this tack we shall have a dirty night of it." Well, we did get round, but we did not run clear. There was a reef on the far side and in avoiding it we became embayed – a lee-shore in a strong gale – heavy seas, tide and current all setting us in – grapnel coming home. We had our dirty night, true enough, but it lasted four mortal days. However, we patched her up more or less – brought her in – it is all over now – and we have earned a thundering good supper.' He pulled the bell and called for the best supper the ship and his cook could produce. But to his distress he saw tears running down that ebony face, and to change the current of Sam's thoughts he said, 'Have you seen the Doctor? I had hoped he would be aboard, but he has not yet returned.'

'Sure I have seen him, sir. I am after leaving him in the mountain.'

'He is quite well? I am so happy. I was anxious for him.'

The first part of the supper came in, cold things the Captain's cook had under his hand with the ship lying off a plentiful market: roast beef yielded up by the gunroom with barely a sigh, chickens, capons, ducks, ham, quantities of vegetables and a great bowl of mayonnaise, decanters of Peruvian wine, a jug of barley-water that Jack emptied without thinking of it. He ate voraciously, swallowing as fast as a wolf; but he both talked at quick intervals between bites and listened. 'We had a prisoner called Dutourd,' he said, spreading butter on his soft-tack. 'We took him out of the *Franklin*, a privateer under American colours. He was a Frenchman with enthusiastic visionary notions about an ideal community in a Polynesian island – no Church, no King, no laws, no money, everything held in common, perfect peace and justice: all to be accomplished, as far as I could make out, by the wholesale slaughter of the islanders. He was a wealthy man, the Doctor told me, and I think he owned the *Franklin*, but that was not clear: at all events he had no letter of marque though he or his skipper had preyed on our whalers and strictly I should have carried him back to England, where they would have hanged him for piracy. I did not like him at all, neither his ideas nor his manners – a confident scrub, very much the foreigner. But he did have some qualities; he was coura-geous and he was good to his people; and it seemed to me – Sam, the bottle stands by you – that piracy where he was concerned was too much like a lawyer's quibble, so I meant to put him ashore here and let him go on parole. He was what is ordinarily called a gentleman: an educated man with money, at all events.' He set about the cold roast beef, and when he had filled their plates he went on, 'An educated man: he knew Greek – you know Greek, Sam, I am sure?'

'A little, sir. We are obliged to, you know, the New Testament being written in Greek.'

'In Greek?' cried Jack, his fork poised in the air. 'I had no idea. I thought it would naturally be written in – what did those wicked Jews speak?'

'Hebrew, sir.'

'Just so. But, however, they wrote it in Greek, the clever dogs? I am amazed.'

'Only the New Testament, sir. And it was not quite the same as Homer or Hesiod.'

'Oh, indeed? Well, I dined in the gunroom one day when he was also invited, and he told the company about those Olympic games.' He gazed round the almost empty table, filled Sam's glass, and said, 'I wonder what comes next.'

Beef steak and mutton chops came next, hot and hot, and a dish of true potatoes, fresh from their native Andes.

'... Olympic games and how they valued the prizes. There was one of these Seven Sages, you know, a cove by the name of Chilon, whose son gained one, and the old gentleman, the Sage, I mean, died of joy. I remembered him and his mates – one of my very few pieces of classical learning – because when I was a little chap they gave me a book with a blue cover and a cut of the Seven Sages in it all looking very much alike, that I had to learn out of; and it began *First Solon, who made the Athenian laws; Then Chilon, in Sparta, renowned for his saws.* But surely, Sam, dropping down dead shows a very wrong set of ideas in a sage?'

'Very wrong indeed, sir,' said Sam looking at his father with great affection.

'To be sure, he was only a sort of ironmonger, but even so ... I once had a splendid filly that I hoped might win the Oaks; but if she had, I hope I should not have dropped down dead. In fact she never ran, and now I come to think of it the Doctor suspected that her lack of barrel betrayed a want of bottom. Yes. But in my pleasure at being in your company, and eating and drinking at last, I talk too much, almost like that French scrub Dutourd; and when you are fagged the wine goes to your head, so I wander from the point.'

'Not at all, sir. Not at all, at all. Will I help you to a chop?'

'By all means. Well, the point is this: when we were lying off Callao I happened to tell the Doctor that I was sending some French prisoners in. "Not Dutourd?" cried he, and then in a low voice, "That might be impolitic." Now this is rather delicate and I am puzzled quite how to put it. Let us eat our pudding, if we are allowed any pudding on such short notice, and when we reach port perhaps my intellects will shine out afresh.'

They were allowed pudding, but only apologetical fancies such as sago, summer's pudding made with what Peru could afford, and mere rice, rather than those true puddings based on suet, which called for hours and hours in the copper.

Jack told Sam of a fine great sago-palm forest in the island of Ceram in which he had walked with his midshipmen and how they had laughed at the spectacle – a sago-forest! These trifles, barely worth attention, were soon dispatched; the cloth was drawn, the port set on Jack's right hand, and Grimble was told that he might turn in.

'Well, now, Sam,' said Jack. 'You must know that when the Doctor goes ashore it is not always just for botanizing or the like. Sometimes it is rather more in the political line, if you follow me. For example, he is very much against slavery; and in this case he might encourage people of the same opinion here in Peru. Certainly, by all means, very praiseworthy: but the authorities might take it amiss – the authorities in a slave-state might take it amiss. So when he said it would perhaps be impolitic for Dutourd, who knows his opinions, to be set ashore he may very well have seen the man as an informer. And there are other aspects that I will not touch upon: shoal water that I am not acquainted with, shoal water and no chart. But to come to the point at last – Sam, you must forgive me for being so slow, roundabout and prosy: I find it hard to concentrate my mind this evening. But the point is this: Dutourd has contrived to get ashore. I am very much afraid he may do the Doctor harm, and I mean to do everything I can to get the fellow back on board. I beg you will help me, Sam.'

'Sir,' said Sam. 'I am yours to command. The Doctor and I understand one another very well where his present activities are concerned. He has consulted me to some extent. I too am very much opposed to slavery and to French domination; so are many men I know; and as you say there are other aspects. As for the miserable Dutourd, I am afraid he is beyond our reach, having been taken up by the Holy Office last Saturday. He is now in the Casa de la Inquisición, and I fear things will go very badly for him, once the questioning has finished; he was a most publicly violent blasphemous atheistical wretch. But he has already done all the harm he could do. The Doctor's friends had arranged a change in government, and since the Viceroy was away everything was moving rapidly and smoothly towards the desired end, troops were being moved and bridges secured, all the necessary precautions for a peaceful change, when Dutourd appeared. He said the Doctor was an English agent and that the whole operation was set a-going with the help of English gold by purchased traitors. Nobody took much notice of such an enthusiast, a Frenchman into the bargain, stained with the crime of their revolution and Napoleon's against the Pope. But a vile official, one Castro, the black thief, thought he might seize upon it to curry favour with the Viceroy, and he made a great noise, hiring a mob to shout in the streets and stone foreigners. The whole city was alive with it. The chief general cried off; the movement collapsed; and his friends advised the Doctor to leave the country at once. He is in the far mountains by now, travelling with a sure experienced guide towards Chile, which has a separate government. We consulted together before he left, and it was agreed that I should tell you he would do his utmost to be in Valparaiso by the last day of next month, staying either with the Benedictines or with don Jaime O'Higgins. Obviously he cannot travel so far over such a country in that period, but once he is in Chile we hope that he will be able to travel on by a series of small coasting vessels from one little port or fishing village to another and so reach Valparaiso in good time. We further agreed, sir, that until the Viceroy's return, which will be in three or four days now, you need have no fear for the ship, and even then direct seizure is unlikely. But we were told on good authority that you would be well advised to move her out of the yard – as indeed Captain Pullings has done – to avoid any vexatious measures, such as detention for some alleged debt or the like. For example a woman is prepared to swear that Joseph Plaice, a member of your crew, has got her with child. Then again our confidential friends, men of business, all assert that you should sell your prizes directly, or if the offer do not suit, send them down to Arica or even Coquimbo. Or even Coquimbo,' repeated Sam in the all-pervading silence. 'But I will tell it you all again, so I will, at half eight tomorrow,' he whispered. 'God bless, now.'

Sam was an even larger man than his father, but he could move even more quietly. Rising now he moved back towards the door, opened it without a sound, stood there for a moment listening to Jack's long, even breathing, and vanished into the shadowy half-deck.

After a week or ten days of steady up and down, but very much more up than down, Stephen was of opinion that his head and lungs had adapted themselves to the thin air of the mountains. He had, after all, walked and ridden all day from their last night's resting-place, rising through the high alpine pastures to perhaps nine thousand feet without discomfort. Admittedly he could not have kept up, hour after hour, with the deep-chested Indians – several of them Aymaras from Eduardo's native Cuzco – who led the train of pack-llamas up the interminable slopes, many of them so desperately barren; yet when he dismounted and walked out with Eduardo over some promising stretch of country he did so as nimbly as if he were treading the Curragh of Kildare.

Three times that day, and at ever-increasing heights, they had left their mules in the hope of a partridge or a guanaco, and three times they had caught up with the llamas not indeed empty-handed, since

Stephen carried a beetle or a low-growing plant for the pack of the animal that carried their collections, but without any sort of game, which meant that their supper would be fried guinea-pig and dried potatoes once more; and each time Eduardo had said that this was a strange, unaccountable year, with weather that made no sense and with animals abandoning customs and territories that had remained unchanged since before the days of Pachacutic Inca. To prove his point on the third occasion he led Stephen to a heap of dung, wonderfully unexpected and even homely in so desolate a landscape, a heap six feet across and several inches high in spite of weathering. Stephen looked at it attentively – ruminants' droppings without a doubt – and Eduardo told him that guanacos always came to the same place to defecate, came from a great way off – it was a natural law among them – but here, in this ancestral heap (so useful as fuel) nothing whatsoever had been deposited for months: the whole surface and the periphery were old, worn, and perfectly dry.

This subversion of all that was right, and the shame of promising birds and beasts that did not appear, made Eduardo as nearly morose as his cheerful, sanguine nature would allow, and for part of the afternoon they rode in silence. During this long stretch, when the faint track rose steadily through broken rocky country towards a far high rounded crest, the train moved on with barely a sound. The Indians, whose high-arched noses and large dark eyes made them look quite like their llamas, talked little, and that in low voices: during all this time Stephen had not been able to establish human relations with a single one of them, any more than he had with their animals, and this in spite of the fact that they were together day and night, since Eduardo kept to remote trails far from all towns and frequented roads, the llamas carrying everything needed for their journey. It is true that they had seen two very long caravans carrying ore down from the isolated mines right up just under the snow-line, but these only accentuated their loneliness, not unlike that of a ship in mid-ocean. One slight consolation was that by now only a few of the more froward llamas spat at him. Up and up: up and up: with his eyes fixed, unseeing, on the gravelly soil and thin grass of the track as it flowed steadily beneath his larboard stirrup (a great hollowed block of wood) Stephen's mind floated off ten thousand miles to Diana and Brigit. How did they do? Was it right in a man to marry and then to sail off to the far side of the world for years on end?

An Aymara Indian of a superior kind with a red worsted cap struck him sharply on the knee, speaking in a severe, disapproving tone and pointing. 'Don Esteban,' called Eduardo again from some little way ahead, 'we are almost on the edge of the puna. If you would like to dismount I believe I could really show you something this time.'

Stephen looked up. Immediately ahead was a low red cliff and on its top the rounded crest towards which they had been travelling so long, now suddenly quite close. They must have mounted another two or three thousand feet, he reflected, taking notice of the still thinner air, the sharper cold. 'We will join them round the next bend,' said Eduardo, leading him towards a shaley path up the cliff while the llamas carried on along the trail, quite broad and distinct at this point.

'This was no doubt a mine,' observed Eduardo, pointing to a tunnel and a spoil-heap. 'Or an attempt at a mine.' Stephen nodded. They had passed no mountain, however bare, remote, waterless and inaccessible, without the mark of men having been there, searching for gold, silver, copper, cinnabar or even tin. He said nothing. His heart was already beating so as to fill his bosom, leaving no room for breath. He reached the top, but only just, and stood there controlling or trying to control his violent gasps while Eduardo named the great shining snowy peaks that soared on either hand and in front, all rising like islands from an orange belt of cloud, one behind the other, brilliant in the cold transparent air. 'Now,' he said, turning to Stephen, 'I believe I shall take your breath away.'

Stephen gave a weak, mechanical smile and followed him carefully over the tufts of coarse yellow grass. Trees had been left behind long, long ago, and here there was not even a hint of a bush, not even of a prostrate bush, only the near-sterility of ichu grass stretching away and away for ever over this high stark plateau. The ground looked flat but in fact it rose and fell, and pausing by a rocky outcrop Eduardo gave Stephen a significant, triumphant look. Stephen, half blind by now, followed his gaze down the slope and to his utter amazement he saw a scattered grove of what for a moment he took to be thick-stemmed palm-trees about fifteen feet high: but some of them had a great solid spike rising as much again above the palm-like crown.

He ran unsteadily to the nearest. The leaves were like those of an agave, fierce-pointed and with hooked thorns all along their sides: the great spike was an ordered mass of close-packed flowers, pale yellow, thousands and thousands of them. 'Mother of God,' he said. And after a while, 'It is a bromeliad.'

'Yes, sir,' said Eduardo, delighted, proprietorial. 'We call it a puya.'

'Ruiz did not know it. Nowhere is it described, still less figured in the *Flora Peruvianae et Chilensis*. What would Linnaeus have made of such a plant? Oh, oh!' he cried, for there, as incongruous in this severity as the bromeliad, flew or rather darted minute green hummingbirds, hovering at an open flower, sipping its honey, flashing on to the next, taking no notice of him whatsoever.

A week later and two thousand feet higher Stephen and Eduardo walked out across the flank of a quiescent volcano at a fine brisk pace: on the left hand a chaos of rocks, some enormous; on the right a vast sweep of volcanic ash, old settled ash, now just blushing green from a recent shower. They were carrying their guns, for in the puna beyond this chaos there was a possibility of Eduardo's partridges; but their main purpose was to contemplate a lofty rock-face with an inaccessible ledge upon which the condor had nested in the past and might well be nesting now.

They threaded the chaos, and although the north-facing boulders were coated with old ice they found several interesting plants among them as well as some droppings that Eduardo pointed out as being those of a vicuña.

'How do they differ from those of a guanaco?' asked Stephen.

'Apart from the fact that they lie separately rather than in a family heap, I should find it difficult to say,' replied Eduardo. 'But if you were to see the two side by side you would distinguish them at once. This is low for a vicuña, however; he must have come down for the fresh green on the other side.'

'Perhaps we may get a shot at him,' said Stephen. 'You yourself said that you were tired of fried guinea-pig and ham.'

'So I did,' said Eduardo, and then, hesitantly, 'But, dear don Esteban, it would grieve me if you were to kill him. The Incas have always protected the vicuña and even the Spaniards leave him alone in general. My followers would take it very ill.'

'Sure, he is safe from me. Yet my best poncho is made from vicuña's wool.'

'Certainly. They are killed from time to time, and by certain people . . . There is our condor.'

There he was indeed, black in a dark blue sky, wheeling towards his still-distant cliff. They watched him out of sight. Stephen did not return to the vicuña: Eduardo was embarrassed and there was obviously some question of the old ways here. He and his followers were no doubt practising Catholics, but this did not prevent them from dipping one finger in their cup and holding it up to thank the sun before drinking, as their ancestors had done time out of mind; and there were other ceremonies of the same nature. 'As you know,' said Eduardo, 'the chick cannot fly until his second year; so if he is there, and if the light is what I could wish, we may see him peering over the edge.'

'Could we not climb up and look down on him?'

'Heavens, no,' cried Eduardo. 'We should never get down before sunset; and it is terrible to be caught by night on the puna. Do but think of the terrible evening winds, the terrible morning winds, and the wicked cold – nothing to eat, nothing to drink, no shelter at all.'

Stephen was thinking of these things as they walked across an accidented stretch of country when, rounding a tumble of rock, they heard the squealing neigh of a guanaco. They stopped short, and there on the left hand stood the guanaco they had heard, while still farther to the left a string of others fled at a great pace, vanishing down the slope.

The guanaco neighed again, louder, still more shrill, stamped the tall spiky ichu grass with his front feet and began rearing and waving his head in a great passion, never yielding a foot as they approached.

'He is challenging you,' said Eduardo. 'He has been fighting – look at the blood on his sides. He may attack you presently. You could not ask for a better shot; nor a better supper.'

'But I must not shoot him?'

'Why, don Esteban,' cried Eduardo, 'how can you speak so? He is no vicuña – he is much too big for a vicuña, and the wrong colour – he is a guanaco, and a perfectly fair quarry for you.'

Stephen's piece had one barrel loaded with shot, the other with ball: he knelt, which enraged the guanaco, took careful aim, and fired. The animal, struck in the heart, gave a great bound and disappeared, apparently collapsing in the long grass.

'The first day we eat steaks, minced very fine,' said Eduardo as they hurried up the slope. 'The next day, in the sun, his shoulders grow quite tender.' Eduardo could be as cheerful as any European, but it was clearly part of his ancestral code to show no adverse emotion: a Stoic calm. Yet now his look of eager expectation changed to one of plain blank undisguised dismay. The guanaco had in fact been capering on the edge of a chasm and its convulsive leap had carried it over.

Two hundred feet below them he lay, and the cliff dropped sheer. They pondered, searching in vain for any way down; they measured the declining sun, the shadows rising below them; unwillingly they turned, and as they turned first the male condor and then his mate began their first wheeling sweeps high overhead.

Another day, on the high puna yet again, coming back from a small alpine lake, the source of a stream that eventually flowed into the Amazon and so on to the Atlantic (though from here on clear mornings they could make out the gleam of the South Sea), a lake on whose frozen bank Eduardo had shown Stephen that handsome goose the huachua with a white body and dark green wings, they paused in still another group of puyas, some of them growing among rocks so conveniently placed that Stephen was able to gather seed from the lower flower. It was late, but for once the evening was as calm as the day, and the llama-train was clearly in sight on the trail below.

'Let us walk down wide,' said Eduardo, looking to his flint. 'I still have hopes.'

'Very well,' said Stephen, and they went down the slope abreast, twenty yards apart. When they were a stone's throw from the trail a fair-sized bird sprang from a tuft with a whirr of wings. It was clearly Eduardo's bird and he fired, hitting it so hard that it bounced again. 'There,' he cried, as happy as a boy, 'here is my partridge at last: or at least what the Spaniards call a partridge.'

'A very handsome bird, too, so it is,' said Stephen, turning it over and over. 'And to be sure there is a superficial resemblance to a partridge: though I doubt it is a gallinaceous bird at all.'

'So do I. We call it and its cousin tuya.'

'I believe it is one of Latham's tinamous.'

'I am sure you are right. A very curious thing about the tuya is that the cock-bird broods the eggs, sometimes the eggs of several hens, like the rhea. Possibly there is some connection.'

'Sure the bill is not unlike . . . But you will never tell me you have rheas at this exorbitant height?'

'We certainly have, and higher still. Not the blundering great rheas of the pampas, but fine grey birds that stand no more than four feet high and run like the wind. God willing I shall bring you in sight of some on the altiplano, soon after we leave the monastery.'

'How good and kind you are, dear Eduardo. I look forward to it with the keenest anticipation,' said Stephen; and having felt the bird's skeleton under its plump breast, 'I fairly long to dissect him.'

'That would mean fried guinea-pig again,' observed Eduardo.

'Not if we confine our attention to his bones,' said Stephen. 'A bird, very gently seethed for some hours, will always leave his bones in the pot. You will say that his flesh is not that of the same bird roasted, which is very true; but how much better, even so, than our eternal guinea-pig.'

The monastery of which Eduardo had spoken was five days journey to the south-east, but the prospect of the altiplano rheas, the salt lakes with their different kinds of flamingo, and the unending deserts of pure white salt itself lent Stephen Maturin wings and, helped by unnaturally kind weather, they reached the high lonely mission in four although they were loaded with the spoils of Lake Titicaca – the skins of two flightless grebes, two different species of ibis, a crested duck and some rails, together with plants and insects.

Eduardo and his train appeared well after what little dusk there was in such a latitude and at such a height. They had to hammer on the outward gate and bawl a great while before it opened; and when at last they were admitted, worried and discontented looks received them. The building had been a mission belonging to the Society of Jesus until that order was suppressed; now it was inhabited by Capuchins, and the friars, though no doubt good-hearted, pious men, lacked both the learning and the dissimulation often attributed to the Jesuits. 'We did not expect you until tomorrow,' said the Prior. 'Today is Wednesday, not Thursday,' said the Sub-Prior. 'There is nothing to eat,' said a friar in the dim background. 'Juan Morales was to bring up a roasted pig tomorrow, and several hens – why did you not send to say you were coming today?' 'If you had sent yesterday morning we could have asked Black Lopez to tell Juan to bring the hog up today.' 'Black Lopez was going down in any case.' After a silence the Brother Porter said, 'Well, there may be a few guinea-pigs left in the scriptorium.' 'Run, Brother Jaime,' cried the Prior. 'Let us lift up our hearts. And at least there is always some wine.'

' "There is always some wine," cried the Prior, my dear,' wrote Stephen, 'and I cannot tell you how well it went down. Nor can I tell you how much I look forward to the next few days, when my amiable companion promises me the wonders of the altiplano, perhaps even of the edge of the Atacama, where rain falls but once in a hundred years. He has already shown me little bright green parakeets in the desolation of bare rock at fifteen thousand feet, mountain viscachas, fat creatures like rabbits with a squirrel's tail that live among the boulders, piping and whistling cheerfully, and many other delights in those prodigious solitudes with snowy peaks on every hand, some of them volcanoes that glow red by night; and he promises more to come, for extreme conditions beget extremities in every form of life. I could however wish that one of the extremities was not the guinea-pig or cavy. He is neither beautiful nor intelligent, and he is the most indifferent eating imaginable – barely edible at all, indeed, after the first half dozen braces. Unhappily he is readily domesticated; he dries, smokes or salts easily; and he can be carried for ever in this dry, dry cold air – a cold air in which the native potato too can be and alas is dried, frozen, dried again and so packed up. I have tried to make this dish a little more palatable by adding mushrooms, our ordinary European mushrooms, Agaricus campestris, which to my perfect stupefaction I found growing here in alpine meadows: but my dear companion told me I should certainly drop down dead, his followers too assured me and one another that I should swell, then drop down dead; and it angered them so when I survived a week that Eduardo had to beg me to stop – I might bring misfortune upon the whole company. They look upon me as an unwholesome being: and I must admit that I cannot congratulate them upon their looks either. At this height, in this cold, and with the incessant effort, their faces grow blue, a dull and somewhat uninviting leaden blue.' He reflected upon these Indians and upon Eduardo for a while, dipped his pen again and wrote, 'Will I tell you two things now before I forget them? The first is that there are no ill smells up here, no smells at all. The second – ' He dipped his pen again, but now the ink had frozen, which did not surprise him; and gathering his vicuña poncho round his meagre form he walked off to his bed, where, when a certain slight degree of warmth had gathered round him, he lay thinking of Eduardo and their conversations all that afternoon as they climbed steadily from La Guayra.

Eduardo had given a detailed account of Pachacutic Inca, the first great conqueror, and of his family down to Huayna Capac, the Great Inca, to Atahualpa, strangled by Pizarro, and the Inca Manco, Eduardo's ancestor, and of the many still-existing collateral families descending from Huayna Capac. It did not surprise Stephen to hear of bitter enmity between cousins, nor of feuds lasting from the earliest times to the present, nor indeed of brother murdering brother – there were after all well-established precedents – but it did surprise him after a while to find that the general drift of his friend's conversation seemed more and more to be in the direction of outside support for one particular branch of the royal line, so that it might neutralize the other Quechua clans and unite a sufficient force of Indians and well-wishers to liberate at least Cuzco, their ancestral home. It surprised him because he would have sworn that a man of Eduardo's intelligence must have seen the impossibility of such a scheme – the unbelievable number of totally conflicting interests – the extreme unlikelihood of reconciliation between the hostile groups – the wretched outcome of Tupac Amaru's rising not long since, drowned in blood by the Spaniards with the help of other Indians, some of the royal blood. He concealed his surprise, but he let the words flow past his ears, deliberately forgetting to record the genealogies, the names of those likely to support the cause, and of those already committed.

Yet as he lay there unsleeping in the cold his perversely retentive memory rehearsed these lists, and he was still with the descendants of Huascar Inca when a barefoot friar came in with a charcoal brazier and asked him whether he was awake, because if he was, the Prior thought he might like to join them in a novena addressed to Saint Isidore of Seville, begging for his intercession in favour of all travellers.

Returning to his now warmer room from this exercise Stephen fell into a dreaming sleep: Diana, sentenced to death for some unques-

tioned murder, stood before the judge in an informal court, guarded
by a civil but reserved jaileress. She was wearing a nightgown, and the
judge, a well-bred man obviously embarrassed by the situation and
by his task, was slowly tying a hangman's knot in a fine new piece of
white cordage. Diana's distress increased as the knot reached completion; she looked at Stephen, her eyes darkening with terror. He could
do nothing.

Still another barefoot friar, looking casually into his cell, expressed
some astonishment that Stephen should not yet have joined don Eduardo and his company. They were there in the courtyard, the pack
llamas already loaded and the sun rising over Anacochani.

So it was: yet the western sky was still dark violet at the lower rim
and as he looked at it Stephen remembered the words he had intended
to write to Diana before he put his letter to the candle: 'in this still
cold air the stars do not twinkle, but hang there like a covey of plan-
ets,' for there they were, clear beads of unwinking gold. He could not
relish them however; his dream still oppressed him, and he had to
force a smile when Eduardo told him he had reserved a piece of bread
for their breakfast instead of dried potatoes, a piece of *wheaten* bread.

The high querulous voice of the llamas as they set off, the steady
clop of his mule striding along the road, the glorious day rising huge
overhead in a sky of immeasurable height, and on every hand brown
mountains capped with white, the thin and piercing air growing
warm as the sun climbed well above the peaks.

Nobody spoke much; nor would they do so until the warmth and
the exercise had loosened their powerful chests – the breath still
came steaming from them all and all seemed totally absorbed by
their own reflections. Yet the train had not gone two miles or three
before a long wavering Aymara howl stopped each man in his stride.

It was a short stocky Indian just coming into sight behind them,
rounding a curve in the mountain-side. He was a great way off, but in
this brilliant clarity Eduardo at once said 'Quipus'; on either side of
him his followers murmured 'Quipus.'

'I am sure you have often seen quipus, don Esteban?' said Eduardo.

'Never in life, my dear,' replied Stephen.

'You will see them presently,' said Eduardo, and they watched the far small man as he came running steadily along the track, his coloured staff rising and falling. 'They are knotted cords and thin strips of cloth: our kind of writing, concise, ingenious, secret. I am a sinful creature, but on no more than a few inches I can record all I must remember at confession; and only I can read it, since the first knot gives the clue to all the rest.'

The messenger came running along the line; his face was blue, but his breath was even, unhurried. He kissed Eduardo's knee, unwound the coloured cords and strips from his staff and handed them up. The train moved on; Stephen gathered his reins. 'No,' said Eduardo. 'Pray watch. You will see me read them as quick as a clearly-written letter.'

This he did, but as he read his expression changed. His pleasant ingenuous young face closed and at the end he said, 'I beg your pardon, don Esteban: I had thought it was just my agent in Cuzco asking whether he might send a draft of llamas to Potosí, this being the runner who usually brings his messages. But now it is quite another matter. We must go no farther south. Gayongos has a ship for Valparaiso that will touch at Arica. We must cut across by the Huechopillan . . . it is a high pass, don Esteban, but *you* will not mind a high pass. I am very sorry I must forego the pleasure of showing you the rheas of the altiplano this time and the great wastes of salt; but not far from the Huechopillan there is a lake on which I can almost promise you some most uncommon ducks and geese: gulls too and rails. Forgive me.' He spurred along the track, and as Stephen slowly followed he heard him giving orders that sent three quarters of the train back along the road, such as it was.

Stephen was intimately convinced that the quipus had brought news of some hostile cousins waiting for Eduardo in the context of that movement for liberation he had touched upon the day before as well as word of Gayongos's ship, which might more sensibly have put in a little farther south, in the realm of Chile. For Arica, as both he and Eduardo knew, was still in the government of Peru: yet pointing out the obvious could only cause distress, fruitless argument, bad blood.

The greater part of the returning band fiowed round him as he sat there on his mule, passing silently, with apparent indifference or at the most a certain veiled disapproval. Riding on to join those who remained he saw Eduardo's face, impassive and firmly in command, though his eyes sometimes wandered towards Stephen with some hint of anxious questioning. Stephen still said nothing, yet he did observe that now their company was made up of the abler-looking (and indeed more amiable) men leading the stronger beasts, and they with larger packs. On, and within half an hour their quiet rhythm had returned.

At noon they were on a broad stony platform, bare flat rock at the convergence of three mountain spurs, hot in the sun; and here their track could no longer be seen at all. Yet neither Eduardo nor his men seemed in any way concerned; they marched steadily across and turned right-handed where the westernmost spur ran down to the little plain, travelling steadily on through a sheltered and relatively fertile stretch of country, green here and there with tola bushes and shaggy with coarse yellow grass.

The going was easier, much clearer in direction and smoother by far. 'We have struck into one of the Inca post-roads,' said Eduardo, breaking the silence. 'In a little while, where there is marshy ground by day, it is paved. My ancestors may not have known the wheel, but they did know how to make roads. Beyond the marshy piece, where we may put up some wildfowl, there is a great tumble of boulders from an earthquake so long ago that they are covered with lichen, and not only lichen but a very curious woody fungus that I believe you may not have seen. It is called yaretta, and it grows at this height from here to the westward; and together with guanaco dung the heads make excellent firing. The rock-fall abounds with viscachas, and if we take our guns we may be spared guinea-pig for a great while: viscachas are capital eating. But Doctor, I am afraid you are sad. I am so sorry to have disappointed you of our altiplano rheas.'

'I am not at all disappointed, friend. I have seen a little flock of white-winged finches and a bird I took to be a mountain caracara.'

Eduardo was unconvinced. He looked into Stephen's face and said, 'Still, if only this weather holds' – glancing anxiously at the pure sky overhead – 'we should reach the pass in three days, and we will surely find wonders on my lake.'

On the morning of the second day the pass was clearly to be seen, a little above the snow-line between two matching peaks that soared another five thousand feet, brilliant white in the almost horizontal sun.

'There is the post-house,' said Eduardo, pointing his glass, 'just under the snow and a little to the right. It was built by Huayna Capac, and it is as strong as ever. The pass is high, as you see, but on the far side there is an easy road, downhill all the way to one of my brother's silver-mines and a village where they grow the best potatoes in Peru as well as corn and barley, and they breed excellent llamas – these animals all came from there, and that is one of the reasons that they step out so well. It is true that after that we have to cross a chasm, with the Uribu flowing far below, but there is a hanging bridge in quite good repair, and you do not dislike heights that fill weak minds with horror. Sailors pay no attention to heights – a circumnavigator is inured to prodigious heights. What have you found, don Esteban?'

'A curious beetle.'

'Very curious indeed. One day I shall really set myself to the study of beetles. My lake too is on the far side. It seems to me that we should reach the post-house in plenty of time for the men to settle in and for you and me to go on to my lake. At this time of year it will not even skim over with ice until well after sunset, and we may find ducks and geese by the hundred. We will take Molina, the best llama, to carry what we shoot.'

'If you are as mistaken about the birds as you are about my head for heights, Molina will have no great burden to carry, at all,' reflected

Stephen, who had often heard, each time with deeper dismay, of the spidery Inca bridges upon which intrepid Indians crossed torrents raging a thousand feet below them, even hauling immobilized animals over by means of a primitive windlass, the whole construction swaying wildly to and fro as even a single traveller reached the middle, the first false step being the last.

'How long does it take to fall a thousand feet?' he asked himself, and as the troop set out he tried to make the calculation; but his arithmetical powers were and always had been weak. 'Long enough to make an act of contrition, at all events,' he said, abandoning the answer of seven hours and odd seconds as absurd.

On and on: up and up. This had been the pattern for a great while, but now the up and up was growing far more pronounced; now it was often a question of leading his mule again; and now he had to concentrate his mind on keeping up wherever the road grew steep. His breath was coming short; his heart beat a hundred and twenty strokes a minute; his eyesight wavered.

'You are in a brown study, I find,' said Eduardo, whose spirits had revived with the altitude.

'I was contemplating on the physiology of animals that live in a rarefied atmosphere,' said Stephen. 'Surely the exact dissection of a vicuña would show some very remarkable adaptations?'

'There can be no doubt of it,' replied Eduardo. 'And at present we too mean to adapt our own persons for the last stretch with a draught of maté. Do you choose to dismount?'

Stephen did so, very carefully avoiding the least hint of unsteadiness. He could scarcely see, but he was most unwilling to show any sign of the mountain-sickness that had certainly come upon him. When his head cleared from the effort of swinging out of the saddle he looked up and saw to his relief that they were now quite near the snow-line, above sixteen thousand feet. He had never been so high, and he had every right to be mountain-sick: this was no discreditable weakness.

Already smoke was rising from the guanaco dung, the woody fungus heads and a few of those bushes that burned green; and presently the gourds of maté were passing round. Stephen drew in the hot cheering gusts through his silver tube, ate a dried peach from Chile, and then like all the rest he drew out his pouch of coca-leaves, preparing a moderate ball spread with quinoa ash, chewed it slightly to start the flow and then eased it into his cheek. The familiar tingling began almost at once, followed by the beginning of that curious numbness which had so started him many years ago.

Mountain-sickness faded, anxiety with it; strength returned. He gazed at the climbing road, the last stretch, three steep traverses zigzagging up to the post-house, into the snow and over the pass. It would be walking every step of the way. He did not mind at all.

'Will you not ride, don Esteban?' asked Eduardo, holding the stirrup for him.

'No, sir,' said Stephen. 'The animal is extremely tired – look at his hanging lip, God be with him – whereas I am now quite recovered, a sprightly popinjay.'

A little less sprightly by the time they reached the massive posthouse, built, like some of those sections of the road cut deep into the mountain-side, of vast rocks so exactly shaped that they outstripped all reasonable conjecture, a little less sprightly, but perfectly human. He took the liveliest interest in the yaretta fungus growing on these rocks and on the inner walls, and Eduardo said to him, 'How glad I am to see you so brisk. Although we reached here in such good time I was afraid you might be too tired to see my lake. Do you think that after say an hour's rest you would like to go? There is some cloud in the east, and as you know winds sometimes get up in the evening; but an hour's rest would still leave us time.'

'Dear Eduardo,' said Stephen, 'the earlier we go the more we shall see. I fairly dote on alpine lakes, and this one as I recall has a fine fringe of reeds.'

It had indeed a fine fringe of reeds, a very fine deep fringe, unique in Stephen Maturin's extensive experience of reeds in that they grew not out of glutinous mud but from a layer of broken stones brought down by some not far distant combination of earthquake and flood from one of the nearby glaciers. This allowed them to walk out dry-foot with their guns and spy-glasses, leaving Molina on a long tether among the clumps of spiny ichu grass.

When first they had seen it from above, at some distance, the lake was clearly full of wildfowl – rafts of duck, geese at the far end where a stream from the northern glacier came in, and gulls over all – but by the time they had made their way through to a sheltered point near the open water that allowed them a clear view although they remained unseen, they found that there were also remarkable numbers of rails, waders and the smaller herons.

'What wealth!' they cried, and began a first eager census of genera at least before the identification or attempted identification of species. Presently they grew calmer, leaving the fine-work until they could obtain specimens, and they sat at their ease, gazing over the water at a distant crowd of flamingoes, gabbling steadily in their goose-like manner. A straggling line of newcomers, pale pink, scarlet and black in the declining sun, passed over to join the rest; and Stephen, watching them as they crossed from left to right, observed, 'For me flamingoes belong essentially to the Mediterranean lagoons, by definition at the level of the sea; and to find them up here, in an air so thin it is a wonder that their wings can bear them, gives the whole landscape something of the qualities of a dream. It is true that their voices are slightly different and that their plumage has a deeper red, but that if anything strengthens the impression, like losing one's way in a familiar town – a sense of . . . ' He broke off as a little band of teal came racing across well within range and both men cocked their fowling-pieces. Eduardo was poised, but seeing Stephen lower his gun he did not fire. 'How absurd,' said Stephen, 'I quite forgot to ask you how you manage without a dog. We could not have brought them down on land, and no man would ever wade far less swim for all love in that cruel bitter cold wetness for anything short of a two-headed phoenix.'

'No,' said Eduardo. 'What we cannot bring down on the shore, we leave where they fall. The lake freezes hard by night and we pick them up in the morning. But it is strange that you should have spoken of a dream – waking dream. I have the same feeling, though not at all for the same clear reason. There is something strange here. The birds are not settled. As you see, they are perpetually moving, the groups breaking up. And there is too much noise. They are uneasy. So is Molina: I have heard him three times now. There is something unnatural. God send there may not be an earthquake.'

'Amen.'

After a long pause Eduardo said, 'I do not believe I shall kill anything this evening, don Esteban . . . What do you say to sitting here and counting and naming as well as we can until the sun is half an hour from Taraluga over there – I have a quipu in my pocket to record them – and then going back across the Huechopillan to the post-house, where you can write them down at your leisure?'

'With all my heart,' said Maturin. It had become increasingly evident to him that there was a whole series of pieties active in Eduardo's breast which had nothing to do with those of Christianity as it was ordinarily understood. Furthermore he was much attached to the young man; and he had not seen him so moved before, even when he received the message from Cuzco.

They sat on, noting the passing birds, watching those farther off with their telescopes, comparing observations; and they were talking about the remarkable sense of the ominous or of impending change in animals – earthquake, eruption, eclipse (even lunar eclipses in certain bats) – when a flock of huachua geese flew straight at them at an extraordinary speed, passing just over their heads and with so great a rush of wings that for a moment their words were lost. The geese all wheeled together, returned at the same height and speed, rose and then pitched on the water, tearing the surface and throwing it wide: they sat in a tight-packed group, their heads stretched up; and high over them the lake gulls turned, screaming, screaming.

Another minute passed and a prodigious noise between a great thunder-clap and a broadside made both men start up, part the tall reeds and look behind them. They saw the snow of the two peaks on either side of the pass streaming out to leeward, streamers a mile long and more: then peaks and the pass itself vanished in a white turmoil.

'It may not last,' cried Eduardo, catching up his gun. Stephen followed him as he went fast through the reeds to the place where they had left the llama. And indeed for some minutes it seemed that this one clap might be the end; but while Eduardo was fastening their belongings to the llama's pack-saddle, Stephen looked at the water. There was scarcely a creature left on it now, and all along the edge birds were pushing in among the reeds.

Moving at that quick familiar short-paced Indian trot Eduardo and the llama set off over the powdering of snow for the true snow-line and the pass. There was still enough day and enough light to cross it, going even at a moderate pace.

A second thunder-clap, a triple roar several times repeated, and first the wind and then the snow engulfed them. Stephen, who weighed no great matter, was thrust first forward, then violently back, then plucked bodily up and flung against a rock. For a while he could see nothing, and crouched there shielding his face so that he should not breathe the flying powdered snow. Eduardo, who like the llama had thrown himself down at the first blast, found him, passed the tether round his waist and told him to hold on and keep moving for the love of God – Eduardo knew the path perfectly well – they would reach the snow-line and move on bent low – much easier up there – no hard falling – and the top of the pass would be blown clear.

But it was not. When at last they had beaten their slow, gasping way up through the roaring, uneven wind in the increasing darkness they found that hitherto they had been in the relatively sheltered lee of the topmost ridge and that the pass itself received not only the full force of the blast but of that blast concentrated and magnified by the two converging sides of rock. The space between was a racing down-ward torrent of air and snow that now partook more and more of the cutting icy crust from the snowfields far to windward. It was quite impassable. The sun had vanished in a white blur at some forgotten or unnoticed point but by the grace of God a four-day moon gleaming at odd moments through breaks in the clouds of flying snow enabled Eduardo to reach a cleft in the rock-face. It just allowed them to shelter from the direct buffeting of the wind if not from its shattering noise, and to some degree from the rapidly increasing and mortal cold.

It was a triangular cleft, the outer part filled with powdered snow. Eduardo kicked it into the mainstream, where it vanished instantly, thrust Stephen right into the sharp apex, followed him, dragging the llama into the opening where it lay on the remaining snow, and squatted between the two. The llama tried to heave itself farther in, but this could not be: after a struggle Eduardo managed to shackle one bent knee and the poor beast gave up, lowering its long neck across them, with its head on Stephen's knee.

Gradually, as they recovered from the immense exertion of the last hundred yards or so, and as their ears grew more accustomed to the wind's countless voices, all different, all enormously loud and oppressive in this shrieking pass, they exchanged a few words. Eduardo begged pardon for leading don Esteban into this – he should have known – there were signs – Tepec had told him it was a haunted, unlucky day – but these winds died with the midnight stars or at least with the rising sun. Would the Doctor like a ball of coca-leaves?

Stephen had been so very near death from a racing heart, an inability to breathe at such a height and physical exhaustion that he had almost forgotten his pouch; and at this point he did not possess the bodily strength or the spiritual resolution to grope for it under his clothes. He accepted gratefully, fumbling across the llama's neck for the proffered quid.

It had not been in his cheek five minutes before the extremity, the almost mortal extremity of fatigue died away. In ten minutes he was perfectly capable of reaching his own supply of leaves and ash, and of rearranging himself with what small degree of physical comfort the space allowed. He also felt a certain grateful warmth from the llama's head; but quite apart from that, mental comfort and a sense

of divorce from time and immediate contingencies were already settling in his mind.

They talked a little, or rather shouted, about the desirability of a
thick drift of snow across the entrance. Yet the steadily increasing
cold made the effort of shouting too great and each relapsed into a
meditative silence, carefully spreading what clothes they had over the
whole of their persons, particularly ears, noses, fingers. What passed
for time or at least a kind of duration no doubt went on. Sleep in
these circumstances seemed wholly out of the question, even if it
had not been for the effect of coca-leaves, stronger by far than any
coffee known to man, above all in the present heavy and steadily
repeated doses.

Yet at some remote given point Stephen's waking mind distinctly
perceived the minute voice of the watch deep in his bosom striking
five and then the half. 'Can this be?' he asked, and feeling deep within
his bosom he pressed the repeating knob. Five said the watch again,
and then the shriller half: at the same moment he realized that the
wind had stopped; that the llama's head and neck were cold, the creature already stiff; that Eduardo was breathing deep; that his own leg,
no longer covered by the poncho these many hours, had no sensibil-
ity whatsoever; and that the mouth of the cleft, now almost entirely
closed by a great deal of fresh snow, had a line of light at the top.

'Eduardo,' he called, when he had digested all these things and
arranged them in order, 'Eduardo, God and Mary be with you: it is
dawn, and the cold is less.'

Eduardo woke at once and with a clearer mind by far. He blessed
God, gathered himself, writhed round the dead llama, pushed the
loose-packed snow away and called back, 'The pass is now swept
quite clear, and there is Tupec coming down, with two other men.'
He pulled the poor beast away. Light came flooding in and Stephen
looked at his morbid leg.

'Eduardo, my dear,' he said hesitantly, after a careful examination,
'I grieve to tell you that my leg is deeply frost-bitten. If I am fortunate

I may lose no more than some toes; but even in that case I cannot do more than creep. Pray pass me a handful of snow.'

As he chafed the pallid leg and the ominously blueing foot with snow Eduardo agreed. 'But,' he said, 'pray do not take it to heart. Many of us have lost toes on the puna without great harm; and as for your reaching Arica, why, never concern yourself at all. You shall have a Peruvian chair. I shall send down to the village and you will travel like Pachacutic Inca himself, cross the bridge, the hills and the valleys in a Peruvian chair.'

At seven bells in the forenoon watch the *Surprise*, under topsails alone, heaved to: the officers began to assemble on the quarter-deck, the midshipmen on the gangway, all carrying their quadrants or sextants, for the sun was approaching the meridian, and they were to take his altitude at the moment he crossed it, thereby finding just how far south of the equator they were at noon. To the landsman, to the mere superficial observer, this might have seemed a work of supererogation, since clear on her larboard bow rose the headland of Punta Angeles, the western extremity of Valparaiso bay, whose position had been laid down with the utmost accuracy time out of mind, while in the brilliantly clear air miles of the great Cordillera could be seen, the peak of Aconcagua a perfect compass-bearing to the north-east: but as far as Jack Aubrey was concerned this was neither here nor there. He liked to run a man-of-war as men-of-war had always been run, with the ship's day beginning at noon; and this was a par-ticularly important day, the last of the month and the first on which he could hope to find Stephen Maturin in Valparaiso. He therefore wished nothing to be done that might break the established pattern or bring ill-luck. It was true that a few years ago some wild enthusi-ast, a Whiggish civilian no doubt, had decreed that day should start at midnight; but Jack, though a scientific, forward-looking officer, agreed with many of his fellow-captains in giving this foolish inno-vation no countenance whatsoever: besides, it had taken him years to persuade Stephen that nautical days really did start at noon, and he did not want his imperfect conviction to be shaken in any way at all. Then again, once this last day of the month had in fact begun, he meant to carry out some physical measurements for his friend the polymath Alexander Humboldt, in whose penguin-filled cold north-ern current the ship was now swimming.

Silence fore and aft: anxious peering through many an eyepiece.

Jack brought his own sun down three times to the fine firm horizon, and on the third it was a trifle below the second, which had been the true altitude. He noted the angle, and turning he found Tom Pullings, who in this anomalous ship played many parts as well as that of first lieutenant, standing there bare-headed beside him. 'Noon and thirty-three degrees south, sir, if you please,' said Tom.

'Very good, Captain Pullings,' replied Jack. 'Make it twelve.'

Pullings turned to Norton, the mate of the watch, and said, 'Make it twelve,' in a strong, hieratic voice. Norton, with equal gravity, hailed the quartermaster, not three feet away, 'Strike eight bells and turn the glass.' The four double strokes rang out, and with the last still in the air, Pullings, directing his words to the bosun, roared, 'Pipe to dinner.'

The lions at the Tower of London made a prodigious and indeed a shocking din on being fed, but theirs was a kittenish mewling compared with that of the *Surprise*; besides, the lions were rarely provided with mess-kids upon which the seamen beat with such zeal, this being Thursday, a salt-pork day, and one upon which an extraordinary plum-duff was to be served out in honour of the birthday of Lord Melville, the brother of Captain Aubrey's particular friend Heneage Dundas and First Lord of the Admiralty at the time of Jack's reinstatement.

The roaring was so usual that Jack barely noticed it, but the ensuing quietness did strike his mind. The *Surprise* was not one of those discontented spit-and-polish ships in which men were not allowed to speak on duty, for not only would this have been abhorrent to Jack Aubrey's feelings and dead contrary to his idea of command ('a happy ship is your only right hard-fighting ship') but with such a ship's company it would not have answered for a moment, and except at times of strong activity there was always a steady low hum of talk on deck. At present the temporary silence made the almost deserted deck seem still more empty; and Jack, addressing Adams, his clerk and factotum in the intellectual line, lowered his voice. 'Mr Adams,' he said, 'when we have taken the temperatures and the salinity, we might try

a sounding. With the two headlands we have a capital triangle, and
I should like to know what the bottom is like at this point, if our
line can reach it. Once that is done we will take the ship a little farther in and you can carry on in the cutter, just as though you were
calling for mail or the like. I will give you the addresses where the
Doctor may be found, and if he is at either you will bring him off
directly. But with the utmost discretion, Mr Adams. The utmost discretion, too, in asking the way. The utmost discretion is called for in
this case: that is why I do not take her in and lie in the road or the
port itself. Things may come to that or to some system of signalling;
but how charming it would be if we could pluck him off the shore
right away.' – lowering his voice still farther – 'You will not repeat
it, but there appears to be some question of a high-placed very furious husband – legal proceedings – every kind of unpleasantness, you
understand me.'

The quietness lasted throughout the scientific observations and
during the time the hands ate their dinner and drank their grog, a
time during which Reade laid out the coils of deep-sea line at given
intervals from the forecastle to the mizzen chains so that the men
could let them go in succession. He had not retired to the midshipmen's berth, because he had been invited to dine in the cabin –
invited to eat a much better dinner than he could hope to find in the
berth, but to eat it more than two hours later than his usual time;
and now, by way of distracting his ravenous, ever-increasing hunger,
he indulged in capers unworthy of his rank or age, such as thumping
the deep-sea lead against the frigate's side. The rhythmic noise broke
in on Jack's calculations and he called out, 'Mr Reade. Mr Reade,
there. Pray attend to your duty.'

His duty materialized in the next two minutes, when the afternoon watch came on deck and those hands who had been told off
for the sounding took up their stations, each with a coil of the stout
waterlaid line in his hand. Reade walked out on the larboard cat-
head swinging the twenty-eight-pound lead in his one hand, watched
with infinite anxiety by the seamen lining the side, dropped it into

the water, calling, 'Lead's away,' and walked back without a stumble. From forward aft each man holding twenty fathoms in his hand, sang out, 'Watch, there, watch,' as he let the last coils go. Each of the ten repeated the call, except for the last, in the mizzen chains, who held the fag-end tight – no coils left at all – looked up at Reade, smiled and shook his head: 'No bottom with this line, sir.'

Reade crossed the quarterdeck, took off his hat, reported to Captain Aubrey, 'No bottom with this line, sir'; and seeing that Jack was no longer vexed with him he went on, 'Oh sir, I do wish you would look out over the larboard beam. There is as odd a craft as you can possibly imagine, a balsa, I think, sailing in the strangest way. It has been brought by the lee three times in the last five minutes, and the poor soul seems to be entangled in his sheet. He is a brave fellow to come on, but he has no more notion of handling a boat than the Doctor.'

Jack glanced at the boat. He covered his poor eye and stared fixedly with the other before crying, 'Mr Norton, jump into the top with this glass. Look at that balsa with the purple sail and tell me what you see. Mr Wilkins, let the red cutter be lowered down at once.'

'On deck, there,' hailed Norton, his voice squeaking with emotion. 'On deck, sir. It is the Doctor – he is overboard – no, he is back again – I believe his tiller has come unshipped.'

The balsa, though wildly overloaded, was by definition unsinkable, and they brought him aboard to the heartiest cheers, helped him up the side with so zealous a welcome that he would have been pitched into the waist if Jack had not clasped him with both hands. 'Welcome aboard, Doctor,' he cried, and the ship's company called out, 'Welcome aboard – aye, aye – hear him – welcome aboard – huzzay, huzzay!' in defiance of all good order and discipline.

As soon as he was in the cabin, and even while Killick and Padeen were taking away his wet clothes and bringing dry, even while a pot of coffee was being brewed, Stephen examined Jack Aubrey's wounds: the leg he passed – an ugly scar, no more – and the eye he gazed at without much comment, only saying that he would need a better light. Then, as they sat down to their fragrant cup, he went on, 'Before I ask you how the ship sails along, how you have done, and how all our people are, will I tell you why I came out to meet you in this precipitate and I might almost say temerarious manner?'

'If you please.'

'I had reasons for not wishing to call any official attention to the *Surprise*, but the chief cause for my haste was that I have some information that you might wish to act upon without the loss of a minute.'

'Oh, indeed?' cried Jack, his good eye lighting with its old predatory gleam.

'As I was leaving Peru because of the unjustified suspicions of a military man who misunderstood my examination of his wife – a deeply stupid but very powerful and bloody-minded military man – ' This was an explanation for some of Stephen's more bizarre movements that both of them understood perfectly: it was calculated, and very well calculated, to satisfy the minds of the seamen, who for a great while had looked upon the Doctor's licentious capers ashore with an indulgent comprehension. ' – a confidential friend came to see me by night, and knowing that I belonged to a British privateer he gave me an account of three American China ships sailing in company from Boston. This document he gave me as a parting present, together with details of their insurance, their ports of call and their estimated progress, in the hope that we might be able to intercept them. At that time and for some hundreds of miles after I paid no great attention to the matter, knowing the uncertainty of sea-voyages: and indeed of my own, by land. Yet no sooner had I reached Valparaiso than I received word from my friend's correspondent in the Argentine: the ships had cleared from Buenos Aires on Candlemas Day; they meant to traverse the Straits le Maire and to carry on, skirting south of Diego Ramirez by the end of the present month and then heading north-east for Canton. I looked at the Abbot's map, and it occurred to me that by spreading every sail and straining every nerve we might get there in time.'

'So we might,' said Jack, after a moment's calculation; and he left the cabin. Returning he cried, 'Oh Stephen, what are we to do with the balsa and all those innumerable boxes, chests and vile bundles that fill it to what would be the gunwale of a Christian boat?'

'Pray let them be brought aboard with the utmost care. As for the boat itself, let it be tossed off with a round turn, if you please, the cantankerous beast, though it is the clear loss of half a crown and eighteen pence for the sail, almost new. It came from the same yard and the same model as that which goes out on Thursdays for the monastery's fish, and the Abbot assured me that one had but to pull a given rope, the escota, towards the back to make it go faster: but this was not the case. Though possibly I may have pulled the wrong rope. There were so many boxes on the floor . . . indeed, there was so little room for me that I almost fell into the sea, at times.'

'Could you not have tossed the worst overboard?'

'The kind almoner had tied them down so tight, and the knots were wet; and in any case the worst, which sat upon three several ropes, held my grebe, my flightless Titicaca grebe. You would never have expected me to throw away a *flightless* grebe, for all love? But, however, the monks had promised to pray for me, and with no more than moderate skill I survived.'

Killick's insistent cough could be heard at the door, then his knock: 'Which your guests have arrived, sir,' he said; but his severity turned to an affectionate gap-toothed leer as his eyes wandered to gaze upon Dr Maturin.

'Could you possibly manage dinner, Stephen?' asked Jack.

'Any dinner at all,' said Stephen with great conviction: he was fresh from a monastery unusually ascetic at all times and now deep in a penitential fast; and in an undertone he added, 'Even one of those infernal cavies.'

Dinner wound on from fresh anchovies, still present in their countless millions, to steak of tunny, to a tolerable sea-pie, and so to an

expected but still heartily welcome spotted dog. Stephen ate in wolf-
ish silence until the very end of the sea-pie; then, being among old
friends eager to hear, he leant back, loosened his waist-band, and told
them something of his botanizing and naturalizing journey south
from Lima to Arica, where he took ship for Valparaiso. 'But to reach
Arica,' he said, 'we had to cross a very high pass, the Huechopillan, at
more than sixteen thousand feet, and there my friend and I and alas
a llama were caught in what in those parts they call a viento blanco
and we should have perished if my friend Eduardo had not found a
little small shelter in the rock. Indeed, the poor llama did die, and I
was mortally frost-bitten.'

'Was it very painful, Doctor?' asked Pullings, looking grave.

'Not at all, at all, until the feeling began to return. And even then
the whole lesion was less severe than I had expected. At one time I
thought to have lost my leg below the knee, but in the event it was
no more than a couple of unimportant toes. For you are to consider,'
he observed, addressing his words to Reade, 'that your foot bases its
impulse and equilibrium on the great toe and the least: the loss of
either is a sad state of affairs entirely, but with the two one does very
well. The ostrich has but two the whole length of her life, and yet she
outruns the wind.'

'Certainly, sir,' said Reade, bowing.

'Yet though the leg was spared, I could not well travel; above all
after I had removed the peccant members.'

'How did you do that, sir?' asked Reade, unwilling to hear though
eager to be told.

'Why, with a chisel, as soon as we came down to the village. They
could not be left to mortify, with gangrene spreading, the grief and
the sorrow. But for a while I was reduced to immobility; and that was
where my noble friend Eduardo showed his magnanimity. He caused
a framework to be made, fitting over a man's chest fore and aft – fore
and aft,' he repeated with a certain satisfaction, 'and allowing me to
be carried on his shoulders or somewhat lower, sitting at my ease and
facing backwards. They call it an Inca chair; and in this Inca chair

I was carried over those terrible Inca bridges that span stupendous chasms – hanging bridges that sway – and I was always carried by fresh and powerful Indians recruited by my friend an Indian himself and a descendant of the Incas too. He generally travelled by my chair, except when the path led along the rocky side of a precipice, which it did far, far too often, where there was no room for two abreast, and a great deal did he tell me about the ancient empire of Peru and the magnificence of its rulers. Surely,' he said, breaking off to listen to the run of the water along the ship's side and the general voice of taut rigging, masts, blocks, sails and yards, 'surely we are going very fast?'

'About eight knots, I believe, sir,' said Pullings, filling Stephen's glass. 'Pray tell us about the magnificence of Peru.'

'Well, if gold is magnificent, and sure there is something imperial about gold in the mass, then Eduardo's account of Huayna Capac, the Great Inca, and his chain will please you. It was made when the birth of his son Huascar was to be celebrated in a ceremony at which the court went through the motions of a formal dance, joining hands, making a circle and moving two steps forward, then one back, thus drawing closer and closer until they were at a proper distance for making their obeisance. The Inca however disapproved of this holding of hands; he thought it too familiar, quite improper, and he gave orders for a chain to be made, a chain which the dancers could hold, thus keeping their formation but avoiding direct physical contact, which might lead to irregularities. Naturally the chain was made of gold. The links were as thick as a man's wrist; the length twice that of the great square at Cuzco, which makes upwards of seven hundred feet; and its weight was such that two hundred Indians could only just lift it from the ground.'

'Oh!' cried his listeners, who naturally enough included Killick and his mate Grimshaw: and while their mouths were still rounded, young Wedell came in with Mr Grainger's compliments and duty to the Captain and might he set the weather studdingsails? The breeze had veered half a point and he reckoned they would stand.

'Oh, by all means, Mr Wedell,' cried Jack. 'Let him crack on till all sneers again.'

Just how it became known throughout the ship that the Captain's chase had a beast in view, and that it was not only the joy of being homeward-bound that caused him to spread so much canvas, to spend so much time on deck, taking every possible advantage of the wind and whipping jibs and staysails in and out, could not be clearly stated; yet known it was, and no officer or master's mate ever had to emphasize, still less repeat, any order that might carry the barky more briskly to the high south latitudes.

Some of the knowledge derived from the obvious fact that the Doctor, though incapable of telling a barque from a ship or a bowline from a midshipman's hitch, was not as simple as he looked – that indeed would have been difficult – and that he did not spend all his time on shore in bowsing up his jib or inspecting ladies in their shifts, but sometimes picked up valuable news: yet this did not account for the 'two or three China ships out of Boston' or the 'south of Diego Ramirez' that could so often be heard on the lower deck, together with the calculation that a steady five knots from noon to noon, day after day, would get them there with time and to spare, which could only come from deliberate eavesdropping or very close attention to all possible clues, such as the Captain's poring over his charts of the desolate regions south of the Horn.

Yet this eagerness for a prize, so natural in the crew of a man-of-war, was curiously coloured and accentuated by Stephen's account of the Inca's great chain, an account that had nothing whatsoever to do with Boston merchantmen launched two hundred and fifty years later: it nevertheless suffused the whole ship's collective state of mind.

'How much do you suppose a tolerably stout Indian could lift?' asked Reade.

'They are natives, you know,' said Wedell, 'and everyone knows that natives can raise prodigious great burdens, though not much above five feet tall.'

'Say two hundredweight,' said Norton.

'That makes four hundred hundredweight for two hundred Indians,' said Reade, writing it on the slate used for his rough day's work. 'Which is twenty tons, or forty-four thousand eight hundred pounds. Which is seven hundred and sixteen thousand eight hundred ounces. What is gold worth an ounce?'

'Three pounds seventeen and ten pence halfpenny,' said Norton. 'That was what Mr Adams reckoned when last prize money was shared out; and all hands agreed.'

'Three, seventeen, ten and a half to be multiplied by seven hundred and sixteen thousand eight hundred,' said Reade. 'There ain't room enough for it on the slate, and anyhow they are avoirdupois ounces instead of Troy. But whichever way you look at it the answer is well over two millions of money. Can you imagine two millions of money?'

Yes, they could – a deer-park, bow windows, a pack of hounds, a private band in a genteel conservatory – and so could others, before the mast and abaft; and although no one was so simple as to confuse these two quite separate ideas, the hypothetical prizes far to the south tended to glow with an additional and quite charming lustre, in spite of the fact that almost every man aboard was already richer than he had ever been in his life from the earlier captures, and that neither the frigate's captain nor her surgeon really needed any more at all.

'There is something profoundly discreditable about this delight in taking other men's property away from them by force,' observed Stephen, tuning his long neglected 'cello, 'taking it away openly, legally, and being praised, caressed and even decorated for doing so. I quell, or attempt to quell, the feeling every time it rises in my bosom; which it does quite often.'

'Pray pass the rosin,' said Jack; and before dashing away into the allegro vivace of their Boccherini he added, 'I may see little of you in the morning: we shall spend much of our time exercising the great guns. But you will never forget that I am to be your guest for dinner in the gunroom, I am sure.' Nothing could have been less certain. Dr Maturin had been so engrossed in the preliminary unpacking, sorting, registering, cleaning and roughly preserving the collections that had come aboard from the balsa that he was perfectly capable of forgetting all ordinary duties other than those of the sick-berth, and all social decencies. 'He is also capable of supposing that the ship's company is still much as he left it,' reflected Jack, and at the end of the movement he said, 'I believe you have not dined in the gunroom yet?'

'I have not,' said Stephen. 'With the sick-berth and my collections to sort, I have scarcely been on deck, either, or asked half my shipmates how they do. You cannot readily conceive the fragility of an undressed bird's skin, my dear.'

'Then perhaps I should tell you of some changes you will see. Vidal has left the ship with two of his Knipperdolling cousins, and he has been replaced in the gunroom by William Sadler, a thorough-going seaman. And then before the mast, there was poor John Proby, who lost the number of his mess two days out of Callao.'

'That I knew. He was in a sad decline, in spite of what little we could do for him in the way of bark and steel and linctus. But Fabien very kindly kept me one of his hands, recollecting my interest in the singular calcification of its sinews. Fabien is a most valuable assistant.'

Jack could still be made uneasy by remarks of this kind, and it was a little while before he went on, 'And you will not see Bulkeley any more, either.'

'The facetious bosun?'

'Just so. He had also been a bosun in the Navy, you know; and with the *Surprise* being run man-of-war fashion he slipped back more and more into his old service ways. You know the expression capabarre, I dare say?'

'Certainly. I am no new-fledged canvas-climber, I believe. It is the topmost summit, the ultimate pinnacle of some towering mast.'

'No doubt. But we commonly use it for that tendency in the bosuns of King's ships to steal all marine stores not immovably screwed down. I checked him once for a missing kedge in Annamooka and again for a coil of three-inch manilla at Moahu, with God knows how many things in between; and he promised to reform. But in Callao he made off with several lengths of chain, a can-hook, and our lightning-conductor, our best Snow Harris lightning-conductor; and when I told him of it he had the provoking effrontery to defend his action on the grounds that everyone knew that metal attracts the flesh and that a glass ball at the masthead was the only true safeguard. And as for the other things, they were quite worn out.'

Discussing the perils of the sea in general and of lightning in particular came very near to talking shop, an act less criminal than sodomy (which carried the death sentence) but not very much so, and the gunroom cast some nervous looks at their guest the Captain, a stickler for naval etiquette; but since it was clear both from his thoroughly amiable expression and his own anecdotes that lightning was this side of the barrier between right and wrong, the subject occupied the company for the not inconsiderable time they took to eat a noble turtle and empty the dish.

The gunroom was less crowded, now that the merchants and ransomers had left, and it was more nearly naval: Jack, Stephen and Tom Pullings were in fact serving officers; Adams had walked the quarterdeck for most of his active life; Wilkins had served in half a dozen King's ships as midshipman or master's mate; and Grainger, together with his brother-in-law Sadler, had taken on the local colour in the most natural way. The conversation therefore had a greater freedom, all the more so since the frigate was homeward-bound.

'This very ship was struck by a levin-flash off Penedo in the Brazils,' observed Stephen, 'and she lost the mast, the spar, the thing in front – the bowsprout. I was asleep at the time, and for a moment I thought we were in the midst of a fleet-action, the noise was so great.'

'Was there anyone killed, Doctor?' asked Grainger.

'There was not.'

'Ah,' said William Sadler, 'my cousin Jackson was carpenter's crew in the *Diligent* when she was struck by *forked* lightning near the Island of a Thursday. Which three hands were killed in the maintop;

and he said their bodies stayed warm till Sunday after church, when they were obliged to be put over the side.'

'The *Repulse* was laying off Spain in the year ten,' said Pullings. 'It was a Thursday too, and all hands had washed clothes. Towards evening clouds began to gather thick, and the watch below, afraid their laundry would be rained upon when the things were nearly dry, jumped aloft to take it in. There was a single flash, and seven dropped down dead on deck, while thirteen more were horribly burnt.'

'When Prince William had the *Pegasus*,' said Jack, 'a single stroke utterly destroyed her mainmast.'

General considerations on lightning followed this – most frequent between the tropics – certain trees more liable to be struck than others: willows, ash, solitary oaks to be avoided – sultry, oppressive weather favourable – tolerably common in the temperate zone – unknown in Finland, Iceland and Hudson's Bay – presumably even more unknown nearer to either pole, probably because of the northern lights. But these remarks together with speculation on the nature of the electric fluid were interrupted by the appearance of a roast sucking-pig, borne in on a splendid Peruvian, silver dish, the rescued merchants' present to the *Surprise*, and set down according to custom before Dr Maturin, whose skill as a carver was intimately known to many of those present. The talk grew more cheerful: pigs at home, how best dressed – pigs, wild, on a remote island in the South China Sea, that had nourished Captain Aubrey and his people for a great while – a little tame black sow at Pullings's father's farm on the edge of the New Forest that would find you a basket of trubs, or truffles as some called them, in a morning, winking and grinning at you with each trub, never eating a single one herself.

By the time they reached the port the conversation was more cheerful still, the words 'homeward-bound' recurring very often, with conjectures about the delightful changes to be seen in children, gardens, shrubberies and the like.

'My grandfather,' said Grainger, 'was sailmaker's mate in the *Centurion* when Commodore Anson took the Acapulco galleon in forty-three: he had his share of the one million, three hundred and thirteen thousand, eight hundred and forty-two pieces of eight they found in her – a figure I always remember – and that made him right glad, as you may well suppose; but when he learnt that now they were to steer for home he used to say it made him happier still.'

'Ha, ha,' cried Wilkins, somewhat flushed with his wine, 'homeward-bound is very well, but homeward-bound with a pocket-ful of prize-money is better still. Huzzay for the Horn!'

There was a good deal of cheerful noise at this, and more chuck-ling among the mess-attendants than was either right or decent; but Jack, recovering his gravity, shook his head, saying, 'Come, gentle-men, do not let us tempt Fate; do not let us say anything presumptu-ous that may prove unlucky. We must not sell the bear's skin before we have locked the stable door. And locked it with a double turn.'

'Very true,' cried Pullings and Grainger. 'Very true. Hear him.'

'For my part,' Jack went on, 'I shall not repine if we meet nothing off the Horn. We have to pass that way in any case; and if our hurry makes us no richer, why, it carries us home the sooner. I long to see my new plantations.'

'I do not like the prospect of this Horn,' said Stephen in a low voice, 'or all this haste to reach it. This is in every way a most excep-tional year – cranes have been seen flying north over Lima! – and the weather down there is sure to be more disagreeable than ever.'

'But you have wonderful sea-legs, Doctor,' said Adams. 'And if we crack on we shall – we may – reach the height of the Horn at a capital time for the passage: barely a ripple, I have been told, with picnics on the island itself.'

'It is my collection I am thinking of,' said Stephen. 'Whatever you may say, the sea around the Horn is bound to be damp, whereas my collections come from one of the driest parts of the whole terrane-ous globe. They need very careful attention, acres of oiled silk, weeks of calm, patient care in describing, figuring, packing. Once they are tumbled and tossed unprepared, on the gelid billows, all is lost – their pristine glory is gone for ever.'

'Well, Doctor,' said Jack, 'some weeks I think I can promise you. Your cranes may have lost their heads, but the trades, or rather the anti-trades, have kept theirs, and they are blowing as sweetly as ever our best friends could wish.'

The promised weeks they had, weeks of pure sailing, with the *Surprise* slanting cross the prevailing wind and often logging two hundred sea-miles between one noon observation and the next: weeks of close, satisfying work for Stephen, who was delighted with Fabien's exact and beautiful watercolours of the many specimens still in their full glory; weeks of ardent sailoring for Jack, with evenings full of music: fresh fish over the side, and penguins in constant attendance. And when at last the anti-trades faltered and left them, within a day the even more favourable westerlies took over.

Those were idyllic weeks; but how difficult it was to remember them, to call them vividly to mind as an experienced reality, a fortnight after the ship had sailed into the true antarctic, and more than antarctic stream, the haunt of the wandering albatross, molly-mawks in all their variety, the great bone-breaking petrel, the stink-pot and the ice-bird – had sailed into that green water at fourteen knots under topsails, forecourses and a jib, impelled by an almighty quartering wind. The change was not unexpected. Well before this ominous parallel the frigate's people had been engaged in shifting, packing and storing her light sails and replacing them with much heavier cloth, with storm-canvas trysails and the like for emergency. Many a watch had been spent in sending up preventer-backstays, braces, shrouds and stays and in attending to new earings, robands, reef-points, reef-tackles for the courses and spilling-lines for the topsails, to say nothing of new sheets and clew-lines fore and aft. Then again all hands had rounded the Horn at least once, some many times, and they took their long woollen drawers, their mittens and their Magellan jackets very seriously when they were served out, while most of those who had had any foresight dug into their chests for Monmouth caps,

Welsh wigs or padded domes with flaps to protect the wearer's ears and strings to tie beneath his chin.

This serving-out happened on a Tuesday in fine clear weather, a pleasant topgallant breeze blowing from the north-west, and it seemed almost absurd: on Friday the ship was tearing eastwards with four men at the wheel, snow blurring both binnacles, hatches battened down, and the muffled watch on deck sheltering in the waist, dreading a call to grapple with the frozen rigging and board-stiff sails.

Presently, in this incessant roar of sea and wind, and in this continual tension, the vision of the warm and mild Pacific faded, leaving little evidence apart from Stephen's collections, neatly labelled, noted and wrapped in oiled silk and then sailcloth, carefully packed into thoroughly watertight casks set up by the cooper, and stowed in the hold; and apart from the remarkable store of provisions Mr Adams had laid in. He had had a free hand; he was not bound by the pinch-penny rules of the King's service, since in her present state the *Surprise* was run on the privateer's tradition of the ship's own money, her personal reserve to be laid out in marine stores, food and drink, a stated share of all the prizes – a very handsome sum after the sale of the *Franklin*, the *Alastor* and the whalers – and she was sailing eastwards deep-laden with provisions of the highest quality, enough to last another circumnavigation.

This was just as well, for after a few days of the first icy blow, when the deathly chill had worked right into the whole ship from keelson to cabin, all hands began to eat with far more than usual eagerness. Their hunger persisted, since the roaring westerly storm had sent the ship a great way, at great speed, south and east into the high fifties, a cold region at the best and now even colder in this unusual year, even without a wind: frequent rain; even more frequent sleet and snow; most hands wet most of the time; all of them always cold.

In such very thick weather observation was impossible for days on end, and in spite of his chronometers and well-worn sextant, and of the presence of three other expert navigators aboard, Jack could not be sure of his longitude or latitude, dead-reckoning in such wind and seas being wonderfully uncertain. He therefore reduced sail, and the frigate moved eastwards at an average of no more than three knots, sometimes under bare poles or with a mere scrap of sail right forward to give her steerage-way when the wind blew a full gale from the west. Yet there were also those strange antarctic calms, when the albatrosses (and half a dozen followed the *Surprise*, together with some Cape pigeons and most of the smaller petrels) sat on the heaving sea, unwilling or unable to rise; and during two of these the drum beat to quarters, as it had done all the way south from Valparaiso, and the gun-crew exercised their pieces, housing them warm, dry and new-charged, with the touch-hole covered and the tompions doubly waterproofed with grease, ready for instant service.

It was after the second of these exercises – two fine rippling broadsides, almost up to the old *Surprise*'s astonishing accuracy and speed – that the sky cleared and Jack had a series of perfect observations of first the sun, then Achernar, and later Mars himself, positions that were confirmed by the other officers and that showed that in spite of this dawdling their initial zeal had brought them almost to the rendezvous far too soon. The China ships intended to pass south of Diego Ramirez with the full moon, and in her present stage she was only three days old: that would mean a great deal of beating to and fro in the most inhospitable seas known to man, with no more than a passable likelihood of success after all. Quite apart from the unpredictable winds, foul weather or fair, state of the sea and so on, merchantmen on such a voyage never attempted any great accuracy of movement.

'We shall have to stand off and on until well past the full,' said Jack at supper – fish soup, a dish of sweetbreads, Peruvian cheese, two bottles of Coquimbo claret – 'The full of the moon, of course.'

'An uninviting prospect,' said Stephen. 'Last night I was unable to control my 'cello because of the erratic jerking of the floor, and this evening most of my soup is spread on my lap; while day after day men

are brought below with cruel bruises, even broken bones, and are falling from the frozen ropes above or slipping on the icy deck below. Do
you not think it would be better to go home?'

'Yes. It often occurs to me, but then my innate nobility of character cries out, "Hey, Jack Aubrey: you mind your duty, d'ye hear me
there?" Do you know about duty, Stephen?'

'I believe I have heard it well spoken of.'

'Well, it exists. And apart from the obvious duty of distressing the
King's enemies – not that I have anything against Americans: they
are capital seamen and they treated us most handsomely in Boston.
But it is my duty. Apart from that, I say, we also have a duty to the
officers and the foremast-jacks. They have brought the barky here in
the hope of three China ships, and if I call out, "Oh be damned to
your three China ships" what will they say? They are not man-of-
war's men; and even if they were . . .'

Stephen nodded. The argument was unanswerable. But he was not
quite satisfied. 'As I was stuffing a green Andean parakeet this afternoon,' he said, 'another thought came to me. As you say, the Americans are capital seamen: they beat us hollow in the *Java*, and carried
us prisoners away. Do you not feel that attacking three of their China
ships is somewhat rash? Does it not smack of that pride which goeth
before destruction?'

'Oh dear no. These are not solid great Indiamen, these are not
thousand-ton Company's ships that you could take for men-of-war,
nor anything like it. They are quite modest private merchantmen with
a few six-pounders and swivels and small-arms, just to beat off the
pirates of the South China Sea: they have nothing like the very heavy
crew of a man-of-war, above all an American man-of-war, and they
could not fire a full broadside even if they carried the guns, which
they don't. No. In the unlikely event of their keeping all together and
manoeuvring just so, they must still fall victims to even a quite small
frigate capable of firing three well-directed hundred and forty-four-
pound broadsides in under five minutes.'

'Well,' said Stephen. And then, 'If we must wait for your more or less mythical Chinamen, if we must wait until your sense of duty is satisfied, may we not go just a little way south, just to the edge of the ice? How charming that would be.'

'With all due respect, Stephen, I must tell you that I utterly decline to go anywhere near any ice whatsoever, however thin, however deeply laden with seals, great auks, or other wonders of the deep. I hate and despise ice. Ever since our mortal time with the ice-island in the horrible old *Leopard*, I have always sworn never to give it any countenance.'

'My dear,' said Stephen, pouring him another glass of wine, 'how well a graceful timidity does become you.'

Stephen Maturin had little room to prate about timidity. In the relatively tranquil forenoon watch of the following day Captain Aubrey caused a crow's nest, in the whaler's manner, to be set up on the main topmast head, a crow's nest stuffed with straw, so that the look-out should not freeze to death. Dr Maturin having publicly expressed a wish to see farther to the south in case, on this clear day, ice might be visible, Jack, in the presence of his officers and several hands, invited him to take a view from this eminence: Stephen looked at the masts (the ship was rolling twenty-one degrees and pitching twelve) and blenched, but he lacked the moral courage to refuse and within minutes he was rising through the maze of rigging, rising on a double whip with several turns about his person and a look of contained horror on his face. Bonden and young Wedell steered him through the shrouds and backstays and their reinforcements, Jack preceded him by foot, and between them they got him safe into the nest.

'Now I come to think of it,' said Jack, who had meant no harm at all, 'I do not believe you have ever been aloft with the ship a little skittish. I hope it don't make you uneasy?'

'Not at all,' said Stephen, glancing over the edge at the absurdly

distant white-streaked sea immediately below on the starboard roll
and closing his eyes again. 'I like it of all things.'

'I am afraid you will not see much in the south,' said Jack. He
pointed his telescope and kept it fixed while the mast upon which he
was poised went through its gyrations, swinging his pigtail left and
then right and then straight out behind.

Watching it as he lay there coiled in the straw, Stephen asked,
'How much do you suppose we move, at all?'

'Well,' said Jack, still sweeping the southern rim of the world, 'we
are rolling about twenty degrees and pitching let us say twelve: so
at this height the roll should carry us some seventy-five feet and the
pitch forty-five. And we describe a tolerably angular ellipse. Are you
sure it don't worry you?'

'Never in life,' said Stephen, bringing himself to look over the edge
again: and having looked, 'Tell me, brother, do people ever come this
way voluntarily? I mean, apart from those that ply up and down the
American coast?'

'Oh yes. With the steady westerlies and the west-wind drift this is
the quickest way from New South Wales to the Cape. Oh dear me,
yes. They began using it at the very beginning of the infernal colony,
you remember, and the Navy still . . . I tell you what, Stephen: there
is something very nasty blowing up in the south. The swell is already
with us and I fear a deadly storm. Bonden. Bonden, there. Clap on to
the line: I am sending the Doctor down. Bear a hand, bear a hand.'

It was a cruel hard blow, and the *Surprise* clawed off from Diego
Ramirez and its long tail of rocks as far and fast as ever she could,
sometimes making fair headway, sometimes lying to under storm
trysails when the prodigious southern swell compelled her to do so,
but always keeping enough sea-room for the comfort of those aboard,
every man-jack of whom dreaded a lee-shore more than anything
in this world and perhaps the next. That however was the only kind
of comfort they knew until at last the storm blew itself out. For the

rest of the time the ship was in very violent motion, with green seas sweeping her deck fore and aft, nobody turning in dry, nobody lying warm, nobody having a hot meal and rarely a hot drink, all hands called night after night.

Yet the storm did blow itself out; the strong westerlies returned, and the frigate made her uneven way back across the southern swell cut into frightful seas by a strong sideways blast. Most very strong irregular winds have freakish effects and this was no exception: no men were lost or seriously injured, but on the other hand the well-lashed and double-griped spare top and topgallant masts on the lee-ward side of the booms flew overboard, together with other valuable spars, like a bundle of twigs, while the Doctor's skiff, stowed inside the untouched launch, was utterly destroyed; and while the Doctor himself, contemplating the apocalyptic scene from a scuttle in the cabin (he was not allowed on deck) saw a sight unique in his experience: an albatross, navigating the great crests and troughs with all its natural skill, was surprised by a flying packet of water plucked from a cross-current and dashed into the sea. It arose from the boil with an enormous wing-stroke and fled across the face of the rising wave: no sound could of course be heard, but Stephen thought he detected a look of extreme indignation on its face.

They were back on their station, with the islands clear on the lar-board beam except in thick weather. But they had brought the cold with them, the right antarctic cold of the high sixties and beyond; and although the midshipmen's berth took a perverse delight in fishing up pieces of drift-ice to freeze their already frigid grog, the older hands, particularly those who had sailed in South Sea whal-ers, looked upon it with sullen disapproval, as a mark of worse, far worse, to come.

This cold, and this for late summer unparallelled show of ice, meant that whenever the westerlies paused, which they sometimes did, without any rhyme or reason that could be made out, the air was filled with mist or even downright fog.

They paused indeed in the middle watch of the Friday after the ship's return, the day after the full moon, and presently they were succeeded by an air from the north; this strengthened with the rising of the sun and immediately after breakfast the man in the crow's nest hailed the deck in an enormous voice of passionate intensity: 'Sail ho! Two sail of ships on the larboard bow.'

The hail reached the cabin, where Jack was drinking coffee in a battered half-pint mug and eating eggs. He had already started up, thrusting both from him when Reade darted in, crying, 'Two sail of ships, sir, fine on the larboard bow.'

Jack ran aloft, straight up without a pause, the hoar-frost scattering from the ratlines under his feet. The look-out moved down on to the yard to leave him room, calling up, 'They have just cleared the middle island, sir. Topsails and courses. Which I saw them clear before the fog closed in.'

Time passed. The intently listening silence on deck was broken by two bells: no one heard the steady heave of the south-western swell at all. In these latitudes a sea-fog could resist almost any amount of wind, being bred from the surface itself; yet the wind could tear gaps in it, and the wind did so just as the cold was beginning to pinch Jack Aubrey's nose and ears. Three miles to the north-east he saw the two ships, their sails white against the black islands of Diego Ramirez: three to four hundred tons, bluff-bowed, broad in the beam. Stout merchantmen, no doubt, capable of cramming a great deal into their hold: but surely very, very slow.

With his glass to his good eye he studied the nearest: she seemed to be getting ready to change course, bringing the wind on to her quarter in order to sail westward round the southern shore of the last island in the group before hauling her wind and steering as near north into the Pacific as the breeze would allow. Both her watches were on deck, of course, a meagre crew: and with so few hands no

brisk manoeuvre could be expected. Yet even so she seemed strangely
hesitant about this sensible, straightforward operation; and all at once
it occurred to Jack that she was the leader, the ship which had been
there before, which pointed out the way, and that she was finding it
very difficult to induce her second astern to take notice of her signals.
Admittedly, the second astern was more often blurred by fog than
not; and in this light flags were difficult to read. His theory was confirmed almost at once: the leading ship fired a gun, and all her people
stared eagerly astern to see what effect it would have. She seemed to
be keeping no look-out at all. In any case he was morally certain that
she had not seen the *Surprise*: the frigate, lying with reefed courses
against a blurred grey background, would have been very hard to see
in any case, and to those who had no notion of any enemy within five
thousand miles she was virtually invisible.

The China ships' intention was perfectly obvious. And if the *Surprise* ran a little way to the east and then steered north she would have
the weather-gage, which would enable her to bring them to action
when she pleased. Yet he would not hurry things: there was the possibility of the third ship. And as they had been as regular as the Bath
to London stage-coach as far as time was concerned there seemed a
strong likelihood that they would be equally exact in number; and it
would be a sad shame not to bag the whole shooting-match. The third
ship must be allowed to sail right through the tangled islands and
join her companions, for once she was in the open sea there was no
return with this breeze. Very soon the wind would back into the west,
and with the *Surprise*'s remarkable powers of sailing close-hauled the
merchantmen could not hope to escape.

He leaned over the edge of the crow's nest and in a quiet voice he
called, 'Captain Pullings.'

'Sir?'

'Pray let all hands go to quarters, but without any noise at all: no
drum. And as soon as the fog closes in on us, make sail, all plain sail:
course north-north-east. For the moment let Mr Norton go into the
mizzentop with a glass and Bonden to the fore.'

The muffled sound of many feet below: guns run out with infinite precaution – no more than the faint squeak of a truck, the inevitable but stifled clash of round-shot. Then the fog closed in and without a single order the sails dropped from their yards or rose silently along their stays.

The frigate gathered way. Pullings could be heard saying, 'Thus, thus, very well thus,' to the helmsman as she settled on her course. Three bells. 'Dowse that God-damn bell,' said Jack, rather loud.

Fifteen minutes more, and as he had expected the breeze freshened, backing westward. He felt a sudden chill waft about him; and he was not alone, for the whalers looked at one another with a meaning nod.

'Sir,' called Bonden. 'Two sail of ships on the larboard beam. No. A brig and a ship.'

'Where away?' asked Jack. His injured eye was now watering extremely in the icy breeze, blurring the sight of both.

'Which I've lost them now, sir,' said Bonden. 'The ship seemed a fair size: topsails and I think forecourse: but they come and go. Sometimes you would say a ship of the line, sometimes only a sloop.'

Silence. Blankness: grey trails of mist wafted through the rigging, leaving ice-crystals on every strand. Jack whipped a handkerchief over his poor eye, and he was still knotting the ends when an eddy tore something of a window in the fog. The China ships, all three of them now, could be seen quite plain: they had cleared the islands and they were well to the south of them, exactly where reason had foretold. But illogically the newcomers, though closer to, indeed between the *Surprise* and her quarry, were much vaguer, mere looming shapes.

Yet they were clear enough for Awkward Davies to bawl out, 'Now there are five of the poor unfortunate buggers. Five!' in an exulting roar, instantly suppressed; and Jack had a fleeting glimpse of gunports on the large vessel before they both merged in the greyness once more, slightly darker forms that soon vanished entirely.

There followed a long period of total uncertainty, with the fog thickening, clearing, thickening again, and both look-outs confusing

the object they reported, sometimes taking the brig for the ship or the
other way about – the two vessels were moving quite fast in relation
to one another – while even the experienced Bonden varied strangely
about their size.

Jack saw virtually nothing. It seemed to him that these were almost
certainly Spaniards, merchantmen bound for Valparaiso and to the
northward; the larger one, if she was really as large as she sometimes
seemed to be, a thousand tons and more, possibly for the Philippines.
The row of gun-ports was neither here nor there: even if they were
real that did not mean there were any guns behind them. Most merchantmen had a full array, real or painted, as some sort of a deterrent.

'Sail ho. Sail on the starboard bow, sir,' called Norton. Jack whipped
round, saw the towering whiteness loom through the mist, thinning
over there, and heard Norton cry, 'Oh no, oh no, sir. I'm sorry. It's an
ice-island.'

Yes. And there was another beyond it, with more appearing in the
south and the east as the fog grew patchy; and now the particular
chill of a breeze blowing off ice was far more pronounced.

By this time the *Surprise* was perfectly well placed for her attack on
the China ships. They were well beyond the islands moving steadily a
little south of west, and with the present breeze she could cross their
wake under a moderate press of sail within an hour or so. The misty
newcomers lay between the *Surprise* and her prey – she would probably pass within hail – and as he contemplated those vague forms, now
remarkably large and even doubled by the odd reflection from frozen
mist particles coupled with what dim shadows they were capable of
casting, it occurred to him that the ship might conceivably be a Spanish man-of-war sent to deal with the *Alastor*, news of her depredation
having reached Cadiz. 'If that is the case,' he reflected, 'I shall ask Stephen to have a civil word with her.'

He leant over, meaning to tell Pullings to wear the ship round on to
her new westward course, but even as he gathered his breath he heard
that never-to-be-forgotten sound of falling ice as a mass the size of a
parish church broke from the nearest island and plunged a hundred

feet into the sea, sending up an immense turmoil of spray and leaping water, and he changed the order to that for tacking, a quicker operation altogether though much less economical in wear and tear and effort. 'The sooner we are out of this the better,' he reflected, glancing astern at the huge forms moving steadily northwards through the fog, although they were already much further to the north than they had any right to be at this time of the year.

The ship was round on her new tack and gathering way; all had been coiled down and hands were laying out on the foretopgallant yards when the brig showed dim on the larboard beam, then plainer and plainer.

'The brig ahoy,' hailed Jack in his powerful voice, now from the quarterdeck. No reply, but in the rapidly clearing air a great deal of activity could be made out.

'Colours,' said Jack to Reade, the signal-midshipman; and then louder, very much louder, as the colours broke out, 'What ship is that? Qué barco está?'

'Noah's Ark, ten days out of Ararat, New Jersey,' replied the brig, with a cackle of maniac laughter. Her big fore-and-aft mainsail was hauled right aft, she heeled violently to leeward, her stern-chaser went off, sending a ball through the *Surprise*'s forestaysail, and she vanished into the mist.

The *Surprise* replied at random. The crack of the single gun, a forecastle carronade, was still echoing to and fro between the curtains of fog when a second dark form heaved up on the starboard bow, grew rapidly distinct, and lit the remaining mist between them with a thundering broadside, eighteen crimson flashes. The guns had been fired on the downward roll and most of the shot fell short, but some hit the *Surprise* by ricochet, breaking through the hammocks in the netting and rolling across the deck: eighteen-pound round-shot. The smoke swept to leeward, much of the mist with it, and clear and plain Jack saw a heavy American frigate, a thirty-eight-gun ship with a three hundred and forty-two pounds broadside, apart from her chasers and carronades.

The *Surprise* was hopelessly outgunned and with her small priva-

teer's crew hopelessly outmanned; while there was also the brig-of-
war ready to infest her disengaged side or rake her from astern. 'Fire
as they bear,' cried Jack. He bore the helm up: the ship's head fell off
from the wind: her starboard guns bore in succession and fired, each
with accurate deliberation.

She had a surprising amount of way on her and in a quick aside Jack
said, 'Tom, I am going to put her about if ever she will stay: do what you
can.' Then aloud, 'Larboard guns: one round as they bear. Sail-trimmers
away.' He put the helm over; the good ship responded, turning, turning,
turning, dead into the wind. If she missed stays, if she fell off, all was
lost. She turned yet, turning just beyond the crucial point, with hands
madly flatting-in forward to help her, filled her jib and head staysails on
the other tack and she was round: and the larboard guns were bearing,
at point-blank range. The moment the last was fired and made fast the
gun-crews all leapt to brace round and to haul aft the sheets that had
been let go and to clear the horrible apparent confusion.

Jack gave the course east-north-east a half east, hoping to weather
the nearest iceberg on his starboard bow, the only way out of this
impossible encounter; and as soon as there were a few hands free he
called, 'Topgallants and weather studdingsails,' while he and those he
could gather together attended to the unloaded guns.

Although he was somewhat taken aback by this shockingly
improper going-about, a manoeuvre that had brought the *Surprise*
so close to his larboard bow that quite apart from the terrible effect
of her round-shot, fragments of glowing wad had come aboard, lighting a spilt cartridge and causing an explosion, the American captain
brought his ship round, spreading canvas at an extraordinary rate
and steering a parallel course, somewhat to leeward, close-hauled to
the strengthening wind, now at north-west.

Obviously he had made his turn later than Jack, which set him
close on a mile behind and almost as much farther east; yet even so
he thought he too might weather the ice-island, although it was moving steadily northwards. This particular island – for there were many
others in sight, south and east – could now be seen as a whole in the

increasing light, full two miles across, rising in steep crags and spires, green in general but ice-blue in the towering middle regions; and its northwestern point, the point which the *Surprise* must weather if she were to have any chance of escaping destruction, and the point for which the American was steering with such energy, ended in a sheer ice-cliff, much worn, fretted into pinnacles.

To begin with the American, with his full man-of-war's complement of hands, had been able to spread more canvas in spite of the damage and slaughter of that brief point-blank engagement and to make up some of the lost distance; but now that the Surprises had set their gun-deck in order they evened the difference and both ships raced through the frigid sea with everything their masts could bear, bowlines twanging taut, both firing chasers as they ran.

Jack left the gunnery to Pullings and Mr Smith. He stood at the con, sailing the ship, getting every inch of windward distance out of the wind's thrust, calculating leeway, gazing at the fatal cliff with his good eye, feeling the pain in his heart as the bows and cutwater hit drifting ice, a terribly frequent sound and sometimes very dangerous. He dared not ship a protective bow-grace: he could not risk the slightest diminution of the frigate's speed.

It was with the horror of a nightmare that he saw the calm, doom-like motion of the ice-island. The vast bulk moved with the apparent ease of a cloud and the slight expanse of safe water to the windward of its tip was narrowing, narrowing every minute.

'Sir,' said Wilkins, 'the brig has altered course.'

Certainly: Jack had expected it. These turns and her own manoeuvres had brought the brig to the westward of both ships, on the *Surprise*'s quarter and somewhat nearer to her than the heavy frigate; and for the last two miles she had been losing steadily. Now, in answer to a signal, she was bearing up with the evident intention of crossing the *Surprise*'s stern and raking her, firing a broadside that would run the whole length of the ship. It was a bold move, since Jack had only to make a slight turn to larboard to bring his own broadside to bear and quite possibly sink her. But the time taken by even a slight turn, by the discharge and the falling off again to her true course would almost certainly make the *Surprise* lose her race against the iceberg's movement.

'My compliments to Captain Pullings,' he said, having looked fore and aft, 'and beg he will direct all his attention to the brig's foremast and yard.'

The stern-chase guns in the cabin below increased their rate of fire. Eight shots in rapid succession, and there was a triumphant roar. Jack turned, saw the brig shoot up into the wind, her square foresail down on deck, her fore-and-aft mainsail swinging her helplessly out of control. He nodded, but the real essence of the matter lay ahead: not half a mile ahead. With his good eye he could now gauge his leeway exactly against a long fissure in the ice. It would be a near-run thing, a damned near-run thing. He had the wheel under his hands, easing her very gently to the rise of each swell, urging her a trifle and still another trifle to windward, to the thin lane at the cliff's very foot itself. Not two cables now, and they were running at eight knots. There was no turning back.

'Sir,' said Wilkins again, 'the frigate ports her helm.'

Again Jack nodded. She had been to the leeward of the *Surprise* from the beginning: now she had no chance whatsoever of weathering the point and she meant to hit the *Surprise* as hard as ever she could, crippling her before she was out of reach. He shrugged: his course was wholly committed now, and again he eased the helm, his eyes as intent upon the lane of green water as they might have been on a tall hedge with God knows what beyond, and he galloping towards it. He was aware of the whiter surf rising on the white ice at the cliff's foot, of a still whiter albatross crossing the swell, and even before he heard the American's broadside he was stunned and deafened by the enormous crash of ice falling from the cliff itself; he felt the ship's hull tremble and then grate on the iceberg's submerged outer shelf, and saw the mizzenmast, shot through in two separate places, sway, break and go slowly over the side.

'Axes, axes,' he roared. 'Cut all away. Cut clear, cut clear.'

Shrouds, backstays, rigging all whipped free; the ship ran past the ice-cliff, her mainyard scraping, past and beyond into the open water: sea-room and to spare for a good three miles. Ice-islands thick beyond.

She answered her helm perfectly: she was an entirely living ship: and there was a prodigious mass of ice between her and the enemies' guns. Jack was aware of some confusion in his mind: just in what order had things happened? Not that it signified. The ship was swimming in clear water. He sent Reade to ask the carpenter to sound the well and then looked for the destruction here on deck. There was surprisingly little. The mizzen had gone as clean as a whistle, and the bosun, together with his mates, was knotting and splicing.

'What damage did it do among the people?' he asked Wilkins.

'None this last bout, sir. The ice missed us by a shaver.'

Pullings came aft, smiling, curiously talkative, a marline-spike in his hand. 'Give you joy of our passage, sir,' he said. 'At one moment I did not think she could do it, and my heart was fairly in my mouth. And then when the ice came down I said, "All up with you, Pullings, old cock." But, however, it missed.'

'You saw what happened?'

'Why, yes, sir. I had just put my head over the top of the ladder when the Yankee opened fire: deliberate shots at first – one hit the mizzen below the hounds – and then when we were weathering the point and running clear, all her remaining guns at once, and some of their shots hit the ice, or perhaps it was just the concussion: anyway a thundering great steeple came down, a thousand ton, I dare say. I never seen the like nor heard it. Plunged into our wake, soaked one and all; and some odd fragments spoilt the gingerbread work on the taffrail.'

Jack perceived that he was indeed deeply soaked behind; and perhaps still somewhat shattered by the fantastic uproar. He said, 'How I regret the mizzen. But a moment's attempt at saving it would have brought us right on the ice. As it was we scraped most horribly, and I tremble for our copper. Yes, Mr Reade?'

'If you please, sir, Chips says . . .'

'What was that, Mr Reade?'

'Beg pardon, sir. Mr Bentley says two inches in the well, no more.'

'Very good. Tom, we must put before the wind or close on until we can ship a jury-mizzen. Pick our oldest whale-men and send them into the crow's nest one after another to pick us a way through the ice: there is a terrible quantity to leeward. Let a stout bow-grace be prepared; and since we are not likely to see that big fellow' – nodding westwards – 'until he has gone about twice, let the galley fires be lit and all hands fed.'

'He may consider it his duty to hurry back and protect his convoy,' said Pullings.

'Let us hope he has a very strong sense of duty, an overwhelming sense of duty,' said Jack.

In fact the big American did not round the point until well on in the afternoon. The devoted brig had not only lost her yard, shot through in the slings, but had also stopped a nine-pounder ball just under the water-line and sprung a butt: water and pieces of ice were pouring into her. By this time the *Surprise*, keeping the wind one and two points on her starboard quarter as far as the ice allowed it, had travelled ten miles in a straight line – more of course when her deviations to avoid icebergs and close-packed ice-fields were counted – and it was from this distance, the fog having largely cleared, that at last her look-out saw the big American. Yet she too would have to thread those devious channels and circumvent the same islands, and Jack sat down to his belated dinner with as easy a mind as was compatible with the loss of a mast, the presence of an active and enterprising enemy, and of an unconscionable amount of ice ahead in the form of floating islands or massive floes.

He had already been down to the sick-berth to see the very moderate casualties – two splinter wounds, one of them the invariably unfortunate Joe Plaice; one man struck into a coma by a falling block but not despaired of; one man with toes and metatarsals crushed by a recoiling gun – and he had told Stephen that dinner would be ready by eight bells, adding, 'Four o'clock, you know,' in case he did not.

He did, however, and at the first stroke he walked eagerly in, wiping his hands. 'I am so sorry if I have kept you, but I had to take that foot off after all: such a mass of comminuted bone. Pray tell me how we do.'

'Pretty well, I thank you. The American is ten miles astern, and I do not think he can possibly come within range before nightfall. Allow me to give you a piece of this fish, a cousin to the cod, it seems.'

'They tell me we have lost a mast. Will this impede our progress to any fatal degree – will it reduce our pace by say a third?'

'I hope not. When we are sailing large the mizzen makes surprisingly little difference; and less than you might think close-hauled. With a side-wind the balance would be upset and she would fall off sadly: I should not like to be chased by a herring-buss in the open ocean with a strong side-wind. But I hope that the westerlies or south-westerlies will go on blowing until some lingering notion of responsibility makes the captain of that frigate turn back to his convoy.'

'I do not believe those ships were his convoy: I believe there was a chance meeting in say the river Plate, no more. But it makes little odds, since I am convinced he will protect them now. My dear, you look sadly done up; and your appetite has failed you. Drink up another glass of wine and breathe as deeply as you can. I shall give you a comfortable dose tonight.'

'No, Stephen: many thanks, but it would not do. I shall not turn in; nor I shall not heave to, neither. I dare not let that cove – a determined and bloody-minded cove if ever there was one – creep up on me in the night. Coffee is more the mark than a dose, however comfortable and kindly intended. Let us toy with these chops. I do love a dry chop, a really well-dried mutton chop, turned twice a day.'

The well-dried chops sustained him all that night, which he spent in the crow's nest, kept if not warm then at least preserved from death by a sequence of whalers and refreshed every other hour by the truly

devoted Killick or his mate who came aloft in mittens, holding a vil-
lainous tin pot of coffee, slung by a loop, in their teeth.

A fairly clear night, particularly at ten or twenty feet above the
surface; a moderate swell for these parts; and above all the blessed
moon, only just past the full and as brilliant as extreme cold could
make her. The watch on deck, muffled in their Magellan jackets, with
flannel shirts over their heads, stood by to shove off floating slabs of
ice with what spars the ship still possessed; and so, with the whalers
advising what lanes to take, the *Surprise* groped her way cautiously
eastwards and as far north of east as ever she could manage. In spite
of the stout bow-grace and the zeal of those employed in shoving-off,
she received some wicked strokes from thick, deep-swimming floes,
and several times the high-perched Jack Aubrey trembled for his
nest – literally trembled with extreme cold, weariness and the grave
tension of guiding his ship through this potentially mortal maze: he
was no longer a young man.

By the strange sun-rise he was older still: a sun rising in a clear sky
that presently grew light sapphire blue, while the sea took on a deeper
tinge and the ice-islands showed at some points pure rosy pink and
at others bright ultramarine. But there, at seven miles or less, consid-
erably farther south, lay the dogged American. In this light her hull
looked black; and she had already begun to set more sail.

Jack swung over the side of the crow's nest, and as he gripped the
topmost shrouds his frozen hand slipped on the coat of ice: he would
have fallen but that his legs, so long at sea, instantly whipped round
the shroud below and held him for the vital moment.

On deck he said, 'Tom, when the hands have had their breakfast
let us shake out our reefs and set the foretopgallant. Look at that
fellow' – nodding southwards – 'he has studdingsails both sides, aloft
and alow.'

'I dare say he has a clear stretch of water, for the moment; but I must
say the ice-field looks right solid down there,' said Pullings hopefully,
and they both staggered as the *Surprise* struck yet another heavy floe.

There was a hanging stove lit in the cabin, still more coffee, endless eggs and bacon, toast, a creditable Peruvian orange marmalade. Jack, stripped to his waistcoat, absorbed these things and the warmth; but he had little conversation, merely observing that he had seen an albatross, several seals, and a most prodigious whale. Stephen spoke, in a desultory fashion, about ice-islands, and the sudden change in colour at the point of cleavage when some great mass fell into the sea. 'This I have observed in a telescope,' he said, then paused, for Jack's head was sinking on his breast.

'If you please, sir,' cried Reade, bouncing in, alive with youthful joy, 'Captain Pullings says would you like to step on deck.'

'Eh?' asked Captain Aubrey.

Reade said it again and Jack heaved himself up, all seventeen stone. Reade led him blinking aft, passed him a telescope and said, 'There, sir: directly to windward.'

Jack gazed, changed the glass to his good eye, gazed again, his tired face lighting with a great smile; he stamped upon the frozen deck, and cried, 'He counted his chickens without his host, by God! Ha, ha, ha!' for the big frigate lay motionless, her sails brailed up; and she was getting her boats over the side.

'On deck, there,' bailed the look-out, one of the *Surprise*'s whalemen. 'Sir, she's gone down a lane in the ice-field, a blind alley, like. A no-thoroughfare, ha, ha, ha. And she'll have to tow back three miles into the wind's eye, oh ha, ha, ha!' And in something of an undertone to his mate at the foremast head, 'Oh, won't he cop it, that poor bleeding sod of a look-out of theirs, ha, ha!'

The distant ship fired a gun to leeward, sending up a cloud of antarctic skuas from a dead and drifting whale.

'The enemy has fired a leeward gun, sir, if you please,' reported the signal-midshipman.

'You astonish me, Mr Reade,' said Jack. 'And now, I perceive, she is throwing out a signal. Be so good as to read it.'

Norton stepped forward; Reade rested the telescope on his shoulder, focussed, and said, 'Alphabetic, sir: our alphabet. H,A,P,P,Y R,E,T,U,R,N, sir.'

'Come,' cried Jack, 'that's handsome. Reply *Same to you*. Who is their president, Tom?'

'Mr Washington, I believe,' said Pullings, after some thought.

'*Compliments to Mr Washington* would be too long by far. No, leave it at that, Mr Reade; and give him a gun in return. Tom,' he went on, 'let us not crack on at all, but proceed east-north-east at a walking-pace until we are out of this infernal ice. Let us not rush upon our doom like a parcel of mad lunatics or gabardine swine. A walking-pace, Captain Pullings; and in the afternoon we will start work on a jury-mast.'

In his happy ease of heart he now went straight to sleep in the warm cabin, never moving until dinner-time, when he woke, fresh and clear-headed, aware that the ship had touched no ice for some hours; he took a turn on deck, observed that although the sky was murky in the north-east the sea was as open as the Channel except far, far to the south, where ice and the reflection of ice could still be seen, with great islands cutting the horizon, and paced the quarter-deck until he heard his steward's shrewish, barely respectful, complaining voice: 'Which the cook says ain't he ever coming, what with everything going cold, spoilt and ruined?'

After dinner Jack, Pullings and Mr Bentley conferred about the jury-mizzen; and now it was found just how grievous the loss of spars in the recent blow had been. Though the ship was heavy with prize-goods such as ambergris and cloth of gold taken from the *Alastor*, with specie, mostly chests of silver, and with provisions of a quantity and above all a quality to make a flagship stare, she had scarcely a stick to call her own.

'After endless lamentations and if only's,' said Jack as he and Stephen were settling to their music, 'it was decided that by using the launch's mast and the rough-tree rail we could raise stump enough and gaff enough to spread a tolerable mizzen. Enough, at all events, to sail with the wind ahead at a moderate pace without straining the rudder right off its pintles; and if it ain't elegant why, be damned to elegance.'

'What are pintles?'

'Those right-angled pieces in the front of the rudder that hook into rings or braces as we say at the back of the stern-post so that the rudder can swing like a door on its hinges.'

And when they had finished their piece, a gentle, meditative anonymous manuscript duet bought at an auction, he said, 'Lord, Stephen, when you remember how hot we were after those China ships so short a while ago, and how simple we should have looked if we had taken them, with that devilish great eighteen-pounder frigate and the brig coming down on us with the weather-gage; and when you consider how happy we are now, to have come off with the loss of no more than our mizzen, why, it makes you think.'

'I do not know that I should go quite so far as that,' said Stephen.

'Oh, very well, very well. You may be as satirical as you please; but I think we have come out of it most uncommon well. I for one never supposed that tonight we could turn in and sleep in peace.'

In peace they slept, profound peace, the peace of physically exhausted but easy-minded and very well fed men, at least until the graveyard watch. On the moonlit deck Wilkins, on being relieved by Grainger at eight bells, said, 'Here you have her: reefed courses, foretopsail atrip; course north-east by north; Captain's orders in the binnacle drawer.' Then, in a conversational tone, 'You may have something of a ducking in an hour or so.'

'Yes,' said Grainger, also looking into the north-east, where low dark clouds quite hid the sky, 'I dare say we shall. A drop of rain and this precious cold will wake me up. Dear Lord, how fast asleep I was, and warm!'

'I shall be the same in two minutes. It was a right hard day and night.' He paused with one foot on the ladder and said, 'Surely it is uncommon to see lightning in these latitudes?'

'Oh, I have known it often enough,' said Grainger. 'Not so often as between the tropics, but pretty often. Only down here you don't linger on deck, so perhaps it seems much rarer.'

Four bells, and it began to snow: the *Surprise* was keeping to her sober five knots.

Six bells, and the wind strengthened, growing so changeable that once the ship was almost taken aback. Grainger close-reefed the foretopsail, and almost immediately afterwards the sky was covered entirely – no moon, no stars – and without a warning a violent rain, mixed with sleet, came hurtling down, so violent and so continued, with water jetting wide from the leeward scuppers and the watch huddled under the break of the quarterdeck, that it was impossible to strike seven bells.

Yet half-past three in the morning it was; Stephen's watch said so, and as it was telling the hour so Stephen, for the second time in his life and in the same ship, was woken by an enormous noise or combination of noises that he instantly recognized. The frigate had surely been struck by lightning.

She had indeed. Her mainmast was utterly shattered, its fragments flung into the sea: its yards, however, lay athwartships, and like the foremast they were quite untouched. The ship had at once put before the wind, whatever the helmsmen might do; but as the snow and rain had calmed the sea she was reasonably steady, though unmanageable, and Stephen was soon called down to the sick-berth.

There were only three casualties: one man, a Knipperdolling named Isaac Rame, apparently uninjured apart from a black mark the size of a shilling over his heart, but completely, profoundly insensible – listening to its completely disordered beat Stephen shook his head – and two other foremast-hands strangely burnt. These burns, though superficial, caused much distress; they were extensive, branching all over the men's backs in a close-set network of divergent lines, and it took Stephen, Padeen and Fabien so long to dress them that a pale daylight was showing upon the table when Stephen came into the cabin for breakfast.

'Well, here's a pretty go,' cried Jack. 'Here's a pretty mess. Have a cup of coffee,' – pouring it. He sounded quite cheerful, as though the loss of the ship's mainmast were of slight importance; and so it was, compared with what followed. 'When we have finished breakfast – pray help yourself to bacon and pass the dish – I will show you something more extraordinary by far. Our rudder has gone by the board.'

'Oh, oh,' cried Stephen, aghast. 'Are we rudderless, so?'

'I will not deceive you, brother: we are without a rudder. Do you remember asking me about pintles?' Stephen nodded, still much concerned. 'Well, it appears that at some point in our dreadful passage through the drift-ice a great floe must have lifted the pintles off the dumb-chalder and the braces, or most of them, and destroyed the wood-locks, so that it was hanging by little more than the tiller. We did not notice it, since we barely touched the helm sailing large; but when the lightning struck the rudder-head, shattering all down to the water-line, why, it dropped clean away.' He pointed to the shattered, blackened rudder-head, now covered by a decent cloth.

'Is there any help for such a state of affairs?'

'Oh, I am sure we shall find something,' said Jack. 'May I trouble you for the marmalade? Capital marmalade, you must confess; though not quite as good as Sophie's.'

Stephen had often heard Jack say, when life at sea grew more trying than the human frame could bear, 'that it was no use whining'; but he had never seen quite this degree of insouciance, or what he felt tempted to call irresponsible levity. How much was assumed as a captain's duty in a virtually hopeless situation? How much was Jack's natural reaction? He was not a man much given to strike attitudes. How hopeless was the situation in fact? Stephen might still confuse braces and pintles, dumb-chalders and sling-dogs, but he knew enough about the sea to feel that a ship far and far from land with only one mast and no rudder at all was in a very sad way: furthermore his knowledge of sailing, though limited, did tell him that one mast and its sails in the very front of the ships could impel a rudderless vessel only directly before the wind, that the wind in these latitudes was nearly always westerly, and that there was no land ahead until they came right round the globe to Cape Horn again.

He did not like to ask directly, but he put these points to various shipmates; to his distress they all, invariably, agreed with him. 'Ah, Doctor, things is wery bad,' said Joe Plaice. 'I have never heard anything so dreadful as the loss of a rudder five thousand miles from land,' said Mr Adams, 'for in our condition, South America, dead to windward, cannot be considered as land at all.' Yet at the same time he detected much of this same cheerfulness throughout the ship and something not very far from apparent unconcern, even in so atrabilious a soul as Killick. 'Have I been plying the ocean with a parcel of Stoics all this time?' he wondered. 'Or in my ignorance am I myself somewhat over-timid?'

But then again in his frequent encounters with the foremast-jacks – and his relations with them were of quite a different nature and in some ways much closer than those of any other officer – he had occasional insights that showed an entirely different aspect of the situation: of the moral situation at all events. The lower deck knew perfectly well that Vidal and his closest Knipperdolling connections had smuggled Dutourd ashore; and they had become convinced that once ashore Dutourd had in some way informed upon the Doctor, putting his life in danger. And it was as though this treachery had brought bad luck on the *Surprise*, however kindly Vidal had meant his action in the first place. Bad luck was a term that embraced a greal deal: other people might have spoken of a curse, a spell, or a divine resentment of impiety. But whatever it was called they had missed the China ships, and they had been near as a toucher sunk by the Americans, by the ice-islands and by the ice-floes. And now the barky had been struck by lightning. But it was a Knipperdolling that had copped it, and once he went over the side the bad luck would be off the ship.

He went the second day after the stroke. His shipmates attended with real concern – they had nothing against Isaac Rame himself, noth-

ing whatsoever – but when the high south-western swell closed over
him without a splash on Tuesday morning they went back to their work
with a particular satisfaction, one that informed their entire attitude.

This satisfaction continued throughout the week, or rather more.
Stephen, who was often, almost invariably, in the way on deck when
complex work was being carried out, wrote a commentary on it for
Diana: *Mariners: Consensus and Cohesion in certain States of Adver-
sity*, together with *Some Remarks on Peruvian Cirripedes* for the
Royal Society.

For the most part the weather was kind, the wind, though often
boisterous, steady in the west; and although they had frequent rain
and two blinding snow-storms there was no ice about and the temperature was nearly always above freezing by day. They were still without
a rudder, but until one could be fashioned and above all hung, they
had a steering oar over the quarter that allowed a point or two of
northerly deviation from their steady eastward course. By the end of
this time three sad little poles rose from where the stately masts had
been: the foremast, standing stark alone; its topmast and topgallant,
both worked into the launch's mast, stood for the shattered main; and
an even stranger assembly took the place of the mizzen, spreading
a pitiful fore-and-aft sail the size of the cabin table-cloth: yet it did
give a certain balance. From the main and the fore yards hung broad
but extraordinarily shallow square sails, so low that when Stephen
was led on deck to see them he asked where they were intended to be
hoisted. 'They *are* hoisted,' he was told, in a voice of strong displeasure. Forward still, and there was the unhurt bowsprit, carrying its
spritsail and spritsail-topsail; and, since the ship was very well found
in bosun's and sailmaker's stores, she wore all the staysails that could
possibly be managed. 'It is just like Bridie Colman's washing day, I
do declare,' cried Stephen, in another unfortunate attempt to please.
'Everything is within an easy hand's reach, so it is.'

'This is an extraordinarily small piece of plum-duff,' he observed at dinner – Sunday dinner – in the cabin. 'I wish it may not be an ignoble stroke of revenge for my innocent words this morning about our harmless, meek, and bargelike appearance – innocent upon my word, and even, I thought, amusing – a mild pleasantry. But not at all: prim faces, wry looks, and now this meagre, despicable pudding. I had thought better of my shipmates.'

'You mistake, brother,' said Jack. 'Mr Adams and I, in our joint character as purser, cast our accounts yesterday, reckoning every last firkin of oatmeal, every bin and locker in the bread-room, and dividing the whole, private stores not excepted, by the number of mouths aboard. That piece of pudding is your full ration, my poor Stephen.'

'Oh, indeed,' said Stephen, looking rather blank.

'Yes. I have told the ship's company of this, and I have told them that unless or until we can fashion and ship a rudder . . . '

'If you spend another two minutes up to your neck in water at this temperature, striving to do so, I will not answer for your life,' said Stephen. 'Last time it was nip and tuck, with hot blanket, fomentations, and half a pint of my best brandy.'

' . . . unless we can ship a rudder that will enable us to haul up for St Helena, I intend to bear away for the Cape, edging north all the time with our steering oar, or perhaps some better gear. It is about three thousand five hundred miles, and although we have logged over a hundred for each of these last three days with this comic rig, as you so rightly call it, and with this steady wind and beautiful eastward current, I have only reckoned on fifty, no more: one seventieth part of the distance. Fifty multiplied by seventy is three thousand five hundred, Stephen. And that succulent, luxurious pudding now in front of you is the seventieth part of all the duff that you will eat before we raise the Table Mountain.'

'God love you, Jack, what things you tell me.'

'Never despond, dear Stephen: remember that Bligh sailed four thousand miles in an open boat, with not a thousandth part of our stores. *You* will never despond, Stephen,' said Jack with a very slight emphasis. 'And I am sure you will never find any of the seamen do so, either.'

'No,' said Stephen, stifling his recollections of the terrible following seas during the frequent storms in these latitudes, the perpetual danger of being pooped, of broaching to, and of being lost with all hands in a turmoil of foam. 'No. I shall not despond.'

'And Stephen, may I beg you not to be facetious when speaking of the barky? The people are surprisingly susceptible, if you know what I mean, about her appearance. And if ever you intend to be complimentary, you might well be advised just to throw up your hands and cry "Oh," or "Superb," or "I have never seen anything better," without being particular.'

'The doctor has been choked off for being a satyr,' said Killick to Grimble.

'What's a satyr?'

'What an ignorant cove you are to be sure, Art Grimble: just ignorant, is all. A satyr is a party that talks sarcastic. Choked off something cruel, he was; and his duff taken away and eaten before his eyes.'

Although the ship was wonderfully busy the news spread forward with its usual speed, and Stephen, making his way to the forecastle to watch albatrosses and the nondescript petrel that had been following the ship for some days, was greeted with particular kindness, brought a coil of soft manilla to sit upon, given a pair of belaying-pins to hold his telescope steady, and told about the birds that had been seen that day, including a numerous band of stink-pots flying south, an infallible sign of clear weather. This was all very much in line with what he had so often known at sea, and once more the evident good-will warmed his spirit.

He thought of it with pleasure as he went to sleep; and its absence the next day, together with a want of that cheerfulness so usual on

deck, struck him with all the more force when he took the air in the
forenoon after a trying, anxious time with the sick-berth, where neither burns nor foot were doing well, and with his collections, where
a vile moth was breeding among the feathers and no pepper, no pepper left in the entire ship to discourage it. He arrived on deck not by
climbing the companion-ladder to the quarterdeck in the usual way
but by the fore-hatchway, having traversed the berth-deck to consider
Dutourd's former cabin for the amputation in case his suspicion of an
incipient pneumonia (that frequent sequel) should prove to be true.
This brought him into the waist of the ship, filled with hands. They
touched their hats and wished him good-day, but mechanically, with
barely a smile, and returned to their low, anxious, intent conversations, frequently calling up in subdued voices to their companions
thick along the starboard gangway.

He pushed through to the quarterdeck; and there were the same
grave faces, grey with cold and discouragement, looking fixedly to
windward, that is to say a little south of the ship's modest wake.
'What is afoot?' he murmured in Reade's ear.

'Stand over here, sir,' said Reade, guiding him to the rail, 'and look
out to windward.'

A topsail schooner sailing large: and some miles beyond her a ship,
also standing north-north-east with topgallants and studdingsails
abroad, a glorious sight; but one that gave no pleasure.

'It is that brutal great American, come to snap us up,' said Reade.

'Shame on him, after such a handsome message,' murmured
Wedel.

'Where is the Captain?'

'Aloft, sir; but,' Reade whispered, 'he don't see very well today. Both
eyes water so in the cold.'

'It is cold, sure,' said Stephen. He focussed his best newly-cleaned
glass, a superlative piece made for him by Dolland with a somewhat
greater magnification than was usual in the Navy, for identifying
birds; and presently he said, 'Tell me, Mr Reade: frigates have but one
row of guns, have they not?'

'Yes, sir. Just one,' said Reade patiently, holding up a single finger.

'Well, this boat, or vessel, has two; as well as some each end.'

'Nay, sir,' said Reade, shaking his head: then urgently, 'Please may I have a look? Oh sir,' he shrieked to Pullings at the taffrail, 'she ain't the Yankee. She's a two decker. A sixty-four-gun ship – the Doctor saw her.'

'On deck, there,' came Jack's voice from on high, cutting through the unworthy hubbub. 'She's a sixty-four-gun ship, the old *Berenice*, I think – yes, the old *Berenice* – from the New South Wales station. Bery nicey too,' he added, with a private chuckle.

'And that, much nearer to us,' said Stephen to the ecstatic Reade, 'is what we at sea term a schooner; but you need not be afraid. She carries little in the way of guns.'

'A Baltimore clipper, sir, I believe,' said Mr Adams.

'Indeed? I could have sworn she was a schooner, in spite of those rectangular sails in front.'

'Certainly, sir. She is certainly a schooner in rig. The clipper part refers to her hull.'

'Oh, she has a hull as well, has she? I was not aware. But pray tell me, Mr Adams, do you think you could find a little small bag of pepper, just half a stone or so, in the Captain's store-room itself?'

'Sir, I have searched it through and through, in spite of that wicked Killick, and – see, she is rounding to.'

The schooner checked her way and a tall young midshipman, standing on her low rail and holding a shroud, hailed, 'The ship ahoy – if ship you can be called, poor hulk [this in an undertone] – what ship is that?'

'His Majesty's hired vessel *Surprise*,' replied Tom. 'Captain Pullings.'

All along her side the schooner's hands stood grinning, staring, making offensive gestures: the Surprises looked back with stony hatred.

'Come aboard with your papers,' said the midshipman.

'Take that American contraption back to the *Berenice*,' roared

Jack, half-way down the ratlines, 'and tell Captain Dundas with Captain Aubrey's compliments that he will wait upon him. D'ye hear me, there?'

'Yes, sir,' replied the midshipman, and on either side of him the simpering stopped dead. 'Aye aye, sir: Captain Aubrey's compliments . . . Sir,' he called across the widening lane, 'may I say Philip Aubrey is aboard?'

Oh the mirth aboard the *Surprise*. Several of the younger men leapt into the rigging, ostentatiously slapping their buttocks at the schooner as she fled away, sailing unbelievably close to the wind. But more, many more of the hands gathered in the waist or on the forecastle, oblivious of the cold, revelling in their prize-money preserved, even as it were restored, laughing, clapping one another on the back.

The ships drew near; nearer. 'I know perfectly well what he is going to say,' murmured Jack to Stephen as they stood there in their boat-cloaks by the gangway stanchions. 'He is going to call out, "Well, Jack, whom the Lord loveth He chastizeth," and all his people will set up a silly cackle. There's Philip! Lord, how he has shot up.' Philip was Jack Aubrey's half-brother, last seen as a youngster aboard Dundas's previous command.

The *Surprise*, with her frail spars, could not easily get her launch over the side, and Dundas was sending his barge for them. It was lowered down in a seamanlike manner, and as it shoved off Captain Dundas, waving his hat from the *Berenice*'s quarterdeck, called, 'Well, Jack, whom the Lord loveth He chastizeth, ha, ha, ha! You must be a prime favourite up above. Heavens, you are in a horrid state.'

'Captain Dundas, sir,' cried Stephen, 'Do you think you could oblige me with a few pounds of fresh black pepper?'

The reply was lost as Jack's bosun and his mates piped their Captain over the side: a howling repeated three minutes later as the *Berenice* piped him aboard.

Stephen, Pullings and Philip withdrew from their splendid dinner quite early, Stephen carrying his pepper; and Jack said, 'Old Hen, what a pleasant young fellow you have made of Philip. I am so grateful.'

'Not at all,' said Dundas. 'He might have been born to the sea. Cobbold says he will rate him master's mate in *Hyperion*, next year, if you would like it.'

'I should like it very much indeed. It is time he was out of leading-strings; though yours I am sure were the kindest in the world.'

They sat comfortably together – very old friends and shipmates – sipping their port, pushing the decanter to and fro. Dundas told the servants to turn in, and presently he said, 'You have had a rough time of it, Jack: and so I think has Maturin.'

'Yes, I have: pretty rough. And he has, too. Then again we have both been away a terrible long time, you know, with very little news, and that adds to the ordinary battering of a distant voyage: not that it was so ordinary on this occasion. Tell me, how are things at home?'

'I was at Ashgrove last July, and they were all blooming – Sophie in splendid looks – her mother is living there with a friend, a Mrs Morris – children very well indeed, and the girls so *pretty*, modest and kind. Well, fairly modest, and very kind. I did not see Diana, though her horses do famously: she was in Ireland during my short leave. But when I called I did see Clarissa Oakes, poor young Oakes's widow, who lives there: what a fine young woman she is.' He paused again; then brightened and went on, 'But tell me, as far as you can, because Melville let me understand that there was something confidential about your voyage' – Melville, or more formally Lord Melville, was Heneage Dundas's elder brother and First Lord of the Admiralty – 'as far as you properly can, then, how your enterprise went.'

'Well, I gathered that the first part, in the East Indies, went well for Stephen – at least the French were discomforted – but I flung the *Diane* on a reef in the South China Sea, a total loss. And then in this second bout, now ending, thanks be, we did take a fair number of prizes to begin with and we destroyed a truly odious pirate; but then I contrived to lose three American China ships: Heavens, such wealth! It is true they were protected by a brig and a thirty-eight-gun frigate that nearly destroyed us. Oh, Hen, such wicked ice south of Diego Ramirez: and north, for that matter. We escaped, true enough; but even so I cannot call the enterprise anything but a failure. And I am very much afraid that Stephen was betrayed, that his plan did not come to good, and that it went right to his heart.'

'I will fetch some brandy,' said Heneage.

They drank it staring at the embers in the hanging stove; and when they had settled what masts and spars the *Berenice* could give the *Surprise*, with a long aside about Dundas's tender the Baltimore clipper, picked up perfect but empty – not a soul, not a scrap of paper – in the south Pacific, and her extraordinary sailing qualities, Jack said, 'No. Harking back to this voyage, I think it was a failure upon the whole, and a costly failure; but,' he said laughing with joy at the thought, 'I am so happy to be homeward-bound, and I am so happy, so very happy, to be alive.'